The Puppet Master

Quentin Black

i

Copyright © 2022 Quentin Black All rights
reserved

The characters and events portrayed in this book
are fictitious. Any similarity to real persons, living or
dead, is coincidental and not intended by the author.

No part of this book may be reproduced, or
stored in a retrieval system, or transmitted in any
form or by any means, electronic, mechanical,
photocopying, recording, or otherwise, without
express written permission of the publisher.

ISBN: 9798418044655

Cover design by : Golden Rivet

https://golden-rivet.com/

ii

An Outlaw's Reprieve – A Connor Reed Novella – For **FREE**

Click here for Free E-Book

DEDICATION

To Donna,

Thanks for being a dedicated Mum to
Paige and Connor.

AUTHORS NOTE

Any specific terms and phrases have been highlighted in italics and can be found in the glossary.

RYDER FAMILY TREE

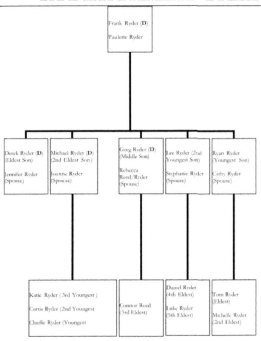

Frank Ryder (**D**)

Paulette Ryder

Derek Ryder (**D**)
(Eldest Son)

Jennifer Ryder
(Spouse)

Michael Ryder (**D**)
(2nd Eldest Son)

Joanne Ryder
(Spouse)

Greg Ryder (**D**)
(Middle Son)

Rebecca
Reed/Ryder
(Spouse)

Lee Ryder (2nd
Youngest Son)

Stephanie Ryder
(Spouse)

Ryan Ryder
(Youngest Son)

Cathy Ryder
(Spouse)

Katie Ryder (3rd Youngest)

Curtis Ryder (2nd Youngest)

Charlie Ryder (Youngest

Connor Reed
(3rd Eldest)

Daniel Ryder
(4th Eldest)

Luke Ryder
(5th Eldest)

Tom Ryder
(Eldest)

Michelle Ryder
(2nd Eldest)

PROLOGUE

"Man matures when he stops believing that politics solves his problems."

—Nicolás Gómez Dávila

ACKNOWLEDGEMENTS

Golden-Rivet for the cover design and promotional video.

Chris Searle his in-depth and polishing critiques.

And Jake Olafsen, the author of *'Wearing the Green Beret: A Canadian with the Royal Marine Commandos'* for his always valuable input.

1

Nineteen months ago

The two men stood side by side looking through the glass screen at the Danish surgical crew clad in either light aqua green or blue scrubs, masks and head coverings resembling shower caps. The medical team crowded the anaesthetised patient, obscuring him from view despite the bright overhead lights.

The Dane stood on the left—middle-aged, tall, light brown hair swept to one side of a face, though jowly when relaxed, was not fat. He inquired in English, "I realise I risk your anger asking, but I am a curious man, and your presence here would suggest that the patient is very valuable."

The Russian—similarly aged, a little taller, wavy brown hair and wearing a well-fitting suit with a touch of flamboyance, answered in the same tongue, "He has been a great servant to me—to my country. Whether he continues to be will be the result of your team's professionalism."

The Danish neuroscientist stiffened, "Their talent and professionalism are unmatched."

Despite the Russian's reputation, the jab at his team's—and therefore his—competence spurred him to answer. They were at the cutting edge of a bio-engineering technology called neuroprosthetics, helping to replace or assist damaged neurons, enhancing their function with external electrical circuitry. And their reputation for excellence had led to a substantial grant for the implementation of BCI—Brain-Computer Interface.

The Russian gave a subtle nod. "Calm yourself, old friend. The statement was not a threat. Tell me again of the…enhancement he will benefit from if this is a success."

The Dane partially relaxed. "If successful, the neural chip will be activated by the host's adrenal system. It will stimulate his vagus nerve and optimise his entire nervous system. The real innovation is that we've found a way of sending signals painlessly through the skin that selectively activate the optimal fibres while leaving the sub-optimal ones unchanged."

"You say it will work off his adrenal system. Will the neural chip be activated during a spoken argument?"

The Dane shrugged. "We have set the parameters high, so it can only be induced once a certain threshold of adrenaline is released—a combat situation, for example. Although, if it is triggered during an argument, the only thing likely to happen is that his verbal fluency, reasoning and decision-making will be enhanced. He will not be snapping the necks of parking attendants. It only acts to enhance his reflexes, sight, decision-making, physical and mental efficiency."

"All the things adrenaline heightens anyway."

"Yes, but not to this degree. And adrenaline only enhances the gross motor skills involving the legs, arms and trunk. It retards the fine motor skills of the hand and wrist."

"Why wouldn't someone want to be in this state as often as possible?"

"Because it'll cause a rapid drain on his body's nutrients, leaving him fatigued in the extreme."

10

The Russian turned to him sharply. "Leaving him vulnerable. How long would it take him to recover?"

"We have created vials of a formula—they trigger an initial release of CO_2 into his system. This tricks the haemoglobin molecules to dump oxygen for use by the muscles and brain, so they can transport the false CO_2 back to the lungs. There's also a concoction of protein nutrients, and iron. If he were to go into near-total depletion, post-injection revival to a 'normal' state should take a minute to ninety seconds. Full restoration to enable the enhancement should be no more than seven minutes."

The Dane mentally grimaced when the Russian asked, "You said 'near-total depletion'—which suggests that if he is in this state too long he could die."

Inserting as much confidence in his voice as he dared, the Dane replied, "That is an improbable scenario."

"But possible."

"If he couldn't find the respite to inject himself, maybe. However, he will be like Superman for a short time, and so able to extract himself from the wrath of the Gods."

The Head of SVR RF (Foreign Intelligence Service of the Russian Federation) remained quiet for a moment. "There was once a time he could do so without enhancement. He is a little older now. Had a long career with many injuries. All men are human, but he is our best asset."

"Maybe with this he will be the first immortal," answered the neuroscientist. "Should he survive the surgery. As you are aware, no human subject has undergone this procedure."

2

Present day

The suited Darren O'Reilly sat in the conference with just over one hundred and twenty European and American power brokers.

The fifty-six-year-old Englishman assumed a posture and expression belying his sense of being an imposter.

It was true the purpose of these Bilderberg meetings—originally at least—was to strengthen *Atlanticism*, the relations between the US, Canada and Europe. And with the British tech tycoon sitting at the head of a company turning over millions of pounds and dollars either side of the Atlantic, he had logically supposed—after the fact—that he would be a natural invitee.

Still, amongst some of the most influential men and women in the world, he had the feeling of being a schoolboy new to an already well-established class—he just hoped no one would ask him to speak.

He understood before he arrived that many of the members represented the *Transnational Capitalist Class*; the top thirty percent that controlled ninety-five percent of the globe's wealth, who were primarily male, Caucasian and predominantly from America or Europe. Realising he was now this class's newest member filled him with mixed feelings.

In the modern neo-feudal society, corporations, CEOs and boards replaced old empires, Kings and senates.

Looking around the cavernous, cream-lit, mahogany-walled conference hall, he recognised barely a handful of faces; even fewer he'd met in person.

His eyes flicked to a grotesque stone statue pressing its finger to its lips. Positioned in the corner, just beneath the ceiling, it seemed to stare down on him.

The female translator's voice came to life in his near-invisible earpieces, as the Norwegian environmental minister addressed the assembly, "….Okay…He is making a complicated joke. Laugh when I say the word 'now'…wait….Okay, now."

O'Reilly chortled on cue with the rest, wondering if their translators had managed to convey the joke or given a similar instruction.

The dark-haired Essex man had initially been reluctant to accept the invite in the knowledge once he had attended, the conspiracy theories swirling around the Bilderberg Group would extend to him.

O'Reilly himself had been curious about what would be discussed, but so far the most interesting had been a fiery debate regarding left-wing ideology in academia. Hardly earth-shattering.

His presence was on an 'undisclosed' invite and not part of the 'official two' representing each attendant country. He had accepted for two reasons; one was to network with the global elite. The other was to provide intelligence to a man who had uncovered the identity of the people responsible for his daughter's murder and helped him take revenge on them.

Having taken a course in body language and social dynamics, he began picking up on the group's behaviour. Before arriving, he had been given a list of the long-standing and regular participants, and so watched their reactions most closely.

Throughout the conference, he had noticed that an elderly gentleman—maybe well into his eighties—attracted a higher portion of glances from the long-time members. O'Reilly did not recognise him.

Others commanded similar attention, such as the towering, bald, commanding presence of Miles Parker, the chief of the UK's Secret Intelligence Service, more commonly known as MI6.

It surprised O'Reilly how some of the politicians, whose renown far exceeded the others present—like his own country's Foreign Minister and the Italian finance minister—seemed to induce vapid boredom on making their speeches.

He knew there would be a social gathering afterwards, and it would be then he would find out the names of those he considered of interest.

Anything he could do for Bruce McQuillan, he would do.

Bruce McQuillan sat with his two nieces overlooking London Bridge. The buzzing, softly lit restaurant was hosting a 'Peter Pan'-themed evening for charity and his niece, Millie, the younger of the two at twenty-one, seemed especially enamoured.

Sarah's smile at her sister's excitement mirrored his.

Once 'Tinker Bell' had taken their order, Millie said, "Awww, I've missed this. Dinner with my favourite uncle and sister."

They smiled—she only had one sister and uncle.

Both girls had been blessed with Bruce's sister Sandra's flashing brown eyes and dark glossy hair—though Millie sported artificial blonde on this occasion and wore a low-cut floral print dress. Sarah had opted for a white button up halterneck blouse.

"How's your mum getting on, Millie? She'd never tell me anything different than she's fine when I talk to her on the phone."

A tight smile appeared on her face. "She still has her ups and downs, but she's nothing like she used to be. And Gordon is a lovely guy too."

Sandra suffered from the same bipolar disorder their mother had. However, whereas the illness eventually claimed Kathleen McQuillan's life through suicide, Sandra had steadfastly managed hers to the point of raising two well-adjusted and University-graduating daughters, while holding down a job for years as a sales manager for a Glasgow metals wholesaler. She also eschewed SSRIs—Selective Serotonin Reuptake Inhibitors—because, she'd said only half-jokingly, *"If I go oan Scoobes, I'll be oan them for the rest of my life."* *Scoobes* being Glaswegian slang for Valium.

Bruce had feared the worst when Sandra's husband, Mick, died. However, the stoicism she showed made Bruce proud to know her. And after his requisite background check on her new partner, Gordon had come back without giving him any undue concerns—something he did with the girls' boyfriends too—he felt glad she had found someone, though a little guilty he had yet to meet him.

Sarah spoke. "Bruce, you know that Aunt Betsy died a couple of weeks ago?"

"Yes," he answered, without guilt. His father's sister barely comprised a few faded childhood memories. It had taken until his adulthood to piece together that the falling out his staunchly Protestant aunt had with his Catholic mother had origins going back to 'The Troubles' emanating from Northern Ireland. He had never pushed his mother on the subject, or used his professional powers to find out.

"Well, Mum received a stack of old letters. Gordon told me on the quiet that she's been very upset reading them but won't tell him why."

"I see," he answered, his mind whirring.

His eldest niece continued, "Something I wanted to ask you, and I know asking it here and now isn't ideal, but I don't get to see you much."

"Go ahead, Sarah," he said, bracing himself for what it might be.

"Well, you don't mention your dad. I don't think I've ever heard you talk about Grandad."

Bruce leant back in his back. "Well…he wasn't around much when we were kids. He worked as a humanitarian aid worker, went all around the world. He'd come back briefly, then he'd be off again."

Millie asked, "And what was he like?"

Bruce searched his recall, despite knowing memories could distort and warp over time, and that they ended before he had reached the age of seven. He thought he remembered one occasion in their living room where his mother had looked up from the paper to ask his dad, *"Don, if you had the choice between winching the most beautiful woman in the world for a million pounds or me for free, which would you choose?"*

Winching, pronounced 'wenching', was Scottish slang for kissing passionately, and his father—as quick as a flash—had answered, *"Silly question, Kathleen, my darling, because you are the bonniest lass in the world."*

His father had motioned an arms' width circle with his hands as he said *world,* causing Bruce and his sister to giggle and their Mum fail to hold back a smile that appeared as a smirk.

"He was a good guy, I think. Funny. Used to bring back presents. Took me fishing."

"Mum said he was a good guy too," said Millie.

Bruce knew this to be more his sister's projection of their father, as he died before her fifth birthday.

"Did they ever find out what had happened to him?" asked Sarah.

Though he didn't show it, the question stung, as Bruce, despite having one of the world's best computer hackers at his disposal, had not been able to find any information outside of the official narrative.

"He went to Lebanon several times during the late seventies to ensure supply chains got into the region during the strife, and he didn't come back after one visit."

"Did they find out the—" began Sarah, only to look up past his shoulder.

Bruce turned to see Adriana Cruz, an Italian-Albanian he had recently grown close to.

Around ten years younger than himself, but fifteen years older than Sarah, the investigative journalist held herself with the quiet assurance of a woman possessing a strong intellect, work ethic and physical attractiveness.

The white straps across her shoulders contrasted her olive skin. The light brown leather belt matched her flat-heeled shoes.

Millie especially seemed to be taken aback by her presence, as Adriana placed a hand on his shoulder, leant down and pecked him on the cheek.

"London traffic—and the damned Satnav tried to send me back to Italy," she said in perfect, though lightly accented English. Her jet black, shiny hair softened into curls at her shoulders.

As Adriana sat down, Sarah's face lit up. "Oh. My. God. Is this an actual girlfriend? I thought I'd see the Loch Ness monster before I saw this."

Before he could respond, Adriana placed a hand on his upper arm and answered for him, "Your uncle feels strange describing me as a girlfriend at his age, so you might have to describe me as Uncle Bruce's special friend."

Though eliciting a broad smile from Sarah, Millie asked, "You seem quite a few years younger."

Adriana answered the loaded statement airily. "I like an older man with money to inherit from. But I cannot have them too old—I do not like to be a maid until I have squeezed a man's finances dry."

As she said this, she clenched her fist, causing a smile to crack Millie's flimsy cool demeanour.

Bruce smiled too. He had recently taken the decision to make a concerted effort to make time for his nieces and Adriana. It had been different back when the Scotsman was solely responsible for the black operations unit known to a select few as The Chameleon Project. He worked in the field back then and could be—and frequently was—pulled away at a moment's notice to various places in the world. A bullet to his knee a few years ago had forced an overdue exit from fieldwork.

The influential political advisor Henry Costner and the head of SIS, Miles Parker, had combined their power and creativity to bring him in from the cold and give him the role of liaison officer between the United Kingdom's various security services.

And he had now begun the process of handing over the reins of The Chameleon Project to one of his protégés.

"Don't worry, Millie. She'll be gone when she finds out I have lied about my wealth just to get a bonnie lass on my arm."

The girls laughed. The Lost Boys and Tinker Bell diverted the girls' attention as they sang 'Happy Birthday' to an elderly lady seated with her family a few tables behind.

Seeing Adriana's tight smile, Bruce asked, "What is it?"

She whispered, "One of my contacts says that Chen Zhao has tended his resignation. He will leave in the Summer."

Zhao, now seemingly the former president of Interpol, had been a distant but extremely influential ally to Bruce, and vice-versa. And had shown no signs of diminishing professional enthusiasm, bad health or a lack of well-being the last time Bruce saw him just over a couple of months ago.

"I'll go see him," said the Scotsman. "I am going to stay up here another day before heading back."

3

Connor Reed felt his eyes getting heavy, as he sat at his kitchen table in front of his laptop, taking in all the information. As a premier agent for the Chameleon Project, a British-based black operations outfit, he had set himself the early morning regime of a cold shower, bodyweight strength training, and then studying various topics pertinent to his role.

Now clad only in his Ron Hill Union Jack shorts, the densely muscled Yorkshireman had been awake for nearly three hours, despite only having four hours sleep.

'The Helena', a lap-dancing club co-owned by his elder cousin, Tom Ryder, had its opening the previous night.

Connor had gone to show his face for the family— that is, his relations making up the criminal element, namely his male cousins and uncles. Though he'd had more to drink than he intended, he managed to steadfastly refuse the premium cocaine offered to him, despite its allure.

Though partial to recreational drugs in the past, Connor's use of them had dwindled as his sense of purpose had grown.

Don't let your serotonin of being a man be taken over by a constant boyish want of dopamine, is what he had told himself when offered.

His fingertips rubbed his temples before splaying into dark blond hair. The study timer told him he had four minutes left until he could creep back into bed for a nap.

"Fucksake," he murmured at the sharp knock at the door. He tapped his phone screen to display the image captured by one of the hidden security cameras; Gran Paulette was standing at his front door.

He frowned as he went to open it—he wasn't expecting an impromptu visit. She scowled, "Is that how you answer the door? I could have been a Jehovah's Witness."

"I have had them already. Bang, bang, banging on the door at six this morning. I had to go down and let them out."

Ordinarily, jokes like that would elicit a crack in her usually icy demeanour, but not this time.

"Mind yourself out of the way," she said, marching past him. "We need to talk."

He closed the door. "I'll put the kettle on. Despite you coming in like the Gestapo looking for Anne Frank."

He clicked on the kettle and turned to see his gran looking around—this was her first visit to his first home.

"It's good you're keeping it clean and tidy," she said, before perching on one of the cushioned stools by the table.

"Thanks." He turned back to the kettle. It had a super-charged heating element, boiling the water within seconds.

"Gosh that was quick."

"I'd turned it on just before you knocked on the door."

Having passed her a sugared, milky tea, he settled opposite her.

She began, "It's nice to see that you can enjoy a cup of coffee without having to bolt off."

Connor felt something stir within his stomach but kept it off his face. Yesterday, he cut short the coffee he'd been having with his gran and her friend and left. Rene had been visibly ecstatic with her new kitchen provided by his family after being ripped off by an out of town gangster.

"It is."

"I found it strange that you left the moment you were told Rene's Granddaughter would be arriving—especially as you've had a thing for the ginger girls since you were a tot."

"I've had girls…acquaintances of all kinds of hair and skin colours," he said, despite knowing his gran was right. A pre-teen crush on a Daniella Sarandon in the school year above had spread to an admiration of celebrities like Isla Fisher, Christina Hendricks and Jessica Chastain.

Paulette sipped her tea. "Well, she's a very pretty girl—surgeon too. And him, he's a real *Bobby Dazzler,* a bit like you were."

"I am still a Bobby Dazzler."

She ignored his weak attempt at deflection. "Strange how the baby's dad isn't on the scene. Jackson is the baby's name, by the way."

"I know. Rene said, remember?"

"What do you think of the name?"

He shrugged against his heartbeat in his ears, "It's a good name."

"Is it what you would have picked for your first son?"

Connor could see his gran had the bit between her teeth and gave way to the inevitable. "I can't say for sure he's mine."

Her tea spilt over the rim as she banged it down. "Christ almighty, Connor! He's the spit of you. And—"

"How's that possible? He is only seven months old."

"Trust me, it's like looking at you at that age. And you never thought to tell me I was a great-grandma?!"

"Calm yourself, Gran. I didn't have any inkling until yesterday."

He could see her taking a few deep breaths before saying, "You better start explaining."

"It's complicated."

"Don't you fucking dare, Connor Ryder, and I don't ever swear."

Now trapped by one of only three people he'd let speak to him like that, he threw her a tea towel. "Fine, wipe the tea up."

When she had done so, he said, "Right, Gran, what I am going to tell you I haven't even told Tom. He's probably guessed but he doesn't know for sure. So, I'd appreciate it if you kept it to yourself."

"I'll keep schtum."

Connor believed her. Women in crime families were often better versed in keeping secrets.

"I don't have as much to do with the family 'business' as you might think. I work…I work for a…a sort of spy unit… secret operations against some very nasty people and organisations."

Connor braced himself for her disdainful disbelief, but she simply asked, "Like who James Bond worked for…MI6?"

He shook his head. "Not exactly. The man I work for works with them, but he's allowed to run his own unit. Don't ask me how."

"So, what's this got to do with you having a son?"

"Grace and I had a relationship, a casual one. Around eighteen months ago, she went to Ukraine on an aid mission to help the hospitals in Crimea. She gets kidnapped and I—in my capacity of working for this unit—was able to get her back safely."

Her forehead creased. "So, she thanks you by letting you get her up the duff?"

"Must have happened before she went."

"So, she lets you get her pregnant. You've rescued her. And then she doesn't tell you that she's carrying your baby?"

"She knows what I know—that the people I go after are amongst the evilest in this world. And not the 'my baby is crying too loud, so I'll throw it in an oven, while I get on with smoking crack' type of evil. These people have the resources for human trafficking, kidnapping, theft, rape and murder on a mass scale. And if Grace and her…Jackson are associated with me, it puts them in danger."

Paulette glared at him wide-eyed. "Don't talk wet. Just quit this work you're doing and—"

"I can't do that, Gran."

"What do you mean you can't do that? No one can force you of all people to do anything."

22

"No. I am meant to do this."

"You're going to give up on your son for a—"

"It's the opposite, alright. I am protecting them both. Even if I quit, certain people could still come out of the woodwork."

She sipped her tea, seemingly absent-mindedly before saying, "Well, I don't know what you're expecting me to do, because I am not going to deny him."

Connor stood. "You'll see him when he's at Rene's. Spoil him, do whatever you like, but you won't tell anyone that he belongs to us. Because if you do, you'll be putting them both in danger."

They held one another's stare for a few moments before she relented. "And what's he going to be told when he starts asking where his dad is?"

"I don't know. Like I said, I'll have to ask his mum."

"Make sure you do. And remember that whoever your boss is, he isn't family."

Bruce pressed the grey composite door's circular chime. The blue light revolved around his finger, and he knew his image would flash up inside.

The three-bedroom, semi-detached in Bothwell lay around twelve miles away from their original family home, and Bruce surmised, even with inflation, it to be worth many times more than the old tenement flat. His last visit to Glasgow had been a while ago.

After a few moments, the door opened to reveal a woman, two years his junior though often mistook to be a little older, if only because of his looking younger than his age. She stood just above medium height, her dark brown hair scraped back into a ponytail.

The surprise on her face irked him, as he knew she hadn't checked the screen before answering the door.

His sister's arm slid around his neck, half-embracing and half pulling him into her home.

"This is a surprise," she said, her broad smile revealing a slightly off-centre front tooth. "You usually call?"

"I didn't want to give your new man a chance to prepare for the interrogation."

"Well he's away. The old firm are playing today," she said, referring to the name given to the derby matches played between the city's two arch-rival football teams, Glasgow Rangers and Glasgow Celtic. And Bruce already knew Gordon would be out.

She continued, "You must think I am buttoned up the back to think I don't know you've already used your powers to check him out."

"A coffee would be great, thanks."

His sister gave him a wry smile as they parted; her for the kitchen and him for the living room.

The dark turquoise rug matched the sofa unit, on which sat coloured cushions.

Pictures of the girls at various ages perched on the cabinet and mantelpiece. Their graduation pictures hung above the television so as to be unmissable to any visitors.

A long time ago, a picture of himself in his beige beret inhabited its place above the television briefly. After Bruce and his sister had engaged in a fierce argument regarding its being displayed, Sandra—for once—had eventually conceded to wrap it up and place it in the loft.

He sank into the corner of the sofa as Sandra placed his drink on the coffee table next to the arm rest. She nestled down on the other end of the sofa. "Well?"

He frowned, "Well what?"

"Why have you really turned up unannounced? And don't give me yer *pish* about checking in on Gordon."

He exhaled a smile from his nose. "Alright. I've heard you've been in receipt of some letters."

"Aye. Received them by recorded delivery from Dad's sister's solicitor. I take it the girls have told you that she's doing the tango with Satan now?"

He nodded. "Sarah also told me the letters have been upsetting you."

"What's in them would make most people *greet*. Drivel about our *maw* having IRA connections and whatever else Betsy thought up on whatever daft planet she was oan."

"If you know it's pish, then why get yerself in a tiz over it," replied Bruce, native dialect coming to the fore in line with his sister's.

"Because there are also letters from Dad to her. Letters from when he was away."

Bruce shrugged, "Saying what?"

"That he was now a target. That he expected to be killed out there. Bruce…"

McQuillan's heart moved into his stomach as he watched his sister fight to compose herself. He restrained himself from comforting her, knowing she wouldn't respond well to it. Finally, she spat, "That fuckin' bitch kept them all these years."

"Kept what?"

"Dad had wrote us…goodbye letters in case he died. I've got yours."

The news momentarily froze him before he said, "Are they dated?"

Her eyes glistening, she nodded. "Early into his final trip. Why did'nae he just come back?"

He said, almost to himself, "Maybe he felt it was his duty."

She snapped, "What about his duty to us? His family? You and I know that Maw would probably still be alive if he'd hav' been around by her side."

"Calm yerself. I wasn't defending the choice," said Bruce quietly, although he hadn't condemned it either. "I'm just playing the devil's advocate."

The aggression in her posture and expression visibly melted under his mild scolding.

"Sorry, I am just so angry about it all."

He knew 'angry' meant 'bitter and full of sorrow'. "Have you done reading them?"

"Aye," she said. "The covering letter said you're getting your 'good-bye' letter sent to your London address by guaranteed next day, so it's down there waiting for you."

Bruce knew what his father had written him was a 'death letter'; standard practice for military personnel about to embark on a tour of duty, and only to be opened by the recipient on the writer's death. However, 'death letters' were left behind, not sent out. And, he surmised, not a general practice for humanitarian aid workers, though he accepted his ignorance on that front.

"I'll need them all," he said. "I'll have to take a copy of yours."

She stared at him for a moment. "Bruce, it's been nearly fifty years. Whoever was behind it will be long gone. And so, what could be done after all this time?"

"Maybe nothing." Bruce stood. "But there's no expiration date on vengeance, Sandra. Now root me out the letters."

4

Bruce opened the door of his Knightsbridge home and picked out the solicitor's letter from inside the clear polycarbonate post box.

Though the curiosity had been burning throughout the near seven-hour drive from his sister's, he fought the urge of rushing to read it. Instead, he replaced his shoes with specialised slippers providing good purchase to the floor and fitting his feet snugly, before carrying out checks of the manual security breach indicators complementing the digital versions linked to his phone.

Once satisfied, he floated across to the window to sit on a high chair overlooking a glittering view of London.

He neatly freed the two sets of papers with the 'Braveheart Sword' sterling silver letter opener—a gift from his niece, Millie. One was a copy of the covering letter from the solicitors, the other a near half century-old death letter.

To My Son,

If you're reading this, Bruce, it means that I have died in Lebanon.

Now, you might be feeling hurt, angry and confused as to why I voluntarily went over to a warzone when I was not a soldier. Well, it was because I needed a break from you weans and yer Maw!

Don't tell her about that joke, she'll give me a skelping in heaven. If that's where I am going.

The truth is that, if I left this place now, I wouldn't forgive myself. Many thousands of innocents are, and will continue to be, affected by this war.

There have been tensions in Lebanon for decades now due to religious tribalism. We Glaswegians know a

little about that, but only a taste—here it is on a scale that would fry your brain to imagine.

But what causes tensions like that to ignite into war? I'll tell you, son, often it is when powerful people ignite it as they stand to profit from it. It won't be their homes destroyed or their children maimed or killed.

I have written letters and sent them anonymously to various western news sources.

A few months after the articles appeared, I began to get 'visits' from what I call the 'TOR Mafia'.

Very polite. Very European. Would never give their names, so I would pick out a characteristic and nickname them. At first, it was one with a pointy chin and ski-slope nose that I called 'Forsyth' after a guy who hosts The Generation Game. But he was replaced by 'Ziggy', after Ziggy Stardust, well Bowie you know (your Maw and I went to him at the Hammersmith Odeon. Only two rows in front of us).

Where was I?

Yes, two weeks ago these tensions exploded into civil war. The UK government is insistent on its citizens leaving but I won't.

Though loud and boisterous, demonstrations about fishing rights were just settling down when Maarouf Saad, an influential Lebanese politician and activist, was shot by a sniper. He died just shy of a fortnight later in hospital.

'They' (meaning the media, and who is behind them) say he was killed by a Lebanese sniper. That, he might have been, but I might have proof that it was sponsored by the West.

Now, the responsible thing to do is to substantiate this before chucking petrol on the flames. But I am unsure who to turn to, because, if the wrong people find out I have it, I'll be a dead man. But I'll find a way.

Bruce, if you are reading this letter, I just want you to know that if you were only going to take away one piece of advice from me it's this—spend your life in such a way that when your time is up, you can look Saint Peter in the eye and tell him that the world was a better place with you in it.

How you choose to do that is up to you (but look after yer maw and sister…that's not up for debate or I'll be giving you a skelping if we end up in the same place!).

Love Dad.

Bruce's eyes stared a hole into the table. He rapidly blinked a few times.

His brain began to contemplate on how to use the information. This focus provided him with a buoyancy aid against his emotions.

Despite what he had said to his sister, Bruce knew he didn't have the luxury of chasing after decades-old vendettas against mysterious ghosts.

Not when the demons of today needed fighting.

Prince Nawwaf bin Salam knew this day would come and had prepared the best he could.

He looked out the windows to the desert city of Riyadh. He had held the position of director general of Saudi Arabia's General Intelligence Directorate (GID) or Al Mukhabarat Al A'amah for almost a year now. Appointed during a time of strife, he'd insisted on two offices to randomly switch between—he had enemies both inside and outside the Kingdom.

Nawwaf had willingly—almost voluntarily—bided his time within the organisation's lower ranks to develop experience and contacts. However, in the wake of the recent murder of a dissident Saudi journalist, the former director general had been implicated by the western press, and a reshuffle had been made to placate the Americans.

From his black snakeskin recliner chair, his eyes followed a plane's take-off from the King Khalid International Airport in the distance.

It had in fact been himself who had ordered it—though the idea had first been proposed by the man in front of him.

His most trusted advisor, the young, soft-eyed Tareq Nabil, knelt with his head bent, delivering his omen. Once Tareq had finished, the Chief of Saudi intelligence said, "You may rise."

Once he had, the Intelligence Chief asked, "And they think this energy will be capable of powering global aviation? I have been told that might not be possible, and even if it was, it would be between one and three decades away?" Prince Nawwaf noticed the younger man's shiftiness.

"That was the scientific consensus, *Emir.*"

The Saudi Prince removed his *Keffiyeh,* rubbing his matted black hair before stroking his beard. "How close are they to mass production?"

"Reports indicate that it could be as little as four months. The Japanese company will begin trials in their smaller cities of Hiroshima and Nagasaki, poetic justice considering those cities were destroyed by such destructive energy and will now win the race to be the first nourished by clean, renewable energy. If successful, the whole of Japan, beginning with Tokyo, will receive the new technology, and then we will not be able to surpass them in this race. We will have to place bids along with the rest of the world, with the Japanese company naming their price."

Nawwaf silently cursed; he had warned the Crown Prince—the nation's de facto leader given his father's old age—over a decade ago regarding Saudi Arabia's need to win the race for sustainable renewable energy. He remembered succinctly the moment he had first brought it up at a conference meeting—there had ensued a deathly silence which he knew, had he been anyone else, would have been replaced with derisory laughter.

"Our king is committed to our quest for sustainable clean energy. It will diversify our economy, lead to future jobs, and let us speak the truth, the less our Kingdom uses oil, the more we have available to sell to the world. And if we become the technological leaders, the world will continue to bend at the knees to the House of Saud. So, my advisor, what do you advise?"

"Under your leadership, the Al Mukhabarat Al A'amah has remained strong, despite the western media's insinuations and lies. However, I realise you might not want to risk antagonising them further."

Nawwaf scoffed, "Our people know the truth—our cyber systems protect them from the lies of non-believers. Besides, now is not the time to be meek."

Nawwaf had been one of the architects behind the pro-regime bot accounts used to crack down on any insidious social media attempts to subvert the people.

"What is your command, Emir?"

"I need a person, or team, of both the highest professionalism and the utmost discretion. Money shall be no object in this sacred mission."

"Forgive me, but I do not understand, your Highness. If it is discretion you require, surely one of our own agents would be the most suitable for this task?"

Nawwaf shook his head, "Should this man or men fail, nothing can lead back to the King. We need an outsider and, crucially, it must not be traced back to us."

Due to the reliance on the Kingdom's oil, Nawwaf knew the world ultimately bent the knee, even though their leaders shrilled their superficial cries of Saudi Arabia's perceived 'industrial and humanitarian infractions'. Unfortunately, this had bred hubris into most members of the Royal Family.

Although he would never show it, this realisation sent a bolt of nerves through him—*If the world no longer relies on us, then it no longer needs to turn a blind eye.*

"I will find the correct man for the mission, your Highness," Tareq stated. "Our enemies might only suspect—but never prove—your mighty hand behind it."

Miles Parker stood and greeted Bruce McQuillan as the Scotsman walked into his office. It occurred to the MI6 Chief that this might be the only man he stood up for, who wasn't his official superior.

The flecks of grey in McQuillan's otherwise black hair, and the wise confidence of his eyes, were the only real indications he was now in his fifties. His movement and sinewy physique were those of a much younger man.

"Bruce, how are you keeping?" asked the bald spy chief, a few inches taller than McQuillan, himself a tall man.

"Cannot complain, Miles. Yourself?"

Parker learnt a long time ago that he shouldn't complain either in the former SAS soldier's presence.

"I'm fine. Please, take a seat."

They faced one another over Parker's large, polished oak desk. A painting depicting the death of Admiral Lord Nelson surrounded by his men, hung behind Bruce, who asked, "And so?"

Parker's fingers drummed once on the table, "A Japanese-owned company called Okada Engineering have made important breakthroughs with regards to renewable energy—both green and carbon neutral."

McQuillan nodded. "Any specifics?"

"Amplification and storage. The amplification is of both solar, wind energy and geo-thermal energy. The science allows for the energy to reproduce in and of itself—an electric form of binary fission. This means that solar panels and wind turbine blades can be much smaller yet can generate vastly more energy. So much so, one house might be able to generate its own energy from a single metre square panel and a small countersunk wind turbine."

"Energy storage?"

"This is the more significant part. Okada has developed a small and light battery that exceeds the miles a car can presently travel on a full fuel tank. A battery can be charged within minutes—much more rapidly than even a fast-charge mobile phone. The prediction is this technology will be improved upon and refined to the point where it can be applied to commercial aviation—something engineers doubted would be possible due to the size and weight of battery previously needed. We might be talking a mere five years until the planet is virtually carbon-free if this is true. This is because the technology can be turned back on itself so that the manufacture of the equipment can also be carbon-free. That has huge implications."

"You said that in five years the planet could be almost carbon-free, but it was my understanding that factory farming contributes a great deal to emissions."

"As you are aware, certain powerful individuals and organisations meet to discuss these matters—in your native Glasgow for instance. In the next few years, the media narrative will be of the merits of tissue culture using cloned cell lines as a more humane way of producing meat. And with this technology, it too will be emission-free."

Bruce stroked his jaw. "Wonderful news."

"Most people would agree with you."

"But the Saudi Arabian royal family aren't most people."

Parker, even after all these years, remained surprised at the man's powers of deduction. He again lamented how Bruce McQuillan should be his successor, a prospect the Scotsman had repeatedly poured cold water on.

"Yes, a family with access to trillions of pounds, hell-bent on keeping that money, even at the expense of the planet's biodiversity, is a sub-optimal situation. That, and the fact the Chinese have placed hundreds of billions of dollars into renewable investments. They'd be loath to see their rivals beat them to the punch for a fraction of their investment capital."

"I can imagine they are not the only ones less than enthusiastic. Last time I checked, not only were the Saudis exporting around eight and a quarter million barrels of oil a day, but Russia was also exporting five and a quarter. The States, three and a quarter. Not to mention the money various companies have pumped into renewables research."

"Yes. There is danger from all sides."

Bruce gave him a small smile, "Now, not to say you're a heartless bastard, Miles, but you don't strike me as the 'save the earth' type, and since the UK itself is in the top twenty for oil exportation, I have to ask why we are having this conversation?"

Miles killed the smile threatening to break out, "Ten years ago, Okada Engineering headhunted British scientist Ronald Sykes to work on solving the problem of amplification and storage. Unfortunately, despite Japan having the world's second highest research and development budget, upheavals at the company caused them to lose money to the point of entering administration, just as serious headway was being made. So, Sykes secretly petitioned British businesses and the UK Government for funds to resurrect the company."

Bruce deduced, "And because the shares were cheap they agreed."

Miles nodded, "A consortium put up half and was matched by the Government. Of course, it helped that Japan agreed to a free trade agreement in the wake of BREXIT. The project's being secretly billed as the 'Twin Isles Project'."

"So, the UK government and commerce own major equity in the most profitable technological potential breakthrough of the last three decades?"

"Potential being the operative word. It is still a prototype, and will be until it has completed trials in Hiroshima and Nagasaki."

"Naturally, we want our investment protected at all costs—obviously because the planet needs saving."

Parker detected the hint of sarcasm he guessed not because Bruce didn't believe in global warming—but more that it was Parker's priority.

"I admit, I think the claims of the earth's imminent demise are exaggerated. But it's irrelevant. If the prototype becomes serviceable, we win—whether 'we' is the planet or the United Kingdom."

The topic of climate change had been one of the more hotly debated topics at the recent Bilderberg meeting he had attended. Not even the man in front of him was privy to the discussions there.

The Scotsman asked, "What is the Yakuza's stance on this?"

Parker leant back. "Much of their income comes from skimming off fossil fuel imports and nuclear energy site maintenance costs. They would only welcome this development if they profited from it. A disinformation campaign seems to have kept them at bay thus far."

McQuillan said, "The Yakuza has strong back channels to law enforcement. They have ties to the government through the *Uyoku dantai*—extreme right wing political groups loyal to the emperor. Don't be surprised if the disinformation game goes both ways."

"Duly noted."

"Why have you come to me? SIS has agents in the area."

"Most will be embedded with the Public Security Intelligence Agency. We cannot dismiss the possibility that certain echelons of the Japanese Government would want the technology under a fully Japanese flagship."

"You telling me we have no assets not known by the PISA?"

"Of course we do," said Parker, trying to keep any defensiveness out of his voice. He didn't want to admit they were mostly native, low-level staffers on retainers in various government organisations. He continued with, "But we have received credible intelligence Prince Nawwaf bin Salam, has gotten wind of it and is planning moves to intercept. And the GID's director general can buy any amount of professionalism he needs. I do not know as yet who he has petitioned for assistance—could be the Chinese, Russians or a freelance organisation. So you see, it's all hands on deck for this one."

"Just Nawwaf bin Salam or his wider counsel?"

Parker looked at him through his eyebrows. "Just the Prince it seems."

Parker felt appreciative of Bruce not asking how he knew. Though if the damn Scotsman would acquiesce to Parker's wishes for him to succeed him as SIS chief, he'd have told him of the chief of Saudi intelligence's favourite mistress run by the UK foreign intelligence service.

Perhaps he already knows.

Parker noticed something strange in McQuillan's posture. He seemed…distracted.

Finally, the Scotsman asked, "Can I ask a favour?"

This was a first—thought Parker, unsure of what to make of it.

"Can I see the files—preferably unredacted—regarding the sparking off of the civil war in Lebanon back in seventy-five?"

The SIS Chief thought for only a moment. "You'll have copies in a timely fashion."

"Thank you."

"Is there anyone you can send?" asked Parker, not wishing to infer that one favour be predicated on the other. The agreement for a long time had been that Parker could only propose, not demand, mission taskings for McQuillan's Chameleon Project.

Bruce regarded him for a moment, "Send me everything you have, and I'll look into it."

"Thank you. With the money these Arabs have, who know who they could send against us."

Mikhail Gorokhov walked the streets of Moscow, the spring breeze buffeting his dark heather-coloured shirt against a physique almost entirely made of muscle, bone and sinew.

In the distance, he could see bronze Greek-like statues of heroes Minin and Pozharsky, oxidised green over the course of two hundred years.

He could almost meditate while strolling there as everything seemed slower in comparison to Tokyo. Being one of the two cities he spent much of his time in, he could appreciate their differences. People in Tokyo had to stand still if using their phones in any capacity other than calling—Muscovites could walk as they texted on theirs.

As a Russian national representative of Judo in his youth, the forty-year-old felt equally at home in either country. He inherited his black hair and almond-shaped eyes from his Japanese mother, his heavy eyebrow and prominent jaw from his Russian father.

His dual heritage had been both a help and a hindrance during his SVR RF (Foreign Intelligence Service of the Russian Federation) career.

The expected Mercedes-Benz S 600 Guard Pullman appeared in the distance and Gorokhov observed the furtive glances in its direction. The Mercedes was the former Presidential State car, gifted to the Head of the SVR.

It pulled up along the street and Gorokhov got in without a word.

Alexey Orlov, the second most feared man in Russia, sat in the back. He wore a red tie with white sparks under the collar of a white shirt. The dark blue of the suit matched the eyes underneath furrowed brows. The wavy brown hair sat on top of an expressionless face.

"Good to see you, Mikhail."

"Thank you," answered Gorokhov. He caught the subtle twitch under Orlov's left eye at his curt response. A few years back, his reply would have included the word *сэр*—sir.

"There's been a development in Japan. Your expertise is needed."

"I believe we had an agreement regarding moves against my mother's country," answered Gorokhov, ensuring disproportionate measures in the assertiveness and respect of his tone.

"I am the messenger," said Orlov. "From our mutual friend."

This stilled the retort on Gorokhov's tongue. Instead, he said, "If that is the truth, then I accept."

"Why would it not be true?"

"Your interests supersede any willingness to be honest."

With eyes narrowing, Orlov replied, "Mikhail, you know that during and even before my tenure as Head of the SVR, I have thrown a shroud of protection over you. Even when my colleagues went so far as to question whether or not you are a double agent, it was I who convinced them otherwise. So, why do you speak to me with such disrespect?"

Gorokhov nodded, "I am appreciative, but I have repaid you with successful missions and loyalty—I have had a—small as it may be—bearing on your ascent to this position. And when I wanted to leave, you attempted to 'persuade me' back."

"You astutely backed the correct chess player in me, Mikhail," said Orlov. "And it is natural to want an asset you have worked to develop to stay. It would have been made clear to you on joining us, that once you're in, you can be called upon forever. You have always known those rules—which I have since broken for you."

When Gorokhov stared back without reply Orlov continued, "We are needlessly arguing, Gorokhov. I am not asking you to attack 'The Land of The Rising Sun'. You know my sole concern is Russia, however I—and our mutual friend—do not wish to see our Japanese counterparts undermined."

"My concern is Russia too," answered Gorokhov, knowing that his superior's declaration was a barb. "Tell me what you need."

"A Japanese company have made breakthroughs in key areas of renewable energy—so much so that our think tank believes in ten to fifteen years, the only significant harmful emissions into the atmosphere may only come through factory farming. Maybe by then, meat will be grown from petri dishes. However, there are people in the race who do not care to be beaten to a prize that could see the victor become the next superpower."

"You said you didn't wish to undermine the Japanese?"

As the Pullman slid around the city, the head of the SVR stroked his chin. "The British have a huge share in Okada Engineering. If this succeeds then there is already a plan in place—'The Twin Isle Project'—that will see both rise on the world stage. Seeing as both are already within the higher echelon of powerful nations, then you understand my concerns."

Gorokhov did understand, the past few years had strained Russian-British relations. The British had the audacity to cry when—a few years back—a GRU officer who had doubled as an agent for them was subsequently poisoned by a Novichok nerve agent. Still, Gorokhov almost respected the move they pulled to have twenty-eight different countries expel an unprecedented 153 Russian diplomats. What he didn't appreciate was the ill-planned attempt not only saw the double agent survive, but led to a British national dying after coming into contact with the nerve agent due to a bungled attempt at disposing of it.

Britain also gleefully imposed sanctions on Russia after his Government took the correct and moral action of protecting the Crimean people from the Ukrainians, who mistook Crimea as their property instead of a gift of alliance from Russia during the Cold War.

"I understand."

Orlov said, "Our patriotism should always be our focus, Gorokhov. However, an opportunity has arisen where you and I can be compensated."

Gone were the days Gorokhov would have found the assumption of his seeking excessive financial gain from his missions for Russia offensive.

"What is this opportunity?"

"Nawwaf bin Salam is keen for this clean energy technology to find its way into Saudi hands—if that isn't possible, they will settle for it being destroyed. An intermediary has reached out for a freelancer."

Gorokhov had heard years ago a rumour that Orlov had a highly placed mole within Saudi's General Intelligence Presidency (GIP). However, he had heard many reports that turned out to be myths. This was the first confirmation of a Russian plant high within the GIP.

"How would that help Russia?"

Orlov treated him to a rare smile. "The Saudis are overfed, pampered dogs. They have never known the struggles of our people. Their nepotism is like wildfire. They will not be difficult to trick. Your...ex-curricular assignments will be enough to confirm that you are an independent contractor. Then, after the mission's successful completion, we simply tell them the technology has been destroyed."

"I sense there is more to this."

Orlov released a throaty laugh. "Yes. This intermediary will tell Nawwaf of your identity."

Gorokhov's felt the vehicle cool.

"That is not acceptable to me. I have gone to great lengths to protect my identity. Intermediaries do not get to see my face."

"Nor shall this one," replied Orlov. "However, not even Naawaf will release that kind of money without knowing your credentials."

"He wants insurance?"

"Insurance he will not receive once he believes you have died. The money you will receive from this contract will ensure your freedom in life, Mikhail. You could do anything you want."

The assassin stared for a few moments. He did not doubt the receipt of at least a share of the money—his new boss would ensure that. For the same reason, he believed that Orlov would report him as KIA and allow him to live in a far distant country.

What he knew to be an untruth was that any future assignments for Orlov would be voluntary. If Gorokhov's new commander—now a very old man—died, then the shark-like Orlov would threaten to expose him to the Saudis if he refused any tasking asked of him.

Gorokhov, despite his insinuated desire to return to full retirement, now liked the idea of taking missions at intervals; what else was he going to do? Bodyguard in Mexico? Teach languages to half-interested home-schooled rich kids? Open a Sambo and Judo school in the United States?

He saw barriers and pitfalls with every endeavour he could think of, but the freedom of a more relaxed schedule, visiting any country he desired might be the best of both worlds. After all, he had developed this skill set for nearly three decades. He didn't know of anything else which he would be prepared to put in the tortuous amount of time to achieve true mastery.

"How will I receive payment if I am 'dead'?"

"You will receive half of the money up front. The other half will come from the old man."

"How much?"

"Twelve million euros has been offered to destroy the technology—which means you'll be able to negotiate fifteen. Thirty million to hand the technology over—which means you'll command forty. Arabs have negotiation in their blood but the Saudis will succumb given the stakes and their untold riches."

The younger man had heard reports of the Saudi Royal family wealth ranging from $100 billion to a trillion.

Gorokhov looked at Orlov and repeated the old Russian quote. "It is better to have one hundred friends than one hundred roubles."

"You have always been intelligent. I am the best friend a man like you could have."

Gorokhov nodded in insincere agreement.

"Yes, if there is to be a dual nation project it should be between Russia and Japan. Not the Americans' puppet—even more so now that they have left Europe."

His boss smiled, "Still hate the Americans, Gorokhov? The Cold War, Hiroshima and Nagasaka were all a long time ago, and excuse me for saying, before your time."

"I may have been a child but I still remember the Cold War well. A strong man forgives but only after seeing repentance. And the way the Americans and British play the champions of moral decency is almost laughable if was not so obscene—or so dangerous to our people."

The SVR head smiled, "It is almost as if you were born for this mission, Mikhail."

5

Ciara Robson sat in the back of the ruby Jaguar XJ (X351). The dark green of the River Thames slithered past on one side with the sun dappling on the beige fortress of Vauxhall Cross opposite.

A faint fragrance of dust and car exhaust fumes slid in through the gap at the top of the window.

Her blonde hair, once highlighted with silver and short to the point of barely skimming the tops of her ears, now stroked her neck like feathers.

She wore a light ash-grey blazer over a white t-shirt, with matching trousers and white flat shoes.

Watching her tall, suited boss walking through the throng, she wondered whether there was another man in the United Kingdom who could claim to have protected the neutral and innocent more than Bruce McQuillan had.

And amid the storms she had witnessed him facing—albeit she had not known him long in relation to his entire career—he had never seemed panicked—scared maybe, once—but never panicked.

Connor Reed shared the same trait. When she had asked the Yorkshireman whether it was a front, he spoke of disguising and channelling his anxiety with an analogy— *'A swan looks splendid when you observe it gliding across the water, but its gipping looking webbed feet are going like fuck underneath.'*

The admission of this 'mask' gladdened her and would be something she would have to develop to an even greater degree.

Though she had worked as one of its agents for more than a few years now, she had barely any idea of its entire personnel, resources, structure and under what criteria it chose its missions.

He got into the car and asked, "Are you going anywhere other than home?"

When she shook her head, Bruce said to the driver, "North Finchley, please—usual address."

When the driver nodded, Bruce pressed the button raising the screen between the front and back seats.

She noted that though he had upgraded to a sleek black metal watch, it didn't look expensive and reminded her of him saying, *'All I need a watch for is to tell me the time and add weight to a punch should I ever need to do that again.'*

He began, "Okada Engineering, a Japanese company dedicated to renewables, have made breakthroughs in the key areas of amplification and storage, especially in the use of photovoltaics—conversion of light into electricity. Are you aware of the problems in relation to clean energy?"

"One of the issues is how intrusive the massive wind turbine farms look in the countryside and how solar panels struggle to provide the energy a family needs all year around."

"Correct. What Okada has done to resolve it is create an amplification of the clean energy collected. Also, a portable storage system, meaning that with this technology the issue of electric cars needing regular charging will be a thing of the past. They have managed to patent a battery made from aluminium. Far more readily available and much cheaper than the potential conflict minerals."

Ciara thought for a moment. "Certain people, organisations, nations might not welcome this news."

His face expressed a hint of approval at her conclusion, which lifted her a little.

"Correct. The Saudis export 10,600,000 barrels of oil a day. The Russians come in second with around half that. The United Kingdom are in twentieth place."

"China has a large interest too."

"That they do—they've been pumping billions into renewables but haven't seen progress like this. Many wealthy and powerful people stand to lose out on a lot of money and power when this comes to fruition—people who might see an opportunity to steal the technology and profit from it."

Ciara shrugged, "I see why the former must be prevented but the latter? I mean, as long as the technology is used, who cares who profits."

"A decade ago, Okada Engineering recruited Brit scientist Ronald Sykes to help solve the issues of amplification and storage. Reading between the lines, the company's business management might not have been on a par with their scientific expertise until Kusama Okada—the Granddaughter of Masayoshi Okada, the founder—took the reins and made changes. But in the meantime they lost money to the point of folding, just as Ronald Sykes was getting somewhere. He secretly petitioned big British businesses and the UK Government for the money to keep the company afloat."

"What percentage of Okada is owned by the UK?"

"Parker did not tell me but Jaime informs me its share stands at forty percent split evenly between the UK government and a group of commercial investors."

"So we are talking billions back into the UK economy."

Bruce nodded. "The primary goal is to see this technology manifest in the world. And whatever is left of the patriot in me, would like to see the UK investors profit from the risk they took."

"I am guessing a plan is forming in your head?"

"You have been to Japan a few times."

"I was under the impression you wanted me out of the field and into the office, so to speak?"

"That I do. But it might be useful to have you do some of the initial surveillance work before rerolling into an advisor for whichever agent I send."

"Were you thinking of Connor?"

"I am not sure. One of the advantages of using Connor, as it was with you, is that there was no need for elaborate legends when conducting operations in Europe. However, what would a British criminal businessman want in Japan?"

Legends in the espionage game were the deep and detailed cover stories the undercover agents needed to memorise and which needed to be 'proofed' against potential enemy investigation.

"Money laundering opportunities?"

"He could obtain that on the continent without the headache of navigating translation and cultural boundaries. There're the Italians, and now the Estonians are making waves in that arena."

Ciara thought for a moment. "You told me once that he wasn't just the best fighter within The Project but the best martial artist too. Maybe he goes there to train, for a break away from everything? Land of the Samurai and such like."

"That might work," replied Bruce. After a few moments he rubbed the stubble of his jaw and asked, "Do you have anything pressing on this afternoon?"

"I can move some tasks around without undue effort."

Bruce pressed the intercom to the driver. "Change of plan. Take us to my personal vehicle."

When the driver replied in the affirmative, and Bruce had lifted his finger off the intercom, she asked, "What are we doing?"

"We are going to visit someone integral to your professional future."

She didn't ask why the driver couldn't take them—he wouldn't be allowed.

Connor sipped his black coffee. It warmed his insides as he had not long stepped out of a cold shower.

He looked out from the hotel balcony bare-chested in a pair of yellow with a black stripe Bruce Lee Game of Death bottoms. The sunrise crept over the hill, illuminating the meadow.

The expanse of pleasure in his diaphragm wasn't only due to the view or the post-workout and shower endorphins; the fact he and his family now owned this hotel played its part.

The Ryder family possessed several businesses, combining to make them millionaires. Not only that, Connor always had a hotel room to retreat to—even though he now owned a beautiful, security customised house of his own.

And he knew a feeling of contentment could be dangerous. As the monies rose, a myriad of challenges came with it. Their profile would be higher—law enforcement, other gangsters and perhaps even the public.

He finished the dregs of his coffee, went inside and fired up his laptop for his morning study. He purposely avoided checking his e-mail or messages until he had completed it.

Today's topic included the intricacies of crypto-currencies, something his brain-box of a cousin, Charlie, knew all about. He smiled at the thought that if Charlie was a purple-belt when it came to information technology, Connor knew someone who had three or four stripes on his black belt.

Finally, he checked the drafts inbox of this week's current 'work' e-mail addresses. The e-mail addresses The Chameleon Project's information technologies magician, Jaime—the said black belt—assigned to him. Any messages were encrypted before being placed in the draft's box to prevent any vulnerability of sending them.

He read the message and smiled—*It'll be good to get back to work.*

Jaime—pronounced 'Haimee' as per his Peruvian descent, sat in his kitchen of black marble, oak, chrome and glass, feeling his nerves bite more than he had in years. This would be the first time he had allowed anyone, other than Bruce, to know the location of his principal residence, let alone inviting them in.

47

As he studied the patterns the fibres made on his rustic cashmere sweater, he thought of how unwarranted his anxiety was; Ciara Robson had been an agent for The Chameleon Project for quite a few years now.

Bruce had shared with him his desire to look for a successor. And Jaime had presumed Connor would be that man; his operational ability in domestic and foreign urban fields had been unsurpassed.

Yuri Kozlov, a friend of Bruce's from the 'old days'—meaning his SAS career—had aided Connor in completing a mission in Ukraine. Afterwards, McQuillan told Jaime that the Eastern European had described the young agent as *Yaskravyy demon*—The Bright Demon.

When Bruce had asked him to elaborate, Kozlov had told him of a fable—left out of the Bible—that the Archangel Michael had convinced one of Satan's demons he would avoid the wrath of God if he killed other demons.

While Bruce said he felt the analogy in relation to Connor to be overly dramatic, Jaime wasn't so sure; the former Commando seemed to derive hilarity and pleasure from torturing the evil people he encountered.

Perhaps this was one of the reasons Bruce had looked elsewhere for his successor.

The air conditioning switching on alerted him to movement on the narrow, winding road almost a mile away.

Tapping a sequence onto what appeared to be a coffee coaster, the cupboards in front of the kitchen table opened to reveal a large screen.

Bruce's Black BMW X5 Security Plus appeared, driving slowly. Within seconds the facial recognition identified both him and Ciara Robson through the windshield. None of the predetermined duress signals were given.

After a couple of minutes, Jaime went to the door to greet them. Ciara did not give off the masculine aura he had observed through videos and pictures, despite walking with straight-backed confidence and her hair not quite reaching her shoulders.

However, though Bruce had told him she had softened her image, her gait and movement hinted at the power her physique possessed.

They ascended the steps and Bruce, after shaking Jaime's hand, announced, "Jaime, this is Ciara Robson. Ciara, this is Jaime."

The Peruvian appreciated that Bruce had not used his surname.

Ciara surprised him by gripping his hand firmly, and instead of a typical greeting, said, "Thank you for everything you have done for me. It felt like a real guardian angel on my shoulder knowing you were supporting me when I have been 'working'."

Jaime could feel himself blushing. "It…it is my job. You are the ones who take on the danger."

"A danger you mitigate, so I thank you."

The Central American gave her an awkward smile and a subtle nod. He had undergone a metamorphism regarding attractive women in recent years, as out of sheer force of will he had pushed himself to meet them. To his pleasant surprise, his boyish looks and his new sense of style— acquired after reading numerous articles and books—along with a study of various techniques used by the pick-up artist community, proved fruitful in attracting members of the opposite sex. That, and his access to millions of pounds.

Despite that, he felt taken aback by the statuesque, broad-shouldered blonde who stood maybe an inch within his personal space.

"Come inside," he said.

He led them into the kitchen and asked her, "Would you like a coffee?"

"Mr McQuillan was insistent I take advantage of your Peruvian coffee."

Within two minutes, due to the hyper-quick machine he had designed, they had their freshly brewed coffees in front of them.

Both he and Ciara looked to Bruce.

"I am fifty-two. So, I am not looking to be going anywhere anytime soon," began the Scotsman. "But no one knows what the future might bring. In the months and years ahead, Ciara will be shadowing me. That she understands our protocols is vital. She will also need to be aware of the wider organisation."

Jaime nodded. "We can start today."

The black operations chief shook his head, "I'll be visiting the others in the next few months. I cannot ethically reveal their identities until they have agreed to continue with the project should I go, and if they accept being under Ciara's command."

Jaime said simply, "They must know to trust you. It would be a risk for you too."

Bruce looked at Ciara and broke the moment's silence with, "Standard practice is that I give Jaime the mission brief. He will then work his magic to collate any data he deems relevant. This can take several days. Then we have meetings to separate the wheat from the chaff, to formulate and polish a plan. This is the first of those meetings with regards to the Okada operation."

"I understand," said Ciara.

Jaime tapped the coaster to again reveal the large screen. His customised keyboard surfaced from an opening in the table.

On the screen appeared various pictures of a man with thick-rimmed glasses and a mop of silvery hair.

"This is Ronald Sykes. He is a sixty-year-old with a doctorate in Renewable Energy. I found the terms innovator and pioneer in reference to him. Politically centrist with left leanings. Seems mildly patriotic but has a great respect for Japanese culture. I have a full dossier for you both. Now, this is very interesting," said Jaime, tapping the keyboard and bringing up the names Inagawa-kai, Yamaguchi-gumi and Sumiyoshi-kai.

"These are the principal clans of the Yakuza. They act as umbrellas for many differing groups. As a collective, they have a substantial interest in nuclear energy. This came under scrutiny after the Fukushima Daiichi nuclear disaster in 2011."

Jamie referred to the series of continuing apparatus failures, reactor collapses, and discharges of radioactive materials at the Fukushima Daiichi Nuclear Power Plant in the wake the Tōhoku earthquake and tsunami. The disaster was the second largest of its kind behind Chernobyl.

"The Sumiyoshi-kai and the Yamaguchi-gumi have been accused of providing illegal worker contracts. Other schemes included fraud in claiming hazard pay. Nothing too out of the ordinary. Some of the nuclear companies benefit from the labour provided by these Yakuza clans in exchange for payoffs. You will know of this already, Miss Robson."

Ciara began, "Extortion in Japan is like snow to the Eskimos. The Yakuza shakedown shop owners by charging them ridiculously high rates for decorations, napkins, coffee, and ice. And there is a term in Japanese culture, *Junkatsuyu*—gift giving—which one businessman told me is the 'the oil that lubricates society'. It is tough to distinguish from bribery."

"That is correct, Miss Robson. And thirty percent of Japan's electricity comes from nuclear energy. Because of their lack of oil they have been vigilant against relying on it since the oil crises of 1973 and 1979. The Yakuza are aware there will always be money in nuclear, so they have deep investments in electricity grids—unlike other developed countries Japan has two not just one—and the electric power companies."

"You said it gets interesting," said Ciara with a hint of a smile.

After a moment, Jaime realised she was teasing and matched her expression before tapping the keyboard to bring up an image of a lean-faced Japanese man in a well-fitting suit

"This is Yasuhiro Takato. Thirty-nine-years old. Previously a highly respected member of the Yamaguchi-gumi family—despite his youth, there was speculation of him taking over on the current Oyabun, Shintaro Goto's, retirement. He had been supervising at the plant when the disaster occurred and became one of the 'Fukushima Fifty'. It would seem voluntarily."

Ciara said, "As far as I was aware, there were hundreds who stayed and braved the radiation to bring the reactors under control."

"That is correct," said Jaime, mildly impressed with her awareness of some of the details. "I am not sure why they called them 'the fifty'. And it is notoriously difficult to find anyone who was there to speak about what happened. I only found out from cross-referenced e-mails and digital police files that Takato was one of them. I am confident this is where his bad feeling towards his clan began."

Bruce said, "I should imagine that surviving a Tsunami followed by a nuclear reactor meltdown would give one a moment's pause."

"He did not just leave the clan. He took other dissenters and formed his own, named Gādian—the guardians. They have been fighting a running battle with the Yamaguchi-gumi family for the last eight years. As you are aware, Yakuza families do not like soldiers breaking away. Yasuhiro Takato's clan is small. But has grown in stature through a combination of brutality and both strategic and street smarts."

"Perhaps due to their greater manoeuvrability too," stated Bruce.

Jaime continued, "The Gādian clan has somehow managed—through various dummy corporations—to lend the Japanese government money in exchange for a sizeable share in Okada. Despite their size, when their renewables project is fully implemented they will be the number one Yakuza clan."

"Do you know what Yasuhiro Takato's thoughts are regarding the UK's share of the company?"

"I do not know. It is difficult to obtain a digital recording of any conversation he has had."

Ciara said, "So, they could be our enemy or our ally?"

Jaime asked Bruce. "Who are you sending?"

"I'll send Connor. All the other agents are tied into long-term operations. Ciara will go too; she has experience over there."

Jaime's bemused expression matched Ciara's. "I thought you were taking Miss Robson out of the field?"

"I am beginning the process of doing that," answered Bruce, before turning his attention to her. "You will be over there for intelligence gathering under the guise of your journalist role."

"What guise is Connor going over in?" asked Ciara.

"I'll let him decide," said Bruce. "I want Connor prepared before I brief him in person. Send him everything you have. Particularly on this Yasuhiro Takato and his Gādian clan."

6

Along with thousands in the crowd, Yasuhiro Takato sat and watched the two sumo wrestlers engage in their four-minute pre-fight ritual. This was his favourite part—the anticipation.

The shiko—foot stomps—could be heard from where he sat in the third row. He did not want to draw attention to himself by sitting right in front of the dohyō—ring.

From the beginning of his forming the Gādian, he'd dismissed the typical Yakuza mode of dress—flashy suits with some colourful garnish, usually the tie—for himself and his clan for the same reason, instead opting for an arctic blue business shirt without a tie.

Not that he wasn't well protected; his side of the arena had several Gādian clan members, inconspicuously and strategically placed.

Yasuhiro appreciated attending events such as this; for years he'd had to hide from the wrath of the wider Yakuza while he built his clan's strength.

Sumo had been one of the many reasons, albeit relatively minor, exacerbating his decision to leave the Yamaguchi-gumi clan. In the same year as the Fukushima disaster, the Yakuza in their greed had caused the cancellation of the tournament in Osaka—the first time since 1946. The result of a match-fixing investigation found fourteen wrestlers and a few stable masters guilty, and the sport tainted.

The arena's atmosphere stilled then crackled as the *Gyōji*—dressed in a beautiful blue kimono patterned with white flowers—went through his pre-match instructions and commands.

When the Gyōji signalled with the *gunbai*—fan—the wrestlers threw themselves at one another in a flurry of muscle, weight and fury.

While expressing admiration for some of the more exotic-looking martial arts, Yasuhiro knew only a remarkable knuckleduster-assisted punch or a gunshot would defeat a sumo wrestler within a confined space. He had a few retired wrestlers on the payroll for that reason.

The last time Yasuhiro had attended a sumo match had been over ten years ago with his Grandfather. He remembered the old man remarking on how much bigger the wrestlers had become since he had first started watching the sport in the sixties.

The smaller wrestler managed to grab his opponents' belt—*mawashi*—before finding himself run backwards by his larger rival. At the last possible moment, the smaller wrestler spun into a superbly executed hip throw, which aided by his challenger's headlong momentum, launched the huge sumo out of the dohyō.

Yasuhiro smiled in the collective applause at the feat.

His attention snapped towards a suited man of similar age to his own near forty years being stopped by one of Yasuhiro's soldiers, who frisked him under the guise of greeting him as a friend. The soldier then allowed the man to cut a pathway to the empty chair beside Yasuhiro, where he remained standing.

"Takato-sama, I have come to speak on behalf of the Inagawa-kai clan."

Yasuhiro dipped his head and the man sat beside him. This had been the first acceptance of any non-violent contact with another Yakuza clan. Of the three families, Yasuhiro held the least enmity for the Tokyo-based Inagawa-kai clan—perhaps because they began modestly until achieving spectacular financial success in the 1980s 'bubble economy' under the guidance of the 'Business Don' Susumu Ishii. Or because one of their most respected former bosses—Haruki Sho—was originally a Chinese national. Or because the clan had sent over a hundred tonnes of supplies to the Tōhoku region in the wake of the earthquake and tsunami.

The Gādian boss noticed a delay in the start of the second match.

The man began, "Takato-sama, we have interests in common. A partnership could be agreed upon."

When Yasuhiro did not reply, the emissary shifted in his seat and added, "We ask for you to share your stakes in any companies you have. Amongst all the services we can offer you, we can help broker peace between you and our friends in Kobe."

"The Yamaguchi-gumi aren't just your friends in Kobe. They are your friends here in Tokyo—ever since your organisation did not fight them hard enough over four decades ago."

"Maybe we were too small back then, but now is different. Together we can drive them out."

A smile briefly flickered on Takato's mouth. "How do you know we have stakes?"

"I am just here to deliver the message, inviting you to a meeting."

Takato understood this to be a fishing expedition to ascertain what holdings his clan had. Not only that, even if the offer to take on the Yamaguchi-gumi was genuine, there would not be equality between his organisation and the Inagawa-kai in the aftermath of victory.

"No."

More shifting.

"Takato-sama," said the man. "Everyone has the greatest respect for you. Your actions at Fukushima are a testament to your heroism. But to continue this fight without allies is lunacy."

Yasuhiro tightened at the man's words. "An event that could have been prevented. And we seem to be achieving our aims this far."

"Takato-sama, the *Kami* took the form of a Tsunami. Men could not have prevented it. It was Yakuza clans that ran to the rescue as we have always done."

Yasuhiro hid his anger at the man's words, and said, "Were you there?"

"No, I was not, Takato-sama."

"Your words of respect are superficial and borne of an attempt to quell my ego so as not to incur my wrath. Your arrogance shines through when you find the courage to tell me your opinions on a disaster you were not present at."

Yasuhiro watched as the victor of the previous match returned to the dohyō. He understood the delay must have been due to an opponent dropping out. His next opponent looked even bigger than the last.

The man bowed his head. "It was not my intention to dishonour you."

Yasuhiro did not speak during the wrestlers' ceremonial warm-up routines—*shikiri*. It pleased him the emissary did not talk either.

Finally, they faced one another. The smaller wrestler, quicker off the mark, slammed himself into the wall of bone, sinew, fat and muscle. Both seemed stuck in a frozen stalemate for a few moments with the smaller one straining intensely, while his hulking opponent appeared only mildly inconvenienced.

Then, with a speed of manoeuvrability not often observed in sumo, the smaller man side-stepped, causing his opponent to stumble forwards. It only took a guiding hand to see the giant out of the dohyō, ending the match.

Yasuhiro suppressed a smile before speaking. "The Gādian will keep its independence in all things. There will be no peace talks with the Yamaguchi-gumi. We do not currently have any serious grievance with Inagawa-kai—do not make that change."

The emissary stared straight ahead in silence for a few moments before responding, "Takato-sama, may I ask you a question? A question for me alone?"

When Yasuhiro nodded, the man continued, "The defiance of you and your clan towards the Inagawa-kai is not unlike a red fox to a wolf. I can understand a fox fighting a wolf who has attacked it, but a Fox biting a wolf's paw—a wolf who can protect it from the Yamaguchi-gumi bear, I cannot. Your Gādian will go the same way as the Ichiwa-kai if you do not accept our help. Can you not see this?"

The man spoke of the gang that broke away from the Yamaguchi-gumi back in the eighties. It lost the ensuing war and dissolved within the same decade.

Yasuhiro smiled. "Your analogy is flawed on more than one level. We have not 'bitten your paw'. I have simply rejected your attempts at subjugation disguised as an alliance. And once they become adult, the bear, wolf and fox cannot grow any further—but organisations and ideas can stretch across the world."

After a few moments, the man slowly got up and left.

The meetings between Bruce and Connor Reed over the past year had needed to become more clandestine. Since Bruce had been given an official role within the security services, and Connor's involvement in his family's criminal enterprises deepened, the days of choosing a random café were gone. They had to choose more carefully.

The Scotsman liked this small hiker's café in Sussex as it afforded him a high, panoramic view of Lewes's yellow and green forest. In addition, the routes in allowed for good counter-surveillance.

Connor walked in wearing a thin, khaki bomber-style jacket over a white shirt, beige chinos and leather loafers. They made eye contact. If either rubbed behind their right ear it indicated they had detected surveillance.

Neither did.

Bruce stood as the man over two decades his junior approached, and they shook hands before sitting.

"How was the drive down?" the Glaswegian asked.

"I am driving a Mitsubishi Evo at the moment. It's a bit noisy when pushing it on the motorway but it's a great drive."

"You din'ae fancy riding your bike down?" asked Bruce with a smile.

"As much as I enjoy the thrill of my grandad's quarter-of-century old Speed Triple, I didn't fancy coming all this way on it."

The bouncy young waitress appeared, addressing Bruce. "What would you like?"

"I'll have the shepherd's pie and a white coffee, no sugar."

She turned to Connor, "And for your son?"

The Yorkshireman began laughing, and she turned and said, "No? I apologise, I shouldn't have presumed."

"Don't you worry yourself, wee lassie," said Bruce in a soothing drawl. "I am old enough right enough. I am more offended by the inference that I couldn't sire a better looking *wean*."

She gave him a sly smile. "I didn't want to say anything."

"Don't dig a hole with both of us," protested Connor to the waitress. "I will have the pork skewers with avocado slices and a black coffee."

When she left, Connor said, "Can't believe they still flirt with you over me. What are you? Sixty-five or summat?"

The fifty-two-year-old McQuillan didn't give him an answer. Many people mistook him as being around his mid-forties. Instead he said, "Character is timeless."

"I bet you said that about Hai-Karate aftershave in the eighties."

"How did you know?"

"You're not the only older Glaswegian I know," answered Connor. "I was going to ask you—my ear caught something called 'The Glasgow effect', about how Glaswegians die younger in comparison to the rest of the UK and Europe and I forgot to research it. Thought it might be a poverty thing. You ken what I mean, like?"

"Firstly, we don't really use the word 'ken' for 'know' as Glaswegians. That's used more in the east of Scotland,"

Bruce said. "It isn't just a poverty thing. Equally deprived areas in the UK have higher life expectancies. The death tolls across all ages and social classes are around fifteen per cent greater."

"What is the cause, or causes, then?"

"There have been a few studies done. One theory is that back in the seventies, new towns around Glasgow were thrown up and most of the city's skilled workers—the steel industry was a mainstay employer in Glasgow before Thatcherism—went there to live. That left the old and people who found it difficult to get employment. I reckon that might be exaggerated but there might be some truth to it—that loss of community for the people who left and the ones who stayed."

"Did you get a sense of that?"

"I was only a wean in the early seventies. My maw— Mum—spoke about it," said Bruce, then wishing to change tack. "If you can't get a job you begin to feel despair at the lack of control of your destiny. The weather up there is'nae warm, there's a takeaway culture—deep fried Pizza etcetera, all kinds of factors can contribute."

Connor sensed Bruce's desire to change the subject and so asked, "What is the nature of today's meeting?"

"Ironically, a country with a very high life-expectancy—Japan."

The waitress came back, set their coffees down and departed with a smile.

"I've always wanted to go," said Connor. "Why do you want me to go?"

"Tell me why renewable energy is important."

"To reduce greenhouse gases which influence the environment—how much of an effect is debated but almost everyone agrees it does have an effect. Horrendous oil spills still occur. Wind, solar, hydro and geothermal don't require transportation so you're saving costs that way. Clean energy is more labour intensive so you have the scope for more jobs, and…," Connor took a sip of his coffee, "because wind, water, and sun are things most countries have. Exploit them fully and the world would no longer need to go into meltdown every time the oil prices go up."

Bruce spoke in depth regarding the breakthroughs in renewable technology the Okada Company had made and the wider situation regarding it.

Connor looked at him. "What you're saying is there is going to be more than a few governments, companies, dynasties and oligarchs that will not welcome this."

"Correct."

"So, who I am dealing with?"

"We don't know as yet. There is another aspect. This isn't one of our organic operations. It comes from Vauxhall Cross's head shed."

By that, Bruce meant it was not an operation identified by himself and Jaime as part of The Chameleon Project; instead it came from Miles Parker, the SIS chief.

"MI6 in the business of global altruism?" asked Connor.

Bruce shook his head. "The head of Okada's clean energy project is a man named Ronald Sykes. He is—"

The waitress interrupted him to give them their meals. He caught her glancing at his left hand. He smiled at her and she left.

Bruce looked at Connor, who wore a blended frown and smirk. The younger man said, "I've wondered why you haven't settled down yet, but I suppose if you can still pull young women then why would you want to."

"Times change. But lassies quite that young wouldn't interest me," said Bruce. "What about you?"

Connor shrugged. "Both professional aspects of my life are not conducive to a long-term relationship."

"Don't look for a girl that you want. Look for a girl that wants you—she'll treat you better."

"I'll have to write that one down," said Connor between mouthfuls. "You were talking about a Ronald Sykes?"

"Ronald Sykes is a Brit who for the past two decades has been considered one of the leading figures in clean energy science and engineering. Now, a few years back the project was ready to run aground. Sykes came back to the UK to petition big business and the UK government for money in exchange for equity in Okada."

"And they accepted. Which is why Parker wants the investment protected."

"That's right," answered Bruce. "The man is a true patriot: queen and country. When the technology successfully completes its trials, then its growth will be exponential. A fact that more than one entity is aware of and interested in."

"Who are the others?"

"Tell me what you know about the Yakuza?"

"I know anti-Yakuza laws have hammered them to the point of bringing their numbers down from 180,000 to 30,000, and a lot of their influence I should imagine."

"There is still a belief amongst some Japanese—law enforcement and politicians included—that the Yakuza are a necessary evil to keep out foreign criminal organisations."

"Better the devil you know?"

"Yes," answered Bruce. "Do you know what triggered these laws coming about?"

"I think when it came to light just how much corruption there was between the government, big corporations and the Yakuza and the Sōkaiya when the eighties 'bubble economy' collapsed, and the Japanese were humiliated on the world stage. Might have taken a long time, but that would have been the ignition point."

Though he didn't let it show, Connor's grasp of both the renewable issue and the geopolitical events pleased Bruce. However, he wanted to test his agent's grasp of the details—an area that he had previously lacked.

"Tell me in depth."

"In 1987, Japan's economy came flying out of a recession and the Bank of Japan was slow to get a grip on the rapid acceleration of assets, foreign investment and the amount of credit being dealt out. So, the Yakuza dove in, buying all these cash flow businesses, including golf courses—apparently the Japs are golf mad—bribing and extorting investment bankers and business moguls."

"Tell me more about the Sōkaiya."

"The Japanese have this overhang from their samurai days regarding their honour being sacred. This 'saving face' culture is the reason why loads of sexual assault cases go under-reported—I digress— so these Sōkaiya are professionals in extortion, offering cash for information about misconduct in companies. Then, through dummy companies they buy enough shares to enable them to sit in on the shareholder meetings. They threaten the board with the exposure of scandals. They made a killing throughout the 'bubble economy' too."

"And what about the anti-Yakuza laws?"

"Well, there are now laws that target businesses paying the Yakuza, and there's a law stipulating they can arrest Yakuza members before a crime is committed. Japan was notoriously slow in allowing its law enforcement to place covert surveillance on criminals. There are laws now preventing Yakuza members owning credit cards, loans, even mobile phone contracts. I think they are still being *divs* by covering themselves with Koi Carp and dragon tattoos, and having their pinkies cut-off."

"Well done," said Bruce, without emotion but with sincerity. "Still, in the West, they talk about the 'war on crime' and eradication. In Japan, it is about containment. There have even been instances of known Yakuza holding public offices. And their police are handicapped in that they do not have a plea bargaining system or witness protection."

"But I've heard their conviction rates are astronomically high—fourteen hour interrogation sessions before being thrown into a birdcage would do that," said Connor.

"Aye," said Bruce. "There seems to be another off-shoot Yakuza clan that seems to agree with you that Irezumi and Yubitsume are archaic."

Bruce gave Connor a rundown of the Yakuza's relationship with certain Japanese oil companies, the Fukushima disaster and the breakaway and rise of Yasuhiro Takato.

Connor whistled. "So, I have to think of a reason to go over, watch over this Ronald Sykes like a stalker, and be ready to fight off the best assassins that Saudi money can buy, not forgetting Japanese criminals on their own turf?"

"Yes," replied Bruce.

"Better get brushing up on my Japanese because *konnichi wa* will only get a Brit so far."

7

Ronald Sykes pushed his thick rimmed glasses back up his nose. He knew it was ridiculous to be still wearing them given he could have his eyes lasered for just a couple of thousand pounds sterling and a day or so of discomfort.

Looking around the sterile white and aqua green laboratory as the Japanese technicians worked in studious silence, he supposed—*With this team, I could make myself a pair of eyes in a few years.*

He found that one of the reasons for the amazing efficiency of the Japanese engineering team was their faithfulness to the concept of *kaizen*—a continual, mostly gradual, adherence to improvement in all areas of work. Everyone in a good Japanese company observed the principle of kaizen from the caretakers to the CEOs, fostering more regular communication up and down the chain than was typical in western businesses.

Not that they would be doing anything other than devoting themselves to the implementation and perfection of the new technologies.

Okada Engineering had many sites within Japan and a few abroad, but Saito 1—Site 1—managed the prioritized projects.

Kenjiro Uda—or Ken to Sykes—walked around the laboratory, clearly out of place in his demeanour and green overalls. Ken had a rolled-up towel wrapped around the back of his neck and stuffed into the front of his shirt. Though the Chief Engineer did not do as much lifting as he used to, Sykes reckoning he kept the towel as a symbol of his factory worker roots.

"Ohayoo gozaimasu, Sykes San,"—Good morning, Mr Sykes. They bowed, with Sykes straightening up three inches taller than the engineering ace's five-foot-seven inches.

"Ohayoo gozaimasu, Ken San."

Ken switched back to English as was the custom amongst all the Japanese here. Sykes was the only Westerner on Saito 1. Though his Japanese had improved immensely in his time there, English was his preference so that nothing was lost in translation at work.

"Why we cannot talk in the manufacture section? Always here?"

Sykes smiled at the thirty-two-year-old engineer—twenty-eight-years his junior. "Ken, we have been through this. No zombies are going to come out of this lab. We work with electricity, not biochemicals, or whatever happens in these Japanese cartoons you insist on watching."

"It not the not real zombies that make worry of me. It is these real zombies," said Ken, gesturing to the laboratory staff working in their white coats and protective visors. Sykes smiled on the inside—Ken could be quite un-Japanese with his insults and arrogant body language.

"Ken, these zombies help design the prototypes that you get to build. And together we are all going to change the world for the better."

"I know this. I make joke. We will change the planet together," Ken nodded. "Will you not come with me to the trials?"

Sykes clapped the slighter man on the shoulder. "I am the man who designs—the genius architect. You are the man who implements—the common sense builder."

Ken blinked a couple of times and Sykes was not sure if the sarcasm got lost in translation.

"Why do you not put this all the know-how on computer? Why do you keep it all in here?" said Ken, tapping the side of his head.

"We have been through this too. I will put it down once the momentum is impossible to disrupt," answered Sykes.

London had told him not to dismiss the Chinese's ability to hack information technology systems to steal whatever they wanted. For this reason, the British scientist had not shared some of the key principles and equations with anyone, especially not on paper or digitally.

"You not trust the security out there."

Indeed Sykes didn't.

On returning to Japan after successfully petitioning for investment, he discovered the Okada family had also secured venture capital from another consortium of Japanese investors.

With the project back on track, and being close to a breakthrough, Sykes had lost interest in the financial aspect and returned to his scientific and engineering work.

Then a set of mysterious visitors arrived to inspect their investment.

Though they did not wear the typical tribal-like suits and slicked-back hair, the demeanour of the Okada upper management towards them let Sykes know what he needed to know.

A man smaller and older than the rest did the talking as the others looked around stony-faced.

Though the Japanese were always deferential and polite to visitors, Sykes also noticed the workers at the site avoided eye contact, and were unusually quiet and fidgety, despite these being the representatives of investors who had saved their jobs.

Ken had been the translator, and the questions struck him as strange in their content and how they were fired.

"How long until completion?"

"Is any of the workers slowing down the process?"

"Are any of your bosses slowing you down?"

Sykes caught sight of tattoos beneath the sleeve cuff of one.

The shoulders of the workers relaxed once the mysterious men departed. The British scientist did not need Ken's confirmation that the men were indeed Yakuza.

Afterwards, Sykes had driven up to the Okada head office, demanding answers, and got them; the Yakuza had also offered their financial assistance. And it had been accepted.

Except, he was told, this was a new clan, separate from the 'big three' of the Yamaguchi-gumi, Sumiyoshi-kai and Inagawa-kai. One sympathetic to their goals.

The news left Sykes reeling. He could not believe the board would have been taken in by any sort of altruistic pitch by a criminal organisation. However, he now faced a severe moral dilemma; should he tell the UK consortium and government of the Yakuza's involvement and risk them rescinding their investment, leading to the project's collapse?

Or remain quiet?

The choice seemed like no choice at all. The future of the planet's wildlife and resources depended on developing and implementing what they were about to accomplish.

However, it seemed to him that this Gādian clan now wanted an intrusive level of oversight on their investment. Okada had accepted their 'offer' for security down in Hiroshima and Nagasaki.

Not that some type of security would not be welcome.

"You're right, I don't trust the security," replied Ronald Sykes. "I do not know why a bunch of armed gangsters would be necessary down there."

Ken scratched his chin. "The Mongoose keeps the Cobra from being many."

The immaculately suited, twenty-one-year-old, six-foot-two, mixed-race doorman from the Chapel Town area of Leeds greeted Connor with a, "Good evening, Mr Reed."

Though Connor's family owned The Dancing Bear lap dancing club and thus could enter outfitted how he liked, he always dressed as per club code. This was to avoid drawing attention to himself, and ensuring the door team weren't put in the situation of having to explain to any queuing customers why he was exempt.

One of Connor's Londoner friends had told him that, *"...people are less inclined to fight when wearing a flash Whistle and Flute."*

Tonight he wore a dark blue suit, burgundy tie and a cream shirt. He'd relax the tie and take off the jacket once inside, as everyone did.

"Fucksake Bambi," exclaimed Connor, looking up at the man near eight years his junior. "Why don't you call me Connor like down at the club?"

He referred to the MMA, mixed martial arts, club Connor had begun to frequent more now since moving back to Leeds where he and the doorman had first met.

"Down there you're one of the lads. Here, you're the Bossman."

"Can you at least not call me Bossman? It makes me feel like Calvin from Django."

Oshain 'Bambi' Riley, in a superb take on how a southern United States black slave would sound, crowed, "No can do Bossman, do you need me to shine yo shoes?"

Connor laughed. "Where's Henryk?"

Tom had chosen the Polish construction worker, Henryk, to be the head doorman of the Dancing Bear. Oshain, despite his youth, usually headed the door for the lap dancing club 'The Helena', and had come down to assess Henryk.

Choosing the security for two of the North of England's most profitable lap dancing clubs had proved a problematic task.

Gone were the days where you could simply approach the best fighters in the city and put them on the door. The new SIA regulations stipulated a lack of a substantive criminal record, which would preclude some. In a day and age of CCTV, required for clubs such as this, litigation and camera phones, the instances of bouncers hitting unruly customers had greatly reduced since 2004.

Still, Tom and Connor didn't want a set of 'shirt-fillers' but a door team that could handle themselves, and a team reflecting the city's growing diversity.

"He's doing a round of the club," said Oshain. "Tom, Luke and Charlie are up in the VIP suite."

As Connor walked into the main area, it reminded him of how far his family had come.

It hadn't been long ago that The Dancing Bear had been a small bar in the centre of Leeds. Now it looked very different. The stage, based on a minor roundabout in Horsforth, had neon ceiling lights that shone blue and purple but could be faded into more rustic colours when a performer came on.

Tonight was 'Ladies Only Night', and as a result young men with shiny, tanned physiques made up of cartoonishly round muscles waited on the hordes of gregarious women.

Three stony-faced 'butch'-looking doorwomen looked on—brought in by Tom Ryder in case of any physical altercations involving the clientele.

Walking to the stairs, he felt a hand stroke the inside of his leg, stopping just shy of his arse.

He turned to a group of giggling women aged around their late thirties and early forties. The dark-haired, curvy woman dressed in a light blue suit jacket, matching skirt and a white blouse with three buttons undone looked back with a smirk. The Botox was subtle enough to enhance, not spoil, her looks.

"Don't touch me unless you're prepared to finish me off," he announced.

He knew that a group of alcohol-infused women would detect nerves like sharks smell blood.

She arched her eyebrows. "Me finish you off? Not the other way around?"

"I can't commit to anything unless I know you're good in bed. For me, how a woman kisses might give an indication of that," he replied with only a hint of a smile.

He caught the collective flicker of eyes towards the woman he was addressing, who didn't flinch, responding, "Then what are you waiting for?"

Consent thought Connor.

He leant down, clasping his hand on the back of her neck and used his thumb to stroke her cheek as they kissed, lightly at first, then with greater urgency as their tongues dabbed.

He broke off the kiss, to see her take a breath. "Yeh," he whispered. "You'll be great in bed."

He straightened up to address the slack-jawed women.

"Ladies," he said with a nonchalant salute before ascending the stairs.

He saw Luke's head looking at him over the balcony, shaking it with mock disapproval.

As he reached the booth, Luke exclaimed, "Fuck me, thirty seconds in here and you're already necking off with the customers."

"She started it."

Tom and Charlie, the youngest of the quartet, stood to embrace him. Then, they all sat back down.

An oiled torso in a bow tie appeared. "Can I get you anything, sir?"

"G&T, lemon and ice," answered Connor.

Connor noticed that his cousins had finally given up deriding him for his choice of alcoholic beverage. They were all on pints.

Charlie asked, "Connor, the Helena's doorman said that you gave him his nickname, 'Bambi', but he said I'd have to ask you why."

"I didn't give him it, I just called him 'Bambi' for a joke down at the MMA club, but it was in front of his cousin, who found it hilarious, and he made sure it stuck."

"Eh," frowned Luke. "I mean pardon, but I don't get the joke. Does he have a glass jaw?"

"Don't you know?" asked Connor. "His mum got shot dead when he was five."

71

After a moment, horrified laughter broke out around the table. Once it had settled, Luke asked him, "Speaking of jaws, have you watched the boxing yet? Ginger fucker must have a chin made of a Nokia 3310."

Connor laughed. "Chin like a Nokia 3310—I like that one. He hits like a panic attack too," before switching his attention to Tom. "How's the door team working out?"

"Pretty good. Henryk seems bob-on, though he ought to be for the money I pay him."

"For fucksake, Tom," exclaimed Connor at his notoriously thrifty cousin's statement. "Now you're a millionaire I thought you were going to stop being tighter than Rihanna's afro."

Luke, along with Charlie, guffawed before saying, "Don't Connor—his dad's the same. Uncle Ryan is deep in his forties and still wears Lynx Africa."

Even Tom smiled at that one before continuing, "I don't know where he got that blond one. Tell him, Luke."

"Oh mate, Rennison is his name," Luke began. "I wandered into the cloakroom and he's getting vexed at his phone, so I asks him what's up and he says the screenshot function isn't working—guess what he's trying to screenshot?"

Connor observed the grins of his cousins and shrugged. "What?"

"The crack on his screen!"

Connor's mouth fell before turning into a broad smile, "Gen?"

"Yes, mate. I just walked out."

Connor looked at Tom who said, "I'll bin him tonight. There's too much money going through this place to have someone who licks his thumb before turning the page on his Kindle."

Connor raised his eyebrows. "Fuck me, Tom. Not only a joke but a funny one at that."

Luke joined him with, "Off the cuff that, as well."

Tom shrugged, "Quality over quantity."

"Well, that's kind of what I wanted to talk about," said Connor as he leant forward with his cousins matching him. "Keep quiet about this but I am off to Japan soon. And I was thinking—what cars does our esteemed cousin here swear by?"

In unison, Luke and Charlie said, "Japanese cars for reliability," parroting out Tom's line about his preference in vehicles. The eldest Ryder cousin had been a superb mechanic for many years.

"It's not just that," said Tom. "Some of the Jap car manufacturers are some of the leaders in electric cars—the future."

Connor opened his hands. "Exactly, maybe we can get in there to become distributors over here."

"You mean get one of our solicitors to draft a proposal?"

"I am going over there."

Luke interrupted the quiet with, "I can come with you. I'd like to see Japan."

"And I'd like the Honey Monster to cuddle me through hangovers while the Pussy Cat Dolls make me a fry-up but that's not going to happen."

Luke answered, "A hangover after your couple of G&Ts? And does a fry-up fit into your ultra-healthy 'I am scared of carbs' lifestyle?"

Connor just smiled along with Charlie and Tom, who asked, "You're saying you're going to go over there, without knowing any Japanese, and negotiate a trade deal for electric cars for us?—a three garage set-up based out of Leeds?"

"Phil Knight did it."

"Who's Phil Knight," asked Luke.

"Co-founder of Nike," answered Connor.

"He'll be a fucking billionaire him," exclaimed Luke. "We're nowhere near that level yet."

"He wasn't at the time, he had fuck all back then, whereas our accounts show millions in profits—look, we still need to launder everything that's coming through our

73

books. I'll go over there, make our pitch—say, a three year contract where we take some of the transportation expenses. Worth a try."

Tom raised his eyebrows. "Doesn't cost us anything to ask—shy bairns don't get any sweets. But why would they choose us over the established distributors?"

"I'll worry about that," said Connor. "If I can get the agreement in place, would you go for it?"

Tom nodded.

"What do you pair think?" asked Connor.

Charlie looked momentarily surprised as Luke looked at him, before saying, "It's like you said, we need to diversify. Speaking of which, I've been doing these ASMR videos and the Japanese love them."

"What? Like cartoon porn?" asked Luke.

"No…eh?...no, they are like sound fetish videos. They are meant to calm you. It's weird but it's using these super-sensitive microphones to pick up and clarify all the sounds in an everyday event like water pouring over ice in a glass, or the opening of a pack of crisps."

"They're fuckin' mental are the Japanese. Remember Takeshi's castle?" said Luke.

"Can't be that mental," said Connor. "Japan ranks second in the world on the Human Development Index that considers life expectancy, education and wages. Must be doing something right, even if some of 'em like watching cartoons of octopuses fucking princesses—so I've heard, obviously."

His cousins smiled, before Luke said, "Guess what I was watching on my Kodi stick—"

Tom interrupted him with, "Are you still using that to watch pirated releases?"

"Yeh."

"You know, a lot of people put a lot of time, effort and money into making those films only for you not to pay."

Luke replied, "A lot of people put time and money into making this Kodi stick so I can steal those films."

As Connor and Charlie grinned, Tom added, "It isn't the Kodi stick that's illegal, it's how you use—never mind."

Connor always thought it strange Tom would argue so voraciously with Luke on downloading illegal films, when he headed the family running the most profitable drug dealing outfit north of Liverpool.

"Anyway, I was watching Forest Gump and I've decided Tom Hanks is the best actor in the last thirty years. Pacino and DeNiro couldn't have pulled that off the same."

Connor smiled inside, knowing what the statement would lead to.

"Seriously?" exclaimed Tom rhetorically. "You think Tom Hanks would have done better than Pacino in Scarface, or DeNiro in Cape Fear? He's never played a bad guy in his life, even Denzel Washington has played bad guys. Tom Hanks just plays a different version of the same character—wholesome, upright, honourable—"

"He played that gangster enforcer in Road to Perdition."

"He wasn't evil though—he only shot up other gangsters."

Luke took a sip of his pint. "I think we can all agree that girl in it is a rancid cunt."

"What girl?" asked Charlie.

"In Forest Gump."

"How?"

"How?" exclaimed Luke. "He loves her. Treats her with respect. Protects her. And what does she do? Leads him on and fucks with his head, while she's getting rattled by hippies. She's like one of those girls who constantly post 'gym' pictures with daft motivational quotes one day, and then how all men are bastards the next. Then that girl—Jenny, named a fucking boat after her, didn't he—gets pregnant by 'im, fucks off again, doesn't tell 'im he's a Dad and only comes back when he's a multimillionaire and she's a single mum with AIDS!"

Connor bit into the edge of his thumb in a failed attempt to quell his laughing. Charlie wore a look of bemusement.

"You might have a point," said Tom with his mouth showing a hint of a smirk. "Anyway, on that note and since most of us are here. I have an announcement to make—Cara is pregnant."

After a moment, Connor, Luke and Charlie burst into sincere congratulations.

"How far along is she?" asked Connor.

"Twelve weeks, past the danger zone now. But keep it quiet until I've told my dad and especially Thatcher or she'll have a fit."

Tom used the nickname he gave their stoic grandma.

Luke said, "First of the next-gen Ryders, eh. Suppose it took us long enough."

Tom, now thirty, looked at Connor who was around two years his junior and said, "It'll be you that Thatcher will be getting at next."

Connor smiled, hiding his jolt of morose guilt. "Not everyone is meant to be a dad. But you'll make a great one, Tom."

Charlie and Luke murmured their agreement before firing questions at Tom. Connor could sense the buoyant mood running through them all, and felt a tinge of sadness that he could not share the news that he might have a son.

He drained his G&T. "Alright. I am going to see if I can take that lady downstairs home. If she gets too attached, I can tell her I am going to Japan."

8

George Follet watched his star pupil enduring a shark tank before his debut in the ONE Championship; a Singapore-based mixed martial arts (MMA), Muay Thai, and kickboxing promotion.

The sound of feet skirting around the cage floor, the cracks and thuds of strikes and grunts of expelled breaths floated through the white-matted and walled London gym.

Old Pride FC fight posters smattered the walls. A blown-up framed black and white photograph of the Russian MMA phenomenon, Fedor Emelianenko, and the Japanese submission grappling wizard, Shinya Aoki, engaging in a light-hearted exhibition, looked down onto the cage.

George thought the cropped-haired Len Broady, being shy of eleven-stone—nearly two stone lighter than himself, would be well-suited to the East Asian promotion that held a swell of talent in the lighter-weight categories. He had put a great deal of time and effort in modifying the former British Thai boxing champion's stand-up fighting skills for mixed-martial-arts, as well as developing his all-round game. The results were on display as the twenty-three-year-old sprawled effortlessly, defending his sparring partner's attempts to take him to the ground.

However, George—a legend of British MMA—knew the ease of these sprawls were in part due to the opponent's lack of inclination to trade strikes; because of this Broady was able to read these take-downs.

The Londoner rubbed the head he hadn't shaved in a couple of weeks, and felt the clipper grade four hair, while thinking back to the first fight between the Greco-Roman wrestling stand-out, Randy Couture, and lethal striker, Chuck Liddel. 'The Natural' Couture had stepped into the storm, trading blows with the former kick-boxer to impose his own attributes via crushing takedowns. The strategy had worked and Couture crowned the dominant performance with a third round technical knockout.

And the fight veteran knew he would have to find sparring partners capable of the same for his charge; or else he might discover the painful lesson in a fight rather than a training session.

George jumped at the Yorkshire brogue.

"Looks mustard, doesn't he."

He turned to Connor Reed, two or three inches taller than his own five-foot-eight, and exclaimed, "Fack me Batman, almost shat my shorts."

"Apologies."

George turned back to the action and said quietly, "It's difficult to tell just how good he is, no facker will stand up with him long enough to make him forget about his sprawl. He's got an important fight coming up."

"You should have got Rayella down here," smiled Connor. Rayella, still a teenager, was his quasi-sister, the real sister of his best friend who died in Afghanistan. She had been a top flight Thai-boxer and now a burgeoning MMA practitioner. To ensure her safety during a gangland war he had become embroiled in, Connor had once temporarily brought her down to London from Leeds, and she had trained at George's Dojo.

"I reckon she would give him more problems than he's had in some of his fights," said the MMA veteran derisively before looking Connor up and down, "You been doing much training?"

"Yeh. The local club in Leeds for the grappling and BJJ. One in Manchester, sometimes, for the submission wrestling."

"What Manchester one?"

When Connor told him the name, George sneered, "You'll facking get a positive steroid test just off the guys' sweat who train there."

Connor shrugged. "Each to their own. It's still a great club."

"You got your training gear?" asked George.

"Of course."

"You fancy a few rounds?"

Connor pulled a face. "He's a professional preparing for a fight."

"Yer over two stone heavier than the cunt. We both know you're good enough."

After a moment the former Royal Marine said, "Alright. Be a few minutes."

"You don't want to warm up after you've got changed?"

"Nah," said Connor. "You don't see lions doing star jumps before they run down a buffalo do you."

"We'll see if you still have that attitude after you've pulled a muscle."

Connor went into the changing room to swap his civilian attire for his shorts and gum shield. Despite what he had told George, he went through a series of joint rotations while thinking about his actions-on.

The only time he had been knocked down, let alone out, had been as a youth by his 'one-punch merchant' boxer of a dad on entering his house. His father had discovered that he'd burgled an elderly couple's home, and hadn't held back on the blow.

Outside of that, Connor hadn't felt the floor despite numerous boxing and Muay Thai bouts, hundreds of sparring sessions, a handful of MMA matches and a multitude of street fights. He attributed this to the quality of his chin, his high level of strength in relation to his weight, his cardiovascular fitness, low centre-of-gravity and defence.

On more than one occasion fighting multiple opponents simultaneously, he'd been dazed and rocked before going down under an onslaught; but never a single strike by a single opponent. However, he knew all about Len Broady—the man's YouTube highlight reels were a testament to his ferocious knockout and stoppage ability— *George is right, you've got two stone on him and it's with the sparring gloves.*

Still, Connor had noted neither Broady nor the lads he was sparring were wearing *shinnies* and the British Thai boxing star had hurt many a man with leg kicks, and knocked out more than his fair share with head kicks. So, he would have to get him to the ground—but he'd first have to spend time convincing Broady that it was not his intention.

Come on—he said to himself—*it's only sparring.*

He walked out to see Broady leaning back against the cage like a lion surveying the savannah. Connor hid the fear slithering in his gut; he used it to remind himself of his strategy as he entered the cage.

George locked it and bellowed. "Alright, away you go."

Since there was no timer set, Connor knew George would end the round at his own choosing.

Connor darted to grab the centre of the cage, before pulling back from a feint.

Neither hit the other in their first exchange of punches due to their parrying and slipping, but Broady angled off behind a jab and whipped in a hurtful kick to Connor's thigh.

The Yorkshireman made sure to press with his feet underneath him; he could not afford to over-reach and get caught on the counter.

The former marine boxer feigned the jab and sat down on a right to the solar plexus, emoting the barest wince.

Connor leashed his instinct to attack more—he'd learnt his lesson of being greedy a long time ago.

Broady attacked with a combination of kicks and punches.

The Yorkshireman tucked his chin tighter, pressing his elbows into his ribs and rode the storm with his body movement.

A spinning elbow skimmed off the top of his head, skittering him a step to the side. Connor feigned losing control of his legs, and spotted the glee of opportunity in Broady's eyes. The younger man tore after him, only to find his legs snatched by a sweetly timed double-leg.

Broady surprised Connor by pinching his hips in a tight closed guard—*maybe he's better on the ground than I thought.*

Still, Connor saw a glimmer of anxiety in the eyes, and steeled himself not to let the man up—*Once on top, stay on top.*

The Yorkshireman began to posture up against the man from Reddish, before crashing down punches and elbows.

The hand fighting of the former Thai boxing star stymied any real damage, and his snake-like hips had almost succeeded in unbalancing Connor.

Broady opened his guard and Connor took the opportunity to knee-slice pass. The younger man shot for an underhook, only for Connor to take an arm-in guillotine choke.

Astonishingly to Connor, the lighter man simply stood up, with him hanging off.

Connor had gotten the take-down easier than he had expected, only to find the striker being more difficult to hold down than he'd anticipated. The black operations agent released the guillotine, breaking away and the two men faced off once more.

Connor tracked him behind his jab—doubling it, feinting it. He checked the low kick, hiding the pain from the clash of shins. He managed to reduce some of the impact from the lightning fast, spinning back kick by stepping back but it pumped out the air through his nostrils.

The flying knee might have seriously hurt him if he had not caught it. Sensing his opponent's wish to harm him, Connor eschewed the more efficient single-leg take down and instead lifted the lighter man high into the air.

Spiking Broady with pile driving force with a mutual explosion of outward breath on impact, Connor quickly passed his legs, and drove his knee into his belly like a hammered tent spike, before raining down punches again.

A couple got through, and Connor waited for the opportunity to snatch an arm bar, or a head and arm choke.

He could not believe it when Broady turned into him while pushing his knee off—accepting a few more digs in the process—and once again, stood up.

Connor threw him away as he fully straightened his legs. With the fatigue evident in both Broady's face and body language, Connor tucked his chin and went for the finish.

"Time!" called out George, and both fighters froze. "You've worked hard today, Len."

The Londoner walked over to Connor. After a moment he stuck out his hand. "Good session that, mate."

"Caught you at the end of your session. Wouldn't have fancied being your first sparring partner."

"Nah, I weren't pushed that hard until you got in," said Broady. "And I need to be. Got my One Championship debut coming up."

"Where?"

"Tokyo."

Connor blurted out. "Fuck off you haven't."

Broady frowned. "Why did you say that? Don't think am good enough or ready or something?"

"No, no. It's…I am genuinely due to go out there myself. Just thought it was too much of a coincidence."

"Fuck off you're not."

"See."

They both laughed. Broady called out to George, "George. Can we get a plane ticket for this lad…fuck sorry, what's your name?"

"Connor," who gave the barest of nods when meeting George's curious gaze.

"It's your training camp," said George.

"I'll pay for my own ticket because I'm not sure how much time I can spend with you out there," said Connor.

82

"And hopefully, I won't be getting into any fisticuffs with anyone harder than you out there."

Mikhail Gorokhov, despite having travelled by air hundreds of times, still enjoyed the thrumming take-off opening the view below.

The sparseness of Frankfurt's high-rise buildings made them stand out amongst the densely urban but more flat plains of Germany's fifth most populous city.

He rarely entered Japan directly from Russia. In the two decades of being an agent, he had amassed funds and separate legends in a vast array of countries. Acquiring the habit of changing flights, identities and constant counter-surveillance had been draining but was now so thoroughly ensconced in his travelling behaviour, he barely noticed it.

Still, he was not above sleeping on a plane. Any potential killer would have to forgo their liberty unless they somehow poisoned his food or drink, in which case he would have to be awake to ingest them. He purposely did not keep hand luggage, so there was no danger of a tracker being placed, unless someone was brazen enough to attach it to his person.

However, besides hanging back on boarding to observe all the other passengers, he also excused himself to the toilet for a second sweep.

Contrary to what some backroom 'experts' might preach, there was no way to identify a shadow by looks alone. Some of the savvier intelligence agencies were not above employing old women or local children in non-combative tasks like shadowing. All he could do was to memorize the facial features and look out for them on his travels in Japan; though a good team used an array of people for human surveillance to create a revolving tail, over a long period the same people would inevitably be used more than once.

He shifted his body sideways to make room for a green-eyed, bobbed-haired, statuesque blonde. Scandinavian perhaps, though the green cardigan and scarf over a white vest top struck him as London fashion.

He enjoyed the shy smile she gave him. Women— indeed, people in general—from that part of the world were a different breed.

Maybe soon he could settle down with such a woman. After this mission he will have accumulated enough money that a woman like her might marry him.

He reined in his desire to speak to her—he was on an operation, and any eroding of his discipline could mean death before he got to marry anyone.

I am the best—he thought—*and the best keep their focus.*

Ciara noted the dark-suited man's face; maybe a blend of oriental and Slavic. The sharpness of his jawline and the broad shoulders hinted at a high level of strength and fitness.

She took in the faces of the other passengers, in the event one of them was a shadow. In the near twelve-hour flight she would have a few opportunities to repeat this without drawing attention to herself.

This would be her fifth time in Japan. She had fallen in love with the country for many reasons. One being how the country blended its steadfast traditions with modern eccentricity; one could walk into—after removing one's footwear—a *Minka*—a traditional Japanese house, through the sliding doors to tread on the tatami mats amid the serene stillness within the rice-paper walls.

Or, you could walk through a densely populated but incredibly clean city, where the high-rises formed giant digital billboards looking down on intersecting shoals of people, before diving into a convenience store full of uniquely flavoured drinks and snacks.

Ciara adored the people most of all; so polite, kind and selfless, even if some could be initially stand-offish with foreigners.

And another reason Ciara loved Japan was that it had the best Kendo schools in the world—the art, along with Judo, was compulsory to the Japanese education system.

She settled back into her seat, and took out an English translation of a book on Kendo she received during her last visit. On the fourth page, the purpose of Kendo had been scribed:

To mould the mind and body.
To cultivate a vigorous spirit
And through correct and structured training,
To strive for improvement in the art of Kendo.
To hold in esteem courtesy and honour.
To associate with others with sincerity.
And to forever pursue the cultivation of oneself.
Thus will one be able:
To love one's country and society;
To contribute to the development of culture;
And to promote peace and prosperity among all people.

She smiled as she thought of Connor's observation—
"So, you throw on a bee keeper's mask and twat the fuck out of one another with sticks?"

Ciara knew the Chameleon Project agent was, and hopefully would continue to be, one of her most important working relationships. She hoped their sharing a bed together several times in the past would not impact that.

In hindsight, she ought not to have slept with him. Especially as she would be due to fill the shoes of a man who never let anything get in the way of his professionalism.

9

Bruce McQuillan watched Kathryn Bainbridge as she stood with the blue-overalled vehicle mechanic across the medium-sized car park. They were outside the back of an open garage with the bold blue and yellow signage of D.M & Sons.

Briefly, he wondered how long Parker would take to collate the information. Bruce knew that despite his request for unredacted documents, the old spymaster would only allow him to see what he wanted him to. Bruce had handed the letters over to Jaime for the tech guru to scan and run through his algorithmic programs.

Though Bruce despised this distraction at this time, he knew to take no action at all would allow it to grow. At least he could put it to the back of his mind for the time being.

Bruce leant against the bonnet of his black BMW X5 Security Plus and let the cool breeze slide through his white open-collared shirt.

A year his elder, Kathryn could be, purely on her appearance, underestimated, but less so than when he had first met her. Her black bob may have a few new grey hairs, but the school teacher look she once sported had morphed into well-fitted suits and subtle make up. Today she wore a short black jacket, matching her knee length skirt, over a light grey shirt.

However, an unmistakable authority riveted her speech when she chose. As she and the garage owner moved around the white Range Rover Sentinel, Bruce could tell by the mechanic's body language that she'd chosen to today.

Both the Security Plus and the Sentinel were armoured cars with an array of in-built security apparatus. Bruce preferred the Security Plus because it drove and looked like a standard X5 and thus did not mark him out as a government official in need of protection. Miles Parker had insisted he have an armoured car, and Bruce made a show of magnanimously relenting in the interests of picking his battles.

During Kathryn's tenure as the director general of the NCA (National Crime Agency), the agency's performance had improved significantly, and Bruce liked her taking protective measures, although he was sure that it had also been on the insistence of the Home Secretary.

In the last few years, Bruce had cultivated a professional relationship with her that had been mutually advantageous.

She had, at what must have been a great effort for a policewoman, curbed her curiosity regarding his past and what he did behind the scenes. But being a highly intelligent woman, she had let him know without expressly stating it that she knew him to be a clandestine force for good.

Now was the time to partially reveal the unspoken. If Ciara Robson was to take over from him, he needed to let certain future allies know, and that meant he would have to let them know in what capacity she would be succeeding him—hence his nerves.

What made it more dangerous was two of the more influential allies he had cultivated had been Kathryn and Chen Zhao, the head of Interpol; both were law enforcement and not in the clandestine services he'd liaised with for decades.

He saw she spotted him and made her way over.

"How are we, Bruce?" she asked in her well-clipped voice.

"Very well, thank you," replied the Glasgow native. "I was lamenting on the general change of your look in the years that we have known one another."

She smiled. "The original frumpy look was a means to come across as unthreatening. It worked well at first, but less as time went on. The power to intimidate has its own merits at times. I might say that in contrast, your edges have softened."

It was true. Since he had stopped partaking in field operations with the black operations unit he now headed, he had allowed his hair to grow longer, his physique—while still impressive for a man in his early-fifties—had become less imposing, and his manner more malleable depending on who he was speaking to.

"Playing the game isn't dirty as long as your intentions are pure. That is why I pretend to enjoy your company."

"Oh, I see," she replied, exaggeratedly narrowing her eyes. "Maybe I have been doing the same."

"Well, I hope not, in light of what I am about to tell you."

Her smile disappeared and she straightened up. "Okay."

"I know you know I work in an extracurricular capacity, in addition to my title as security services liaison officer."

Kathryn said nothing, which he had anticipated and hoped for. If she did not confirm anything then she retained deniability. And he appreciated her not probing now he had to lower his guard.

"I wish to groom someone else in that extracurricular position should I become unable to continue in that role."

"Succession," she said simply. "Little point in creating something great only for it to turn to ashes once its founder has gone."

Her answer surprised and heartened him. She continued, "When am I to meet him?"

Her ability to think ahead was one of her more formidable assets.

"It's a her—you should know better than anyone, especially in this day and age."

"My apologies. When do I get to meet her?"

"I will be in touch on that," said Bruce. "How are things your end?"

Kathryn looked at him and said, "Bruce, I wasn't going to bring it up until I had more to tell you but Zhao might be—will be—stepping down come the summer."

As President of Interpol, Chen Zhao had proved an important friend to Bruce and Kathryn.

"He has over a year left on his mandate. Health issue?"

"I am not sure what it is, but I've never known Zhao to be in anything but the best of health."

"Yes, the Chinese seem to have a wealth of knowledge in that area," mused Bruce aloud. "I appreciate you telling me, Kathryn."

"What are pretend friends for?"

Ciara sat on the straw mat straight-backed and cross-legged with her ankles together in the Burmese position. The view of the shimmering lake framed by forest-covered mountains lay before her.

She closed her eyes so as not to be distracted by the calm beauty or the cold biting her through her dark blue floral-patterned kimono.

Focusing on her breath at her *Hara*—belly—thoughts wandered into her mind uninvited. She observed them as taught and returned to her breathing.

On her earlier arrival at the Kazuyoshi Kendo school, a senior student greeted and instructed her to change into the kimono.

Then, he drove her to this disused Buddhist temple. On arrival, she found the Sensei kneeling on a long roll of white parchment paper, holding a black-inked brush. Writing Kanji symbols and characters in what she knew to be a challenging form of calligraphy known as *Shodō*, without even looking up, he dismissed her in grunted and simple Japanese, instructing her to meditate.

She had made great strides in speaking the language. However, her ear still struggled with rapidly spoken Japanese, especially in one of the more difficult to decipher dialects of the primary twelve. Therefore, she had initially focused on the words and phrases pertaining to Kendo.

On her first visit to Japan, her fascination with blades had led her to the Kazuyoshi Kendo School on the outskirts of Tokyo. The Sensei had treated her with a gruff indifference in the beginning. On her second visit, his demeanour seemed to thaw a little, which she put down to her improvement brought about by her training in the UK.

Before this visit, she had e-mailed him asking for intensive private training to maximise her time with him. She knew people would think the money she had paid to make this happen was strange but she considered it an investment in herself.

She returned to her breathing, berating herself for how many thoughts had passed through her mind before she'd even noticed.

Finally—as she began to shiver—her Sensei Kazuyoshi called out from behind her in his stilted English, "Ciara-san. Stand."

She did so and turned to face him.

The wizened master swordsman stood around her height, and she believed she could outmatch him for physical strength.

He held up a black and white Iaido uniform which resembled a short Gi jacket with willowy trousers, before gesturing his head in the direction of a side room within the thatch-roofed dojo.

She took the uniform with a bow and changed into it in the side room, pleasantly surprised that it fitted well.

She found Sensei Kazuyoshi outside, on the training mat, holding two wooden bokken - wooden practice swords. From her prior research, she recognised the katana-shaped swords were made from red oak, as opposed to the much softer and more flexible bamboo *shinai* blades customarily used for practice.

The breeze passed through her garment as she bowed and stepped onto the mat.

Her Sensei said, "Kendo. Iaido. Bokken. All Kenjutsu."

Ciara understood—in his opinion all the blade arts should come under a single umbrella.

"Wakarimasu," she answered—*I understand.*

He gestured to the spot on the edge of the mat where she had just been meditating. "Zazen good for mind."

He tapped her forehead. Then raised his sword. "Good fear, good for fighting. Bad fear, bad for fighting."

The simplicity of his English clarified his meaning perfectly for her. Controlled adrenaline aided performance, unadulterated fear led to bad decisions or even freezing.

He afforded her a low laugh. "Good pain good for memories."

She knew the truth of this more than most. *That must be why neither of us has any protective gear and we're using hardwood swords.*

His hand slid up and down the wooden blade. "All is okay."

In Kendo, to score a point one must hit with the end, twenty-five centimetres from the tip. Here, now, the entire blade was legal.

He pointed to her legs before waving his hand in a circle encompassing her entire body before doing the same to himself. "All is okay."

In Kendo, attacking four areas achieves a score: the head, wrists, torso or throat. Her sensei was letting her know the entire body was fair game.

She steadied her breathing as she walked to the opposite corner of the mat to him.

"Begin!" he grunted, which meant the same in Japanese.

She brought her bokken high to block the downward strike, only for a thudding pain to crease her around the back of her thigh under her backside. His hand snatched her sword, gripping it like a vice, before his bokken tip punched the air out of her diaphragm.

91

A sweeping stroke and she found herself on her back with the wooden sword pressing against her throat.

He stepped back, allowing her to stand.

"Futatabi," he announced —*Again.*

Ciara knew he did this without malice; she guessed he had struck her around the meatier part of her thigh as not to disable her with a strike aimed more against her femur.

The Chameleon Project agent made a mental note not to overreact to his feints.

She faked her swing, only to step back in anticipation of his counter blow. She felt mild embarrassment at his complete lack of reaction.

She gave a stuttering feint before committing to a thrust, effortlessly parried. The hilt of his bokken banged underneath her jaw, shunting her head back as he spun her around by the wrist. He tapped the bokken tip into her back behind her heart.

When she turned to face him, he lifted his sword, "You fear bokken sword, not fear Shinai. Zazen, remember."

She nodded her understanding—the anticipation of pain was clouding her mind, not focusing it. Adhering to her Sensei's instruction, their following exchanges lasted a few moves longer, despite her losing every time.

As she rose from her knees after another sweep, he grunted, "Good."

She frowned, "I didn't land anything on you."

He gave a low laugh before pointing to himself, "I years of sword. You not. Small victory, small victory, small victory makes big victory. Understand?"

She kicked herself—*You know this from Thai boxing you 'nana.*

"Tomorrow we practise again," he said, concluding the session, and they bowed to one another.

10

Connor had decided to arrive in Tokyo at the Narita International airport instead of the less busy, and more domestic, Haneda. This increased the difficulty of potential surveillance on him despite being further away from where he would stay, west of Tokyo.

He swerved and angled his head away from the small camera crew waiting to interview newly arrived tourists for Japanese television.

The glass-ceilinged, quarter-dome-shaped airport buzzed all around him, and he familiarised himself with being taller than average—*Finally*.

His khaki jacket crept down past his waist over a black t-shirt and met his dark jeans. Connor felt glad that the only tattoo he had was on his chest; exposed tattoos were generally seen as impolite in Japan with some places outright banning their display.

Waiting for his Yen at the ATM, he switched on his pocket Wifi—his prior research told him Tokyo and the surrounding area could be murder for internet reception.

After picking up his prepaid Japan Rail Pass, he managed to decipher the underground rail route map. The extreme punctuality of the train arriving at the Tokyo station did not disappoint.

Connor kept his head still, his eyes looking for any potential shadows in the reflective windows.

He felt a swirl of vulnerability around him here more than in other countries he had operated in. Being Caucasian in the UK, Ukraine and Italy had afforded him a sense of blending in; here, though there were plenty of white tourists, he felt exposed. The quiet murmur of the unfamiliar language exacerbated this.

His phone vibrated in his pocket and he answered it quietly. "Hello."

"Just making sure you arrived and got on the train safely," said Ciara.

"Yeh, easy-peasy Japanesy."

"I'll message you the details of both the car rental and your residence."

"Okay."

"I'd recommend only driving outside the cities if you can help it as the congestion can get pretty bad. And remember, left side."

"Thank you," replied Connor, restraining his sarcastic reply. Ciara was his boss now, and would be in charge of the Chameleon Project in its entirety one day. He thought a degree of formality between them would be more professional.

"You're welcome," she replied before ending the call.

He felt a small relief the call ended just as he got on the train, knowing the Japanese considered it rude to talk on the phone within the confines of a railway carriage.

Instead of the 'sardine-like' feel he had expected, the carriage was relatively sparse of people as he began his journey. He sat as far as he could away from other passengers and, though he resented it, donned a mask because he'd read a sizeable portion of the population had begun the practice even pre-COVID.

Some of the advertising signage seemed vaguely comical to him, while other more suggestive adverts seemed to have models younger than would be common in the UK.

He took out a Kindle but his mind drifted to his relatively short career working for McQuillan.

The new dynamic of his and Ciara's relationship would take some getting used to. They had met just three years ago when Bruce had seconded her to Connor to investigate a human trafficking operation for illegal organ donation.

Though his instincts in the field exceeded hers back then, she had proved a formidable ally; possessing an uncommon physicality and fighting ability for a woman, she also had a sharp intellect, as well as an almost regal attractiveness. This meant she could adapt to most situations she found herself in during operations. They had eventually slept together—she had been more the instigator. Though Connor loved it, he had on more than one occasion suggested that they curtail their sexual relationship only for her to agree with a wry smile, and for him to cave in the next time.

Those times were over now.

And Connor knew why the old man had chosen to take her out of field operations despite her abilities; aside from her distinctive appearance being memorable, Connor could see she had the attributes to take over from McQuillan one day, should he choose to take a step back or down.

He opened the document and it pleased him to see the rental car to be a green Alfa Romeo Giulia. He had anticipated she would get him something cheaper and smaller in the reasoning it would be less conspicuous.

He would now live in an isolated house in a small town called Hinode, around thirty-five miles from the centre of Tokyo. He could see the reasoning; the town's size was sufficient for him to play the western tourist without being the centre of attention, but offered a house isolated enough that he might spot unwanted visitors. Jaime had provided tiny wireless cameras that he was to put up in and around the residence.

Connor watched who he presumed to be a father being shown something by his young son on his phone.

His diaphragm cooled as he thought about the high probability he was now a father, and how if he led a 'regular type' life he'd have been ecstatic for Grace to be the mother of his children. And in half a year he would be an uncle. His father, however, and two of his uncles, now lay murdered.

The smoke of melancholy swirled as he thought of his dad.

Connor had lived with his mother in the more upmarket Roundhay area of Leeds, and used to visit his father's side of his family periodically on weekends and school holidays,

While his grandparents, uncles, aunties and cousins always made a fuss of him, his father would be more reserved. Connor was shocked when told more than once of his father boasting to people about his son's boxing exploits—he rarely told him, himself. Connor thought him a good dad though, encouraging in him a protectiveness of others and offering him life guidance in the form of speeches or one-liners. He had several ingrained into him:

"Try and talk yourself out of fights. If it's going past the point of no return then get the first punch in—don't do this pulling and shoving shit. If they're an okay lad, then you'll be able to talk yourself out of it. If they are cretins they'll take your trying to talk yourself out of it as weakness, which is good because it means they deserve a smack and they have underestimated you, which will make the first punch a shock."

"Consistent hard effort over a long time are your best friends in getting good at something."

"Highs from drugs, drink, shagging women are temporary. A sense of being the best man you can be is in you all the time—when you're brushing your teeth, eating, getting showered, getting dressed, driving—all the time."

"Start something now that your ten-year-older self will thank you for."

And one that Connor found out his dad stole off Jack Nicholson, *"Do unto others: How much deeper into religion do we need to go?"*

His father had also given him several *hidings*. He knew the social services and the law would deem them cruel and illegal but Connor thought it was the intention behind such an act that determined whether it was abusive or not, like the adage of both a mugger and a surgeon cutting you. Only once had his dad hit him in anger, and it had never been for no reason. Connor did not think he could bring himself to strike someone so much smaller than himself, but he understood that his dad was doing what he had to do to keep an unruly son in check. In this, Greg Ryder had only been somewhat successful at curbing his son's rebellious and aggressive nature; Connor had served a short stint in Wetherby Youth Offender Institution, something that had deeply disappointed his father.

But Connor liked the man he had become and knew it was partly down to his father; not necessarily the hidings themselves, but the 'talking tos' that came afterwards.

The beatings had been used to *"…help you remember."*

With this memory, Connor steeled himself to remember why he was here—*To prevent greedy men interfering with the earth's sustainability—like Captain Planet.*

The walls of Ronald Sykes's office were adorned with an eclectic mix of Japanese and British paintings. He sat, staring at the Newton Cradle, or *"Steel Ball swing"* as his niece used to call it.

He gently lifted three of the steel spheres before releasing them. Watching how the trio in motion kept switching from one side to the other had a meditative effect on him.

Ken's opening of his door broke his moment of absent-mindedness.

As the engineer closed the door behind him, Sykes could see that the usual crankiness did not show on his face, instead replaced by nervousness.

"What is it, Ken?"

"A man has come to meet you."

Sykes frowned, "Well don't keep me in suspense. Who?"

Ken dropped his voice to a whisper, "He is dangerous man. He is Yasuhiro Takato, the head of the Gādian."

Sykes felt the whitening of his face. He steadied himself. "What does he want?"

"I do not know."

"Does he speak English?"

Ken nodded gravely. "Yes. He speaks very well."

Sykes took a breath. "Okay. Send him in."

He stood as Ken opened the door, bowing as the suited, flint-eyed man Sykes guessed to be around forty, walked in. His face made no attempt to be either threatening or friendly. His left eyelid seemed ever so slightly lower than the right.

Sykes mirrored Takato's deep bow—a good initial sign. In Japanese culture, the deeper the bow, the greater the respect. However, Sykes and Takato were strangers, so a deep bow could just be customary.

Takato stared at Sykes for a moment before saying in superb English, "Relax, Mr Sykes. You have nothing to fear from me."

Sykes felt his shoulders lower—he hadn't even registered they were trying to reach his ears.

"I think most people would fear you, Takato-san."

"You are not most people. You are the man who history might thank for preserving this planet," replied Takato. "May I sit?"

Sykes nodded numbly. Sitting, Yasuhiro Takato continued, "You are now aware that my clan has a sizeable stake in Okada. I think you dislike this. And I understand. It is true we are a criminal organisation. You might not believe my words but I am committed to seeing you be successful— to succeed—in your clean energy technology. Not just for my family's stake but for the world."

Sykes searched the crime lord's face for signs of insincerity but failed to find any.

Then again, these types will be masters in subterfuge, he thought.

"That is good to know, Takato-san."

Yasuhiro's right hand fingers spread his collar V-gap, almost as if to emphasize the absence of a tie. "I am sure you are aware of how much money some individuals, companies, organisations and governments will lose if Okada succeeds?"

Sykes nodded. "I am fully aware."

"You and I live in different worlds. And I want us to continue to live in different worlds. Do not be naïve, to kill you to stop this would be the easiest thing in the world."

Sykes shifted in his seat. "Then why haven't they done it yet?"

"Because they need to know if the information in your head is also in the heads of others. And if it is stored digitally."

"The Okada board does not want me publishing the studies until the trials are completed."

"Does anyone else know what you know?"

It took a few moments for him to answer. The reality was there were only two people who knew what he knew; and neither had quite such a tight a grasp as he did— together maybe, but not as individuals.

Ken had to know much of the theory to help design and manufacture specific machinery. However, there had been more than one time where the Japanese engineer had thrown his hands in the air and said, *"I do what you say, boss."*

In truth, the person who had grasped the science the most had been Chisato Fukuhara.

He had explained everything to her, and even though this was not his girlfriend's field, her intelligence was such that she understood.

Still, he did not want to tell the man before him this.

"The team is aware of the science."

Takato shook his head. "Can anyone do what you can do?"

Sykes opened his mouth to speak, then closed it until finally, "Not to the same extent, no. I have been working in this field for decades."

The outlaw's eyes stared into his. "Then you understand your importance in the world?"

The gravity of the words finally hit Sykes as he realised the veracity of them. If something did happen to him then the project, if not lost, would be set back years.

His conclusion to all his years of study suggested it was critical to stem the rise in global warming sooner rather than later. Major storms, droughts, rising sea levels and disease were expected to increase. Certain animals and plants were on the brink of extinction—the threat to coral reefs and krill being perilous. Parts of the earth were likely to become uninhabitable by humans, causing mass migration from inhospitable climates—and the conflicts that went with it.

"I understand," Sykes sighed. "So, what is next? House arrest?"

Takato shook his head. "No. If you are in just one place, it is easy to target you. My family are small compared to the other Yakuza groups—if they want you, they will pay the police and attack you in numbers. My family fight like guerrillas—I mean like small band soldiers not the—" with that Takato banged his fists in tandem on his chest, and smiled. Because the action and smile appeared from nowhere, Sykes could not help smiling himself.

Takato continued, "Maybe, yes, like the animal and the small band soldiers. We need to keep you moving, so they find it hard to track you."

"This might be for months," stated Sykes without self-pity.

"Yes," nodded Takato. "Do you have any loved ones here in Japan?"

"No," he said, before changing the subject. "What about here? Is this place vulnerable? We run a lot of the sensitive equipment from here."

Takato said, "The Okada Company has strong security systems that link to the police. The Yakuza would not risk attacking here. Our government would be humiliated and revenge would be fast and strong."

"When will your security measures begin?"

"I will give you three days of freedom. Because once the trials begin, then Okada will have to make a media announcement. And then we cannot control who will discover your name and you will have to be under our close protection."

Sykes looked at him. "I understand this has to happen. But I do not want to be protected if other staff members are not."

Takato looked away, seemingly in thought before locking his eyes back onto Ronald Sykes's. "My organisation is not large. We will look after key personnel. But make no mistake. It is you who will be the target, Mr Sykes, and I am here not to let them succeed."

11

Bruce sat on a buffet stall in Jaime's kitchen, sipping coffee from a stainless steel mug.

He listened to the tech guru's report of Ciara and Connor's arrival in the Land of the Rising Sun. Across the table, the cupboards had rotated in on themselves to reveal a screen, on which various images pertaining to Jaime's briefing flashed up.

The black operations chief usually had these initial briefs sent by encrypted e-mail, with the details in pre-arranged code in case a crack hacker somehow managed to get hold of it.

He knew his presence in Jaime's house would alert the hyper-sensitive information technology genius for another reason.

"Jaime, you know this thing we have built, this Chameleon Project, I am proud of what we've achieved."

He saw a ghost of a gratified smile before Jaime answered, "Yes, I am too."

"And this is something we both want to endure, isn't it," Bruce stated rhetorically.

Jaime gave him a shrug with a frowning nod.

The Scotsman continued, "Even after we have gone?"

Jaime's eyes widened. "Yes."

Bruce knew the former recluse had come a long way in the last few years and it had been a big step allowing Ciara into his home. However, what he was about to say next would be difficult for the younger man to hear.

"We need to find you an assistant. Someone to fulfil the dual purpose of lightening the workload, but also taking the reins should anything ever happen to you."

Jaime took a deep inhalation before breathing out slowly. He looked at Bruce and responded, "I know this is true. Ben had the brain but he liked to build things."

Ben Shaw, his best friend, had died as a result of a Chameleon Project operation.

"Naturally, no one will be selected without your consent. But we must start looking. If it is even possible to get someone to your standard, it will take thousands of hours, so we cannot put this off."

"Do you have any candidates in mind?"

Bruce shook his head. "No. I will petition Darren O'Reilly to see if he has any high talent he'd be willing to give over. He owes us, after all."

Darren O'Reilly owned one of the most profitable UK companies called Verbatim Cyber Securities. A few years ago, on O'Reilly's pleading, Bruce had taken on an investigation into his daughter's murder the police had mistakenly believed they had solved.

The enquiry not only led to the uncovering of a kidnap-for-organs ring, but afforded O'Reilly justice over his daughter's real killer. And Bruce had helped negotiate a contract between Verbatim and the CIA for the provision of various security systems.

"His staff might have the IQ…maybe…but will lack ingenuity," said Jaime derisively.

"Do you have any better ideas?"

"I might," the Peruvian answered. "Did you know that Connor's cousin Charlie has been in my world for a few years?"

Bruce felt a jolt of surprise. "I did not know that."

"He is not inadequate given the equipment he has. He is inexperienced but has innovation. I know it would be a…conflict of interest. Just thought you would like to know."

"It's always good to have options," stated Bruce. "What about the Chen Zhao situation?"

Jaime nodded. "Yes. I have obtained a screenshot of his letter of resignation."

It appeared on the screen. Bruce read the formulaic, formal and vague resignation letter citing 'personal reasons' made out to Interpol's congress made up of its 194 member states.

Jaime continued, "Seems strange, given his high standing and recent successes."

The recent successes included his passing on vital information to Italian law enforcement. This led to the discovery of an island internment centre used for the brainwashing of kidnapped subjects. That intelligence had been given to him by Bruce himself.

"I'll go over there to talk to him," said Bruce. "But it'll have to be an unexpected visit. And one not observed by others."

"I will begin to canvas," said Jaime. "Bruce, I have completed the run through of the letters you gave me. I cannot find any definitive leads on the men your father says threatened him in Lebanon. There are no other references to them except in the letter he sent you—and those descriptions are not detailed enough."

Bruce gave him a solemn smile of gratitude for trying. The chance for vengeance had been virtually non-existent from the outset, even if it was true his father had been murdered. And maybe nothing would come of searching any harder.

"I appreciate your efforts anyway, Jaime."

The younger man gave a shy nod. "I will also be updating you once Miss Robson has finished her meeting."

Detecting an edge of nerves in his voice, Bruce replied, "Relax, Jaime. Not even they would carry out an assassination of a foreign journalist during an official interview…possibly at another time, further down the line, when least expected, maybe."

Ciara could not fathom why she had been granted an interview so easily with the *Kumicho*—chairman—of Yamaguchi-gumi, Shintaro Goto.

She had made the six hour journey through the smattering of rain showers from Tokyo to Kobe alone in a black Lexus IS F. The journey was freer of traffic and smoother than expected.

Arriving at the Yamaguchi-gumi headquarters, she was met at her car by three suited men. Her loosely fitted charcoal suit lay over a white t-shirt and flat brown shoes.

As she alighted from the car, the smaller man in the middle of the three held up his hand after the perfunctory bows.

"Robson-san, we will park your car."

Ciara feigned a hint of surprise at the request, before handing the keys over. In truth, she knew it was standard practice for them to check the car in the owner's absence.

A black and white Japanese wagtail looked down on her from the moist branches.

As one man took the car, the remaining two led her around to the front of the headquarters; she could see the building had two faces. The back resembled a grey prison block with steel-shuttered windows one side and nothing but a drainage pipe and a telephone line on the other.

As they curved around to the front, the sun stroked her face, and she saw the frontage had the look of a commercial office, painted beige by the sun's rays.

She did not have to hide the nerves buzzing through her veins; any British journalist would feel uneasy.

The twenty-eight-year-old felt a jolt on seeing the inside was made up almost entirely of red wood, which harshly juxtaposed the building's exterior. The hanging, bulb-like plants and flowers further heightened the contrast.

She had expected more 'soldiers' in an effort to intimidate and to prevent intruders from entering. Then it occurred to her, the Yamaguchi-gumi's reputation alone would keep errant drunks and gregarious youths away, and the crime group would not deem it prudent to have many of their people around in case of a police, or rival gang, raid.

Ciara pretended not to notice the glint in the plants, knowing them to be security cameras.

"Robson-san. Our Kumicho will see you now. The door is at the top of the stairs," said one of the men who had escorted her in.

She ascended the stairs until the copper *Mempo*—Samurai mask—embedded in the large wooden door, came into view.

As she got to the top, the door creaked open and she entered.

If she hadn't known better, she would have guessed the eighty-year-old to be at least ten years younger. His skull held his skin tight against it, with his grey hair thin but still keeping its hairline.

The Osaka native had joined the Yakuza in the early sixties. After a storied career including shoot-outs, brawls, armed robberies and prison sentences for drug dealing, pimping and fraud, Shintaro Goto became the Kumicho of the Yamaguchi-gumi. A contact had told her that, 'If Tokyo is like New York, then Osaka is like Chicago'.

Though not common knowledge, Ciara knew that Goto had expanded investments internationally during the eighties; gunning in and out of Hawaii and the sex tourism industry throughout various south-east Asian countries. This diversification had helped him survive the crash of the 'bubble economy'.

In the nineties and early two-thousands, Goto also helped export Japanese pornography into Los Angeles which included the digital superimposing of minors' faces onto barely age-legal actresses with child-like bodies. She remembered recoiling when reading a quote attributed to him that the practice was akin to '...*throwing vampires rats for blood so that they don't harm humans.*'

His flamboyant suit surprised her—dark green and blue, with a loose lilac tie. The eyebrows sloped at the corners over dark eyes.

A man, whose age she guessed to be around thirty, slight-framed, wearing glasses and a black suit stood beside him. The faint contrast of his little finger's colour on the right hand compared to the rest of his skin drew her eye before she saw it as a fake.

The pair stood back, banged their palms against their sides and bowed theatrically, which she hurriedly mirrored.

"Robson-san, thank you for meeting me," said Shintaro Goto through the translator.

"It is I that should be thanking you, Goto-san. I am aware that you rarely give interviews—to journalists, at least."

The man beside him translated. She saw her risk rewarded with a slight smile.

Her journalist contact had instructed her not to ask him a direct question regarding the criminal nature of the organisation—the largest of the Yakuza clans.

Still, she could hint.

The translator said, "You are the first westerner he has agreed to."

"Then I am honoured."

For the next few minutes, Ciara steered the conversation towards flattering the Kumicho's entrepreneurial acumen. Most crime lords she had spoken to liked to think of themselves as businessmen.

However, Connor had said that the gap between wholesale cost and profits were usually so substantial that 'criminal businessmen' were rarely under pressure to streamline their businesses with regards to outgoings. She also remembered him saying, *"...with drugs, customer satisfaction isn't really an issue—a pisshead doesn't give a fuck what goes up their nose. And it's not like a drug dealer has to worry about advertising costs is it."*

But he had also noted even low-level criminals had to deal with the added layers of navigating the risks of death, being maimed and imprisonment that straight businessmen usually didn't.

She sensed Goto's ego responding to her questions as he leant forward and spoke more animatedly. After a long monologue with his translator, Ciara thought she heard him use the phrase *ninkyō dantai*—which she understood the Yakuza used to describe themselves, roughly translated as 'chivalrous organizations'.

The translator confirmed this, saying, "We are noble groups. Some of the safest places in Japan are in areas that are under our control. If you ever walk in Tokyo's Kabukicho entertainment district, you will never have to worry about being attacked or robbed because we control it better than the police ever could. When the earthquake hit this city in 1995, or when the tsunami hit Tohoku, who were the ones who moved food, blankets and medicine? It was we, not the government."

Ciara nodded. She had heard this before, and although she didn't doubt the validity of the stories, she did question the motives—good public relations served as an insulator. Also, Ciara would have asked how much money Yakuza clans made from the construction contracts in the aftermath.

"Speaking of tsunamis," Ciara began. "What are Goto-san's thoughts on the disaster at the Fukushima Daiichi Nuclear Power Plant?"

"He says it was the hand of the divine. This hand has protected Nippon—I mean Japan—over the centuries, but she needs to remind us of her power."

Ciara said with an insincere naivety, "Do you think the fact it was a nuclear plant that caused the divine's wrath? I mean, nuclear power is not of nature."

Goto gave a gruff laugh at the translation before speaking.

The translator said, "Nuclear energy has a much lower impact on the environment than fossil fuels. It does not produce greenhouse gases like fossil fuels do. Even better than solar and wind."

Ciara's grasp of the language indicated that the translator had expanded on his bosses answer, but she simply nodded and said, "That is true. But if clean energy technology without carbon emissions came into existence, would Goto-san support it?"

On translation, perhaps Japan's most powerful crime lord stared at her for a few moments. Despite the language barrier she heard his voice lose its congenial tone.

"We are an evolving organisation. If such technology existed, of course we would support it. However, we must be aware that if Japan is the nation to produce such a technology, it is not dangerous and remains under protection."

"Absolutely," she replied. "Whichever country developed it should prosper from it. But I am glad he agrees it should be protected—we are talking about the future of the planet, after all."

Shintaro Goto's short laugh sounded from his chest and came without opening his mouth, before he fired his opinion at her through his translator.

"Goto-san says the experts cannot even agree amongst themselves. They first predicted we'd be underwater now. It is something the west's politicians say because they do not control the oil reserves. This is not the first time the planet has warmed up. And do humans have that much influence over nature?"

Ciara knew some pre-eminent scientists would agree with the sentiment. She also knew the vast majority of people latched onto evidence supporting their own hypothesis. She had heard more than once—but first from a university professor—that one must vigorously research against their own argument.

"Of course, Goto-san," she said agreeably. "You would have to admit, it would be nice to breathe cleaner air in Tokyo."

A non-committal shrug met the translation.

Ciara spoke to Goto with a rehearsed statement, "Kono-ji no shitsumon wa sukoshi binkan kamo

109

shiremasen. Kotaeru hitsuyō wa arimasen."—*This next question may be a little sensitive. You don't have to answer.*

As she anticipated from the powerful underworld king, he grunted with a wave of his hand, a gesture that said—*no question is too sensitive for me.*

Keeping her eyes on Goto, she continued with, "How much of your business expertise was passed to, and therefore helped, Yasuhiro Takato? He has become an excellent businessman in his own right."

She observed a ghost of a sneer appear at the mention of his rival's name.

The venom edged into every sentence of his reply, being almost matched in the translator's English. "Yasuhiro Takato is not a businessman, he is a disloyal rat. His greed saw him split away from us and he has been running ever since."

She saw little reason to push further.

"I understand," she replied. "I thank you for seeing me, Goto-san."

She heard the softening in his speech.

"Goto-san asks if you would like to meet some of Japan's most influential people?"

She took a moment to reply. "Yes, I would be honoured to."

As the meeting broke up, Ciara felt a coolness about her person. Anyone they wanted her to meet, she would have to encounter on her own.

She suddenly felt empathy for Ronald Sykes—he now found himself caught in this deadly game through his altruistic pursuits.

And he was a mere civilian.

Ronald Sykes stood with his hands thrust into the pockets of his black Parka jacket.

The vast panoramic view of Tokyo from the Roppongi Hills Mori Tower included the Tokyo Tower and

Tokyo Skytree. The night's dark blue sky still had wisps of clouds through it as it looked down on the city lit by blues, oranges, whites, reds and hints of green.

When he first arrived in Tokyo, going to observatories became one of his favourite things in the Japanese capital.

His visits got sparser as his workload increased, dwindling to nil in the past six months. It had only been because of the woman, who now came up behind him to squeeze his right triceps that he was here.

"Hello, Ronald," she said in a high, lilted English.

"Ikaga desu ka Chisato-san,"—*How are you Chisato?*

Twelve-years his junior, Chisato Fukuhara smiled as she always did at his Japanese. In the beginning, it had been to hide her embarrassment. Now, it was in admiration for the correctness of his pronunciation.

A former student from the University of Tokyo—known as Todai—the diminutive Osaka native had disproved low expectations and graduated within the top percentile of her intake and become a highly respected professor of Pharmacology.

They had met in Germany at the Albert Ludwigs University of Freiburg. Chisato had been there to visit a friend, and they both dropped into his lecture.

One of the lecture attendees recognised her, and her blushes had amused Sykes.

"I am fine, thank you. You look tired."

He smiled, "In a few months the workload will calm down."

"If you do not take a rest, you will be calmed down on a hospital bed."

"I can't take too much rest at the moment. There is too much at stake."

"You should let me help you. I know the principles," she said without any edge of arrogance, for this was the truth. At first, she'd had to coax and cajole him. But with her rapid understanding of the concepts, the drip of information became a tidal wave. He had been pleased to

111

have someone to share it with. Still, he had not shared with her all the intricacies.

"We are nearly there now. Little reason to add to your workload, my dear."

She gave him a tight smile. Sykes wanted to kiss her, but public displays of affection in Japanese culture did not go further than hand-holding.

He felt aggrieved their day-long dates—customary in Japan—were a thing of the past. Looking at her, knowing the focus of her concern was centred solely on him, caused a bloom of warmth within him.

"Soon, it will be taken over and we will be able to travel the world for a year."

"I know. I look with happiness to it."

As they gazed over the city, Ronald Sykes felt they were the only two people in the world, unaware another person at the back of the observatory was watching him.

Mikhail Gorokhov strolled the smooth stoned paths of Shinjuku Gyo-en National Garden with a sense of calm he rarely felt in other parts of congested Tokyo.

The land had been a gift from the shogun to Lord Naitō, who had the garden finished in 1772.

The Japanese-Russian found the smell and brightness of the various floral colours serene to walk through, and had come early to enjoy it before his meeting.

Gorokhov had met Shohei Nomura fifteen years ago when the Japanese narcotics officer had been deep within the Yamaguchi-gumi. Gorokhov had assassinated a potential whistle-blower, thus preserving Nomura's cover and life. The Tokyo native's sense of honour meant Gorokhov could call upon him from time to time for intelligence.

The former SVR agent took care with the frequency and how intrusive the information he inquired for; a man's patience could be tested by anyone, his kids, his wife, boss, and even a man who had saved his life, in the wrong circumstances.

Gorokhov stopped and looked out onto the rippling Naka no ike lake.

Through the red-leaved trees, he saw the taller than the Japanese-average forty-two-year-old man from a distance but feigned he hadn't; experience and history had taught him allies could easily turn into enemies in time.

"Hello, Mikhail-san," said Nomura as he crept up and stood two metres to the SVR assassin's left.

"Hello Shohei-san," replied Gorokhov. They spoke in Japanese, and used the less formal first names.

"What brings you to Nippon?"

He asked every time Gorokhov met with him, and Gorokhov never failed to ignore the question.

"I have heard that Japanese law enforcement are particularly on edge regarding one Yasuhiro Takato upsetting the apple cart."

"Upsetting the apple cart?"

"It is a phrase meaning to spoil things, to upset the natural order of things. I believe the Romans first used the term. Maybe you should travel more, Shohei-san."

"You should tell my boss that."

"One day you will be the boss."

Gorokhov knew Nomura to be now a mere two positions from heading the Japanese Organized Crime Division. This was largely due to the reputation gained during his tenure as an undercover agent earlier in his career.

As the spring breeze feathered the water, Nomura blew into his hands and said, "The three major clans have well-oiled communication lines. Though they are technically rivals, none wish to see the heat an all-out war would bring down. But Yasuhiro Takato seems not to care. His clan— the Gādian—have already pulled on the tails of the tigers."

"I understand that the Yakuza clans are not what they once were, but I thought that would invite the destruction of the Gādian?"

Nomura stooped down to pick up a smooth pebble that looked out of place amongst the rest of the stones. He skimmed it for eight bounces across the water and replied, "The Gādian have three elements on their side as far as I can see. They have proven to be more ruthless—latest being cutting through the Achilles tendons of those who defy them. They are more manoeuvrable. If I were to guess, I think they might have a system where the first and second lieutenants are much freer to make decisions and take immediate actions."

Nomura had used the words *wakagashira* and *shateigashira* for the respective ranks.

"What is the third?"

"Mystery," said Nomura. "There are myths that they live underground in the forests of Oyama and Hachikokuyama Ryokuchi. That they are secretly funded and given intelligence by all sorts of rich and powerful people. Maybe this is all untrue but no one knows for sure. That is what makes certain people nervous."

"Does it make you nervous, Shohei-san?"

The policeman took a moment to reply. "The quiet gets boring at times. Although, the warm comfort of fire is pleasant until you get too close and it burns you."

Gorokhov smiled, "Unless someone puts out the flames first."

He caught Nomura looking at him briefly in his peripheral vision.

"You know I am grateful for that day, Mikhail-san."

"I know," said Gorokhov. "You are a brave man. A brave young man doing hazardous work."

"I was—am—an ambitious man, and you gave me time to develop the strength to control that ambition before it consumed me," answered the Japanese law enforcement officer. "The flashpoint regarding this potential all-out war will be the rights to the technologies developed at Okada Company."

Gorokhov kept his triumph off his face. A sense of duty—*Giri*—formed a staple of Japanese culture in general, let alone amongst its law enforcement. That Nomura had brought it up without him asking was a victory.

"Our just standing here looks suspicious to anyone observing, Shohei-san," said the man with Russian blood. "Let's take a walk."

When the policeman sidled up beside him, Gorokhov asked, "What technologies?"

"I am unsure of the details but it centres on dramatic breakthroughs in renewable energy. The rumour—that I know to be the truth—is the Gādian has a major stake in the company. If and when these technologies become mainstream, the company will become the richest in the world. This is why I think the rumours of the Gādian being secretly funded by the government and other wealthy men is accurate—the country will benefit from Okada's success, and with that type of money behind them, the Gādian will rule Japan. The other Yakuza clans do not wish for that to happen."

"Are you aware of the three tigers' plans to prevent this?"

"It centres on a British scientist. They have an idea that he is the key. Except, they have had difficulty tracking him outside of the laboratory he works at—it is huge with many exits. The whole site is rigged to security systems that alert Special Assault Teams who are rotated on stand-by. So, no one will attempt to kidnap him there. However, outside of there is different. Which is why I am glad you are here."

Before Gorokhov's brain could restrain the question, he had already asked, "Why?"

Nomura shot him a glance. "Because I am presuming you are here to protect Japan's investment. I know it has been quite a while since we last met, but I have never questioned your commitment to Japan since the death of your brother, Mikhail-san."

A rush of understanding burst in Gorokhov's mind. He hadn't forgotten exactly, but at Nomura's words, the memories stepped out of the dark forest in the back of his mind.

"Of course I am here for Japan, you should never question that," answered Gorokhov, using all his will power keep control of his demeanour in the rush of his renewed recollections.

His elder half-brother, Makar, had gone into deep cover with the Solntsevskaya Bratva many years ago and had been accepted as one of its most respected members. When Makar had been killed by a shot to the throat—fired from behind him—in London three years ago, Gorokhov had demanded answers but been stonewalled.

"What is it Mikhail-san?"

"Just thinking of my brother."

"The bonds of family are strong, even if one's government does not value them. You understand."

Indeed, Gorokhov did, which is why he left the SVR for a life of civilian peace.

However, his world view had been modified when he had been taken to the island. The old man with the white coat and thick glasses had shown him a new path to follow, one that involved him giving the inquiring agencies the perception he had gone freelance. He had offered his services to Japan's Public Security Intelligence Agency, and word of his exploits had reached Nomura's ears.

He asked the law enforcement officer, "Why wouldn't the National Police Agency give the scientist day and night protection?"

"I do not know. My guess is they believe it is the site itself holding the technology. My department's concerns have been escalated—whether they are taken notice of, I do not know."

"Why wouldn't they?"

"There has been…friction, between the departments."

Gorokhov halted with Nomura following suit. "I know you still have strong contacts, not only within the Yakuza, but the other law enforcement departments. When you hear of this scientist's whereabouts—will you tell me?"

Shohei Nomura did not speak for a moment and Gorokhov could see contemplation of the request.

Finally, the law enforcement officer said, "Yes."

"I need to know if he has any friends or loved ones here in Japan. He'll go to them."

"There is a woman. I will get you the details."

12

Connor put the half empty packet of crab-flavoured crisps into the bin, before weaving through the fast moving, crammed shoal of Japanese residents and tourist shoppers.

He lamented the Shibuya shopping district of Japan for being one of the hardest places in the world to track someone.

The multi-coloured neon lights raked over the entirety of the skyscrapers and tall commerce centres. The shops sold an array of bizarre items he hadn't time to get drawn into. The chattering hum of people and the sounds of nearby traffic converged into a loud thrum.

And of all the people to track in this crowd, a physically non-descript Japanese woman might be one of the more difficult.

Twenty minutes previously, Connor had managed to surreptitiously stripe her fur-lined, light brown jacket with a thumb of special IR paint.

The glasses he wore looked like a regular pair, but had been designed by Verbatim Cyber Securities, a company on the cutting edge of surveillance technologies; the owner of which held a deep allegiance to Bruce McQuillan.

At times like this, Connor felt a little like Bond—*except Bond wouldn't be following a middle-aged woman like a stalker.*

Through a digital report sent to him by Jaime, Connor knew tracking Ronald Sykes would be dangerous and invite suspicion. With Sykes already under the protection of the Gādian, the only way to get to him would be through his loved ones.

The former Royal Marine had watched them together at the observatory. Although Japanese custom meant that it would be hard to distinguish if they were a couple, Connor's understanding of body language meant he immediately identified it.

He had also spotted a second watcher—the creased shirt with the flared collar the Japanese man had worn indicated to Connor a freshly removed suit jacket and tie. Yakuza soldiers dressed distinctively, and Connor surmised the character may have wished to stay incognito the closer he got Sykes.

He had taken a picture of the gentleman on his phone and forwarded it to Jaime. The response was immediate—a Yamaguchi-gumi *Shatei*—'Little Brother'—meaning a lower rung soldier.

As Connor had followed the couple, and the watcher, back down from the high point, it perturbed him that as the couple parted at the entrance, it was the woman who the watcher had followed, not Sykes.

And so, now here he was, playing the unobtrusive bodyguard. Not that he was sure how he'd deal with multiple men attempting a kidnap.

He had chosen not to arm himself.

Japan had one of the lowest gun crime rates globally and an outright ban on handguns. To obtain a shotgun required day classes, written examinations, a high shooting range pass mark, mental health and drugs tests, a criminal record check and a thorough investigation into your background, including friends, colleagues and family. Even the Japanese police rarely used guns, instead employing *taiho-jutsu*—arresting technique—and were encouraged to reach a high level in Judo.

He realised he could be tailing her only for her not to be the target, and though he hoped that was the case, his intuition told him otherwise.

He had planned to track her to her vehicle and attach a GPS monitor. Then it occurred to him that in the time it would take to make it back to his own vehicle and follow her, she would be vulnerable.

Proper surveillance required multiple revolving teams, as did close-protection.

He could request more personnel but knew the use of UK nationals for these operations could cause a major diplomatic incident and risk exposing The Chameleon Project.

He knew Chisato Fukuhara's address—he would head there.

Ronald Sykes thought the blend of navy blue-blazered law enforcement and the black-suited Gādian standing on the peripheries of the Okada engineering section loading bay to be a surreal scene.

The parking lights illuminated the early night to show the drivers of the bright white trucks conversing with the various Okada staff as they loaded equipment into them. This would be the first of several trips to Nagasaki.

He had wished Chisato goodbye at the Okada office reception desk. He would be away for a while.

The way Ken busied himself between the parties seemed like he was on fast forward.

He came up to Sykes and said, "Those are Gādian men. Why are they here when the police are here?"

Sykes sighed, "The contract Mr Takato had the board sign allows to provide security when they want. The police might not like it, but have to allow it."

"They have gun licenses?"

Sykes tilted his chin. "I think yes. They must have powerful friends."

Sykes caught a look on Ken's face. "It was you who said that mongeese, mongooses rather, keep the cobras at bay. Besides, it would take an army to overcome this many armed men. You will be quite safe."

Ken looked up at him. "That is problem—maybe. If an enemy knows that then they might send army. Like Russian invasion of Manchuria, with all of us in the centre."

Sykes acknowledged his logic but wanted to assuage his highly-strung engineer's nerves. "There is no organised

120

crime group that will risk the wrath of the Japanese government to undermine our efforts in plain sight. Don't worry."

Ken remained quiet, before nodding his head. "You are right. I think of how they will attack then? Maybe you should have security?"

"I already do."

"That is good," said Ken. "It is good that your family is in England. The Yakuza maybe use them to get to you."

Sykes felt a cold ball bearing materialise in his brain at the words. He replied on a kind of autopilot. "I believe the British government is keeping a discreet eye on them."

Ken's face broke out into a wide smile. "That is good, my friend."

He patted Sykes's arm with force and left to berate a driver loading up some equipment.

Sykes's hand began for his phone, before the conscious part of his brain understood why.

The realisation dawned as the screen showed two missed calls from Chisato.

His legs went hollow as his heart threatened to strangle him.

Frantically tapping the phone's screen, he prayed for the wave of relief that her voice would bring.

The street lights lit Chisato's face as she drove for home. She lived over half an hour outside Tokyo's city centre. Her residence in Inokashira provided a quiet relief from the flashing claustrophobia she sometimes felt in the capital.

Though to call Inokashira a quiet area would be laughable to other countries; she remembered how the space in Germany had taken time to get used to. She now lived on the water, the only houses she could see being on the opposite shore, the forests on three sides giving her a sense of tranquillity.

She thought about Ronald Sykes and worried about his health. The enthusiastic energy still surged, pushing a tired man toward exhaustion. He would constantly affirm he would take her up on her suggestion of a short and straightforward meditation routine, but his attempts always ended in his fidgeting—*a brain that refused to slow*.

She was convinced her own meditation had guarded against burnout, improved her health and helped her become more aware.

Chisato would miss him of course, but this hadn't been the first time they had time apart. Her cat, Momo—*Peach*—would provide her company.

Using the controls on the steering wheel, she selected Ronalds's number—just to say goodnight. It went to voicemail after a few rings and she clicked off, not knowing what message to leave.

As she eased her car into the forest for the short journey home, she felt prickles in the hair behind her ears.

I must be tired myself, she thought, imagining silhouettes of vehicles through the black trees.

As she slowed the car to a crawl, she felt puzzled by Momo's absence from her usual position, awaiting her return perched on the wooden porch's railing. Ronald had told Chisato that he'd seen Momo run out of the house to greet her a full minute or two before he could even hear her car.

She brought her vehicle to a stop. Instinct caused her to dab down the driver side window an inch without knowing why. The quiet gave way to the sounds of the Koorogi—Japanese Crickets—singing and fighting in the darkness.

Her hand went for the door handle, but instead she gave in to the urge to phone Ronald. Her heart rate began to simmer as the ringing received no reply.

Pushing the off button, her driver side window exploded, showering her with glass shards.

With the door prised open, a rough hand clamped off her scream and another viced her arm. Unceremoniously wrenched out, her kicking legs banging underneath the steering wheel and then the door. Another set of steel-like fingers collected them up as one of the other suited gentlemen looked on.

She found herself struggling hopelessly as they faded with her into the terror of the cold woods.

The black silhouette of a vehicle morphed into a dark blue van. A hand muffled her screams.

She guessed the one man not holding her to be a low-ranking sumo wrestler. The Yakuza sometimes paid them for 'heavy work'.

He darted around the trio with surprising agility and opened the sliding door of the van.

Then came a sudden drop of her ankles.

Her wide eyes took in that the man who'd held them now stood still, open mouthed, eyes bulging. His head tilted as the blade tip sliced out from his throat's centre to the side, spraying a warm wet all over her.

A glimpse of a *Hakujin*—Caucasian man—behind him snatched across her eyes a split second before the ground thumped the air from her lungs.

Feet scrambled over her. The sounds of men fighting cut through the night. Her diaphragm clawed for air, and she craned her neck forward.

Her mind could barely compute the carnage. The man who had held her legs now lay flat on his back. The one who had held her arms knelt upright, eyes wide open with the hilt of a dagger protruding at a perfect right-angle to his left temple.

The sumo—a mass of muscle and fat—dwarfed the Hakujin despite not being much taller.

Both adopted fighting stances; the white man with his chin down, shoulders hunched and hands up in loose fists—a glint came from inside the right one. The small giant confirmed her suspicions of him being sumo with his *Sonkyo* stance; a wide half-squat with the upper body tucked in.

The thought of running away did not occur to her.

The dialect in Hakujin's following taunt indicated to her that he was an Englishman.

"Not so brave now you're faced with a man and not a dainty woman. Not exactly Samurai-like, you fucking fat *yowamushi.*"

On being called a 'weak, cowardly insect', the colossus charged, flinging downward slaps.

The sandy-haired man whipped to the side, kicking the man's bulbous calf before his hands became a blur of pile-driving punches into the side of the sumo's head.

Eventually, the *hundred and seventy-five kin*—two-hundred and thirty pounds—hulk crumpled to the ground.

What looked to be a cigarette lighter dropped out of the Englishman's hand, landing with a thud.

From behind, he punched in a *Hadaka-jime*—rear-naked choke—before pitching forward with his feet on the ample hips, trapping his prey between his body and the ground.

Still frozen still, she sensed the Englishman meant no harm to her.

Her heart rose in her chest, as the huge henchman came to life, rising to his hands and knees, seemingly unencumbered by the man on his back, choking him.

Just as his banana-fingered hands grabbed for the smaller man's clasped ones, the sumo's tree-like legs buckled, pitching him forwards and toppling him.

The Hakujin stayed on his back like a rodeo rider and held the choke a long time after she heard the Yakuza soldier emit a curdling snore. It dawned on her— *I am witnessing a murder.*

Finally, as the Englishman rose so did her fear, and he said quietly, "Sayonara E.Honda."

He stepped around the hulk and crouched a few metres away. "Chisato Fukuhara. I am aware you speak

124

English fluently. My name is Connor Reed. I am not here to hurt you. Understand?"

Her head slowly nodded.

"Say it," he commanded.

"You are not here to hurt me."

"Good," said Connor.

He stood, walked a few paces and retrieved a handgun from the ground. Her legs fired into life in an attempt to get away. Instead, she found her ankle gripped.

Connor hissed venomously, "Stop it, now."

She immediately ceased and he continued, "Look at me."

When she did so, he opened his unzipped brown leather jacket further and pulled up his black t-shirt before spinning three-hundred and sixty degrees. Next, he pulled up his trousers to reveal his socks.

He knelt beside her and held up the pistol to her eyes. "This is an MP-443 Grach. The Yakuza used to smuggle these weapons in from Russia, especially back in the 2000s."

He pulled back the top slide a few millimetres, and she could see a stripe of brass. "This shows that a round is seated—that it's loaded. And this red dot shows that the safety catch is off and ready to fire. All you have to do is point and squeeze. Understand?"

"I understand."

He flipped the gun around so the grip faced her. "I have shown you that I am unarmed. Take this gun if it makes you feel safer, because you won't survive without my help."

Her hand reached out before her mind computed his offer. She caught a flicker in his eyes as her fingers snaked around the grip and his fingers left it.

He stood up. "I am going to retrieve my knife. It has sentimental value."

Stepping on the current owner's head, he prised the blade free like the English myth she had enjoyed of King Arthur pulling the sword Excalibur from a stone.

"Okay. Let's go."

Her voice came out stronger than she anticipated. "Not without Momo."

His face scrunched briefly. "Who's Momo?"

"My cat."

He stood still for a moment. "We've already been here too long. We're not going back to your house for a fucking cat. If you are that hungry, we can stop off for Sushi, or whatever."

She climbed to her feet. "It is the Koreans and Chinese that are known for eating cats," she said, before pointing the pistol at him. "And we are going back for Momo."

Connor Reed looked at her with a faint incredulity. "Looks like we're going back for your cat, then."

13

Chen Zhao sat on the large balcony of his apartment watching the fading sun take the glitter away from the river Rhône. His hands nursed a warm drink of Chivas mixed with green tea.

In the first few weeks of the blackmail, he had abstained from his usual—moderate—consumption of alcohol, so as not to tempt himself towards drunkenness.

However, now, on the acceptance of his situation, he allowed himself these moments. Out of his suit and dressed in a dark navy turtle-neck and comfortable grey slacks, the fifty-five-year-old realised how few quiet moments such as these there had been since his tenure of President of Interpol began.

He hadn't appreciated how beautiful a city Lyon could be.

The past few weeks had been the most emotional of his life. It had begun with a visit to his native China, welcomed by his wife Chyou, if not by his eleven-year-old daughter Daiyu, who considered France her home country.

For him, the stay had been a harangue of meetings and conferences, but for Chyou and Daiyu it had been a holiday of visiting relatives and touring the country. So, he hadn't been too disappointed when told he was urgently needed back in Lyon and his wife and daughter would meet him back there.

With his glass now empty, he succumbed to a brief mental battle and got up to make himself another drink.

He made his way back through the bedroom, along his hallway adorned with art, and entered the kitchen, where he grabbed the bottle of Chivas.

The Glaswegian voice made him jump, mid pour.

"Best make it two, but leave out the green tea for me."

His head jerked towards the hawkish features of Bruce McQuillan, whose frame now filled the doorway.

Fear must have etched his face, because the British black operations chief said, "I've activated a device that intercepts audio bugs in a way that isn't suspicious. And we'll stay away from the windows."

This had a calming effect on Zhao, who said, "So you know?"

"Not everything, but I know you resigned two days after you returned from Beijing, despite Chyou and Daiyu still being over there."

Zhao squeezed his eyes tight, and quietly said, "They have them. They can travel around, visit friends and family, but eyes are on them at all times. Their phones will be tapped. Chyou doesn't even know the danger she is in—and will continue to be in danger until I officially step down."

"Who are they?"

"The Chinese government, but I sense something else at play," said Zhao, handing Bruce a glass of Chivas whisky.

"Why?"

"I have no major cases currently ongoing in my home country; indeed, I know of the whispers that I have been lenient with regards to my home nation."

"Any truth to the whispers?"

Zhao shrugged, "I do not turn blind eyes, but nor have I been very aggressive following all leads to conclusion. A crusade to penetrate the web of corruption over there would take far too many resources."

"If I could get your family back, would you rescind your resignation?"

Zhao blinked—surely not even Bruce McQuillan could extract his family from beneath the gaze of the Chinese Ministry of State Security. He shook his head. "They have collected evidence of corruption and bribery against me, and will be prepared to use it."

The Scotsman's eyebrows rose. "False evidence?"

"Mostly," said Zhao. "I have never profited beyond my pay cheque. But you don't rise through Chinese law enforcement without having to turn your eyes to certain things or…greasing the wheels to ensure justice. There is enough in it all to ensure my dismissal—enough in the lies to ensure I lose my freedom."

"And this evidence—the genuine evidence—would have taken some digging up?"

"From many sources too. I do not know why my government would want to scandalize one of their nationals. Especially as any successor would likely be more proactive in targeting Chinese businesses and government corruption."

"Which are two of the reasons you think an entity outside of China is influencing this move?" said McQuillan rhetorically.

"Yes. I have been able to keep my hands clean, but only after washing them," said Zhao without any contriteness.

"Your intentions have always been pure, Chen," said McQuillan, seemingly with sincerity.

"Which is why I am not going to make a commotion. It had to end someh—"

"We'll see about that," interrupted the Scotsman, draining his glass off and preparing to leave. "We exist to keep the wolves off the prey."

Ciara looked through the second floor window down at the three small aircraft and the sea beyond. She stood in the large room with metal walls. Old flight plans and safety regulations in Japanese with English translations adorned the walls.

Chisato Fukuhara sat on the far side of the room, speaking quietly and reassuringly into her phone. A white cat—one eye blue and the other brown—sat contently on her lap with a tail more akin to a rabbit's than a feline.

The door opened and Connor walked in. He went over to Chisato to hand her a can of cola. The bobtail's head craned up and it began meowing as if talking to him.

He came over to Ciara, cracked open his own cola and took a sip.

"I thought you being Mr Healthy you would steer clear of that? Ten teaspoons of sugar in one of them."

"It's handy as a pick-me-up when I'm shattered. It wasn't just taking three of 'em out, we had to look for her 'Resident Evil' cat afterwards."

"What are different coloured eyes on the same face called?" she asked.

"Heterochromatic. Kate Bosworth and the late Da—"

She cut him off with, "You should have just said no to looking for the cat."

"There was an extenuating circumstance," he replied. "What now?"

"She'll take a series of charter flights to get her back safely to the UK," answered Ciara. "The thing is, I am not sure she'll ever come back. Whichever clan those guys belonged to, the bosses aren't going to easily forget three of their guys are dead."

"I couldn't risk temporarily incapacitating all three. I was lucky only one was armed."

She turned to look at him. "I wasn't questioning your judgement."

"I know. I'm just angry about it."

She nodded. "Not that she'll be out of reach, although the Yakuza may look to make a direct bid for Ronald Sykes now."

"The backlash would destroy them. They aren't what they were."

"Jaime has picked up chatter there will be a high level meeting between all three of the major clan heads. He's struggling to decipher the codes they use, so hasn't got any idea where or when the meeting will be at the moment."

"When did Jaime know this?

"Yesterday afternoon. Before you rescued Chisato."

"Then why would they agree to a grand meeting? If they had succeeded—which they had no reason to suspect they wouldn't—why would the clan behind it risk the exposure?"

"Perhaps so they could go into the meeting with the greater hand? Or maybe they would have simply pulled out once they had her."

"Maybe," said Connor, rubbing beneath his eye. "Does Ronald Sykes have anyone else close to him in Japan?"

"No."

"If that's the case, I guess I'm redundant here, aren't I?"

"Can you hang around for a few days?"

"Yeh," he said. "Shouldn't you be commanding me rather than asking me?"

"Old habits. Stay where you are until I say so."

"Of course."

He did not tell her he was planning to anyway. In addition to aiding Len Broady in sparring, he had visits to make to various electric car companies and things to tick off his 'visiting Japan' bucket list.

Luckily, he had not left any witnesses when killing the three Yakuza soldiers, which would have made staying in the country undetected near-impossible.

As he stared out to the hillside opposite glittering with lights, he looked forward to the rest of his stay, knowing that his work was done and the danger gone.

Gorokhov's camera more resembled the small telescope which it doubled as. With infrared and thermal settings, it was handy in a variety of situations.

Though it might not have access to some of the more hyper-advanced technologies the CIA, or the Guoanbu—Chinese Intelligence—had, the SVR could still be relied on for state of the art equipment.

He focused on the face of the man with the dark-blond hair and blue eyes. Gorokhov had been impressed with the man's dispatching of the three Yakuza soldiers, which included a sumo wrestler. Still, he calculated he could have achieved the result eight-to-nine seconds quicker while minimizing the risk.

Gorokhov had planned on intercepting the pair, only to curse on seeing the man taking Chisato Fukuhara to a small military airfield.

Studying his northern European features, Gorokhov guessed them to be predominantly Anglo-Saxon. However, he found it more challenging to be confident of the ethnicity of the short-haired blonde female stood next to him.

As he studied her features, it dawned on him he had seen her before—*The flight over.*

If the man was indeed British, it would make sense they would send an agent to protect their investment. However, Gorokhov was sure the man was not among the MI6 agents or Special Forces soldiers that the SVR had identified and held on file.

Not that the Russian intelligence agency knew of all the UK's on the ground assets but Gorokhov reckoned on the vast majority; it was amazing what went out on cyberspace now, and he took pains to memorise at least the names and faces of those they had on file, and the biographies of the majority.

Gorokhov took photographs of the plane, ready to forward onto Alexey Orlov who, unlike the Japanese, had numerous assets throughout Europe and the UK. Gorokhov presumed they would take Chisato there. And the SVR's cyber technicians might be able to retrieve a manifest of the flight he had shared with the blonde woman.

He knew now his best play was to contact the hierarchy of the biggest organised crime clan in Nippon—the Yamaguchi-gumi.

Shintaro Goto's rage fired his body with the energy of a twenty-five-year-old. He came around his desk to stand over three of his wakagashira.

"You sent three men—including Shiina, who was like two men!—to take a diminutive woman and you are telling me she has disappeared, they are all dead and you do not know who is responsible?" he fumed in Japanese.

The lieutenants kept their heads bowed in fear. And it was only this action preventing him from asking for their atonement through Yubitsume.

Still, he prided himself on not acting rashly and never liked demanding his soldiers take portions of their little fingers off. Over a long career, a man was bound to make a few mistakes, and inhibiting the individual's physical ability was not the wisest course of action unless Goto wanted to run them out.

"We have reached out to our police contacts in the area. They will hand over what they have and we will find out who is behind this. And—"

"We know who is behind this. Yasuhiro Takato is a cockroach that should have been squashed years ago. Now he has grown and we need a huge shoe to stomp him with."

One of his other wakashira found the bravery to look at him and said, "One thing that has changed is we now know where they all are. The Okada Company has made their big move to Hiroshima and Nagasaki. Our scouts have recognised several Gādian members."

Another lieutenant declared, "And they are protected by the law. A shoot out would destroy us."

Goto felt a calmness descend on him. The others seemed to sense this as they quietened too. Finally, he declared, "Maybe this is just the opportunity we need. A chance to regain our former power. If we can unite the clans, we can devise a strategy that will bring the government to its knees."

He hid his anger on catching their furtive eyes. A comfortable existence had smoothed the edges of their warrior instincts, and was the result of a protracted period of affluence and peace. The men of the Yakuza had softened—but more disturbing was that some of this generation wanted to be seen to be Yakuza rather than be Yakuza; some of the other clans had even allowed their underlings to sport small tattoos done with modern tattoo guns rather than the more expansive, time consuming and painful *irezumi*, and this disgusted him.

"We will need allies other than other Yakuza clans, Oyabun."

"When you set forth strongly with your intentions clear, allies will come to find you, not the other way around," said Goto. "And I would rather see this clean energy technology destroyed than to have Takato possess it—there is no telling what he would be capable of should his wealth exceed ours. And the men who invented, or know how this technology works, need to be made accountable to me, or else die."

Clad in his striped pyjamas, Ronald Sykes lay back on the soft bed of the small, sparse hotel room, and thanked God in a remorseful prayer. He felt guilty; this would be his first attempt in months to communicate with a higher power, a deity that had saved Chisato.

On the phone, she had whispered to him that an Englishman had appeared from the darkness like a cross between *Yōkai* —a supernatural spirit in Japanese folklore, and a *Tennin*—a spiritual being found in Buddhism akin to western angels.

What were the odds of one of his countrymen, with the ability to dispatch three violent Yakuza, was watching over his Chisato that night? *God must have sent him.*

Tomorrow would be D-day—the first time they set up on the site in Sapporo and begin the process of turning it into the first cost-effective, aesthetically pleasing city completely sustained on renewable energy.

The announcement that Hiroshima and Nagasaki would be the test sites had been a ruse; with the eyes of the media and other nefarious entities searching in the south of the nation, the real work could proceed unhindered in the north.

If all the markers were implemented and sustained, the roll-out would be truly global. Sykes knew it alone could not cure all the threats to the earth presented by an ever expanding world population, but it would be a great step forward.

The more he thought that there were people willing to sabotage it for the sake of money, the more a burning sphere of anger and determination built within him.

The Gādian and the police would watch over the project, protecting it from evil hands. And the bilateral investment would elevate the power and prosperity of his twin homes of the United Kingdom and Japan. And he could retire and travel the world with Chisato.

He fell into a peaceful sleep.

14

Shintaro Goto closed his eyes and allowed the live jazz orchestra to envelope him. The Velvet Figurine was one of the few nightspots in Kobe the immaculately suited Yamaguchi-gumi boss helped support without taking a share.

He had been coming for decades and the place had barely changed. At the reception, the bare brick frame encapsulated the glass logo of a curvaceous woman in a cocktail dress, complete with microphone. The alluring purple and cream lighting percolated through the hanging glasses above the bar. The tables were intimately close, situated in a rough semi-circle facing the small stage.

The jazz band sat on high stools in a formation mirroring the crowd. A porcelain-like Japanese woman, with the bottom curls of her jet black hair disappearing into the cocktail dress of the same colour, sang centre stage.

This would be the last song of the evening, hence his closed eyes; risky, but then again there were two of his bodyguard—armed—present, one sat beside him and the other at the bar.

In addition, he had his driver—also armed—outside.

The melody finished to the sound of a gentle applause blooming to become rapturous.

He stood and donned his soft brown fedora hat.

Patrons began to leave, as did he, though his exit was via the kitchen.

The cold air hit him, and he began to ascend the spiral stairs. He felt a pique of anger that the black Infiniti Q60 had not already pulled up.

With his two bodyguards beside him, one said, "I will go find him boss."

As he skipped away into the darkness, stood with his lone protector, Goto began to feel the cold.

His sole bodyguard lunged forward, falling onto his front. It took a second for Goto to realise his guard had been kicked by the phantom behind. A ghost who now spoke in crystal clear, rapid Japanese, with the barest hint of an accent.

"Goto-san, do not make any sudden movements and listen."

As his bodyguard scrambled to get up, the same voice commanded, "Remain seated with your palms facing up. If I wanted your boss dead, he would be dead."

The uncertainty on the guard's face confirmed to Goto the man behind him was armed.

"It is okay, Wataru. Do as he says."

The voice said, "Good. Now, here comes the other guard. Calm him and tell him to put his pistol away."

The second bodyguard emerged through the darkness at a sprint while unholstering a pistol.

Goto called out, "Jun. It is okay. We are just talking. Put your weapon away."

Jun said, "Hideo is dead."

"He is not dead," said the voice. "He has been tranquilised. Believe me when I tell you, I have the experience and knowledge to sedate someone without killing them, now please holster your weapon."

Goto gave a brief nod, and Jun slowly complied.

The voice said, "My name is Mikhail Gorokhov. I am a former intelligence agent of the Foreign Intelligence Service of the Russian Federation. Tell me, Goto-san, do you believe the proverb 'The enemy of my enemy is my friend'?"

"Yes," replied the crime lord. "That is a strategy of war."

"And your clan must go to war to save itself. Yasuhiro Takato wants to destroy you all, Mr Goto. And with the revenue gained from his share in Okada, I have no doubt he will succeed."

"What do you propose?"

"I will make my proposal to you in a warm room facing you, not here in the cold behind you."

"Okay, when and where?"

"You have a restaurant named the Kobe Grill. I'll meet you there at 1 P.M. Reserve the central table, and we'll eat and talk."

"I will look forward to hearing your proposal."

"Good," said Gorokhov. "Hold out your hand."

Goto did so, and found the pistol placed in it.

"It belongs to your driver. Have mercy on him, I am just very good at what I do."

As the man slid away, the bodyguards scrambled for their weapons, only for Shintaro Goto to stop them with a gesture.

Connor sat in the reception at the top of the multi-storey Okada Company. He wore a conservative business suit of dark navy over a white shirt, with a light blue-striped tie.

His highly polished oxford shoes matched the brown leather strap of his watch.

The glass windows encompassed the entire sitting area, giving a panoramic view of Tokyo's urban skyline and a mountain in the far distance.

Connor did not know if it was Mount Fuji, the highest mountain in Japan at 3,776 metres, but over sixty miles away as the crow flies, or Mount Takao, a mere 599 metres tall but only around twenty miles in the same south-easterly direction.

He nudged the Japanese translator he had hired.

"Noguci-san, which mountain is that? Fuji or Takao?"

"That is Mount Fuji, Reed-san. We are very high up and this is a clear day. Perhaps a good promise."

"Omen is a better word."

"Omen. Thank You," replied the twenty-four-year-old Tokyo University business graduate.

While on operations in the Ukraine a time back, Connor had hired a high-class escort for a few days for the sole tasks of showing him around the city of Odesa and translating.

This time, Ciara had provided him with a man who she had met at her kendo class. Connor could not understand why his future boss would devote so much time to pursuing a skill she was unlikely to use. That was the sole reason why he had lost interest in the marines post-Afghanistan; the realisation that all the hard training would never be put to use. Many others felt the same, opting to try out for Special Forces selection, repeating the mantra, 'SF or Civvy Street'.

The fastidious Jun Noguci interrupted his thoughts with, "Reed-san, can you go over some of the business practices here."

Connor answered, "I'll have to wait before sitting down, which is standard anyway. The gicho—the meeting leader, will sit in the centre but the most important person in the room will be sat next to him, but could be either to the left or right. So I go in and ask, 'Which one of you is more important than the other?'."

"No, No, No Reed-san, you cannot ask that, it is considered—"

"Noguci-san, it's a joke."

"Oh. Sorry. Ha ha."

"You'll have to work on that 'career laugh' more."

Jun frowned, "What is a career laugh?"

"It's just a term we used back when I was in the marines—the military—for people who fake-laughed at their superior's jokes to climb higher on the career ladder. I know with you, it is just your Japanese politeness."

"Okay," said Jun frowning, before saying, "What is the etiquette if they offer you their business card?"

"I can't just slip it into my jacket after receiving it, which would imply I am brushing it aside instead of giving it the respect it deserves. But I can't leave it on the table like a lost child for the meeting's duration. I'll have to slip it into my jacket when people are perusing documents."

Jun said, "That is correct. Now tell me—"

"Listen, Jun, just relax. It should be me who is nervous."

"Yes, of course.

One of the receptionists came over. "Reed-san. They are ready to meet you now."

Connor stood and smoothed his suit. At the tinted glass door, he rapped the requisite three times; he knew the Japanese would only knock twice to see if a toilet cubicle was empty.

A strong voice cut through the glass.

"Hairu."—*Enter.*

As Connor pushed through the door and bowed deeply, he avoided revealing any sign he recognised the man sitting to the female meeting leader's immediate right.

It was Yasuhiro Takato—Head of the Gādian.

15

Mikhail Gorokhov alighted from the taxi at the urban intersection around a hundred metres away from the Kobe Grill. He did so to allow Shintaro Goto's soldiers to see him approaching, and to give himself a view of the restaurant.

He admired the signage of white wood with dark wood lettering. The greeting lady stood at the door in traditional Japanese dress.

Through the spotless windows, he could see the surreal scene of empty seating around Goto, and the bustling waiting staff attending to the patrons dining on tables set around the periphery.

The greeting lady looked at him expectantly, and he spoke in Japanese, "My name is Mikhail Gorokhov. I am expected."

He had anticipated what she would say before she said it, "You are to enter through the kitchen. Two buildings down is an alleyway. Go down it, turn right and you will arrive at the rear. Someone will meet you there."

He gave her a cross between a nod and a bow.

His heart rate rose by five beats per minute as he rounded into the dark alleyway. Chances were that the 'someone' would be a 'they' who wanted to frisk him. Still, nothing could be certain when dealing with the Japanese criminal element with their convoluted rules of honour and respect.

He walked down the path and opened the gate to his right. Gorokhov could smell the nervousness of the four men despite their sharp-suited posturing. In his desire not antagonise—or encourage—them unnecessarily, he kept his body language and facial expression neutral.

Still, none of them were from the previous night, which meant he might not have to deal with inflamed egos.

In stark contrast to the elegance of the front, the back consisted of overflowing bins with flies hovering, and a huge, dirty-coated Tosa fighting dog chained in the corner.

The tallest man in the centre said, "We believe you can speak Japanese?"

Gorokhov nodded.

"We must search you. Is there anything on your person that might be considered a weapon?"

"Nothing outside of my own body."

He caught the slight shift in their postures.

"Gorokhov-san, would you please stand a large pace away from the wall to your right and lean forward with just your fingertips for support against it."

Gorokhov knew then they were more proficient than the bodyguards he'd encountered previously. Being placed in this mild stress position made it more difficult for the person being searched to explode into action.

The assassin complied, glad of their professionalism; it meant a greater chance of their keeping a grip of any inflamed emotions.

They came close but not too close. The speed and thoroughness of the search impressed him.

"I will lead you through, Gorokhov-san."

It heartened Gorokhov to see the uniformed kitchen staff meeting the hygiene protocols, while rapidly ping-ponging commands and replies between themselves over and between sizzling pans and boiling pots.

The aromas of rice, Sushi, Sashimi meat and fish danced in the air free of the heavy smell of oil that permeated a lot of western kitchens.

None of them made eye contact.

The Yakuza man handed the Russian-Japanese off to a waitress who led him to Goto's table.

To Gorokhov's mild surprise, the crime lord stood and the two men bowed deep, before seating themselves.

"I am glad to put a face to the voice," said Goto, regarding him. "I was impressed with your Japanese. Now I can see why. Which side does it come from?"

"My mother's."

"Is she still alive?"

Gorokhov ignored the question. "Shall we order, Goto-san?"

The Yamaguchi-gumi boss tilted his jaw and a waitress came over at speed.

"I will have the grilled eel on rice," ordered Goto.

"And I will have the Sukiyaki," said Gorokhov, referring to thin slices of beef, green onions, tomatoes, mushrooms, and tofu cooked in a shallow pan with sukiyaki sauce.

"Drinks, sirs?"

Goto ordered a Royal Tea and Gorokhov an Aloe drink.

"Do you come to Japan often?" asked Goto. The question reminded Gorokhov of the clichéd line that American males used to initiate conversation with females they were interested in.

"Enough to maintain certain relationships."

"You have loved ones here."

"I consider Japan herself as a loved one," said the Japanese-Russian. "One of the reasons I have requested this discussion."

Goto ignored him and said, "So, your loved ones are in Russia?"

Gorokhov briefly thought of his deceased half-brother, but answered, "I consider Russia to be a loved one too."

"Since you are the one who requested this meeting, I will allow you to speak on this first."

The waitress came back with their drinks, set them down and vanished.

Gorokhov sipped his, before saying, "Yasuhiro Takato has been allowed to grow from a pest to a serious adversary. I understand he was part of your clan originally and so your

143

responsibility to bring to heel. He has secured a sizeable holding in a company on the cusp of the biggest breakthrough in renewable energy. When that happens, every other Yakuza clan will be subservient to him or else be destroyed."

Goto smirked, "Japanese companies are always making 'breakthroughs'. The people who control the electricity grids make a lot of money from them—this is why past attempts at renewable energy have failed here. Besides, Japan does not have enough land mass for these wind turbines and hydro dams."

He punctuated his point with a dismissive wave of his hand.

"This is different."

"Explain."

"A photovoltaic system employs solar modules, each comprising a number of solar cells, which generate electrical power. The Okada—"

"Solar panels? Summer only," frowned Goto.

Gorokhov carried on as if he hadn't been interrupted. "The Okada Company have made two breakthroughs. One in the amplification of energy, and one in the storage of it. So, it will not be necessary for a house to be connected to a collective grid—it can power itself even through many weeks of dark, cloudy days. Imagine electric cars that can be charged from home and able to exceed the range of fossil fuel-powered cars by hundreds of kilometres."

"This is true?"

The assassin replied with the barest of nods. "There are even rumours of an electrical battery in development, small enough, and potent enough, to power a commercial aircraft in a few years' time—a feat anticipated to be decades away. Who knows—maybe 'clean energy' space travel will become possible in the not so distant future."

After a few moments, Goto said, "You said you are 'former' SVR. Which leads to me ask how you got this information while I have been unaware?"

144

"My former employers still request my services. In this instance, I have politely declined."

"They have allowed you to 'politely' decline after they have given you this sensitive information? If I was a cynical man, I would think you were still a servant of Russia. A nation whose economy relies on its natural resources. You would like to see this technology destroyed."

Destroying the technology was not Gorokhov's first aim. His brief was to steal it and bring it back to Russia if he could.

His superior had told him that, *"With the technology in hand, Russia could return to its position of being the superpower of the world. No more hypocritical sanctions, no more ingrates waving placards after being hypnotised by western media. No more uncertainty. And there would be greater stability in the world."*

"There are certain members of the Japanese Organized Crime Division and the PSIA who are aware of just where my loyalties lie. You should ask around."

Goto sipped his drink. "Maybe even the KGB are soft now."

Gorokhov ignored the barb. "I want to retire with the type of money that will allow me to live comfortably for the rest of my life. That type of money is noticeable when deposited in a lump sum. I want a monthly payment into an account of my choosing once this is done."

"Once what is done?"

Gorokhov held his tongue as the waitress came and set their meals down. He did not especially like eating in front of strangers, but needs must.

After a few minutes, Goto indicated to the Japanese-Russian's dish and asked, "Good?"

"Great," replied Gorokhov. Though he meant it, he knew any answer other than a positive one would result in a beating for the kitchen staff.

"So, then…until what is done?"

"Until the Gādian are destroyed and the Yamaguchi-gumi have a controlling share in Okada. The work will be dirty, dangerous and demanding. Perfect for a foreigner like me."

Gorokhov had used the terms *kitanai, kiken, kitsui*, forming a Japanese expression used to describe migrant labour, with the word 'demanding' interchangeable with 'demeaning' or 'difficult'.

"I have Korean blood in my veins," said Goto, straightening his back, "You must know my organisation would have to fight a major war against the government and its law enforcement agencies if the technology was to be destroyed."

"Even if all the clans are united?"

"That is extremely difficult to achieve. Ceasefires when territories are agreed upon maybe. Alliances are different."

Gorokhov chewed his food, and washed it down with his Aloe drink.

"What if attention could be diverted to a different party?"

Goto regarded him for a moment. "If you are who you say you are, then I do not think you will be diverting that attention onto yourself, your agency, or your country."

"I said a different party. I did not say my party."

The rows of cylindrical lights encased in polished wood hung from the ceiling, reminding Connor of a box of Ferrero Rocher.

He watched the potential investors converse with one another in Japanese. It was clear from how the others vied for his attention, the influence Yasuhiro Takato held.

Due to his diligent preparation for the meeting, Connor knew of all the conference's attendees, and a significant amount of information on each.

The suited, dark pony-tailed Kusama Okada was the granddaughter of the company's deceased founder, and held a controlling share in the firm. Only a few years Connor's senior, she had vast experience from working in some capacity or another for the corporation since she was ten years old. Her demeanour came across as a blend of demure but professionally confident.

The cheerful-faced Keizo Mori, sixty-one-years old but looking a decade younger despite grey-flecked hair, was a senior partner and head of their automobile division. Connor had read that Kusama's grandfather, Masayoshi, acquired the car engineer turned businessman in the late eighties. Mori, in turn, had helped turn the medium-sized business into a national giant.

Yasuhiro Takato spoke in clear English, "You can provide transport and sale for our prototype vehicles?"

"I can. It's all in the documentation."

"Do you know what one of the biggest challenges Tesla faced?"

"That it was not just about the car, it was to provide an apparatus for charging the cars to prevent the inconvenience in searching for them."

"Very good," said Takato. "Then a man such as yourself must know that Okada does not have this type of system in place. My question is, why you would part with such a large amount of money to transport and sell our cars?"

"Long answer or short, Mr Takato?"

"Long…but slow for your translator."

"I have read deeply into the company's history and the country's history. It fascinated me that Japan quickly built itself into a strong economic power in the wake of the 1930s to 40s war. I came across this principle of gradual and continual improvement—*kaizen*. And I am aware the company's founder, Mr Hiroshi Okada, amplified not only that philosophy but one of innovation."

When the translator had finished, Connor said to him, "Just translate as I go. I'll speak slowly."

The interpreter nodded his affirmation and the Englishman continued, "I read a passage in the novel Musashi by Eiji Yoshikawa, *Looks like in any field only the first generation counts for much. The next gets lacklustre, and by the third, everything falls apart.'* This is true as a general rule. But not with the Okada family, which has seen a steady rise in net profits, even as the baton has been passed."

He waited for the translator to finish.

"I believe this commitment to kaizen and innovation will lead to this company developing ground-breaking technologies, and that my investment will one day be a small one."

Connor thought he saw a faint smile on the face of Takato upon translation of the last sentence.

The Chameleon Project agent then looked directly at Kusama Okada and said, "Okada-san, your father brought in Mori-san here for what people at the time thought was an exorbitant price. However, Mori-san has shown he was a bargain and helped take the Okada Company to the next level. I believe my family could also help you and the company."

She stared at him for a few moments and began speaking in rapid Japanese.

"Miss Okada wants you to outline all the challenges facing the implementation of renewables in Japan," said Takato before Jun had a chance.

Connor took a breath, and began to speak, leaving pauses to help the translation. "The electricity companies have monopolized the transmission lines, so charge extortionate rates for them. They can also hold the government to ransom, ensuring difficulty in obtaining them. Japan is also the leader in fuel—gasoline—powered cars, and the government might be nervous of seeing a substantial dent in that industry's profits. And a lot of people make a lot of money through nuclear energy and fossil fuels. Powerful people who will resist major changes over to renewables."

Takato answered him, not Kusama. "And you still wish to be our partner in this?"

Connor looked at him and said, "Yes. You and I can have a private conversation regarding how I might help you from a security perspective."

Takato looked at him and said, "We Japanese will always have a suspicion of outsiders in our lands. It is of our culture. Nearly four hundred years ago, the Tokugawa Shogunate forbade all foreigners to enter our country. Some say this good, some bad. Do you know what they used to call the western boats to come here?"

"Black Ships," the Englishman answered. "And yes, they might have been good for some. And bad for others. Just like me."

16

Gorokhov sat in the white and black interior of the grey-blue Mazda 6 sedan. The air freshener picturing two peacocks hung from the interior mirror added to the 'new car smell'.

The private airfield, where he had tracked the man who had saved Chisato, lay two hundred metres away. The overhanging trees at the entrance of the closed factory helped surround the car, and he had settled down to wait for his target.

Alexey Orlov had come through with the intelligence based on the pictures he had sent. The man he had tracked here a few nights previously was called Connor Reed. The woman had been a Ciara Robson.

The rudimentary background reports seemed strange to the former SVR agent. Connor Reed had had a military career complete with operational tours, but it had not been with the UK's Special Forces, which he had expected when observing his skill set. Gorokhov had detailed knowledge of the British military. Though the Royal Marines, which Reed had been a part of, were the most elite unit—along with the country's Parachute Regiment—that a British or Commonwealth civilian could join, they were not Special Forces. UKSF required the individual to already be in the military before attempting the globally respected 'selection' process.

According to the file, Reed was from the burgeoning Ryder family criminal empire based out of the region—named counties in the United Kingdom and Ireland—of Yorkshire, in the north of England. Gorokhov guessed why this former Royal Marine had chosen to keep his mother's maiden name of Reed.

But it seemed strange that though the Ryder family's home city of Leeds was one of the bigger metropolises in the United Kingdom, Russian intelligence had not identified it as one of the 'big five' criminal hubs of London, Liverpool, Manchester, Birmingham or Glasgow. Yet, the family was now in the top five Caucasian crime families on the isle. How they went from a mid-level organisation to such prominence could be seen as startling, especially as the media coverage was minimal.

Ciara Robson's file had also made him curious; a well-travelled freelance journalist who had the power to extradite foreign nationals?

If they were indeed part of the British security services, it impressed him that they'd stayed beneath the radar. Not that he'd ever lost his respect for that country's intelligence agencies—despite despising them. The initial dislike had grown to loathing since his half-brother's disappearance in England.

On the night he'd observed the pair, he had misjudged the entrances they both left from, and being alone, could not track them. Even with their names and descriptions, it would be near impossible to locate them in a country as densely populated as Japan.

Gorokhov had done his own research on the small airfield's staff. The ultimate control of this airport lay in the hands of four commissioners who rotated their shifts.

The commissioner that night was one Atsushi Fukuda. And Fukuda's shift officially ended ten minutes ago.

He would be due out soon.

With the dual purpose of maintaining her cover and because she took being a journalist seriously, Ciara now sat across from one of the richest men in Japan, a retail magnate named Akio Shigeta in a bar made almost entirely of chrome.

The shimmering and revolving overhead light threw glimmers over the surfaces, drawing the eye. The glass panelling around them—so clear that it seemed at times invisible—filtered out the decibel level so a conversation could be had.

Shigeta's blue suit jacket lay crumpled beside him with his discarded tie decorating it. Despite not being particularly overweight, he had a round face and kind, expressive dark eyes underneath full, jet black hair. He looked a few years younger than the forty-eight he had lived.

A billowing denim shirt dress clad her physique, concealing the short blade taped to the small of her back, and pressed beneath a brown leather belt. She had used a gel-pencil liner to touch up her eyes and a lip liner that matched her natural tone, but not much else.

She noticed and appreciated the billionaire's confident but not overbearing admiration of her appearance.

As a side venture, Shigeta had established a modelling agency eschewing the general Japanese modelling taste for very young-looking girls. Whether or not it was a PR stunt, Ciara did not know.

Shigeta—who spoke flawless English—had an appearance and manner in sharp contrast to the serious and keen-eyed security. Ciara had been taught in her training that close protection usually fell into two camps; visual deterrents and professionals. These were the latter.

"So, why would a man in charge of one of Asia's largest online retailers, not only branch out with a modelling agency, but go against the cultural and industry grain by hiring older, more curvaceous models."

He smiled, "There are two reasons. One is for business. And one is for humanity. Which would you like first?"

She tapped her foot. "Let's go for your business reasons."

"I became aware of these childlike models when they were brought in to promote the brands I sell. I saw them and decided to do some research. The percentage of Japan's population that are girls under the age of fourteen is barely six percent. And their spending power is either low or dependent on their parents. So, why would you use them to promote clothes?—this is a business not an artist's delight. Japanese women from fifteen to fifty-four comprise around twenty-three percent. They are the ones who can spend money. I wanted to cater directly to them. To say, 'You can look good in these clothes'."

She used her fingers to comb her hair behind her ear. "I expected nothing less from a businessman such as yourself. I appreciate you being so open with me in regards to the money to be made. Plenty in the public eye would simply steer the conversation towards their altruistic reasons."

He waved his hand dismissively. "A man without power is reduced to waving cardboard signs in the streets."

Ciara frowned. "Are you saying the Boston Tea Party and the Women's Suffrage Parade did not accomplish their goals?"

A smile crept across his mouth. "I do not wish to wave placards. Especially not in the cold."

Ciara could not help but find him endearing.

"Okay. What about your altruistic reasons?"

His face became serious, and he placed his fingertips on his breastbone. "You are correct. The fashion modelling industry in this country has become obsessed with child-like models. I pay investigators and what they've discovered is very…sad."

"I am listening."

"Take an agency for the Japanese taste. They might use former models as scouts—models who have made a living from their looks but have not developed their skills in the job market. They are addicted to the jet-setting of their former careers."

He took a sip of his drink. "The scouts are sent to poor areas in other countries to find…exotic recruits. They tell the girls they are guaranteed to make money. The poor parents trust them because they are kind-looking women—not sneaky men—and allow their thirteen-year-old daughters

153

to go to Japan with strangers. Except, the girls' dreams become nightmares once here. You might have similar stories to this."

She shook her head. "It isn't a subject I knew too much about before my preparations for this interview."

"They come. They have their photographs taken for a shoot. They are told they have not got the job. But the photographs are kept and sold in secret. The girls are sent back—often in debt. Sometimes their photographs are used by magazines, but if the girls ever did find out, their families are too poor to even think about suing through the courts. But sometimes the photographs are purchased for worse reasons than that."

"For paedophiles," she stated.

"Yes," he nodded. "Creating my own agency will not directly solve this problem, but by speaking to journalists such as yourself, the issue can be highlighted. Eventually, we as a culture can remove this practice from our society."

Ciara felt a warm admiration. "Since you are first-generation rich and are now one of the wealthiest men in Japan, I am inclined not to take your words as mere hyperbole."

"What is this word? Hi-per-bolee?"

"Exaggerated statements."

"No. I intend on achieving this," said Akio Shigeta, before seemingly staring off into his own world. Then his attention snapped back to her, and he said, "I am throwing a fund-raiser for the project. A lot of important people. But it is a little different."

"In what way."

He did not answer. Instead, he took out a pen and business card, and wrote on it. He handed it to her. "I will put your name on the guest list, Robson-san. I will understand perfectly if you do not wish to attend. If that is true or not, I thank you for speaking with me."

With that, he signalled to one of his security staff, and indirectly to Ciara, that the meeting was over.

154

17

Connor left his pitching meeting after being told they would be in touch. The Yorkshireman had left his phone number and decided to make the best use of his time in Japan.

George told him the address of where he was training Len Broady.

The Chameleon Project agent noticed a silver Toyota Prius with a driver and front passenger pull out of the carpark shortly after him. After a few minutes, he made a right turn four times in a row to ascertain that the Prius was following him and memorised the registration number. He slowed to a near-crawl when approaching the traffic lights on blue—the 'Go' colour in Japan—with his left indicator on. Once they turned red, he accelerated through them to the right. The Prius stalled, and Connor drove as swiftly as he could for a few miles before pulling over and checking for trackers. Once satisfied, he uploaded the registration number to Jaime, who identified the vehicle as being rented under a probable alias.

Connor decided to put the incident out of his mind for now, and continued his journey.

He had been hoping for some kind of temple in the Japanese hills. Maybe overlooking a river with an eagle looking down on the training a la Jean Claude Van Damme's 'Kickboxer'—*fucking loved that film*, he thought as he drove.

Instead, the SatNav took him to a place that he might have mistaken for a corporate car repair shop had it not been for the logo 'Gotch Ya' emblazoned on the front.

Gotch, Connor knew, was in reference to the renowned professional American wrestler Frank Gotch, who wrestled in the early years of the twentieth century. Back then, not only were wrestling matches legitimate, in addition to a pin, a win could be obtained by submission, essentially making them 'catch' wrestling matches.

However, it was Charles Istaz—better known by his ring moniker Karl Gotch, who brought the style of catch-as-catch-can wrestling over to Japanese professional wrestling in the 1970s.

Ribbed metal, powder-coated grey, formed the outside of the two storey complex. A smaller building stuck out to one side, and through the glass doors, Connor recognised it to be a reception.

As he went through the doors, mentally rehearsing his rudimentary Japanese greetings for the female receptionist, the London-accented voice boomed out, "Here he is. It's okay, Luv, he don't have to pay!"

George appeared from the white, matted area to Connor's right.

He spoke to the receptionist in rapid Japanese—presumably translating what he had just said.

She smiled and gave Connor a bow.

"Len's finished training for the day, mucker."

Connor frowned, "Why didn't you tell me? I could have gone to the Kodokan?"

The Kodokan Judo Institute had been founded by Kanō Jigorō back 1882, and remained the most famous Judo Dojo in the world.

George, despite being shorter, threw a strong arm around his shoulders, and guided him towards the training area.

"Relax. I am taking this training session. You can get yourself thrown around in your pyjamas another day. Today, you'll train with some real catch wrestlers."

As they crossed the threshold, Connor saw several strong, athletic Japanese men in shorts. Some topless, some with plain t-shirts, others with colourful *rash guards*. All wore wrestling shoes.

These guys would be versed in the art correctly termed as 'catch-as-catch-can' and as such, did not rely on the 'position before submission' mantra of Brazilian jiu-jitsu which emphasised securing a pin before attempting a choke,

157

strangle or joint lock. Instead, combatants were encouraged to snatch whatever limb was available.

Another difference was, a real catch wrestler was encouraged to cause pain to an opponent to force them into giving up position or an arm, or a leg, or exposing the throat, in a way that would cause affront to some practitioners of the 'gentle art'. As did the legality of neck cranks and spinal manipulations.

"You got your boots?" George asked him.

"Yes," admitted Connor reluctantly. He'd have preferred everyone to be bare-footed. Wrestling boots meant escaping single leg take-downs and more pertinently leg locks leading to heel-hooks and knee bars, a lot more difficult.

Stop it with your victim mentality, he admonished himself, *it's harder for them to escape too.*

The Mixed Martial Arts master shouted something in rapid Japanese and Connor saw the group's attention snap onto him.

"What have you said to 'em?" asked Connor. "They are looking at me like Ted Bundy looked at girls walking home alone."

The Londoner grinned, "I just said that you're my protégé and will be able to wrestle the fack out of any of 'em."

Reed kept the disconcertion off his face and asked, "Are you joining in?"

"There's a saying that a good coach teaching his students the art of fighting is like a snake charmer training cobras to strike him. Now, you've come the closest to biting me so far, and you'll get your chance again in the future, but today I think I'll enjoy throwing you into the vipers nest. Now, chop, chop."

The Yorkshireman turned away with a murmur of, "For fucksake."

Connor got changed as quickly as possible before joining the class running around the mat.

Framed and signed pictures of various mixed marital artists adorned the white walls, including one of Shinya Aoki, Connor's favourite mixed martial arts submission specialist and of Kazushi Sakuraba, a man who exemplified the effectiveness of this style in no-holds-barred fighting.

Throughout the 1990s, the Gracie family had dominated mixed martial arts with their own brand of jiu-jitsu. However, starting with Royce Gracie, the UFC's first champion, Sakuraba acquired wins over four of the family's members. In some circles, it was suggested—though disputed by others—that the family's best practitioner, Rickson Gracie, had avoided the decade younger and theatrical Sakuraba.

George shouted instructions in Japanese and the class went through routines of tumbling, cartwheeling, dry sprawling and shooting takedowns. Next, they performed a head stand before lowering into a full-bridge, taking their hands away and rolling on their foreheads to stretch and strengthen their necks.

Then, disconcertingly for Connor, George began to teach the class.

It dawned on Connor that he had never sat in on a George Follet class before. All their previous sessions, of which there had now been many, were one-on-ones, where they had usually engaged in hard sparring first, and afterwards he would receive his directions for improvement. The MMA legend remained the best instructor Connor had come across.

He partnered up with a man roughly his height and build, topless with multi-coloured *spats*.

George showed the class a leg-lock that involved under-hooking the top leg while in an opponent's half guard. It didn't look like anything Connor had seen in a Brazilian jiu-jitsu class before. However, he could see the simple efficacy of it while drilling it with his partner.

Next was a No-Gi Harai Goshi (Sweeping hip throw). Connor had found a well-executed throw to be one of the most beautiful things to observe in grappling. Not only that, but the crushing follow-through of the thrower's body onto the one being thrown was termed 'hitting your opponent with the ground', and the thrower was usually automatically past the opponent's 'guard'—their defensive legs—on impact.

However, due to having to 'give your back' to the opponent for most throws, they were dangerous to do in Gi BJJ and doubly so in NoGi submission wrestling due to a lack of grips. Therefore, most MMA fighters chose the safer leg takedown options, even though more often than not, one would land inside their opponent's guard.

Japan had recently reclaimed their historic dominance in Judo after an embarrassing 2012 Olympics. To ensure muscle memory during combat stress, the Japanese would typically drill the same technique many more times than their international counterparts. Although this was still the Japanese way, they had incorporated ideas and methods from Russian and Eastern Europe.

And Connor knew that despite once having been a competitive Judoka, his proficiency in the art would likely be rudimentary in comparison to these lads.

Finally, the technique session came to an end with George shouting, "Matchisu!"

Due to the relative smallness of the room, there could only be one match at a time. This was good in that the coach could assess the wrestlers with greater and longer focus. However, the lengthier rest in between did not lend itself to grinding, soul-searching conditioning, unless…

"Connor in the centre," called out George, before addressing the rest of the class with, "Same no tanku!"

The men gave a low chuckle and the Englishman guessed that 'Same no tanku' meant 'Shark Tank'; he would have to grapple each in turn without a break.

His first partner for the session stood across from him.

"Begin," called out George, which stood for the same in both English and Japanese.

160

They circled one another, exchanging foot and hand feints.

Connor snatched an arm drag, and though his opponent had been quick to right his position, the Englishman's arm caught him in a front headlock with the other under-hooking him. Connor swept his foot out and behind him, dragging his opponent down into a modified guillotine choke.

The tap came within two seconds.

His next rival took considerably longer to subdue as they exchanged multiple wrestling takedowns and reversals. Finally, Connor escaped his adversary's loose leg lock to snake around to his opponent's back and sank in a rear naked choke.

The third opponent, bigger, stronger and more technically adept than the previous two, wrestled him to near exhaustion. Connor had considered pulling guard to conserve energy, but considering this was a club with a catch-wrestling lineage, his pride wouldn't allow him to.

His opponent slid around behind him with his hands clasped in a vice-like grip.

The former marine, anticipating being tripped backwards, had the shock of being hoisted into the air before being suplexed square onto his shoulders.

The shock and embarrassment—compounded by George's shout of, "It's like a dad play-fighting with his son!" fired energy into him.

Connor spun like a shark, driving his opponent's clasped hands into the mat, releasing the grip.

Turning back, he used his legs to elevate his foe before snapping on a leg lock, followed by a heel hook. His opponent's hand hammered his surrender into the mat.

Connor, now spent, lowered his aim from winning to surviving as long as possible. He had observed in people when they were too exhausted to win, they would give up fighting altogether. When he got to that point, he lowered his goals to defensive duties.

He spent the next nine minutes stuffing takedowns, scrambling up from trips, enduring one particularly horrendous crank before finally succumbing to a knee bar.

His survival time gradually decreased until he was being submitted within ninety seconds.

Finally, his suffering ended with George shouting, "Yameru! Steady there."

With effort, Connor stood up. The subtle nods from the class meant more to his ego than applause would have.

As the Chameleon Project agent stood off to the side, George paired off another match and joined him.

"Facking hell Geez, proud of ya. Weren't expecting that—these boys are mustard. You did well."

"Been keeping up with it the best I can," said Connor. "There is always someone harder, faster, stronger and better."

18

Though Connor's body felt drained, the ten minute cold shower had revived his mind.

Walking outside the Dojo, he spotted the silver eight-seater Toyota Estima with the tinted windows parked across from his car.

His heart jolted. The Englishman stood straight and hid any outward sign of fatigue.

A single man alighted and approached with his suit flapping in the breeze. Connor had expected more.

"Reed-san, Takato-san sent me for escort to meeting."

Connor chose not to challenge him over not introducing himself. Instead, he said, "Well, he hasn't just sent you over, has he?"

The man shook his head. "Security must protect you in group."

Connor nodded, "We British are taught very young not get into vehicles with strangers. And you don't even have any Haribo."

The man stood as if in thought for a few seconds. He then turned back to the vehicle.

Is this the part where they come team-handed and bundle me in?

He did not think he'd have the strength to run if that was the case. And he cursed himself—Bruce had always told him never to unnecessarily exhaust himself while on operations.

He braced himself to fight as one of the doors slid open to reveal three other suited men, with Yasuhiro Takato being one of them.

Connor walked towards the eight-seater. Takato addressed him, "Caution is a good sign, Reed-san."

"I think so," replied Connor. "I am going to put my training bag away."

"Of course."

He returned, and climbed in the back, facing Takato.

Connor spoke first, "How did you find me?"

"How did you know that I did not have you followed since our meeting?"

"I know you did, but as you know I slipped them."

"Interesting a man with your background could do such thing. The men I used had special training in following people."

Connor smiled. "We all have our hidden talents. Like your talent for speaking impeccable English."

"Thank you," answered Takato without elaborating. "And yours for submission wrestling."

"I see," said Connor. "So, it was the girl at the reception who alerted you to my presence."

"You have a sharp mind," said Takato. "Maybe I could acquire your services."

"You want to use me in your war with the Yamaguchi-gumi."

Takato said, "I am thinking about it."

"No you're not. You have decided you want me to help you and you're acting nonchalant as you know a negotiation is about to commence."

Connor thought he saw a jarring of the shoulders in one of the men before Takato laughed—*must not be a regular occurrence.*

"You might be correct. But you are just one man. And a man who can easily be seen in these parts. You must not push negotiations too far."

"Maybe we should negotiate on the results, not the likelihood of me achieving them. Since the odds are stacked against your renegade Gādian. Until these new technologies come online, not only will your enemies have vastly greater manpower, the Yamaguchi-gumi have perfected the art of turning violence into money—they massively outstrip you in revenue."

"You do not believe we can be victorious?"

164

Connor took a moment before answering. "Before I came over, I studied Japan's past. Do you know what my favourite saga in your history is?"

Takato said without expression, "Our defence against the Mongol invaders?"

The correct answer gave Connor a jolt of surprise before he smiled and replied, "That's right. When the most powerful man in the world—which the warlord Kublai Khan must have been at the time, with the most feared army behind him—asks politely for a tribute from a nation of rice-agriculturists, and is told to fuck off…well, not told to fuck off, but it's insinuated by sending back his emissaries without a reply—very Japanese—then that would seem like inviting disaster. A bit like when you broke away from Japan's biggest clan to form your own."

"Yes, I understand—"

"Apologies for interrupting but my favourite part is when the Japs—Japanese rather—during the second invasion, swam out to the ships at night, slicing up the Mongols as they slept, before setting fire to their ships. More Ninja than Samurai, but a win is a win."

"You believe there should not be honour in how a victory is achieved?"

"To a degree, but I think the Gods will forgive the rules being bent by a smaller defensive force. More important is the reason why you are striving for victory. If it is just to be the next criminal enterprise, then that will not be sufficient to win."

"We have not engaged in any criminal activity that harms society."

"I should imagine that is debatable."

"I should also imagine a lot of the actions you have taken might be debatable," answered Takato.

"To others maybe, not to me. But then, maybe that has been the attitude of a lot of tyrants in history."

"Then you want to know the reason."

"Yes."

"The Yakuza will not give up nuclear power or its interests in fossil fuels."

"I don't understand. Japan imports its fossil fuels."

"Precisely. And the Yakuza receive money from the Saudis by way of Russia to ensure that fossil fuels remain in Japan. This is a practise they have enacted through various hidden shadows throughout the world."

"The Saudis pay criminal organisations in different countries to ensure their oil is the main source of energy?"

"I do not believe it is just the Saudis. Other forces in the world care about the control power brings. Japan and Britain owning the most profitable company in the world would upset global powers—and some do not want to see that happen."

"Not to be disrespectful, but the last statement seems about as vague as a horoscope," said Connor. "I mean, who are these 'forces' of which you speak?"

"Not just criminal organisations. Government officials, hedge fund managers, charity boards, and businesses," said Takato. "They are more effective in some countries than others, but they have been successful."

"Instead of paying millions and millions to keep hold of fossil fuel dominance, why didn't they just plough their money into recruiting the best scientists and become the leader in renewables?"

"Because there will not be a leader. Okada and its owners will make the initial money, but after that the technology will be given out—if we refuse then it will be reverse-engineered anyway. The Saudis are wealthy because their land is full of oil. But this technology will be used everywhere."

"I see. And with Japan being the largest importer of liquefied natural gas, fourth largest oil importer and third largest importer of coal, if this renewable technology is implemented here then the momentum will be impossible to stop?"

"Yes," said the Japanese outlaw leader. "My intelligence contacts have informed me the heads of all major clans are due to meet to form an alliance against the Gādian and Okada Company. Most Yakuza soldiers are *Kumi-in*—enlisted men. But if the three clans unite, they will also have many true killers. That is very bad."

"So, you're saying that if I help you win this war, I would be saving the entire planet?"

Yasuhiro Takato blinked a couple of times. "Yes."

Akio Shigeta's heart dropped as he walked into the freshly-lit boardroom. This meeting was meant to have been to welcome the shareholders who, between them, had bought a forty-nine percent share of Shigeta Electronics, one of his smaller but proportionally most profitable businesses.

He had expected five men but instead there was only three—and one he did not recognise.

The man was dressed in a suit just the same as the other members; however, besides being a *Hāfuburīdo*—half breed—and younger than the other two, instead of a black tie he wore a white one with blue and red stripes, dramatically contrasting with his jacket.

Like all Japanese businessmen, Shigeta had had to deal with the Yakuza in some form or other. However, he had been highly disciplined and managed to keep them out of upper-level decision-making.

The modern Yakuza, unlike the Italian mafia, did not tend to target small businesses. Instead, they used specialist racketeers known as Sōkaiya to seek out and investigate 'vulnerable' ones. Once a suitable target company had been identified, enough stock would be purchased through intermediaries to allow the Sōkaiya to sit at board meetings. At these conferences, the corporation would be extorted under the threat of exposure of any shameful secrets that the Sōkaiya had uncovered in its investigative phase. With the concept of shame being so taboo within Japanese culture, the practice was almost unique to the Land of the Rising Sun.

Shigeta believed these men to be Sōkaiya or Yakuza.

Though not all Yakuza were full Japanese, with many being part Korean or other ethnicities, especially as they had branched out internationally, most were. But unusually, Shigeta made a guess the man to be half Russian.

"I do not believe we have met," said Shigeta. He was more angry than scared. Being one of the wealthiest men in Japan gave him power, but it also meant he had more to lose.

The man stood without any attempt at intimidation, smoothed his jacket and with a bow replied in perfect Japanese, "My name is Mikhail Gorokhov."

"I was expecting three other men in your place."

"Those three men allowed my company to make a purchase of shares through them in order to facilitate this meeting with you."

Shigeta looked into the man's expressionless eyes to find they belonged to a shark, who then addressed the other two men, "Gentlemen, please would you excuse us and wait outside."

The other two men nodded curtly and left.

The room seemed to cool and Shigeta asked, "What do you want?"

"It is not shares in this company."

"I find that hard to believe since it must have taken much 'work' to acquire them."

Gorokhov nodded, "That it did. But it was for an ulterior purpose."

"So, you are Yakuza. Which clan?"

Gorokhov smiled, "Would a Yakuza clan give back their stocks in a company like this once in their possession?"

After a moment, Shigeta replied, "Perhaps not."

"You met with a journalist named Ciara Robson."

"I meet with many journalists."

Gorokhov shook his head. "You do not."

168

"Yes, I met with her," answered Shigeta, before regretting giving even that much away.

"The company I am temporarily contracted to would like to speak with her."

Shigeta took a breath. "I can pass your contact details on to her."

"No. I do not wish for Miss Robson to be able to prepare her answers."

A plate of adrenaline spun in his stomach.

"The answer is no."

"You will receive the shares back. This business is essential to your future plans and your employees."

"What do you want her for?"

"To ask her questions. If she is a journalist, then no harm will come to her—she will be too scared not to answer truthfully. And then she will simply be released. She will not go to the authorities—especially as she is a foreign national."

They stared at one another for a time, before Shigeta broke the stalemate. "She is invited to a gathering of mine. You may question her there. She will not be leaving with you. My security will wait outside for you to ask your questions."

The man took a moment to answer. "It will not be me interviewing her. It will be three men—"

"Two is all you need for a woman reporter."

Shigeta thought he saw a flicker in the man's eyes. "Okay. Two men. They will present themselves to your security staff, who will lead them to the meeting place."

"Will they be armed?"

"That is the personal choice for the men."

"And it is a personal choice for me not to have strangers arriving with weapons at a party of mine."

Gorokhov's eyes diverted for a moment. "Maybe they just appear to be armed—to smooth the questioning. A compromise."

Akio Shigeta nodded. "Yes, a compromise."

Connor performed his condensed 'cleaning run' to meet Ciara after he had sent her a coded message indicating the alliance of the Yakuza clans.

Whatever she was going to discuss with him must have been important as meetings in foreign countries were meant to be avoided. His rescue of Chisato Fukuhara being an exceptional circumstance.

Cleaning runs were originally used by the KGB during the cold war to 'clean' themselves of any potential surveillance. A full one could take hours depending on the geography and enemy, involving several changes of transport and perhaps identities.

Due to time constraints, Connor simply drove in a confusing route, doubling back on himself several times in an effort to identify 'tics'.

Once satisfied he drove into one of Tokyo's inner city carparks—a strange experience that involved driving into a perforated steel box before the crane placed the vehicle into a designated spot.

From there, he performed a similar cleaning run on foot. The automated voice of his phone's app directed him through his near invisible earpiece to Shinjuku City rental complex.

As he walked, he took in the ambience of the mixture of multi-coloured low roofed and high rise buildings, the blend of indecipherable Japanese signage with stores titled 'Liquor World' and 'Co-Op'.

While many young people zipped around on mopeds, Connor had noticed Japan had more, and spryer, elderly walking around than the average UK street, with a number on pedal bikes.

He entered the Toblerone bar-shaped tower block and found the door. It opened after he rapped a pre-determined pattern on the door, and Ciara, in stretch jeans and a collared egg-shell shirt, ushered him in.

Dark turquoise carpets, white plastic and wood panelling made up the room comprising of the bed, wardrobes and kitchen unit with a separate bathroom.

After an exchange of greetings, she poured them both a black coffee from the already brewed pot into glass cups, and they stood across from one another with the table unit separating them.

Ciara said, "Jaime has found information backing up your intel that the Yakuza clans are looking to unite—for the time being at least. He's also worked up a projection of just how devastating that would be to our goals. Their combined political clout and informants within the police would make protecting Sykes and Okada impossible."

"Yeh," he answered. "It's not ideal."

"Listen Connor. I want you to know two things," she began with a seriousness of expression that piqued his curiosity. "One is, is that I have thought about the mission I am about to give you a lot. Thought of less dangerous ways we could go about achieving the objective and have decided that this—if it's possible—to be the best course of action given the time we have."

"Okay," he said stretching out the word.

"And two is that you can say 'No' and we'll get our heads together to think of something else."

His smile overpowered his frown. "Do you, knowing me like you do, seriously think I am going to reject whatever tasking you're about to give me on the grounds of it being too dangerous?"

"No I don't. But it makes me feel better that I have said it," she said. "Especially as the day in question, I'll be attending…an event and won't be able to provide a tactical overwatch. You'll be operating alone."

"Tell me. The anticipation is killing me."

19

Ciara sat high in the black Nissan GTR, admiring its drive quality. Though the AWD (All-Wheel Drive) system softened the dangerous edges, the car still reminded her of its daring high performance on the Japanese highways.

She had overruled Akio Shigeta's request to have her picked up in style; she wanted the option to leave of her own accord. Still, she hadn't wanted to embarrass or draw attention to herself by turning up in a cheap car.

Ciara wore a black and white chequered dress, giving off an optical illusion of movement if one stared too hard. Though it clung to her hard physique, the stretch fabric afforded her freedom of movement.

As she manoeuvred the GTR onto the quieter roads, she slipped it into its comfort mode and ran her hand through her short, silvery-blonde hair and thought about the evening ahead.

Despite the gadgetry at her disposal, she had chosen not to bring any. Akio Shigeta, aside from being wealthy in the extreme, owned a cutting-edge electronics company and might not leave any stone unturned to ensure his guests' privacy.

Though Ciara had studied the high-tech coastal building complex as much as she could through Google Street View and a dark website, she admired its architectural beauty as the GTR approached.

And she knew that this was not even Shigeta's main residence.

The sides were made up of reflective glass, obscuring an outsider's view of the inside, depending on the tint setting. She could see tonight some were darkened while others allowed the amber lights of the party to be seen.

A smooth, stone-tiled path skirted around the mansion. It split, one section leading to an enormous pool on the right hand side, so large it jutted out into the sea, making it appear like a white marble ring in the ocean.

Though the Bonsai trees swayed welcomingly, Ciara guessed they housed hidden security cameras, as none were visible anywhere else.

The GTR prowled into the giant, circular parking area paved with white marble. It already sported vehicles many times the cost of the Nissan. She pulled in next to a red 1967 Toyota 2000GT she knew to be worth anywhere between half and one million US dollars.

Two black-suited men—taller and heavier than the average Japanese man—stood at the high arches.

Approaching them, the man to her right spoke English like a privately schooled upper class British native would.

"Good evening, Miss Robson."

"Good evening."

"Would you like me to take anything for you for the duration of your stay?"

"I don't think that is necessary, unless you are insisting?"

He shook his head. "You will be guided into the main room where all official business is held. There is no alcohol in that room. In effect, Mr Shigeta will bribe you to don a Kimono and leave your possessions in a security box, so you can enjoy the frivolities."

She smiled, "Oh my, I wasn't expecting you to say something like that."

He smiled back, "Come, Miss Robson, I will lead the way."

They entered a small room where an array of shoes had been arranged in a neat line, each pair separated by floral painted wooden dividers. She removed her shoes—black satin heel and toe caps, clear gauze on the sides—only to be handed a pair resembling those ballerinas use, except with a less pointed front, made of silk with an elaborate bow.

"They will be discarded after you've worn them. Such is the extravagance of the ultra-wealthy," said the suit.

"I would think these are worth more than the pair I have removed."

He looked over and said, "That would be an accurate assumption. But wealth cannot buy you taste, I am sure you are familiar with this already."

She gave him a frowning smile. "You're demeanour isn't very 'Japanese Security man' is it?"

"My father sent me to boarding school in England. I can alter my manner depending on the company I am in?"

"In that case, before we go in there, can I ask what to expect?"

"The Japanese class system has four tiers—the old middle class, the new middle class, the working class and these people, the capitalists. However, Japan's wealthy elite is a little more subtle than their western counterparts. As a rule they value food and shelter over clothes and transport. For example, this house has layers—every room has been thought about deeply. The food you will be served will be amongst the best in Japan. The clothes they will wear will be of the greatest expense but the colours will be muted."

"Thank you," she said, though she had wanted more of an insight into their manner.

As though reading her mind, he said, "Japanese people are always very polite, even when they dislike someone."

"Excellent."

The suit led her through a corridor of cherry trees whose top branches intersected to make a fully enclosed arch. The faint aroma calmed her.

Opening the door revealed a great hall. At a glance, she estimated there to be around seventy guests, almost all flashing her a look, but no one stared.

That they were wearing western attire as opposed to traditional Japanese dress pleasantly surprised her—she would not stand out as much, indeed she spotted a western couple in the corner.

She surmised the dress code might have been a way to distinguish themselves from the all-female waiting staff who wore uniform Kimonos of red and white. They carried wooden trays of small delicacies and small cups of drinks.

The music of delicately plucked strings flowed through the sounds of Japanese conversation. They emanated from the corner, where a lady with elaborately woven hair, played what Ciara recognised as a Koto. The traditional Japanese instrument had thirteen strings stretched over a half-tube of hollow, polished wood the width of a piano.

A path gently parted through the crowd to allow Akio Shigeta, suited in a black, button-down dinner jacket, to approach her.

"Miss Ciara Robson. It was good of you to come."

"Not every day a woman like me is invited to a billionaire's party."

He raised his right arm at the elbow, and one of the waitresses appeared seemingly from nowhere.

"What would you like to drink?"

"What do you have?" Ciara answered.

"Everything."

"A lemon chuhai, please," she asked.

"I will have one too," said Shigeta.

The waitress gave a shallow bow and disappeared.

Shigeta asked, "So, you've never been to a party like this?"

"I have been to a wealthy man's party before," she said, shooing away the mental images of how that ended. "But not like this one. It's more demure and tasteful. More—"

"Japanese."

"Precisely."

"People will have a natural curiosity about you. This will increase when I give my speech in English, while my translator repeats it in Japanese. Since you are the only native English speaker here, people will of course make the correct assumption the speech is for you."

The Englishwoman knew to protest would only be met with an amused insistence.

The waitress appeared with their drinks, startling Ciara with how quickly the order had been turned around. She took a sip—*perfect*.

"Does anyone here know what my profession is?"

"If they do, they do not know from me."

They made conversation for a few minutes until the host raised his right hand again and a different waitress came to take away his barely touched drink.

He must have caught the wry expression on her face for he said, "In our culture, to be subservient is seen to be noble. Besides, the money they are paid far exceeds their western counterparts."

He turned and made his way onto the stage. A hush ascended, and one of the serving staff stood off to his right. The Kato still played soothingly in the background.

True to his word, he spoke English with long pauses to allow the girl to translate his words.

"Ladies and gentlemen. I have seen how we humans take great precautions to protect ourselves from an instant death but behave to encourage a slow one. This can be seen in the man who drinks, smokes and eats to excess every day, but will never fail to fasten his seat belt."

Quiet laughter.

"And this does not just apply to the individual. Most parents would risk their lives for their childrens', but many—especially in other cultures—do not do all that is necessary to help them develop as adults. So, what is the point, I ask myself, to rescue them from fire only to see them commit suicide through mental health problems?"

Ciara presumed this to be a veiled reference to the West.

"We now live in a time where this phenomenon threatens the entire planet. Mankind has so far been adept at preventing the immediate danger of a nuclear holocaust, with only our nation being the victim of atomic weapons. But the danger of global warming and overconsumption of the planet's resources has been allowed to grow like a painless tumour—painless to us at least, as wildlife and the ecosystem have been steadily destroyed over the decades."

David Attenborough would be proud—she thought.

"Now, as some of you know, I am a huge comic book fan. Not only of our Anime but of our American counterparts. Mr Stan Lee was a genius. In the comic Amazing Fantasy, issue fifteen in 1962 was written the line, 'With great power there must also come great responsibility'. And this is an idea I think is important to us in this room. We have power—we have wealth. But money is simply energy—it can be used for bad or good. In this crucial time in history, I think we with money should be stepping forward like a Samurai, not in service to a lord, but in service to the people…although, not like Bruce Wayne."

More quiet laughter. The serving staff began handing out leaflets. Ciara got hers in English. Before she could start reading it, Shigeta began, "The Okada Company needs our finance and resources. They are on the verge of a remarkable breakthrough—I have seen it with my own eyes. They can save the world and we can help them. Thank you for listening."

He stood down to polite applause and approached Ciara.

"Come, Miss Robson. I will begin to introduce you to my guests."

She nodded and put out of her mind how her agent would be faring—there wasn't much she could do for him now.

As Connor drove the green Alfa Romeo Giulia down the highway, he marvelled on seeing Shinjuku, one of Tokyo's busiest wards, a few miles away.

Not that he could miss it even at this distance—a kaleidoscope of skyscrapers and buildings lit with multicoloured electric lights and commercial billboards.

An epileptic's nightmare—he thought.

178

The black wig felt like a mildly cumbersome hat, as he felt the pinpricks of sweat beneath it. Luckily, the brown contact lenses were of such high quality that the coloured filter did not obscure his vision.

As he got closer to Shinjuku, he picked out a billboard displaying two provocatively clad Japanese women. Connor himself was not particularly attracted to oriental women as a general rule, preferring curvy women with a touch of height, and he had a taste for redheads. However, he smiled at the words of John Foley, his Essex born headcase of a friend from the Parachute Regiment;

"Connor, if you've never been to Thailand and 'ad the level of service off a bird over there, then you're letting the best in life pass you by. Could never be with a round-eye now."

Indeed, Connor knew of several Royal Marines who could attest to his Maroon-bereted friend's words.

Prior to Japan, Connor, as an agent, had only operated in Europe. Though he remembered southern Ukraine being foreboding, Tokyo just seemed alien. The language had no Latin structure, the characters were too many and varied to readily assimilate, and in just about every respect the culture was radically different to his own. And yet, he liked the place.

Ciara had once lamented they could not fully enjoy the places they were sent to as they couldn't ever relax when on operations. He had not said anything at the time, but he realised he felt the opposite way. The danger of operations heightened his senses; he heard more, the colours seemed brighter, the sensations of air against his skin more prominent.

Being on operations in places like this captured a small part of the wonderment of childhood. He remembered when aged around six, staring out of the bedroom window of his maternal grandparents' rural home over farmland, and wondering what kind of magical land lay beyond it.

He felt grateful it was only spring and not summer. Not only did this part of Japan have a temperate climate, but

Tokyo was an urban heat island, especially places like the Shinjuku ward.

Concentrating on following the Sat Nav kept him distracted from his quietly singing nerves as he hit the busy metropolis.

Finally, he reached the underground car park of the huge, glittering hotel opposite the street from another enormous hotel where the targets were situated. He took a few deep breaths and licked saliva around his gums—a trick to convince his system to ease back on the adrenaline release. A little epinephrine helped induce speed, strength and focus but too much frayed the fine motor skills he would need, even if the club-swinging ancient men hadn't in the face of Sabre-toothed predators or enemy tribes.

Yasuhiro Takato's men had given him the intelligence he needed. And he had Jaime verify it the best he could. Still, Connor knew he was now trusting an organisation that owed him zero loyalty.

However, since youth, Connor had been adept at ascertaining people's motivations through their behaviour and words. And he concluded Takato wanted to win his war, and saw that Connor could help him do that. The British outlaw could not see why the Japanese crime lord would want him dead or in prison.

Still, trust had limits, and Connor would never accept a weapon system without firing it first. Takato had obtained a Heckler & Koch UMP 45 with a suppressor for him. That impressed Connor, not only because a host of laws made the weapon difficult to import, but because it also came with the fitted accessories of rails, a hand stop and a tritium front sight.

He had modified the trigger pressure down a lb before taking it deep into the woods outside his residence to zero it.

He found it functioned flawlessly. The former Commando liked it for several reasons; its mechanical simplicity equalled reliability, the calibre had more than enough stopping power for what he'd likely encounter, as would the twenty-five-round magazine, of which he had three. He preferred the ergonomics of it over the MP5.

The trigger group this one came with included semi-automatic, burst mode—three rounds as opposed to two, and full-automatic.

However, it had its drawbacks; the cyclical rate and recoil made groupings challenging to keep tight—for an average shooter at least, the round was susceptible to the wind at range—not that he planned on firing outside or at distance.

Before he climbed out of the car into the noise of one of Tokyo's busiest districts, he donned a squash snapback, which matched his simple designer black shorts and t-shirt. Rubber-soled court shoes covered his feet.

Flicking up the boot of the vehicle, he took out the multi-racket bag. Due to its six racket design, it did not bulge in odd places as a single racket holder would have done with the UMP 45 inside.

He began to breathe slowly and deeply as he approached the hotel. He turned the corner, and at a distance could see that the exit door of the kitchen was ajar—just as Takato told him it would be.

Still, he walked past to perform his counter surveillance duties. He rounded the next corner to the car park mirroring the one he had parked in. He could not see any sign of an ambush, by either law enforcement or a criminal group. He turned back and headed to the door.

Stepping into the empty kitchen, he waited ninety seconds—no one followed. The room full of stainless steel and polished wood led to another door.

An image flickered in his head of the door morphing into a dragon's mouth.

No turning back once you walk through that door—he said to himself—*Fuck this, you're the dragon here.*

Through her prior study, Ciara had knowledge of most of the guests who courted her attention. Akio Shigeta would introduce her as an international business consultant. Shigeta's manipulation of the other guests made them act in deference towards her, despite them being among the most influential people in one of the most developed nations on earth, and it seemed surreal. Maybe he had manipulated her also, as she found herself espousing the benefits of backing the Okada Company.

She would periodically catch Shigeta's wry smile and sensed his amusement at the party's attendees' responsiveness towards her.

As the crowd's consumption of sake and other alcohol grew, their cultural inhibitions began to loosen. Shortly after observing this, Shigeta got up onto the stage—again with the translator by his side.

"Ladies and gentlemen. The recreational part of my residence is now open to you. If you wish to indulge, you will be given a necklace with a key and led to an individual room where you will change into a Kimono without pockets. There is a selection of masks to choose from if you wish to wear one. Then, you may be a voyeur or participate in anything that is on offer. For those who do not wish to participate, you can stay here."

A Japanese 'Eyes Wide Shut', thought Ciara.

As Shigeta stepped down, no one made a move for the door. She understood the hesitancy, as Shigeta stood by her. He whispered, "The couple walking slowly to the corner will be the first to go in. I think after three minutes. Once they have, the rest will follow."

"Not your first time?"

"No, but the first time with this crowd."

"So, beyond those doors will be masked figures in red robes and gold masks, chanting, swinging pots of burning incense?"

He frowned, "Chanting?"

She smiled, "Never mind."

She sipped her lemon chuhai, "I wasn't aware you were a sponsor for Okada."

"They might change the world."

"Indeed," she said. "So your motives are purely altruistic?"

Shigeta didn't speak for a moment, but then said, "Doing a good thing and making a profit, or obtaining a service, does not have be mutually exclusive. We have spoken about this."

She gave a seemingly absent-minded nod, but noted the 'obtaining a service' part."

She nudged him and said, "Well done."

His eyes followed hers to his predicted couple entering the doors first.

"Ahh yes," he smiled. "Knowing a person's motivation is a crucial business skill."

Ciara replied, "It is a crucial skill in a lot of areas."

He nodded before gesturing with his palm to the open doors. "Shall we? You will have your own room to change in, of course."

"Of course," she smiled. "Let's go."

He led her through the entrance on the far right—closed until they reached it. Everyone else had gone through the other open doors. Her senses began to sharpen—*maybe it is to exacerbate this illusion of me being special.*

Polished wood and spotless white paper made up the left side of the corridor, with huge glass windows on the right. The red-leafed trees watched them both walk down.

A heavy-looking, iron bird feeder hung mid-way down with its roof resembling a temple.

She felt the cold the same instant as noticing one of the apertures ajar. Then, in anticipation of her question, a bird of around eight inches, with a brownish-red head, blue wings with black tips, and a black stripe wrapping around its beak and eyes like a robber's mask, flew in and onto the bird feeder.

"What is that?"

"It is a Japanese shrike."

"That's very nice of you to keep it uncaged."

Shigeta replied, "I am in fear I have unknowingly caged it. For you see, it should have migrated with its friends and family, but the prospect of easy to get food and shelter has kept it chained here. And now I must leave the door open or else it would not survive."

They walked past the feeding bird, which made no move to distance itself.

He stopped them at a Shoji—sliding outer door, comprising wooden frames covered in tough, white paper, obscuring any view but allowing in light. He slid it back to reveal a traditional wood and cream Japanese room with flickering fire lamps.

A clear sheet of toughened glass constituted around seventy-five percent of the floor, displaying a huge shoal of brightly coloured fish beneath it.

To her right hung a painting of a weeping woman in the foreground with menacing, uniformed oriental soldiers in the background.

On a beautifully carved table lay a simple oak box with a strip of green light underneath. An embedded black shiny patch glinted from the box.

Three masks lay to its left and another three to its right. All were of radically different styles; a white cat, a werewolf, a traditional Oni mask, one remarkably realistic and disturbing mask of a beautiful Japanese woman's face, a caricature of the US president's face, and a floral painted porcelain mask.

Though she noticed them all, the mounted katana blade with its scabbard beneath snared her attention.

The black cord wrap snaked tightly around the *Tsuka*—handle.

Authentically crafted samurai sword blades had three sections; the *Mune*—back, the *ha*—the edge, and the *Boshi*—

curved edge ending in the *Kissaki*—the point. The *Hi*—groove or fuller—ran up the blade's centre.

A fuller she knew had three purposes; to make the blade lighter and strengthen it structurally against pressure in the same way a builder uses I-beams instead of rectangular box beams. The third—though disputed—was to act as a channel for the blood, making its withdrawal easier.

"Go ahead, Miss Robson."

Ciara nodded her thanks and approached. As she neared she could see the crafting of the *Tsuba*—handguard—made so that five iron dragons revolved nose to tail above the gripping hand.

The light reflected off the different parts of the blade.

"Can I?" she asked Shigeta, still stood at the door.

"Of course," he said. "For it is yours."

She turned to look at him with suspicion edging the plume of pleasure inside.

"Why?"

He pointed two fingers at the portrait.

"I think a good journalist such as you has done her research and knows I have Korean blood through my great-grandmother. You might not know she was a 'comfort woman', pressed into the service of a battalion that my grandfather was part of during World War Two. He liked her so much he brought her back—a very cruel man."

Ciara was aware of how the Japanese imperial army had forced women and girls of the countries they occupied into sex slavery for the soldiers.

"Part of me feels guilty that I am grateful he did—for I am alive. But guilt on its own is useless. I look at that picture and think of how helpless those girls must have been. Of how, if they were given the means to fight back would they have taken it?"

"I guess it is an individual choice," said Ciara.

"Yes. But confidence comes from ability," he said. "Now, I will leave you to get changed. The box has a finger scanner, once you press it the light will turn red on locking and will only be able to be opened by you."

"Alright."

"Remember, Miss Robson, here no one has the right to make you do anything you do not wish. And I will support you against anyone who attempts to."

"Thank you," she said. As he closed the door, she did not immediately change. It wasn't exactly what he said—he could be seen as simply reassuring his single female guest in the face of being in a strange place in a foreign country. However, she would have expected him to be more…nonchalant in his delivery.

She replaced the samurai sword, not quite believing he had given it to her. Her long-time fascination with blades swelled within her—*He must know somehow.*

She began to remove her clothes, carefully folding them and placing them into the box. Naked, aside from her black satin knickers, she reached out for the black kimono enhanced with pink flowers.

The sliding doors suddenly opened to reveal three suited young men with slicked back hair. They entered. She took note of the tattoos peaking beyond their sleeves.

Shigeta's words echoed in her mind—*No one has the right to make you do anything you do not wish.*

The intel Connor possessed had been that the Sumiyoshi-kai soldiers—the second largest Yakuza clan, booked out all the courts. One reason was to ensure they all got a game, and the second was they were able to remove their tops, thereby exposing their *Irezumi* tattoos, which was still taboo, even in modern day Japan, and therefore kept from the public's gaze.

As he walked, Connor admonished himself—*stop whistling, you're not the Pink Panther.*

His diaphragm began to pulse as he heard the echoes of squash balls pinging off the walls—though they were barely audible above the loud, banging techno music. Probably another reason why they wanted to book the courts out for themselves only—book not pay.

He rounded the corner to be confronted by the final corridor. The entrance door faced him, approximately twenty metres away and with a youth guarding it. Connor guessed him to be in his early twenties, in all probability a *Wakagashira-hosa* (underling). A young lad who'd had his head turned by stories and films depicting the glamour of crime.

He might get out. Go on to raise a family. Do some good— fucking stop will you. This needs to be done.

The youth approached, shaking his head and wagging his finger. Connor kept walking, performing the role of a western buffoon.

"Back, back…no come in," barked the lad over the din.

The Englishman kept walking, cupping his ear. "I am a salesman. These are the best rackets in Japan."

The man jogged up to him and snapped, "You stop!"

"I can do a group discount," exclaimed Connor, lifting the nose of the bag level with the Wakagashira-hosa's face.

The youth viciously slapped the bag in the same instant as the Commando dagger blade punched through his throat, taking his voice with it.

The former marine whipped around his victim to avoid the blood geyser, drawing the blade one hundred-and-eighty degrees.

The corpse fell off his knife with a wet thud into the expanding blood pool.

Connor quickly wiped the blade clean on the cadaver's pants and sheathed it back under his t-shirt. He rifled the bag open, aware someone behind the door might have heard the exchange, and pulled out the Heckler & Koch UMP 45.

Out of barely conscious habit, he flicked the safety off, checked the setting of 'burst' on the change lever, the sights and the correct housing of the magazine.

187

Alright, killing the men behind this door helps the sustainability of the planet and its inhabitants. No one forced these cunts to join the Yakuza.

He walked forward.

Ciara, to feign fright rather than any genuine modesty, clutched the kimono to her naked breasts.

The one on the left barked, "Put on clothes and come with us."

They did not move further towards her initially, which was good as it indicated they were oblivious to her skill set.

Ciara gestured to the box and began to edge over to it. She half turned before turning back.

"Who are you?"

"It not matter. Come. Now."

The one on the far right brushed the bottom edge of his jacket to reveal the pistol tucked into his waistband.

"I don't want to," she said.

The mouthpiece jerked his head towards the other two and they stepped forward.

"Okay. Okay," she exclaimed turning around.

Snatching the Tsuka, the katana sang as it skimmed the air.

Streams of surprise and adrenaline whooshed into her diaphragm as a head toppled off the shoulders with little resistance.

Switching its arc and her stance, the katana lopped off the raised hand and parted the face of the central gangster like a macabre grapefruit.

The mouthpiece knocked the blade to one side and flung his arms around her neck and shoulders.

She torqued her body around to avoid a crushing bear hug. Then, stepping back to make room, the back of her calves caught the crouching man whose face she had sliced.

Her assailant's eyes gleamed at her fall. A flicker appeared in his eye before he spun for the headless corpse.

The gun, she thought. She knew she would not have the time to stand up and close the distance before he shot her.

Fuck it.

She snapped the sword into a reverse grip, performed a sit-up and threw it javelin style. The reality did not match her anticipation as the blade entered a third of its length deep into his back.

No sound came forth. A rigidity seized the man into a dead lift stance.

She stood, took a stride, placed a foot on his arse and slid the sword out while pushing him away.

The man with half his face sliced had now assumed a foetal position. She fought her bloodlust now he posed no threat. The British black operations officer knew the image of the sliced cheek—which pulled down the flesh, revealing his lower eye, hanging upper jaw, and the entirety of the tongue, would be burned into her psyche, and would chase her through her nightmares.

She leapt toward the doors as they slid open, only to halt in the face of a non-threatening and smiling Akio Shigeta.

"You led me into an ambush," she hissed.

He laughed, "I led them into an ambush."

"At least one had a gun."

"With the bullets removed by my security. That was one of the agreements."

She stared at him. "Then why did the other feel the need to go for it?"

Shigeta shrugged, "To scare you maybe. Check."

Keeping her eyes on Shigeta, she did so—empty.

She looked at him. "So I have murdered three unarmed men?"

"Believe me, Miss Robson, if you had allowed them to take you then you would have been hurt before being killed."

"Why did you not warn me?"

189

"I couldn't, but I gave you the means to protect yourself, and—"

"How did you know I was capable of using it?"

"I have my sources," he said. "Now, Miss Robson, you are in grave danger. My security team is on standby to take you to anywhere you need to go."

"Who were they?"

"Members of the Yamaguchi-gumi Yakuza clan."

"Why?"

"I am sure you know better than I do. Now, when the security tapes are reviewed it'll show them coming in, and then a short time afterwards you walking me out under the threat of your sword. You will lead me to your car. We will drive a while before you release me to walk back. That is when I call their representatives."

She stared at him a moment. "Why are you helping me?"

The back of his hand waved towards the hanging picture. "You already know."

Connor—adhering to the principles of speed, surprise and violence of action, booted the flimsy door open and dialled in on targets.

The long wooden walkway ran along the four courts to its left with the bleachers on its right.

Already a challenge emerged in that the intel indicated there would be no more than eight people, and they'd be solely Sumiyoshi-kai.

He assessed six men in the bleachers, eight playing squash and three women.

The plan had been to kill everyone before leaving a Yamaguchi-gumi symbol.

He had also been told they'd unlikely be armed due to both Japanese anti-gun laws and the recent Yakuza crackdown.

But one sat with his right arm around a girl, his left hand twirling a shiny Colt 1911 pistol with his finger inside the trigger guard. The shock froze in his eyes as the UMP's burst imploded his jaw and throat inwards before spewing them out the back.

Feminine screams and male shouts bounced off the walls. Not wishing to harm the women, Connor kept the selector on burst and began scything down targets.

His peripheral vision caught the two players on his left diving for holdall bags placed on the edges.

The Chameleon Project agent shot them through the glass before stepping into the shard-littered court.

A *wasp* hissed past his ear, and he performed his turn and life-saving step simultaneously.

Squeezing the trigger tipped his pistol-firing assailant back over the seats.

He leapt to the corner and took up a knelt firing position. The barrel of his UMP switched around the corner in time with his aim.

The former soldier barely fired two bursts at the amassed group before an avalanche of fire came back like a spotlight of death.

Angry but confident Japanese commands pinged between the kill team.

Adrenaline spiked Connor's system with the realisation he'd trapped himself. With no grenades to take advantage of their crowding, he set the selector to automatic and fired a long burst blind.

Taking a step back, he reloaded in two seconds, reset to burst, took a breath and exploded around the corner.

Four—clearly adrenaline startled—aimed at him.

Connor and the UMP danced in the fire—burst—step left—burst—step right—burst—crouch—burst.

Am I hit…No…no fucking way…hurry up.

He stood on aim. He checked left to see one of the girls dead from the indiscriminate return fire he had caused. Hearing sobbing, he deemed the other girls to be no threat—*If they were that good as actresses they would be movie stars for Toho, not watching their gangster boyfriends in leisure centres.*

He rapidly cleared the area, ran back and inserted the UMP back into the racket bag.

Connor had worn gloves when he had charged the magazines, so leaving the empty casings did not bother him. In addition, the dried superglue on his fingertips helped negate prints in the absence of his usual silicone caulk.

But the girls had seen his face.

He aggressively jumped up onto the seats and they cowered. He pointed at them before covering his eyes briefly, wagging his finger before pressing it to his lips. He took out the business cards of companies under Yamaguchi-gumi control and scattered them over the girls.

He knew their silence would be a fool's hope; right now they were terrified, but under the protective coddling of the police, their lips would probably loosen—to describe a man with black hair and brown eyes.

He ran off towards the exit. He knew if the police had been called after the first unsuppressed shot, he was nearing the seven-minute response time for Japanese police—unless they'd had a unit close by.

Pulling out some baby wipes, he took forty seconds to scrub his face, ears and remove a splash of blood off his leg. The black fabric of the t-shirt and shorts camouflaged the rest.

His brain took a second to decide either to exit as if frightened of the gunshots or nonchalantly. If a crowd had gathered or the police had arrived then being unhurried might look suspicious. However, if neither of those had occurred and he burst out, then he might draw the eye.

He decided on the latter, and rushed out into the cold only to be warmed by the lack of crowds or police presence.

He had expected a melee, but could only surmise the loud music throughout the sports centre had masked the gunshots.

Slowing to a stroll, he rounded the corner, keeping his eyes searching for watchers. Finally, he reached the underground carpark, got into his car and left the scene.

20

Gorokhov stood on top of the Tokyo Metropolitan Government Building Observatory. At just over two hundred metres high, it held a spectacular view of the Tokyo skyscrapers in the east and Mount Fuji in the south-west.

He lamented how there were few historical buildings left in Japan's capital, especially in comparison to Moscow. Twice in the last hundred years, the city had been left in ruins. The 1923 Great Kantō earthquake had decimated it, as did the firebombing during The Great Patriotic War, as the Russian in him called it.

Both of his peoples had risen from the ashes of war and the breakdown of previous political structures, to take their places high among the global power players.

In his mind, they should be the two nations holding the greatest influence in the world, and not the US and China. If his beloved countries formed a closer alliance, they could be. Gorokhov's anger at the British interference crystallised into a determination to stop them.

He thought about Makar. In truth, it was his brother— the elder by two years—who had been his hero. He respected his father, a one-time factory worker who became an influential spokesperson for the FNPR (Federation of Independent Trade Unions of Russia), but it was Makar he followed to the Sambo training hall. In wanting to impress his only sibling, he had participated in the rigours of training and competing in full combat Sambo. One of his happier memories had been when he threw his larger, heavier brother—albeit for a *waza-ari* rather than a full score *Ippon* during a Judo Randori (practice)—before transitioning into Hadaka Jime (Rear naked choke).

This occurred on his return from a year's stay with his mother in Japan in order to attend Tenri University. The eighteen-year-old Mikhail Gorokhov had made use of the time by training brutally hard at the University's highly respected dojo. He'd also competed in Kosen Judo, a form that emphasized *Ne-waza*—ground techniques—than did traditional judo.

The joy had not come from briefly besting his older sibling, but in Makar's enthusiastic approval of him doing so.

His daydream broke on spotting Shohei Nomura, his law enforcement contact, in the reflection of the window.

Nomura approached and spoke in Japanese, "You were right. He was a Caucasian. However, he had black hair and brown eyes."

Gorokhov thought for a moment. "Nothing that hair dye or a wig, and coloured contact lenses might take care of. Besides, the recall of stressful events can be notoriously inaccurate."

"Perhaps, but no fingerprints were left at the scene," said Nomura. "But several cards belonging to Yamaguchi-gumi businesses were left there."

"A transparent attempt at misinformation."

"Perhaps for you," shrugged Nomura. "But the Sumiyoshi-kai clan will presume it to be true. If we shy away from investigations, then the perception will be that we have too close a relationship with the Yamaguchi-gumi. Certain law enforcement and government figures have been looking for a reason to declare war on the Yakuza. This might be it."

Gorokhov could not help but admire the intent of the plan, and the ruthlessness and audacity of the execution.

"Security footage?"

"An unidentified man leaves the sports centre around the time of the shootings. He's wearing a cap and has a multi-racket carrying bag—large enough to carry an assault rifle. He walks into the multi-storey. Then it gets strange."

"What is strange?"

"The security feed is disrupted inside for seven minutes by an outside electrical interference."

"Or perhaps paid off security staff?"

"I don't think so. The feed goes to a central hub where the shift is rotated."

"Did you get the cars coming out?"

"We recorded the cars leaving half an hour after the man left, yes."

Gorokhov felt a twinge in his brain. "And?"

"They all check out."

"Why only half an hour?"

"That is ample time for a man to get into a vehicle and drive away."

"Unless they or he anticipated it and decided to wait?"

"It would take some nerve to wait so close to the scene of the crime."

"The type of nerve that allows a man to enter a foreign country and assassinate members of a ruthless criminal organisation?"

Nomura at least afforded him a look of sheepishness. So as not to draw out the silence, Gorokhov said, "Can you get the feed for the rest of the day?"

Nomura slowly nodded. "It'll be part of our ongoing investigation."

Gorokhov knew given Nomura's status within law enforcement, he would be aware of Okada.

"I understand that. But I believe he's a British national. If that is true then the diplomatic situation will detonate. Neither of us want that for Nippon just when it is so close to its ultimate resurgence."

"Why do you think he's a British national?"

"I do not want to tell you," said Gorokhov.

"You believe he is here to help prevent the Yamaguchi-gumi from interfering with Okada's rumoured project?"

"Yes."

"Then, that is good."

"It will not be good when civilians die in the streets when the clans go to war," said Gorokhov. "When the trials are completed, the attention of the world will be on Nippon.

And Nippon is considered a very safe country—in the top ten on the global peace index—and you don't want that perception shattered. Bad for your career."

Nomura asked, "What do you propose?"

"Allow me to look over the security footage."

Nomura gave a snort of derision. "You are pushing the limits of our arrangement."

"Am I?" asked Gorokhov rhetorically. "If you go ahead and attempt to arrest this man, I believe it would cause a diplomatic incident. But, if you allow me to handle it, I'll do it discreetly. And I'll smooth over tensions before it explodes. The last thing you need when this British scientist is about to change the world."

Shohei Nomura remained quiet for a few moments. "I will arrange it."

Sykes's anxiety had receded as the last few days had passed without any security incidences. And his excitement began to build with the installation of his technology within households.

He stood overlooking a hissing, clinking, whirring car assembly line, specifically the robotic arms applying adhesive to a suspended car chassis. Men dressed in work attire, including hats, not unlike a restaurant kitchen staff uniform, operated other factory sections. He could almost sense their resentment towards the robotic arms that signified their future employment would soon be obsolete.

Sykes espoused enthusiastically to the factory owner—through Ken translating—the possibilities now he had allowed the installation of Okada technology.

The irony was not lost on Sykes that the owner might have helped end his own business of manufacturing fossil fuel-powered cars with the installation of this technology. The owner might be okay for a short time from the government's subsidization grant in allowing his factory to be a guinea pig. But unless he diversified into building electric cars then he would go under.

Sykes decided to keep this to himself; as far as the owner knew, this technology would be used to power household appliances and factory machinery exceptionally cheaply.

Sykes also chose to downplay the threat to his factory now they had been implemented.

Ken said to Sykes, "He says he understands why his security system is being upgraded but does not understand why he now needs to employ security guards."

The head of the project frowned. "He doesn't. Okada will provide the security guards and pay for them too."

The owner visibly relaxed, and Sykes felt less sorry for him.

Sykes stuck out his hand to the owner. "We are pleased to have you on board."

The owner shook it after translation and they bowed.

The Englishman tilted his head. "Let's go outside, Ken."

The exit took them out at the south-western corner, overlooking Hiroshima Bay. As they leant against the green round railings, he enjoyed the cool sea air and the view of the mountains of Okurokami Island in the distance.

Sykes asked Ken, "How are we so far?"

"Progressing as planned. I like this better— businesses, not homes."

"Every system we install has a sophisticated anti-tamper device that alerts the security."

"When more and more houses have the technology, the security will take longer and longer to come," said Ken straightening his back. "All this for a big hoax."

"It's not a hoax, Ken. You know it is to distract potential enemies from stealing the real technology, or these business owners attempting to sell it."

"I still think I should be up in Sapporo implementing the real stuff. I am the chief engineer."

"We have been through this, Ken," sighed the Brit. "The people who may want to destroy these inventions will follow the chief engineer, while the real installations are going on in Sapporo."

"I know, I know. But these business owners think they are getting this technology."

"It is not a scam, Ken. At this moment, they are receiving state-of-the-art systems, albeit from two years ago. When our new systems are fully approved, they will be the first beneficiaries of it."

"But the family homes—colours them for the bulls."

Sykes understood Ken meant 'Paints them as targets' and replied, "Why would they hurt families? It is not as if they can remove the installations without the anti-tamper alert going off."

"Going off?"

"It means coming on—it's a peculiarity of the English language."

"Oh," said Ken. "Let us hope that no one comes."

"Yes," answered Sykes, thinking of Chisato. "Let's hope."

21

The kneeling former Russian Special Forces soldier observed the super mansion from among the trees. He was glad of the cover of darkness.

Mikhail Gorokhov had been assured of Akio Shigeta's guilt as soon as he observed the beefed-up security around him. The billionaire now did not go anywhere without a full team, consisting of four bodyguards from a rotation of sixteen men.

In observing this, Gorokhov knew if he could get the business mogul alone, he would be able to pry a useful lead from him—though making a dangerous enemy in return.

Gorokhov did not want to get into an altercation with Shigeta's security team, despite his ultra-confidence of overcoming them. Dead bodies triggered investigations. Fortunately, Shigeta dismissed them on entry to his home.

And the former SVR assassin did not necessarily believe this was hubris on the Japanese businessman's part; the location protection was several layers deep.

Though Akio Shigeta owned estates abroad, he only had listed two residential properties in Japan; one where he held parties and meetings, and this, his more private home.

Gorokhov had conducted a detailed investigation of the security apparatus both through digital searches and a scoped inspection.

The SVR cyber analysts, who had proven their sophistication in recent times, not least in penetrating the United States political apparatus, had unearthed old e-mails between Akio Shigeta and the architect. Within these messages, amongst other things, were general descriptions of the rooms.

An unusual design in that the structure's shape was of a giant truncated wedge. The front—on the opposite side of where he now hid—rose to two storeys made of reinforced, dimmable glass and housed the majority of guest bedrooms, bathrooms, recreation quarters, the library, a private cinema and indoor pool.

It slid back on a shallow slant into a multitude of different angled thatched roofs—some being flat and expansive clearing out onto a limb, and other nooks and apertures at one storey high forming the back side of the building. It housed some more bedrooms—including Shigeta's own—and the ones, though now empty, for his close friends and family when they visited. However, though Gorokhov knew the bedroom windows were dimmed to black at night, he did not know exactly which bedroom Shigeta slept in—hence his wariness of making sounds on the roof.

Other rooms included more bathrooms, the gym, storage cupboards, an office and a kitchen to the dining room.

Gorokhov's architectural knowledge—though not expert—was at a level where he appreciated the aesthetically pleasing front juxtaposed with the 'ugly' practical traditionalism of the back.

In addition to the six metre wide, man-made swimming moat encircling the entire estate, his computer findings showed the home to be guarded by an array of measures, including motion sensors that alerted the local police of intrusion, automatic room locking, 4K vision and extreme zoom hooked to the mobile devices of both Shigeta and his security team.

The intelligence agent, having extensive knowledge of security systems, knew the company manufacturing the equipment and the company who installed it were usually different, as was the case here.

He had spent two nights observing; identifying the potential blind spot on the first night before confirming it on the second, as well as the distance and route selection to the kitchen extractor fan unit.

Now was the time to execute.

The security posted a single sentry, who took an hour to patrol the entire perimeter outside of the moat.

Gorokhov slid on his operational backpack after removing the highly advanced rappelling gun from it. He had never used it in a live situation but tested it extensively ever since he'd had it made by an engineer in Yokohama. Fixing it to his harness as per design, he felt assured of its reliability.

The device could be aimed and fired from both ends, either separately or simultaneously depending on the setting. The new Enhanced Projectile Propulsion (EPP) firing mechanism meant it could be adjusted to fire deep into the ground, through a large tree or embed into brickwork. The spindle lock, multi-directional spring-operated hooks ensured the bolts' security even under the necessary tension of supporting the weight of a large human. Their specialist design meant the operator could disengage them easily as the hooks could turn back in on themselves to prevent snagging.

Another enhancement had been coiled tension-line manufactured from a rare form of spider silk with a tensile strength many times greater than steel, but with the ductility reduced; this meant that over a hundred metres of the line could be coiled within the rappelling gun without its design becoming overly bulky or heavy.

He pressed the rappelling gun's rear barrel against a large, strong isunoki tree and fired a bolt into it.

He then broke from the treeline and strolled up to within fifteen metres of the moat. Beyond the water lay a pristine, glinting lawn stretching ten metres from the moat to an internal corner where two windowless walls met.

Two mounted and moving cameras cast their serpentine eyes a metre and a half forward of this incut.

Gorokhov had established their patterns; both would face in, then the left would sweep out, followed by the right—generating a seven second blind spot before the right would turn back in.

The wandering sentry would be on the opposite side of the estate.

This next part he knew would be crucial. If the bolt failed to gain purchase on the roof, the spider-silk wire would fall with the bolt setting off the motion sensors.

Also, Gorokhov could not be sure which of the back bedrooms Shigeta's was. Gorokhov knew beneath the thatched overlay lay strengthened EPDM rubber—good for resisting his body weight, bad in that the thump of the hook piercing through it would likely wake Shigeta if his room happened to be the room below.

Inhaling the night air, he timed it and fired—the spear shot out on a straight path with only a hint of a curve at the end of its trajectory.

It hammered into the angled roof and he heard the wire strain against the immediate snap of tension.

The agent froze as the motion sensitive cameras swung back in. If Shigeta had woken, and was quick enough, he might check his phone, accessing the images from the cameras.

Gorokhov felt sure he had done all he could to negate the chance.

The cameras began to rotate away. He pressed the trigger and with a jerk, flew through the night air. Using the gun's speed selector, he slowed when passing the cameras.

He controlled his hitting the wall the way a gymnast would a landing off the vaulting platform. Deeply etched forearm muscle striations rose as he held himself still for three minutes; after being awoken from deep or REM sleep, people would usually fall back to slumber if quiet ensued for a minute or so afterwards.

He climbed up and over the lip. Remaining prone to prevent skylining himself, he gingerly removed the attachment to his harness. He decided beforehand that bringing back the rear hook past the cameras would be the lesser of the two evils in comparison to leaving it for the wandering sentry to find.

Again timing the cameras' outward motion, he selected the disengagement and return of the rear bolt. His eyes creased at the faint sound of the wire speeding back into the device.

Though still wearing the relatively light harness, he chose to leave the front bolt secured, and the device in place in case an emergency escape would be needed.

And he had been assured that the rappelling gun had been pre-contaminated with the DNA of an agent of Chinese Ministry of State Security, so if and when found it would lead back to them.

He began to crawl, pausing every so often until he had covered the twenty-six metres to the extraction vent.

Taking out his tools, he removed the front panelling. The menacing-looking fans were still, presumably due to the relative cool of the spring night. To squeeze down without snagging on the fan blades, he removed his backpack and harness and placed them on the right hand side of the unit.

Pressing his hands and feet against the sides, he stretched headfirst down into the shaft. After three-quarters of a metre, it curved horizontal to crawl across the ceiling.

In Gorokhov's initial planning, the SVR cyber cell had snatched the installation company's digital files. In reading the electronic invoice's comments, he discovered that Shigeta had chosen not to have any security cameras placed within the house due to privacy concerns.

Barring a secret dog, the only thing that could give away his presence was for noise to alert Shigeta himself.

Touching his feet down from the vertical shaft, he lay on his front and began to crawl slowly to the vent opening in the kitchen. Finding it, he used a specialist multi-tool he'd possessed since his Alpha group counter terrorism days to silently remove the grill.

He decided against poking his head out to observe for danger, not wishing to risk giving away his location when he wouldn't be in an adequate position to defend himself.

Instead, he swung his feet around, took out his boot knife and dropped.

His brain slowed to catch the pistol pointed at him.

And the recognition of an ash-blond man gripping it.

Connor—expecting the intruder to freeze on landing— barely dodged the blade darting at his throat.

Before he was able to draw down, the black clad man leapt at him like a panther.

His eyes barely registered the movement that seared pain through his wrist, sending the pistol clattering across the steel table.

The Englishman's short, sharp left hook skimmed over the ghost's head. A grabbing push of his left shoulder spun Connor, and steel forearms clamped his waist, launching him into the air.

Connor shifted enough to take the crashing impact on his shoulder and not his head. His foot hooked the man's ankle as he sprung to his feet, causing him to stumble forwards into the hanging utensils.

The man righted himself to snatch the pistol and bring it to bear on Connor.

Shigeta's security burst through the door, only to be overwhelmed by the force of nature cutting through them like a katana through bamboo.

After disarming the first man, the next three went down under the pistol's rapid burst.

Connor leapt on the man's back, snatching the pistol's top slide back to prevent further shots from being fired. Digging his heels inside his opponent's thighs he slung his right hand over to reinforce his gripping left, astonished at the man's strength.

The rest of the security did not fire, presumably as not to risk hitting Connor. The assailant's thighs whipped in and around, detaching the Englishman's 'hooks' and he charged forward, barrelling them both into the Japanese men like a bowling ball into tenpins.

They fell into a mass of punches, elbows and headbutts, as Connor once again sailed over the intruder's head. His double grip and falling bodyweight prized the pistol from his adversary's hand, who bolted for the door over the scramble.

Connor, now with the pistol in hand, clambered up to tear after the phantom.

He cut around the corner only to encounter a fist to the jaw and sweeping foot to his ankles.

The Chameleon Project agent fired as he fell, seeing his enemy's right shoulder jerk, unable to tell if from being hit by the round or avoiding it. The toe-punting boot shot the gun out of his hand.

The shadow raced away at unnatural speed down the long corridor. Connor—a fast sprinter himself—knowing he wouldn't catch the man, nonetheless snatched up the pistol and ran hard. Wariness of rounding another corner slowed him enough to glimpse the man disappearing beyond the next.

He couldn't shake the image of a Great White attempting to chase a Killer Whale.

But I have a gun.

The sound of smashing glass punched anxiety into his chest, making him run harder.

Bursting into a room, the curtains at the broken window flapped a mocking wave at him.

Connor, gun raised, cleared the immediate outside space around the window, and leapt out.

With his weapon following his eyes, he spun around to catch any sudden movement in the darkness.

Nothing—*disappeared into thin air.*

Was he still in the house? The security team bundled in and Connor commanded, "Check every space large enough to fit a man. Start with this room and work out."

One of the men translated his orders, as Connor stood off to the side of the window, his pistol held in the 'low port' position.

After a couple of moments, the distant nagging in the back of his brain came forth with clarity—*the roof.*

Gorokhov had leapt for the roof, his iron-strong fingers allowing him to pull himself up before crawling back towards his operations pack beside the vent.

He knew I was coming—that's why he snuck in the extra security.

Though Connor Reed's bullet had barely grazed the Japanese-Russian's shoulder, it disconcerted him that the Englishman had touched him at all in his artificially enhanced hyper-alert state.

And now that state seemed to be waning, getting further and further away. Fatigue washed over him as he crawled through invisible mud—warm and with a distant invitation to sleep. He fought against it, towards the salvation of his operations pack and the vials within it.

Finally reaching it, his brain screamed for his hands to work quicker as they slid out the needle, syringe and vial. He concentrated hard to extract the liquid. Locating a vein, he slid the needle in and pressed the plunger.

He knew the immediate alertness he felt to be part placebo. The concoction typically took a few minutes to fully take effect. Though he would feel normal in a minute or so, his enhancement could not come back until complete restoration.

His energy flamed within him. As he reached for his operational harness, he heard a sound behind him.

Instinctively, he knew it was his pursuer and turned around. He ran at him but not before Reed had vaulted onto the ledge and adopted a crouching position.

He knew until the concoction had fully run through his system, this would be a more even fight.

As the Englishman brought his pistol to bear, Gorokhov snatched it with a wrenching twist.

The gun clattered off the edge as Reed's head smashed into Gorokhov's cheekbone. The Sambo master stumbled back, his rival darting forward with a furious storm of precision punches.

Though Gorokhov covered up, the impacts thudded pain into his liver, ear and solar plexus. Just at the point of becoming overwhelming, he snatched hold of his opponent and swept his foot out with an inside reap while driving hard into him.

His adversary stumbled but remained upright.

Exchanging hellish blows, their defensive slips, blocks, ducks and rides prevented knockdowns.

When he heard the chorus of Japanese voices below, his soul sang on feeling his inhuman sharpness and strength return. When the blue-eyed Reed snatched a standing Kimura trap on his left wrist, Gorokhov's sheer strength torqued his arm free. His Hiza Guruma—placing his foot on his enemy's knee and wheeling him over it with a drag of his hands—sent his adversary flying.

The airborne Reed tumbled into men attempting to ascend onto the roof. Though they dropped from the ledge, their presence had prevented him falling along with them.

He clicked the attachment of the rappelling gun back on his harness, thanking grace he'd left the bolt attached.

Seeing Reed running at him, and confident the Englishman couldn't disengage the bolt or snap the wire with his bare hands, Gorokhov ran and leapt off the lowest edge of the huge roof. He landed with a feline grace, whipping into a forward roll to dissipate as much of the kinetic energy as possible.

As the Japanese calls went up like flares, Gorokhov switched the selector to 'single fire'. Aiming the rearsight—now the foresight—end of the rappelling gun at the original isunoki trunk beyond the moat.

Squeezing the trigger, the hook shot out before the spider-wire pulled taut on impacting the tree. He flew through the gunfire.

Clearing the moat, his feet began to skim the ground and he ran hard, disengaging the hooks, zipping the wire back in before sprinting into the darkness of the wood.

His relief gave way to the feeling of his pride burning—*I failed.*

22

Shintaro Goto outwardly displayed the same confident posture and demeanour as he would have done twenty years ago if visited by law enforcement. However, today clarified to him the loss of power the Yakuza had experienced.

Goto had been arrested several times in his life, and once even as boss, but never summoned.

Now he sat, with an allowance of a single bodyguard, in a room with five police officers present. Sitting in front of him was The Chief of the Tokyo Metropolitan Police Department, Ryohei Ohno, the second most powerful man in Japanese law enforcement outside of The Chief of the National Police Agency.

It was the man next to him who concerned Goto more. Hiroki Kobayashi was a Public Security Intelligence (PSI) officer whose activities were generally not well known to the public. However, Goto's awareness of him came about three years ago when the young officer helped destroy the Yamaguchi-gumi's human trafficking operations in Vietnam and Korea.

The other three police officers were set about the flanks, each with the fingers of their right hand resting on their holstered New Nambu M60 pistols.

Ohno spoke, "Why did you order the assassination of Sumiyoshi-kai members, Goto-san? We cannot understand it. In a public sports hall no less."

Goto remained silent.

"We thought a *Tengu* might have possessed you, Goto-san," said Kobayashi. "But you need the spirit to speak through your mouth now. Staying silent will not save you."

Goto considered the implications of the younger man's words—had they brought him here to kill him? He dismissed the thought; they would not be so blatant—not yet.

But staying silent might not be the best course of action. If Goto had to guess, he would have reckoned on Kobayashi facilitating the meeting with Superintendent General Ohno, and insisting any refusal to attend or remaining silent would be an admission of guilt.

Goto cleared his throat. "I did not order this."

"Maybe someone else in your organisation then? Someone…respected," said Kobayashi slyly.

"No one would dare order a strike like this unless I had authorised it. The Yamaguchi-gumi are not responsible for this."

"Forgive my rudeness, Goto-san," answered Kobayashi. "But we predicted that answer."

Goto smiled, "Of course. A denial would be the same if I were telling the truth or lying. Anticipation of me not confirming I ordered such reckless killings is nothing to boast about."

Kobayashi disappointed him with a complete non-reaction, and so he pressed on with, "But it is like you say, why would we harm ourselves by instigating a feud like this?"

It became evident to Goto he was now in a negotiation for the future of the Yamaguchi-gumi. He knew Kobayashi hated organised crime of any kind, and was itching to be let off his leash entirely.

He suspected Ryohei Ohno, one generation forward to Goto's own, to be more pragmatic regarding the Yakuza's place in Japanese society, and the fallout from an all-out war with them.

If Goto failed to convince him to allow the Yamaguchi-gumi boss to handle the strife internally, then this meeting could be the striking of the match that saw the Yakuza burn to ashes.

Kobayashi said, "Why else do organisations of your kind come into armed conflict? Money, power, territory…vengeance?"

Goto frowned. "Vengeance for what, young man?"

The intelligence officer's hand disappeared beneath the table before reappearing clutching three enlarged photographs.

Goto remained expressionless; they were old mugshot pictures of the three soldiers he had sent to accost the journalist.

"Recognise these men?" said the younger man, in what Goto recognised to be an attempt to bait him.

"Yes."

"When did you last see them?"

"I am not sure," said Goto. "A week ago, maybe."

"Do you know of their whereabouts now?" asked Ohno.

The Yakuza boss felt a knot form at the probing questions regarding three comparatively low-level underlings.

"I have many employees. I cannot know all their whereabouts at all times."

"He did not ask you if you knew the whereabouts of all your employees," said Kobayashi, his voice edged with derision. "He asked you if you knew where these three are?"

Goto understood; at least one of them must have been an informant, or worse—undercover.

"I could find out," the crime lord stated, seething that he did not send his best to take the gaijin woman.

Ohno declared, "You have until the end of the day. And if there is any hint of a gangland war, then this year will see the beginning of the end for Yamaguchi-gumi as we know it."

Ciara knocked in a prearranged pattern on the solid wood back door. She knew Connor would be able to see her through the tiny cameras posted around. Jaime, the Chameleon Project's tech wizard, had provided them.

Though she had conducted a thorough cleaning run, she felt uneasy that this would be the third face to face she'd had with him since the operation began. However, she had decided she needed to assess the situation with him in person after the events of the past few days.

The door opened to reveal the Yorkshireman. The bruising on his face did not concern her—she had seen his face marked more than once—it was the hyper-alertness in his eyes.

He stepped back to let her into a kitchen comprising polished grey woods, black ceramic surfaces, and the silver of utensils.

After the perfunctory greetings, he asked, "You want a coffee?"

"Please."

Soon they sat across from one another. She couldn't remember him seeming quite so…distracted.

"A few days you've had," she said.

"And you. How did you survive being taken by three Yakuza? They must have been armed. I never asked Mr Shigeta the other night."

She sensed he might be deflecting but indulged him anyway. "Aoki Shigeta in addition to insisting their guns were emptied of bullets before they came in, also left me in a room with a beautiful katana mounted on the wall. You can imagine what ensued."

A smile, threatening to turn into a chuckle, broke out on his face.

"What happened?" she asked, avoiding her urge to be gentle, knowing he would find it patronising. He had already debriefed her digitally regarding the squash court attack.

He began to speak, seemingly almost to himself.

"I have been doing this kind of work for more than a few years now. I know I might be one of the best shooters the UK has—I came out unscathed from the squash courts when no man had a right to. And I can hold my own with professional mixed martial artists," he said without arrogance. "But that guy made me feel like Batman when he's getting filled in by Bane the first time they fought."

"How much bigger was he?"

The Yorkshireman shook his head. "He was about the same size. Just so fast and strong. His anticipation wasn't normal. It was like getting battered off a half-Japanese Jason Bourne."

Ciara asked, "Half Japanese?"

"His features seemed a cross between Japanese and a Slav race—I reckon eastern Slav but I can't be sure. Pale, square-faced, strong jaw, eyes angled down."

He sipped his coffee, and continued, "The firing sequence that dispatched three of Akio's men was fucking rapid but he managed to catch them all square in the point of the chin—the spot to aim for if you want to hit the medulla."

"I'll make a request for more men to be sent. More agents from the Project, it'll—"

"No, don't," he said, before looking at her. "I mean, as the man on the ground, I am asking you not to."

"Why?" Ciara appreciated that he was making a concerted effort to address her as his superior, especially as it had been him teaching her instead of the other way around. Still, she couldn't afford for his ego to jeopardize the mission.

"By the time you get them here, and brief them, it could be too late. And the more Brits we've got over here, the greater we risk a diplomatic incident."

"Connor, if this man is what you say he is, then you're going need help."

She watched him stare into his cup, before replying, "You're right."

When he did not say anything further, she asked, "What are you thinking about?"

"About how, when you blow out with a 'Hhhaaaa' your breath is warm, but when you blow out 'Oooohh' its cold."

Her forehead knotted, "What?"

"I meant, I know a guy who might help."

23

Carlo Andaloro generally enjoyed his trips to Canada. He surmised the country's air must be some of the cleanest in the world, especially here in Alberta, around five miles south-east of the town of Slave Lake.

Carlo was perhaps the 'Ndrangheta's first pick for more 'overt' assassinations. There might be one or two better at making it look like an accident, but if stealth wasn't an issue, and dangerous people needed killing, the southern Italian mafia bosses turned to him.

The peaked military-style cap kept the cold off the thirty-two-year old's bald head, and he kept the camouflaged jacket unzipped at the top to let out his body heat.

The straps of his Bergen pressed into his clavicles. Negotiating the harsh, steep forest terrain teased Carlo, a man a little below average height for an Italian, though densely muscled. He was not in quite the shape he had been as a young soldier. Forced marches had been regular in that life, albeit in more of a desert environment than the bitter cold.

With years in the French Foreign Legion, Carlo was one of the Calabrian mafia's few former military soldiers; thus equally adept at killing in both urban and rural environments.

Despite the world's glamorized view of the Legion, Carlo knew though elite, they were not Special Forces. Carlo mused that basic training turned him into just as good a cleaner as a soldier.

However, the training and experience he had received in the legion's only airborne regiment, the 2nd Foreign Parachute Regiment, had been of an exalted standard. The "Shaping up" period alone for *2e R.E.P* (2e Régiment étranger de parachutists) took twelve months of physical, mental and psychological tests across all terrain and weather conditions, including special operations training.

His performance had led to him—though almost unheard of for a non-French national—to be selected for several unofficial joint missions with the GIGN, an elite police unit that, amongst other things, dealt with counter-terrorism and hostage rescue.

Now, the hitman had arrived in Alberta under the guise of wolf hunting. As romantic as that might sound to a civilian, the idea of sitting protected in an insulated and heated box for hours on end waiting for a baited wolf seemed both boring and unmanly to him. Especially as Carlo, at eleven years old, had killed a wolf in self-defence when it burst unexpectedly from a nearby treeline.

It had been that incident which first turned him on to the high octane rush of surviving dangerous situations, and he had been putting himself in them ever since.

Like the one he was embarking on now.

The 'Ndrangheta affiliate Siderno Group—named because the majority of its members either came from, or had ancestry tracing back to the town of Siderno on the Ionian coast in Calabria—had progressively grown into a powerful mafia group. Though also active in Italy and Australia, it had been in the Greater Toronto area of Canada where they had made their name and forged a stronghold.

However, civil war had threatened to take root, and the Siderno Group high council had petitioned Calabria for house-cleaning—and so here Carlo was, his breath expelling against the cold air like a white fire from a dragon.

The assassin had done a thorough map study of the landscape before plotting the waypoints into his GPS watch. He'd wipe them later, but preferred it to marking a map and using a compass.

On cresting a peak, the snow-covered trees saved him from being skylined and he began his descent.

This was easier on the cardiovascular system but harder on the knees.

Finally, he reached the edge of the forest and crouched to survey the scene.

Because stilts supported the underside of the wooden lodge complex, it gave the impression of floating above the snow.

A single light shone in one of the windows, and the intermittent wafts of smoke from the chimney indicated the first party had already arrived.

This proved the intelligence he had received to be correct. The group under Marco Bianchi had broken away from the larger Siderno Group. The nucleus of the Bianchi contingent now waited for the leadership of the Romano family based out of Montreal to discuss the formation of an alliance.

A coalition between the two would pose a crisis risk to Siderno dominance.

He had arrived an hour before the Romanos were due to arrive. The Siderno Group's orders to him were to attack the Romanos on arrival. In the fallout, disinformation would be pumped out that Marco Bianchi was behind it in order to make a name for himself.

Knowing his targets had no formal military experience and were not expecting a guy like him, he had not taken the measure of building a hide and laying up overnight.

Although exceedingly adept at hide construction, he did not particularly enjoy extended stays in them.

And though highly skilled with a sniper rifle, kills with them felt sterile—unless there were counter-snipers in the vicinity—as the victims did not present any danger to him.

It had never just been about killing; it was surviving combat situations that held the real attraction.

A thought occurred—the overarching purpose of his being there was to cripple the breakaway group led by Marco Bianchi. The Siderno Group had wished for this to be accomplished via a false flag operation to see the Romano family turn on Bianchi.

But if the Bianchi men in that lodge were to die, their uprising collapses, thought Carlo.

Though he understood orders were orders, he also knew to kill double the men, leaving a scene that could be convincingly interpreted as the two groups turning on one another without a survivor would be neigh impossible. Because he had received the orders through an intermediary, he had not had recourse to question them but accepted anyway due to the allure of combat.

Now here he decided to change the play. In the end, they'd be grateful the overall objective had been achieved.

He tried to shake the thought; his secondary weapon was the new Berretta APX. He had familiarized himself with the pistol the best he could in the few hours he had been given on a private range.

One of the things he liked about the 9MM polymer-framed, striker-fired semi-automatic, was that the foresight dot was larger than the two back sight dots; this meant all three appeared the same size when the APX was held at arm's length, making for quicker target acquisition.

The two wolves in his mind began to circle one another. He could not be sure of the numbers or what they were armed with.

But in meetings such as this, the unspoken code of respect demanded that weapons were never on display—which meant they'd be carrying pistols, because even an amateur wielding a sub-machine gun could scythe down a pistol-armed professional in an enclosed space.

Without a silencer, he'd give away his presence on firing the initial shots. But he had his knife.

He shifted on his stomach—*If you're going to do it, you need to do it now before the others turn up.*

He estimated he'd get within thirty metres of a side entry point by using the treeline and dead ground.

Carlo got off his belly, collected his gear and slid back into the trees.

Though confident they had not posted wandering sentries, he stopped every so often during his jog in a wide arc to the spot he'd picked out earlier.

He set down his backpack and sniper rifle. After checking that his top round was seated correctly, he stalked forward using the trees as cover.

Crouching behind a large tamarack tree, he remained still.

At this angle, he could see the building had a small porch with a door facing the vast stretch of snow-coated farmland to his right.

The end window of the lodge faced about twenty degrees off to his left.

He estimated that if there were wandering look-outs around the house, one would appear every minute or so.

A dark-haired man with a hard face appeared at the window, scanning the area before receding back and vanishing. Carlo waited five minutes to establish the sentry's pattern; he appeared every thirty to forty seconds.

Though he could easily make the distance, he would leave footprints—*No stealth. Just speed and ferocity then.*

As the sentry's face disappeared from the window, crackling energy roared in Carlo's ears. He counted the seconds while bursting from the trees in a hard sprint.

Reaching the door, he crashed a boot through it.

The shock on the sentry's face turned to imploding red and white fleshy pulp and bone. Carlo, not knowing the numbers facing him, had opted for single shots.

His nose barely registered the mix of nitro-glycerine, sawdust, graphite and burnt meat.

The lodge came alive with hoarse shouts in English and Italian.

Dropping to one knee, his next shot punched through the throat of a man rushing down the hallway.

Wishing to take advantage of the collective panic, he moved as quickly as he could, crouching, his Beretta up.

220

The nose of a submachine gun poked around the corner.

Time compressed his decision-making, causing him to leap backwards and to his left, crashing through a door.

Scrambling to clear the 'kill zone' of the doorway, the floor splintered under the punching hail of bullets.

Spinning around into a knelt firing position, he let out an injury-feigning moan. He found himself rewarded with the appearance of the Uzi-wielding aggressor.

Carlo fired three times in rapid succession; two to the chest and one to the head.

His enemy tipped backwards, his death twitch clamping down on the trigger, spraying rounds in a wide arc. The magazine expended rapidly, allowing the former 2 REP paratrooper to dart for the window.

God must have been on his side as the frame sprang open when struck by his desperate palms, and he leapt through.

He landed with a deep knee-bend in the snow before tearing down the side of the lodge.

The assassin had banked on his actions creating panic in the bodyguards, hoping their lack of skill and experience would prevent them rushing outside to cut him off.

The point of his Beretta whipped around the corners of the lodge in line with his eyes. In seconds, he had reached the opposite side's window.

Through the pane he observed the back of another guard. Glass shattered and the force of his 9MM rounds flung the man forward.

Carlo did not want to risk being caught by return fire while climbing through the window. Instead, he turned and sprinted back. The former Legionnaire rolled his sights on the window he originally exited the building from but saw no one. He ran on, heading towards his original point of entry.

He used a *CQB* technique, *Couper la tarte*—Cutting the Tart—named by his French CQB instructors, peering incrementally around the corner, his weapon up so as not to unnecessarily expose himself.

This technique enabled him to shoot the first of the three men clutching their Uzis and simultaneously scan the area.

Already firing before properly aiming at Carlo, the second died with a pair of the Berretta's rounds punching his chest.

Carlo ducked back around the corner just as the Uzi rounds of the third turned it into a mass of flying splinters. He stilled his urge to run back and waited for it—the click of an empty magazine.

Stepping back out, he shot the man hurriedly trying to reload.

The 'Ndrangeta assassin moved into the building and began to clear it.

No armed men appeared.

He found a room where Marco Bianchi and three of his deputies were hiding.

The elation Carlo felt coursing through his veins had nothing to do with shooting all four dead with just five shots. Instead, it was his victory in death-defying combat.

Having performed a dead check on all his victims, he made off back into the forest just as the Romano contingent came into view in the distance.

He pulled out his phone to alert the extraction team to change his *PUP*—pick-up point. A message fragment appeared across the screen. He recognised the code on opening the message.

His adrenaline-euphoria prevented the frown appearing.

He hadn't expected Connor Reed to cash in on the debt Carlo owed to him so quickly.

It must be something or someone important and extremely dangerous.

Gorokhov sat beside Shintaro Goto, knowing this meeting might have historical significance.

The traditional-style communal room looked huge in comparison to the round table. The green of the walls heightened the paintings of wild seas and ancient samurai battles, and contrasted the cream, light browns and amber of the floors, ceiling, and hanging lights.

Three groups of three suited men with bulges in their jackets stood in separate huddles around the room, all out of ear-shot of the table, where their masters sat with their advisors.

Ryoichi Hori, the *Sosai*—director-general—of the second largest Yakuza syndicate, the Sumiyoshi-kai, sat across from Gorokhov and Goto at a forty-five-degree angle, with his older advisor beside him.

The Sumiyoshi-kai differed from Goto's Yamaguchi-gumi in that they were a collection of smaller gangs making up their federation. Although supreme leadership rested with Hori, he had to share a portion of his powers with other men. One of the reasons, Gorokhov knew, why Goto did not see him as equal. That and the slick-haired, sharp suited Hori being nearly two decades younger.

Gorokhov recognised the Yamaguchi-gumi and Sumiyoshi-kai had a peculiar relationship of partnering on some projects and fighting over others. It had been more of the latter than the former in recent years.

Kingo Teruaki sat in a mirroring position opposite Hori, so the three formed a triangle. Between Hori and Goto in age, Teruaki held the title of first *kaicho*—first chairman—of the Inagawa-kai, the third largest clan in the Yakuza.

Operating out of the Kantō region that included greater Tokyo, the Inagawa-kai was originally formed in the 1950s by traditional travelling gamblers, named the *bakuto*. And although they now involved themselves in a variety of criminal activities, their primary source of income remained gambling.

The square-jawed Teruaki, sitting with his younger advisor, seemed to Gorokhov the most relaxed of the trio, as he stroked his cropped, salt and pepper hair.

Ryoichi Hori spoke, "You request a meeting, Shintaro, after having my men killed in a public place and in daylight. I admire your nerve, if not your intelligence."

Goto retorted, "So easily manipulated you are, Ryoichi, if you think I would be that reckless."

Gorokhov noted the Yamaguchi-gumi leader did not say he wouldn't have ordered it, just that he would have been more subtle. And that the two men addressed one another by their first names in veiled disrespect.

"There is only you with the motive to do so."

"That is not so, Ryoichi, and we have evidence."

"Before we get to this 'evidence', I want to know who is this Hāfu, and why he is permitted to attend this meeting?"

Hāfu was a loanword from English, referring to a person of both Japanese and non-Japanese heritage. It was not an offensive term, as the Yakuza saw themselves as society's perennial outsiders too, many having Korean blood flowing through their veins.

However, it was obvious to the half-Russian that the Sumiyoshi-kai leader used it to highlight he was an outsider and therefore not welcome.

"The agreement was an advisor of our own choice, along with three bodyguards, Hori-san," interjected Kingo Teruaki calmly. "Let us not change the rules."

"I am not Teruaki-san. But given what is to be discussed, I think we would all be more comfortable knowing who he is. This is not unreasonable—our advisors are known to everyone else around this table."

Gorokhov rose and bowed in turn as he addressed the Yakuza leaders. "Hori-san, Terukai-san, my name is Mikhail Gorokhov . I am a former agent for Russian intelligence. My father is from St Petersburg and my mother from Osaka."

"Former?" sneered Hori. "The Russians would never let a *good* agent go. Especially one who speaks Japanese like a native."

"You are correct, Hori-san, and I am a superb agent. However, I agreed with my former masters that I be allowed to go freelance, as long as my tasks do not conflict with the interests of Russia. This is one such task that does not."

"And what task is that? And who gave it to you?"

"It is the destruction of this new technology. As to who…there are wealthy people in the Middle East who do not wish for this technology to materialise—unless they are the ones profiting from it. Same as yourselves, and I am your best hope of making sure you all profit from it."

Gorokhov sat.

Hori stated, "So, you were the one who killed my men?"

The assassin shook his head. "I would have been much cleaner."

"Then who?"

Gorokhov raised his hand before slowly reaching inside his suit jacket and removing photographs.

"These photographs are the stills from security footage on the day your men were assassinated."

He handed both Yakuza bosses the photographs. Hori peered into the first one and said, "A man with a large squash bag walking away from the sports centre? Is that your evidence?"

"There is a time stamp in the bottom left corner."

"Yes, I have eyes," snapped Hori. "What is its significance?"

"A man exits the sports centre a few seconds after a mass murder involving unsuppressed firearms seemingly without a care in the world. With a bag large enough to hide a weapon system."

Before Hori could retort, Terukai said, "These are photographs. Perhaps the man was running."

Gorokhov produced two USB sticks and handed them over. "These show the security footage from that day."

Hori snatched his, whereas Terukai gave him a nod of his head and asked, "Have you progressed with your investigation?"

Before Gorokhov could answer, Hori interjected with, "Investigations? We cannot allow this tale and a few photographs—possibly doctored—to deceive us."

"Can I ask you what motive Shintaro-san would have to do that?" asked Gorokhov.

"It is obvious—he is afraid of our group's power. He wanted to make a display of dominance. And this will not—"

Terukai placed a hand on Hori's forearm and said calmly, "If that was the motive, this would have happened before now. This is something different, which Gorokhov-san will be sure to explain."

"The Gādian have a large percentage share in the Okada Company. I am sure you are aware, Okada have been pursuing the research and development of renewable energy. They made use of the government grant scheme issued post-Fukushima to recruit the best, including foreigners. It seems they have made breakthroughs that will change the world—and also change your worlds, because the Gādian's revenue will grow to dwarf yours combined, and given his...enmity for you all, that does not bode well. This technology needs to be destroyed."

Hori sniffed. "He hates you, Shintaro-san, most of all."

The Yamaguchi-gumi finally spoke, "He is young. Maybe he'll understand it is difficult to oversee everything at once."

When no one spoke for a few moments, Gorokhov continued, "To answer your earlier question, we have identified the rental vehicle and traced it back. We have begun to look into the digital records of who booked the vehicle. A forensic team have so far not been able to obtain DNA."

Hori frowned. "What forensics team? We have not heard of the investigation getting that far. And we have strong back channels."

Goto said, "We have our own. And this team isn't part of the official investigation. They have made more progress."

Terukai cut Hori's intended angry retort before it began with, "And what progress is that?"

Gorokhov said, "The stills you have in your hand show who we believe to be the same man coming out of the rental building—"

"These, where you can barely see his face? And with different clothes and hair colour?"

"You don't change your clothes, Hori-san, from one day to the next?" asked Goto rhetorically.

Gorokhov quickly said, "A man capable of assassinating multiple armed men without leaving a trace of DNA would take the rudimentary measures of angling his face away from the cameras. But you can see by his jawline that it is the same man."

Terukai said, "Even if this is true, how do we find this man?"

"We will deal with that," said Gorokhov. "I cannot guarantee I can bring him to you alive but I will bring him back—"

"You will not touch this man," interjected Hori. "It was Sumiyoshi-kai men who were—according to you— ambushed and slaughtered by this man, and it will be the Sumiyoshi-kai who will avenge them."

"Of course, Hori-san, but this man is extremely dangerous. We would like to assist you."

"You can assist us by locating him, but we will bring him in, and ask him questions. Why would a foreigner attack my men?"

"I suspect it was a false flag operation to pre-emptively destroy an alliance between the three of you," stated Gorokhov. "If you are to destroy, or capture, this technology, and reclaim your position as masters of Japan, you will need to unite—the full weight of the government will oppose you, but with your co-ordinated efforts and pooled resources and contacts, you will succeed, and Japan will be yours once again."

The silence rang in Gorokhov's ears.

Terukai said, "We have been accepting a shrinking slice of the pie for too long. The authorities have taken our reasonableness for weakness and taken more than is owed. Or, maybe we have become weak. Whatever we have become, I wish for it to change."

All eyes settled on Hori, who met Goto's eyes and said, "If I find out you have lied to me there will be war."

"I am not lying to you, Hori."

After a moment, Hori stood and the other Yakuza bosses followed suit.

Hori said, "It is time to take back what is ours. I will press to the leadership my desire for our clans to unite."

Gorokhov hid his elation—if Hori wanted an alliance, the Sumiyoshi-kai leadership would grant it.

Terukai said, "I will do the same."

"Then…brothers…I will look forward to your response," said Shintaro Goto. "Hori-san, I will locate this man for you. The vengeance will belong to the Sumiyoshi-kai alone."

He bowed with Hori, Terukai mirroring him.

"What about the man responsible for inventing this technology?"

"Leave him to us," said Gorokhov.

Bruce edged his black X5 up to the nineteenth century wrought iron gate and briefly admired the intricate swirls in the flower pattern design.

It opened without his getting out.

That Miles Parker had requested to meet him at the Surrey home of their mutual acquaintance, Henry Costner, and not at Vauxhall Cross, had compelled him to cut a lunch date with Adrianna.

The political fixer's UK home went from an expensive apartment in the city to the eight-bedroom, fifteenth-century grade II manor house in time with his move from Westminster to Brussels.

Bruce knew Costner's children had flown the nest, leaving just him and his wife, and the eight-bedrooms were only filled around half-a-dozen times a year when various European, and sometimes global, power players needed to discuss subjects privately.

After motoring slowly for a few hundred metres on the beige stone driveway, the red-brick, thatched-roofed manor house came into view.

A cluster of crown-topped chimneys seemed to rivet the grand house to the ground like tent pegs.

Beneath the archway of a wall leading around to the disused stables stood Costner, looking more relaxed and fresher than when Bruce had last seen him. His green shooting jacket matched his trousers and wrapped itself around a light brown, chunky jumper.

Bruce got out of the car and approached the fifty-four-year-old former public schoolboy, who smoothed back a silvery-brown fringe and offered a handshake.

"How are we, Bruce? It's been a long time."

"Around two years. You're looking well," replied the Scotsman, now suspecting a touch of Botox on closer inspection.

The black operations chief did not exert too much pressure on the politician's manicured hand.

"The pace in Brussels is more…leisurely," he answered with a smile. "And we won't pretend you didn't notice that I've had work done."

Bruce smiled, "Less is more with that from what I have seen."

"Duly noted," said Costner, stepping back and gesturing. "Shall we?"

Bruce followed Henry through the enclosed, sunlit garden and empty stables.

Miles Parker stood tall in the conservatory resembling a dwarf's house attached to the manor.

The two men shook hands hard as he crossed the threshold.

Fresh flowers entwined themselves throughout the room feathering the air with a pleasant scent. An assortment of tea, coffee and biscuits—none which would be touched by the two men—lay on a wicker table between a pair of yellow and orange sofa chairs.

"Gentlemen," announced Costner, clapping his hands together theatrically. "I will give you your privacy."

When he had closed the bi-doors, Bruce turned back to Parker and said, "It must be sensitive if you've excused him. Can't imagine he took it well."

The SIS chief shrugged. "He didn't assume or ask, and I didn't invite him."

The thought briefly appeared that maybe Costner did not have to attend the meeting to hear it. Henry had proved his loyalty to the good fight in the past, but Bruce knew that men could change. Still, he remained quiet, as he was here to gain information not to share it.

"And so?" asked Bruce.

Parker skipped any preamble to hand him a steel-jacketed USB in a clear plastic case.

So he doesn't have his fingerprints on the USB, thought Bruce.

"Cross-reference the information using whatever…off-site means you might have. Destroy it afterwards."

Before the Scotsman could answer, the Englishman brushed past him and left.

24

Sykes powered off his phone and nestled further into the pillows of his hotel bed.

The windows covered one entire wall, floor to ceiling. As he stared out at the night-lit city of Sapporo, he felt a sense of peace for the first time in weeks.

He had just finished his phone call to Chisato. He was glad to hear she had been given an unobtrusive protection team whilst in her United Kingdom asylum.

The declaration that the renewable energy technology trials would take place in Hiroshima and Nagasaki had been a publicity stunt and a ruse. Whilst old-model—though top of the range—systems were being placed there, here in Japan's most northern prefecture of Hokkaido, commenced the quiet installation of the truly new, revolutionary systems.

Now spring, the remnants of the winter snow could be seen in patches on the rooves of the buildings.

Installation had its challenges but were now satisfactorily implemented and there had not been any security breaches so far.

Sykes knew the difficulties would come once the area of installation expanded. The resources of the Okada security teams—both official and unofficial—would be stretched. Live feed cameras were placed over each installed renewable energy system as well as the area around it.

For the international distribution to go ahead the trials would need three months of proven effectiveness.

The business owners and residents who accepted the installations had been made to sign legal affidavits of strict secrecy.

The people who wanted to steal or sabotage the technology would be looking in the wrong places.

Ken would be arriving sometime during the night. Sykes left his keycard at the reception desk for him so the

Japanese engineer could take the bed beside him before being issued a separate room the next day.

The middle-aged scientist sunk into the bed in tandem with his eyelids. His brain's images began to detach themselves from his consciousness, and he soon fell asleep.

Sykes did not know if the click woke him or not. His eyes flew open as he processed that a revolver was aimed at his face.

"Ken! What the hell are you doing?" he exclaimed.

His heart pounded as he watched his friend's red, tear-stained eyes.

"I am so sorry, Ronald-san. They have my family."

"Whoa, whoa. Who has your family?"

"Them…the Yakuza. They send me a video. This is true. I must kill you. I am sorry my friend."

Ken shut his eyes tight and scrunched his face. The barrel moved to the side slightly before it blasted a slug into his pillow.

Sykes, with his ear popped into ringing, dived out of his bed like a twenty-one-year-old, tackling the smaller man to the floor.

The fight seemed to go out of Ken as he released the weapon. Sykes scrambled forward off his friend and snatched up the revolver.

He stood up to see Ken in the foetal position, sobbing.

The door to the room burst open, revealing two men of the Takato security, guns in hand.

Sykes raised a calming hand at the pair, who stood at his shoulder, their weapons pointing at Ken.

They barked at Ken in Japanese, one roughly frisking him, the other covering. They dragged the quivering engineer to his feet.

"Stop," said Sykes, forcefully enough for the two guards to comply. "We can use this to our advantage."

The guard to his left shook his head. "Takato-san must know. Police will now come. Guns are very serious in Japan."

"I am sure you can smooth that over," said Sykes, knowing the Gādian had already heavily baited the local police with hefty bribes. "This man's family has been threatened and that's why he's done this. But there is no reason why they can't be led to believe he has succeeded."

A glimmer of understanding shone from the bodyguard's eyes. "I speak to Takato-san."

Sykes just hoped Yasuhiro Takato had men cunning enough to seize back the initiative.

Akio Shigeta felt a near total relaxation he hadn't experienced in a long time. The stone-framed *onsen*—hot water spring—stroked his naked body with its soothing heat. Perched on the volcanic mountainside, the sights and sounds of nature and trickling water acted as a balm to the billionaire's constantly active mind.

The crystal glass of lemon chuhai with ice proved particularly refreshing.

The onsen seemed to be having a similar effect on the younger PSI officer. Hiroki Kobayashi had served Japan as well as any man he knew, and saw fit to reward him.

With only one way to and off the high platform in the form of a spiralling pebble path, Akio had posted his substantial security out of sight—and conversational earshot—of the pair.

Finally, Akio asked, "How did the mighty Yakuza boss act at the meeting?"

He saw Kobayashi smile before opening his eyes. "Like a cat trying to impersonate a lion."

"What about the Shinjuku squash court massacre?" asked Shingeta, referring to the name the media had given to it.

"He denies it of course. I must say that it did seem strange that he would order such a public shooting of mere underlings. I thought he might have targeted Ryoichi Hori himself, or at least one of the leadership council of the Sumiyoshi-kai," said Hiroki, taking his own lemon sour and sipping it before saying, "Good choice."

"It was recommended to me recently."

Shigeta felt a pang of guilt for not informing Hiroki of his suspicions of the true killer; the man named Connor. He had been the only one who gave the invader of his mansion, and destroyer of his security team, a fight.

He had been close to asking Ciara Robson if Connor had indeed been the Shinjuku hitman but decided he did not wish to know.

The entrepreneur saw no reason to tell Kobayashi of that night at his mansion; the attacker had somehow kept the security cameras from capturing his face and any DNA combing would just as likely turn up Connor's as much as the ghost's, which could lead to a diplomatic incident and public embarrassment to himself.

Instead, he offered, "Maybe that was the point. A grand statement of the Yamaguchi-gumi's fearlessness."

Kobayashi shrugged, "Then I would have expected his usual silence than his strenuous denial."

"I am not a fool, Hiroki-san, I realise there will always be organised crime, but once Okada sustains this technological breakthrough, the Yakuza's reliance on fossil fuel and nuclear energy will be their downfall."

The intelligence officer locked his eyes on his and said, "That will be a long, hard road, Akio-san. The Yakuza have been part of Japanese society for over three hundred years. They will not go down without a fight."

"If this was thirty years ago I might agree, but they are not what they once were. You have said so yourself, this younger generation are soft—and more like rats."

"And rats will fight when cornered. You should not be too confident. The Yakuza still have their claws in every layer of our society, and have many favours to draw upon."

"I will continue to support you financially, Hiroki," said Shigeta sincerely.

Given the PSI officer's recent successful operations against the Yakuza, in particular the Yamaguchi-gumi, the business mogul felt certain Kobayashi was honouring their agreement that the monies be used to 'grease the wheels' for operations against the Yakuza.

"I know and appreciate it. Although it is a dangerous risk—if people were to discover that I was taking money from one of Japan's richest men, then they will not listen to any explanation."

Men's shouts rose up the mountainside. Kobayashi bolted upright, swishing water over the lip, and exclaiming, "What is that?"

"I am sure it is just my security forbidding access to hikers. It often happens."

The shouts were cut short, giving credence to his hypothesis. However, Kobayashi looked agitated and said, "Do you hear that?"

"Hear what?" asked Shigeta, though the distant and faint clacks answered his own question.

"That."

When much louder—and closer— Akio Shigeta called out to his head of security, "Ichiro! What is that?!"

Kobayashi leapt out of the onsen, snatching a towel and roughly drying himself. As the younger man whipped a kimono on, Akio exclaimed, "Relax, Hiroki, I am sure it is—"

His words were cut short by Kobayashi's backwards jump into the onsen to the sound of clacks.

Shock froze Shigeta, as the intelligence officer's ripped face began to dye the water crimson.

Shigeta's eyes slowly rose to take in the sight of his trusted head of security, with a silenced pistol raised.

235

"Ichiro," he gasped. "What have you done?"

"I had to, boss," answered his chief protector, his voice tremoring, but then steeling when Shigeta attempted to get out of the onsen, "Stay where you are."

The pointing of the weapon emphasized his command.

Mikhail Gorokhov appeared beside Ichiro, with a similarly silenced weapon in his right hand, and a case in his left hand.

The Hāfu whispered, "It's done, Ichiro. Your family will now be released."

Shigeta's once most trusted employee's head and arms slumped before he slunk away.

The billionaire tried to muster strength in his voice. "What do you want?"

"The truthful answer to all my questions," said Gorokhov, before setting down the suitcase and continuing with, "Although it is doubtful you would lie or refuse after one attempt to."

Suddenly, Akio Shigeta felt very cold in the water.

Keizo Mori sat looking down through the glass at the passing street-lit traffic and pedestrians.

He found his usual anticipation of the first bite of the Full Moon Cheese Tsukimi Burger marred by the company of the three men sat at tables around him. Their milkshakes remained untouched.

He resented the Gādian bodyguards having to be with him for every single public outing. When a teenager spilled his Coca Cola on the floor just a minute ago, the trio jumped up like Habu Snakes. This compounded the youngster's embarrassment, who shot down the stairs, no doubt to inform the staff of his accident.

Keizo had been working for Okada for over four decades, and visiting McDonalds for nearly thirty, but could never have foreseen the day he would need an armed—though not displayed—escort for his bi-weekly visit.

He took his bite and admonished himself for his self-pity.

Surely it wouldn't be forever, and it was a small price to pay if it kept Kusama happy. He knew she saw him as family, especially since the death of her grandad—and his dear friend—Akebono Okada. She constantly scolded him on his love of fast food despite being, if anything, a touch under the ideal weight for his height and age.

He reciprocated her familial feelings. His pride had grown in watching her develop from a timid teenager to a highly competent businesswoman.

In the window's reflection, he caught the arrival of four uniformed McDonald's staffers, buckets in hand with the mops sticking out.

His jaws froze mid-bite as they pointed the bottom of their buckets directly at his bodyguards.

A cacophony of gunfire, screams, smashing glass and shouting exploded.

Keizo managed to turn to face the gunmen just as invisible, steel fists punched him in his chest.

He fell but did not land.

The realisation of flying away from the building hit a moment before the impact did. He became vaguely aware of people rushing past him on street, where he lay.

As the gunmen exited, and circled him with their submachine guns, the last thing he saw was a giant plastic carton of fries above the entrance smiling down at him.

25

Ciara sat in the cheap hotel room comprising beige walls and a floral bedspread—booked under a false identity earlier that day—at the small desk in front of her 'work' laptop.

Dressed in a loose khaki tracksuit, she fired up the computer and after a minute, Bruce's face appeared. After they went through their challenges and codes, the Scotsman asked, "How bad?"

"Very," she said, before giving him a rundown of the massacre of Akio Shigeta, his security team and the PSI officer named Hiroki Kobayashi, and finally the public murder of Keizo Mori.

Regarding several other attacks on Okada personnel, the Gādian had resisted without fatalities to those in their charge. Though one had been hospitalised by being 'winged' by a bullet.

She finished with, "Kusama Okada is said to be distraught and is laying the blame of Mori's murder on the Gādian's war with the rest of the Yakuza. If she shuns the Gādian assistance of security for her main players, then that is bad. The Yakuza still have various ties with law enforcement, but Yosuhiro Takato's hate for the other clans ensures against his corruption."

Bruce replied, "I am guessing Miss Okada's reaction is more of the knee-jerk variety. I have read the file our friend has worked up and understand she was very close to Mr Mori, but is a very pragmatic lassie."

"I hope so," answered Ciara. "Parts of the media are pointing the finger at the Gādian. No doubt stirred up with Yakuza money to put pressure on Okada and the government."

"Our tech friend believes that various government officials and wealthy patrons have been threatened. Which leads me on to Akio Shigeta."

"He was found dead in a mountainside onsen in Hakone, Fuji Hakone Izu National Park, along with his security team and a high-flying PSI officer, named Hiroki Kobayashi. From the little I have been able to glean, everyone died by being shot at close range, except Akio. He was found with his wrists handcuffed behind his back—heart failure was listed as the official cause of death."

She watched her boss's eyes dip for a moment before rising to meet hers. "Because he was interrogated with electricity. What did he know?"

"Aside from my killing the three Yakuza sent to 'question' me, he knew about Okada's breakthroughs, although it seems now like half of Japan knows about that. Other than that, I am not sure. I suspect he knows I am not simply a journalist. I guessed Akio had been 'questioned', which is why I dumped the rental car and booked another, and changed hotel rooms, under an alias."

"Good," he answered. "What's the plan now?"

"We've managed to get a possible location on where Kenjiro Uda's family is being held. Connor is organising an extraction. It needs to be done fast, given the circumstances."

"How does he seem?"

"When I last saw him, he seemed…muted. Said he'd never encountered a man like the one who broke into Akio's mansion. Did you manage get his identity?"

"His name is Mikhail Gorokhov. He is an SVR agent—went off the grid a few years back before returning to the fold. He was one of the most dependable operatives they have. I will send you a digital file of what we know of him so far."

"Okay."

"Who is assisting Connor?"

"An…acquaintance of his. He said you've met him before."

Connor held his crossed-legged forward bend on the green carpet of the bedroom of his temporary residence in Hinode. He began to 'box-breathe'—four seconds in, four seconds hold, four seconds out, four seconds hold—waiting for the tension to release.

The morning sun's rays warmed his face through glass framed by wooden-slatted walls.

He had taken a more aggressive approach to his flexibility after finding it nigh-on-impossible to pass the jiu-jitsu guard of a man back in Leeds, whom Connor was convinced could sleep with his feet behind his ears.

He thought about the brief Ciara had given him earlier—he realised, before she did, the Yakuza clans must have united to be this brazen. No single gang would have actioned so much carnage on their own for fear the other families would gain favour from the State.

The pointlessness of his killing spree at the squash court dawned.

Despite the mildness of the guilt—mainly centred on the initial youth he had murdered—he knew he wouldn't have had that sensation even a couple of years ago. And he felt a residue of unease to feel any repentance at all.

He began to cycle through the reasons he would feel remorse, before cutting the thought process off—it was not going to help.

Instead, as he changed stretching position, and began to think of the extraction of Uda's family, the IPad in front of him lit up. It showed the image of a Nissan X-Trail approaching the house.

Carlo Andaloro had forewarned him of the vehicle he would be driving. Still, Connor observed the screen until he saw the Italian stop and alight from the car alone.

He made his way down the stairs and opened the door to the 'Ndrangheta assassin, stepping back to allow him in.

The former marine noticed all the former 2REP paratrooper had, luggage-wise, was a green leather holdall.

"Travel light, I see," said Connor.

"Is this what the English call 'small talk'?"

"You're right…you don't look the type of man who'd want easing in, so to speak."

"I do want coffee before we talk," said the Italian, dumping his bag to one side of the kitchen door.

They sat facing one another across the kitchen table. Carlo took a sip, scrunched his face and said, "Better than I expected but still shit."

"You're welcome," said Connor sardonically.

"I would like to thank you. I understand you talked to the main man—vouched for me. Saved my life."

"I only did that so that you would end up owing me."

When Carlo looked at him, Connor could see him trying to work out if he was serious.

"You seem to forget I saved your life in real-time back in Castel Volturno."

The former Legionnaire referred to an incident where Connor, less than six months ago, had been tasked by the 'Ndrangheta to conduct a false flag operation to ignite a war between the Nigerian mafia operating on Italy's west coast and the Camorra based in Naples.

Despite Connor killing swathes of armed African gangsters, he found himself hemmed in and facing imminent death, before Carlo intervened with his superb sniping.

"I haven't forgotten, but if you don't owe me—which you don't—then why have you come over?"

The Italian took a moment to reply. "I like the thrill of combat. You guessed this, and this is why you called me. So, tell me the details."

"The first thing I will tell you is that in addition to helping look after my family's foreign business interests, I am an agent for a black operations unit."

241

Carlo sipped his coffee, and said, "That night in Castel Volturno showed me you were no criminal, or any mere soldier. I knew there was something. So, you were targeting us?"

By 'us' he meant the 'Ndrangheta. Connor had thought long and hard over how to answer this question. He could easily lie and claim that the Chameleon Project was targeting 'Ndrangheta underboss Salvatore Mancuso. The powerful Mancuso had been conducting activities independent of the 'Ndrangheta, including the global kidnap of 'useful' people to brainwash them before selling them on.

He remembered what his father had once told him—*There is a difference between refusing to answer and lying. People lie because they are scared…scared of the consequences of telling the truth…only pussies lie.*

Still, if Carlo told his bosses back in Calabria, it would not only be Connor's head, but his family's.

"Yes."

A Berretta M9 appeared in Carlo's right hand. "Why should I not kill you right now?"

Connor breathed slowly through his nose, and shrugged, "Why shouldn't you?"

The moments seemed to stretch out, as Connor's heartbeat tapped his eardrums.

"Because you could be too much fun," Carlo laughed, while keeping the Berretta pointed at him. "You are a man of honour. I need you to swear that you will never go against us again."

"I can't swear to that. My allegiance isn't to you or the 'Ndrangheta."

"Even with a pistol pointed at you by a killer, you refuse to say what must be said to save your own life."

"I don't know what to tell you," answered Connor. "Other than it would be difficult to conduct operations against your organisation now that their best assassin knows my identity."

Connor could feel his face vibrating as he watched Carlo's eyes.

The Italian slid his Beretta beneath the table. "Give me the details of why I am here."

Takato hid his rising concern as he faced his men. He could only hear the soft chirps of Lidth's jays and the rushing water of the brook outside this make-shift temple.

The five men—dressed in attire suitable for the outdoors—stood around him in a semi-circle, forming his inner council.

One of his advisors said, "In protecting the Okada staffers, we are exposing ourselves. Our strength has always been in our guerrilla stance and tactics—we do not have the numbers to endure a standing defence of these people for long."

Takato answered, "Leaving Okada personnel unprotected is not an option. We will ride the storm for however long it might take."

He studied their reactions and continued with, "There might be an opportunity. The location of Keniro Uda's family might be soon discovered. A rescue attempt will be mounted."

"Where is the engineer now?" asked another. "I heard that he attempted to murder Ronald Sykes."

Takato answered, "He failed either from his nerve abandoning him or his incompetence. Mercifully, the police were never called, despite a shot being fired—through a pillow."

"What has happened to the engineer?"

"We have him. We could use this situation to our advantage. We could feed our enemies' disinformation for the time being, but they will kill the family as soon as they know he has been successful. I have a suspicion that at least one of the clan bosses might be holed up at the same place."

"Boss, how can we rescue them without the hostages being killed? I am not aware of anyone within our ranks who might have the skills needed to extract them without harm."

"I might know someone who can," answered the outlaw leader. "But if they are unsuccessful, we might have the opportunity to strike back at the heart of our enemies."

26

Kasumi Uda held her children as they slept in her arms. Her rage at their kidnapper's attempts to separate her from the children had convinced the captors to leave them together.

The morning light began to illuminate the surreal direness of their situation.

A couple of mattresses had been thrown into a room, bare apart from a crude, make-shift toilet which had at least been afforded the decency of a taut ivory rice paper shield.

Five days ago, they had snatched her and the two boys in the night. They had ensured their calm silence with the threat, *'If you boys are not silent, we will kill your mum. And if you make a scene, we will kill one of your boys'*.

They had endured the drive blindfolded for what seemed like hours and hours. Unsure whether or not she had slept, she recalled the bumpy ascent on the last part of the journey.

When they prodded her and the kids out of the van, her heart sunk on seeing the run-down wooden building surrounded by the mountain forest. Even if she could escape, she had no clue where they were or how far from civilisation.

She had guessed who these men were and deduced it must have been to get to Kenjiro.

The boot to the door shocked her boys awake. They pressed into her hard.

The suited man looked prestigious in comparison to their dirty and dishevelled appearance.

He held a sectioned tray with rice, steamed vegetables and fish. He placed it on the floor and said, "You will eat. Then you will empty the bucket and be washed."

"I will not leave my children's side for a moment."

The man smiled, "We choose that, not you. For now it makes sense for you to comfort your children but do not test us. You have no power—especially not here. Be obedient, and maybe if your husband is too, you and your sons might live."

Kasumi painted an expression of belief on her face, and said, "We will not be any trouble."

"Good."

He left, and she shooed her sons to eat. She felt cold, despite the sun skimming her skin—*If they were going to let us go, why would they be so bold as to show their faces?*

Kenjiro sat staring at the orange, black and white painting of the underside of a Koi fish. It taunted him with its freedom out of a net.

The men had smuggled him to one of the Okada offices in Sapporo. Sykes had assured him he would be okay to be taken by his protective team, but in truth he had not cared about his own well-being since receiving the pictures of his wife and sons, followed by a phone call.

He had drifted in and out of sleep after eating a bowl of buckwheat and fish.

The father of two hadn't smoked in a long time but found himself craving one now.

He straightened up at the opening of the door.

Ronald Sykes came in and Kenjiro fought back tears. "I am sorry, so sorry, Ronald-san, I—"

"Do not be silly, Kenjiro-san. They have your family, you were doing what any loving husband and father would have done."

Kenjiro hung his head at the words. Sykes continued, "A man is about to enter. He can help, Kenjiro-san."

Sykes walked to the door and tapped on it.

A *Gaijin* with dark blond hair and blue eyes entered. Though he towered over Kenjiro, he was not overly tall or heavy for a European, despite seeming to fill the room. The brown leather, fur-lined jacket parted at the front to show

246

his muscle definition through a white t-shirt. He held a laptop case in his left hand.

Sykes said to the man, "Kenjiro knows you're here to help."

"I appreciate it," he replied.

Sykes turned to Kenjiro. "You're in good hands, Ken-san."

He clapped Kenjiro on the shoulder and left. The Japanese man briefly wondered if the closing of the door signified the end of their personal and professional relationships.

The man spoke first, "I have been told you speak English very well, Uda-san. Which is good, as my Japanese is rudimentary."

He placed the laptop case on the chrome table to his left, Kenjiro's right, and sat on the chair opposite.

"Who are you?"

"My name is Connor. I am here to get your family back."

"Ho…how?"

"You've been given a contact number. We are going to trace it."

Kenjiro's heart pulsated in his chest. "You cannot. They warned me they will know if traced and they would kill my family. Please no. Please no. Please—"

"Will you pack it in," said Connor sharply. "I understand it's stressful for you, but you aren't going to be any help to anyone, least of all your wife and kids, if you let emotion control you. That's basic Jap Zen."

Kenjiro opened his mouth to retort, but closed it on looking into Connor's eyes. He slowly nodded but said calmly, "Please do not trace the call."

The Englishman sat next to him and said, "Calls to mobiles—cell phones, can be traced when the police get access to phone companies' cell towers. With you being an Einstein, you'll already know it's the strength of the signal that determines the distance, and three towers can triangulate it."

"Yes, I know of this," said Kenjiro. "I also know the Yakuza control much of the phone companies. They are everywhere. As soon as the police or anyone makes a request, my family die."

Connor reached into his pocket and opened his palm to reveal a SIM card in a clear plastic casing.

"This can mimic any number. When you call from it, it can pinpoint the exact GPS position of the receiver, without being detected."

"Impossible," exclaimed Kenjiro, angry that the man would try to deceive him like this. "You are lying."

The Japanese man's head snapped forward under the smacking clamp of a hand on the back of his neck. The Gaijin's steel fingers torqued his head to face his flaming blue eyes.

"I am many things, but I am not a fucking liar—don't call me one again," hissed the Englishman, before releasing him and saying in a softer tone, "I'll convince you. Do you know anyone you can call right now to test?"

Kenjiro, after thawing from the shock, thought for a moment. "I have a friend I can call."

"Okay," said Connor, handing Kenjiro the case. "Stick that in your phone."

The Japanese man did so after subduing his suspicion. The Brit took out the laptop and fired it up.

After a few seconds he asked, "Tell me friend's number."

Kenjiro did so as Connor's fingers tapped away.

He said to Ken, "When you call him, I'll show you on this screen exactly where he is. You can confirm by asking him whatever questions you like. *Rikai?*"

"Yes. I understand."

"Repeat what I have just said."

"I call him. You show me where he is. I ask him questions to know the truth."

"Exactly. Go ahead."

Kozo, his old University drinking partner, answered after three rings, answering in their native tongue. "Hello you invisible bastard. How are you?"

"I am good. I am good. Just been very busy."

A silence passed. "You do not sound good."

"It is a very stressful time," replied Kenjiro truthfully. Connor spun the laptop around to show a Google Maps image of his friend's exact location. "Where are you Kozo?"

"I am in Tokyo buying my wife a handbag."

"Where exactly in Tokyo?"

"Why? Are you close? Want to meet for food and drink?"

"No, I am just curious."

"Ginza district."

"Which shop?"

His friend chuckled, "You want to know what handbag shop I am in?"

"Please, Kozo. It is important."

"I am in Kanematsu."

Kenjiro looked up at the Englishman, who turned the laptop back around once he'd nodded.

"Kozo, I have to go. Something important has arisen. One day I wish to meet you for food and drinks."

He hung up before his friend could answer, and said in English, "I maybe believe you. But they might have a system to know the call is traced."

"Believe me, they don't."

"If you find them, can you save my family?"

The dark-blond looked at him a moment. "There will be no guarantees. But these are your options. You can do nothing—in which case your family's captors will start to 'convince' you to act. You can go to the police—you will have to lie about how you know where they are being held, and hope your report isn't leaked to whoever is holding your family. Or you can choose to allow me to help you."

249

Kenjiro's brain, though greased with fear, still retained its analytical processes. Sykes said this man could help him. He had shown the technology worked. And if Kenjiro did go to the police, he estimated there was a seventy-five percent chance he'll have signed his family's death warrant.

He looked at the Koi fish painting and then back at Connor Reed. "You are the best option."

"Good. Let's make this call," said the Englishman.

Kenjiro noticed the expression on his face and asked, "What is it?"

Connor Reed murmured, "Let's hope the Yakuza believed you and have not sent a team up here."

27

Gorokhov sat back from his hotel window, peering through the high-powered mounted telescopic. He watched Ronald Sykes step out onto the street as if the Brit stood three metres away and not the three-hundred and thirteen displayed on the bottom-left of the sight's picture.

He had an easier time picking out the Englishman than he'd usually have due to the scientist's security detail highlighting him. Not that the average civilian would notice them, but to the former SVR agent Sykes may as well have worn a halo.

The Japanese-Russian clicked the tiny communications set clipped to his collar. "He's walking south on Soseigawa-dori Avenue. Has a significant security detail around him, so maintain your distance at all times. Losing him is a lesser evil than being spotted."

Gorokhov had felt a sense of unease at not being able to use professionals for this type of work. None of the Yakuza foot-soldiers had been exposed to the level of instruction and practice needed to become an effective shadow.

Though the three Yakuza clans had formed an uneasy alliance which had proved effective so far, Gorokhov knew their rivalry could spur them into mistakes.

He did not yet know if members of Japanese law enforcement or the Gādian made up Sykes's security team.

As the sight-picture of the telescope framed Sykes's face, Gorokhov contemplated how easy it would be to simply shoot him.

However, they needed to interrogate him to discover where any backup files were, and who else might have sufficient knowledge of the technology.

All he needed was to get to know the man's routine, and he'd deal with the security team and snatch Ronald Sykes himself.

He could not tell if he felt glad or disappointed that he could not see the man with the dark blond hair within the security detail.

Then he realised he was professionally glad, as it would make the task easier, but personally disappointed—as he needed to put the man down.

The pair of red wine glasses clinking down on the table broke his attention.

Bruce snapped hold of his urge to cover the laptop screen. Instead, he focused his strained eyes on the faint moon through his apartment window.

Adrianna's fingers instantly relaxed his shoulders.

"You have been staring at that screen for over two hours," she said softly.

"Chasing ghosts," he murmured.

"Can I help?"

Ordinarily, he would have turned her down. However, now he had exhausted all reasonable avenues, he felt the exercise to be hypothetical.

"Numerous conspiracy theories surround the Lebanese Civil war, as well as other conflicts pertaining to the middle-east. People want a silver bullet explanation to a multi-faceted situation. However, that does not mean people stood to benefit from the situation. Aside from the usual suspects, arms companies, Israel, America and the Soviet Union."

"Why are you discounting them?"

"I have my reasons."

Adriana sat on the chair beside him, pulling her satin black dressing gown to cover her chest. She sipped her wine. "Western Europe prospered in the post-war era. The middle-east has land mass and oil wealth, but first found themselves as a major chess board on which the cold war was played out. Even when the IRA, ETA, OAS were at their height, the deaths, injury and damage they did are very, very small in scale compared to Lebanon—no matter the rest of the middle-east. No refugees from the United Kingdom, France, Germany, Spain or Italy."

The Scotsman knew the fatalities from the Lebanese Civil War alone stood at around 150,000 and precipitated a mass exodus of close to a million.

"I'll pop it in the think tank to see if it floats," he said, closing the laptop. "There are other challenges for now needing attention."

Shintaro Goto stood alone in his office.

Unable to contain his temper, he shouted down the secure line at his Sumiyoshi-kai counterpart, "How could you be so foolish, Ryoichi? And reckless? Killing the British inventor will not solve our problems—this technology will have back-ups, and there might be others."

The retort barked down the line. "He is the architect, you said so yourself."

"Don't you understand? If we simply kill him and get rid of the technology, we will become pariahs and will be hunted to the end. But if we control the technology, we bend anyone to our will."

"That was not what you said at the meeting."

"We must be mindful of what we say to outsiders. I did not realise I would have to explain that to you."

"*Your* outsider."

"Outsiders can be useful as long as you control them and not the other way around. And I did not think you would take matters into your own hands without consulting Terukai-san or I first."

"And you consult me on all your actions Shintaro? Do I have to call you when I need to take a shit?"

Goto pinched the bridge of his nose. At one time he would have engineered a war just to kill the upstart, and perhaps that time would come again, but for now he knew had to assuage the ego of the younger man.

"Of course not, Hori-san. The westerners have an expression, that it is bad when the left hand does not know what the right hand is doing," said Goto, smoothing his tone. "I will, with yours and Teruaki's permission, arrange for the inventor to be taken. You have done good work locating him. That is something that we could not do."

After a moment, Ryoichi Hori said, "I will agree if Teruaki-san does."

"I need to action this immediately to close any chance of his escape. If you say yes, I will proceed."

"Then you have my consent."

Goto smiled, and said, "Could you petition him, Hori-san? Your ability of persuasion exceeds mine."

"Yes, Goto-san, he will see the logic of our plan," said Hori, before changing tack. "And you can relax. The inside man is one of the British engineer's closest colleagues. He has not reported that he has killed Sykes-san, and I can call him off—if there is time. And we can keep him as an inside man."

"I am impressed, Hori-san. How?"

"We have his family."

After a moment, Goto asked, "Where?"

"They are with me at an undisclosed location."

The Yamaguchi-gumi boss did not want to give the younger man the satisfaction of refusing to answer the question of where.

"Thank you for agreeing to convince Terukai-san," said Goto. "Remember, Hori-san, this inside man may delay passing on any knowledge of Sykes-san's location because of their friendship. Maybe you can send him a reminder of what will happen if he is uncooperative."

Goto could almost see the younger crimelord's smile.

"I think that is a good idea."

The call ended and Goto relaxed into the chair. Ryoichi had a flaming insecurity that proved easy to manipulate. He could become a useful ally if handled correctly. When he had surpassed his usefulness, Goto would find a way to discard him—as in much the same manner as Ryoichi Hori would discard the engineer's family.

28

Connor crouched down in the forest of Akiogahara, known as the sea of trees, surrounded by a surreal silence. The density of the trees helped block any animal noises, with the hardened lava of the 864 BC eruption of Mount Fuji absorbing the rest of the sounds.

Known as the 'Suicide Forest', though he had kept off any obvious tracks, he saw a sign which, although he could not precisely decipher, he knew to be urging any potential suicide visitors to think of their families.

He had asked Yasuhiro Takato that he and Carlo be inserted two hours ahead of the Gādian strike team; he knew the chances of the Udas surviving a clan-on-clan shoot-out would be slimmer than his and Carlo's attempt at a stealth extraction.

Low-level anxiety simmered within the agent, not because of the danger of what he was about to attempt—that would come when he stood on the precipice of doing it—but because he was late.

Not to be late had been drilled into him by his father, who told him, *"You can recover from illness and injury. Lots of millionaires have previously gone bankrupt—some more than once. But time is something you can't get back once it's gone—the people who think it's acceptable to be late for someone are either losers who aren't doing anything with their time and so don't realise how precious it is to someone else, or people who don't respect you enough. Don't be late for anyone you respect."*

And the notion of punctuality had been ruthlessly reinforced in his recruit training for the Royal Marines, *"From now on, you will be five minutes early for every single detail or else your arms will be bending and stretching* (Press Ups) *until your eyes bleed. If you're on ops and the helo* (Helicopter) *is due to leave at a certain time it isn't going to wait for 'Marine Fucknuts' to hurry up."*

His lateness now had been due to the Gādian driver having to negotiate various law enforcement road blocks leading up to the DOP (Drop-off point). Connor had reluctantly accepted the Gādian's offer to insert him due to the time constraints the Uda family were under, and had been impressed that they had sent civilian scouts up ahead to report back on such unexpected events.

Still, they hadn't quite left enough time to ensure punctuality.

Eventually, Connor insisted on being dropped off in the general vicinity to make his own way to the LOD (Line of Departure). However, due to the dense forest affecting the short-range PRRs—Personal Role-Radios—they had chosen to use, he could not raise Carlo to warn him of the potential delay.

In addition to the FIWAF training—Fighting In Woods And Forests—and the operations conducted in the 'green zones' of Afghanistan as a Royal Marine, Connor had undertaken a month-long course with Finnish Special Forces. During the hundred-and-five day winter campaign against the Russians during World War II, some estimates had the Finns claiming five Soviet lives to every one of theirs.

The insertion in had been hard. Although of a high level of physical fitness, his days of hard *yomping*—marching under heavy weight—had been years ago and he had so far covered eighteen kilometres in just under three hours. Not that he carried as much weight now as he did back then—his current operational daysack being a third of the poundage of a full field Bergen.

He shielded his GPS watch to check the time and his direction and distance to the target. He was still behind the agreed on ETA.

Connor began hiking with more ferocity through the conifers and broadleaf trees, though ensuring he did not snap any of the branches; there wasn't anything he could do regarding leaving footprints.

He became aware of sacrificing his ability to hear any potential patrols before they could hear him, but dismissed it as the lesser of the two evils.

Cupping the face of the watch, he glanced down to see that he had exceeded the check-in time by nearly two minutes with his position being still fifty-seven metres away.

He cut through the forest harder, aware Carlo would likely give him no more than a five-minute grace period.

The sweat slid down his camouflaged-creamed forehead as he reached the lip overlooking the wooden fortress holding the Uda family hostage.

He heard it before he saw it—loud grunts interspersed with hissing.

Connor turned slowly. His heart leapt into his throat.

The two-hundred and fifty pound, black-furred beast stared through him with white, pupil-less eyes.

Though the British Isles had an almost complete lack of wild animals able to kill humans, watching the Japanese black bear coil into a crouch, he instinctively knew it wanted to slay him.

Connor's thinking compressed into microseconds in the face of death. He carried an FN Five-Seven pistol in a holster on his hip, but the suppressed Heckler & Koch UMP 45 lay in his operational daysack.

It had been decided it would be improbable that the Yakuza kidnappers would conduct security patrols due to the density of the forest and their lack of military training. And if he were to detect them, he was to skirt around and not engage them; therefore his only 'silenced' weapon immediately to hand was his Commando dagger.

His screaming primal survival instinct almost completely drowned out the realisation any gunshots would be heard by the guards below.

The bear charged with roaring, saliva-dripping fangs displayed.

Carlo felt a sense of unease as the check-in time approached. He had expected Connor Reed to arrive at his LUP—Lay-up point—in good time, as had he.

The former Legionnaire—clad in a *ghillie suit*—had spent the hour observing the small clearing through the scope of his FR F2 sniper rifle. Behind him lay a drag bag—a daysack designed to carry a sniper rifle—as well as his rations, ghillie suit and optics.

There did not seem to be any discernible sentry routine, with the Yakuza members milling in and around the structure, some coming out to smoke while leaning against vehicles, a white Lexus RX, a Blue Hyundai i20 and a black Nissan Qashqai, inappropriate for the carved-out forest vehicle paths. Their pistols were displayed in their belts and the submachine guns hung beneath their armpits.

It both heartened and disappointed him to watch their unprofessionalism. Glad their chances of success in this rush of a mission seemed greater, but disappointed that they might not be a test.

Also, Carlo did not like amateurs' unpredictability, especially when the stakes included the lives of two children and their mother.

He glanced at his watch—*he's late, something must be wrong.*

The Italian knew why he didn't kill the Englishman when it was perfectly reasonable, and perhaps even prudent, to do so; he knew of the deceptive masks of betrayal worn by men of supposed honour and thus respected a man who could unflinchingly tell him a life-threatening truth.

Nevertheless, the former 2 REP soldier now knew to stay would make him the amateur—cut-off times were implemented for a reason. However, on the precipice of combat, he could not bring himself to abort just yet.

Five minutes, not a second longer, he decided.

His eyes flickered across the clearing to the lip on the higher ground where Connor was meant to be.

Carlo thought he had imagined the sound of a large animal roaring, but realised it was real when the heads of the men below snapped towards the noise too.

The four cracks of gunfire boomed out across the clearing.

His earpiece crackled for a brief second before the Englishman's voice came alive, "Bear attacked me. I am okay. Abort or proceed? Your call."

Due to there only being two of them, they had decided in the planning stage to dispense with the use of call signs to shave off time in their communications with one another.

"We've been compromised," stated Carlo. "Let's proceed."

"This is why we are mates," replied Connor. "I'll use the same *LOD*, out."

A strange swirl of both hope and fear expanded in Kasumi Uda's chest at the sound of gunshots.

The quiet breezed in before an explosion of cries and shouts reverberated through the walls, followed by gunfire much closer than the previous four shots.

She grasped her sons by their shoulders and pulled them down, hissing, "On your stomachs. Flat as jellyfish."

Her heart bled to see the terrified face of her youngest.

The door burst open to reveal Ryoichi Hori—the man whose feet she and her sons had been thrown at on arrival. The man they all either called Sosai—director-general, or Oyabun—Boss.

He had a pistol in his hand.

The menace marched straight over, snatched a fistful of her hair, dragging her back into the corner.

Her eldest boy ran at the man in a fury, only to fly backwards after receiving the back of the man's snapping hand.

Hori's soft-skinned hand wrenched her hair, stretching her throat taut, as he barked, "I will fucking shoot your mother if you do not keep still."

The threat froze her boys as, outside, the gunfire intensified.

"Keep away from the windows boys," she yelped, the barrel pressed firmly into the back of her head.

Connor stepped over the skull-smashed bear as he began fitting the suppressor to his UMP 45 while on the move.

A tiny part of him had hoped Carlo would call it off. Even before his agent training with The Chameleon Project, Connor trained in assaulting buildings with both the fast, aggressive US MOUT (Military Operations in Urban Terrain) and the more systematic British version FIBUA (Fighting In Built-Up Areas).

However, both systems relied on manpower. He remembered on his agent's course by the cockney instructor that attempting a building assault against multiple armed adversaries was '…*a pretty fackin' gnarly way to commit suicide. Unless yer Neo off The Matrix, only do it if there is no other way.*'

He scolded himself for insisting he and Carlo go up ahead of the rest. At the time, he preferred to go in alone with Carlo as a sniper over watch than with a load of Gādian gunslingers.

You've put in thousands of hours training. You have a tonne of operational experience. You're one of the best small arms shooters in the world. You have body armour. You'll be okay.

His earpiece came alive. "I have eliminated four. Others are now hidden from view on your side of the building. I will watch for runners, over."

"Acknowledged, out."

Using the treeline, Connor ascended in a curve towards the original LOD facing the building on a ninety-degree angle to Carlo's elevated position.

In addition to the four corpses, seven armed men had their backs to the building, hidden from Carlo's field of fire, and were pointing their weapons up towards his previous position. Though the numbers posed a dangerous challenge, he reckoned he'd dealt with worse.

Just as he lined the crosshairs of the scope onto his first target, three black motorcycles—including both a helmeted rider and a gun-wielding pillion—and a blue Toyota Tundra 4x4 rumbled up the vehicle path on the far side of the compound. The men in the flatbed fired AK variants wildly in the general direction of Carlo's position.

With their numbers and firepower now bolstered, Connor knew the best tactical and strategic decision would be to withdraw. With Kenjiro Uda in Takato's possession, and his lack of knowledge regarding the renewable sites, it meant saving his family was now superfluous to the overall objective. He would be asking Carlo to trade the high risk of losing his life for the low probability of success.

He briefly scrunched his eyes as the picture of Grace and her son—maybe his son—entered his mind.

Carlo's voice, crisp and calm, came over the Net, "They have pushed me off position. Awaiting your orders for reposition, over."

Connor smiled, *Crazy Italian cunt wants to fight it out.*

He replied, "Skirt around the east side. I'll draw them on."

"Acknowledged, out."

Not knowing where the hostages were located inside, Connor and Carlo had opted for flash-bangs and smoke over frag grenades; a decision he now regretted seeing the seven bunched as they were. In addition, open spaces reduced the effectiveness of stun grenades.

Beggars can't be choosers.

After a minute, the former Legionnaire's voice sounded. "In position. The north side of the building is clear. There is an entrance on the end closest to you."

"Acknowledged, out."

262

With that, the former Royal Marine threw the flash-bang so that it bounced off the south-facing roof before detonating above their heads in a blinding bang.

As the collective staggered, Connor fired on the run, making short work of the first four. A burst of automatic AK return fire from a death twitch caused him to dive to his left.

Scrambling up, he kept his barrel facing the south side's corner as he reversed to the north side.

"They are using the vehicles as cover," said Carlo. "I am pinned here and they are entering the house, over."

Connor knew the 7.62MM calibre rounds the AKs fired could still be lethal even after punching through wood.

He spun around the corner to face the entrance and crashed his boot through it. One target fell under the two clacks of his UMP.

The wooden frame shredded into screaming splinters under a hail of heavy rounds. Connor dropped to a crouching position. For a split second he contemplated simply firing off a burst around the corner without exposing his head. However, without his eyes being on the hostages, he decided against it.

He knew the panicked shouting was alerting everyone to his presence inside.

Risking two seconds to take his supporting left hand off the UMP, he ripped out and pulled the pin on the flash-bang. Letting the fly-off lever go, he waited two seconds before throwing it around the corner. With a fuse delay of three and a half seconds, he barely had time to clamp the heels of his palms to his ears before the reverberation of the explosion hit his body.

Rising to his feet, he spun around the corner and supported his firing position against the partially destroyed doorframe.

The three AK-wielding black-suited and helmeted men resembled staggering Xenomorphs from the Alien film franchise. Their shiny black domes impacted inwards,

263

spitting out black polycarbonate plastic and a glob of blood under the *phuft* of his trigger squeeze.

Carlo blasted in his ear. "Get out. North side. Now."

The Yorkshireman exploded back out the door as a fusillade of bullets tore into the south side wall. Carlo's voice instructed him. "East side is clear. Head there. I'll cover you."

The Chameleon Project agent's adrenaline-pumped legs flew him along, as he fitted a fresh magazine.

Seeing the east side's door, he prepared himself to enter when Carlo stopped him. "I think they are preparing to come down and around the north side. If we wait, we can eliminate them in the open. Over."

Connor, weapon still facing the entrance, replied, "Give me the order and I'll throw a flashbang."

The seconds past slowly as he remained poised.

"Throw out fifteen metres…right…about…now."

The former marine did so. He took a crouching, supported position, and began shooting.

Caught out in the open, they fell like skittles under Carlo's and Connor's combined fire, and the Yorkshireman felt a shade of guilt.

Seeing the strewn gaggle no longer possessing a threat, he withdrew back to the east side's door.

He reloaded, despite knowing he had almost half the magazine left, and refocused.

Having watched another soldier spending a full minute booting a door in on a marine training exercise, only for his corporal to open it by the handle, Connor did the same.

The door swung in and Connor 'pied' it off as much as possible before entering.

The silence blended with familiar smells of nitroglycerine, sawdust, graphite and blood iron. One of the shot-up Yakuza men writhed a little too energetically for his liking. He removed his Commando dagger, spun it into a *Psycho*-grip and hammered the blade into the point where the

264

spine met the base of the skull. His victim vibrated into stillness and Connor used a boot between the shoulder blades as traction to remove the deeply embedded knife.

He heard fast breathing and muffled groans coming from behind the door to his right. Opening it with his foot, he looked in.

A little boy, he recognised to be the younger of the two brothers, Tamio, bled from a wound to the side of his belly, his head cradled by a boy marginally bigger, his elder brother, Keiji.

Connor recognised the wild-eyed man to be Ryoichi Hori, the sosai of the Sumiyoshi-kai clan. And the woman, whose head he had the pistol pressed against, to be Kasumi Uda; her eyes weeping desperate tears.

The back of her head covered her restrainer's lower face and thus his medulla oblongata—the brain's messaging centre located at the base of the skull. Connor could not risk a shot as even if his round hit the man in the head before he could consciously squeeze his own trigger; his death twitch might kill her.

If Tamio could be saved, it had to be now.

Ryoichi barked, "Put down weapons."

Connor surreptitiously pushed down the communication-opening pressel button of his PRR with his elbow.

"Calm down, Hori-san. I'll let you escape by jumping out that window."

The Yakuza boss shouted, "Put down weapons. I will kill her."

"You won't, Hori-san, because I will kill you," said Connor with injected confidence. "Now just stand up, climb out of that window and go."

The Japanese man's voice turned icy. "I will escape when you empty hands. Talk long time and the boy empty of blood—die."

Connor's peripheral vision caught the treeline through the window. Taking a guess at the man's confidence

265

in using a pistol at range, Connor walked backwards, passing the boys to the far right corner.

"Okay. You win. I am laying down my weapon."

The moment Connor unslung and laid down his UMP and stood, the man violently threw Kasumi to one side.

Levelling his pistol at Connor, he marched forward. Passing the window both his gun and the hand holding it exploded like a pomegranate filled with metal shards.

Connor charged forward, putting his full weight and leverage into a blockbusting right hand through the point of the Yakuza sosai's jaw. The unconscious body collapsed to one side.

Connor rushed to Tamio, his hand ripping open the webbing pouch containing his first aid kit.

He touched the pressel. "Target down. One of the boys is hit. Over."

"On my way, out."

Keiji clutched his brother, whose eyelids fluttered.

Connor ripped away the clothing, exposing the bleeding site. He recognised it to be shrapnel instead of a gunshot, but being a catastrophic bleed, he treated that first by way of a quick sterilisation and applied pressure with specialist bandage.

He shook the boy gently by the shoulders and called out, "Tamio."

No response.

Ear pinch—no response.

Connor checked his airway—clear, breathing— shallow, pulse—weak, disability—no evidence of any broken bones.

The heads of Kasumi and Keiji wheeled towards the doorway, their eyes wide with fear.

He admired Carlo's fitness in arriving so quickly.

Connor gestured behind him. "It's okay. Friend. Friend."

He turned.

It wasn't Carlo

A Yakuza foot soldier had an AK47 aimed directly at him. The AK47, due to the space between the working parts, meant though bad for accuracy—negligible at this range—it very rarely jammed.

Connor felt a bolt of anger at himself and fear for Tamio. Even civilian first-aiders were taught a version of the acronym DRABC where the 'D' stood for 'assess for Danger' before carrying out the Response, Airway, Breathing and Circulation checks.

Now everyone's going to die because of your incompetence.

The man's head snapped to his left, presumably at the sound of Carlo's entry.

Connor unholstered his FN Five-Seven, extended his arm and fired, all within a fraction of a second.

The Yakuza's face spewed bone and blood as he fell.

Carlo appeared and Connor said, "I haven't cleared the building but this lad hasn't got long."

"I will cover you. Let's go."

"I have to make sure that this guy is still here for Takato's lads to question," said Connor, who rapidly shot the Sumiyoshi-kai crime lord in the knees, ankles and his 'good' hand. He knew where to hit to minimalize the risk of death through blood loss—and preferred it to the unreliable pistol whip because of the greater degree of physical and psychological damage it would cause.

Next he scooped Tamio up as Carlo barked at Kasumi and Keiji to rise and follow.

Bursting out of the door, they found the keys still in the ignition of the Tundras.

With Carlo gunning the engine, Connor, feeling the wetness of the bandage beneath his fingers, asked God for help for only the second time in his adult life.

29

Ciara stood in the hospital corridor watching the surgeon speaking to the huddled Uda family outside the room where the young boy was being operated on.

Her phone vibrated, and she turned away from the scene to answer.

"Hello."

Bruce McQuillan's voice sounded clear. "Give me an update."

Ciara turned and began walking back down the corridor.

"Give me one minute."

She reached the glass exit doors into the cold air, removed the mask covering her mouth and said, "The extraction was a success but the youngest boy caught shrapnel. His condition is critical but stable. And Ryoichi Hori has been taken alive by the Gādian. I am not entirely sure how they are going to use him."

She looked out onto the next block, where white-helmeted Japanese construction labourers worked with seemingly ruthless efficiency.

"Where's Connor?" asked Bruce.

"Making his way back up to Sapporo."

"How does he seem?"

"Better. He seemed initially affected by his encounter with the unknown man who invaded Akio Shigeta's mansion."

"Who is watching over Sykes now?"

"A mixed security team of Gādian members and law enforcement."

"How far is Okada from implementing all their systems?"

"Sixty-three percent complete. The fact that all information is kept with Ronald Sykes is a double-edged sword. The risk of leaks is minimised but if anything happens to him then the whole show collapses."

"We best make sure nothing happens to him then. There are powers at play that I don't even know about yet."

Alexey Orlov stared out on the arctic wasteland of the Russian archipelago of Novaya Zemlya.

The warmth of the high-tech dacha juxtaposed with the scene of a distant polar bear sniffing around the steel apparatus of an on-land oil drilling rig. The room's specialised glass seemed absent until touched.

The Russian SVR Chief stiffened at the sound of the voice.

"Thank you for meeting me, Alexey," said the voice in flawless Russian, despite Orlov knowing it not to be the man's first language.

Orlov turned to greet the tall—only a hint of a stoop—eighty-nine-year-old, bald oligarch. The man's white beard and grey, flecked moustache contrasted with his black eyebrows, highlighting the blue right eye and the brown left.

He stood at the door wearing an open-collar blue shirt beneath a long, fur-lined brown button-down coat, black trousers and highly polished shoes.

Until recently, Orlov could only remember truly fearing two men. One had been his middle schoolmaster, and the other had been his grandfather.

Neither dread survived his teenage years. It had taken until his fifties for Daniel Fridman to imbue him with similar anxiety.

"Not at all, Daniel," replied Orlov, despite them both knowing that he did not have a choice.

Orlov knew that Fridman's influence had not simply been obtained through the billions he had made in secret investments in oil, gas and chemicals, before diversifying into telecommunications. Even billionaires could be arrested, imprisoned or exiled, with their assets 'frozen' by a disgruntled government.

Fridman had survived by providing value to, and bringing together, the correct people. Rumour and myth shrouded Orlov's knowledge of the geopolitical advisor's background.

From what the SVR Chief had heard and managed to piece together, Fridman's family had been part of the Polish cultural elite at the outset of the Great War, and thus later became targets of the Nazis. In addition to the persecution of the Polish people, Hilter's Germany also implemented a suppression and destruction of Polish cultural treasures, artefacts, and institutions.

It had been alleged that Fridman's father was one of the founding members of the Polish Underground State, a union of political and military resistance against both the Nazi and Soviet occupiers.

The rest of the information Orlov had come across had been conflicting; some purported that the family were Jewish, whilst others said strict Catholics. Travel documents suggested the family exiled to London in 1940, whereas others showed Switzerland.

No concrete data materialised until Daniel Fridman began his university education at Cambridge in 1950.

And Orlov knew enough to know Fridman had been the *éminence grise* behind some of the major geo-political manoeuvres made by various countries, mainly European and Middle-Eastern. The mystery made the old man even more intimidating.

In helping to grease the wheels for the wants and needs of the rich and powerful, Fridman had integrated himself to such an extent that to remove him would leave a vacuum too powerful for anyone to contain. All over the world, political leaders, business moguls, investment firms and Royalty relied on the support of Fridman and his 'advisory' group.

Fridman stepped closer to him, "Arrhh, the polar bear. Do you remember what happened to the 'problem bears' when they invaded on mass, looking for food scraps last year?"

The old man referred to the state of emergency that occurred when around fifty polar bears entered the main settlement on the island of Belushya Guba.

"They were removed."

"Yes…sanitized terminology but correct. Because the sources of sustainment of their native area became scarce, they had to go looking, which led to their…removal."

"I understand, Daniel."

"What do you understand?"

"It is a metaphor for what will happen to Russia if the resources of my country become scarce."

"It is a certainty. Even if natural gas and oil resources were infinite, their value will plummet once this renewable technology is implemented. It is imperative for your nation to reclaim its position as the leader of the world, that it is us who possess this technology."

It surprised Orlov to suspect Daniel was not motivated by patriotism but by his own power and international friends. His true friends, not the ones he made believe that they were, such as members of the Saudi royal family.

The way the magnate had manipulated the Chief of Saudi Intelligence, Nawwaf bin Salam into laying out a financial transaction trail for Gorokhov's services had been masterful. The Saudis would never benefit from the assassin's work but could be held accountable during the international fallout.

Not that the global cabal of which Daniel was a member was anti-Arabic; of what little Orlov knew, they could make a bizarre poster of diversity and religious inclusion.

"The asset is in the field."

271

"Considering that the asset's renewed sense of patriotism and enhanced abilities were a result of two well-funded and cutting edge scientific experiments, I would have expected his success by now."

When Gorokhov decided to leave the SVR, Alexey had made the decision to terminate him. The attempt had been disastrous with two of his better assassins slain.

It was then that Fridman presented himself, promising he could bring his best agent back into the fold.

The spymaster had never tried to substantiate the rumours of an island dedicated to the scientific altering of one's mind. All he knew was that Gorokhov returned with a fierce sense of fidelity to Russia, though Orlov doubted the agent's loyalty to he himself.

This allegiance to Russia had been proven to the spy chief when Gorokhov unflinchingly accepted to undergo the procedure to implant an experimental neural link inside his skull.

"There is a multitude of complexities that have now been resolved. I am confident that he will obtain the information which we need shortly."

"Are the British one of these complexities?"

Orlov felt his diaphragm expand—*He always knows*.

"My asset within MI6 says that no assets have been dispatched to Japan. However, I have reason to believe there might be British assets in the country."

"I feel the hand of The Guardian in this," announced Daniel. "Have you uncovered his identity?"

The Russian Intelligence Chief felt a swirl in his stomach. Daniel had used the word *Opekun,* which was the name that a select few within the Russian intelligence community gave the almost two-decade-long myth that had stymied a number of their operations, as well as hitting them back.

Despite the high-level moles and contacts the SVR had within Britain's security services, and the various cyber infiltrations inflicted, his existence, let alone his identity, had not been fully confirmed.

Not that the spymaster doubted his existence. And Orlov felt certain the man was one Bruce McQuillan—a former SAS trooper who had disappeared from official MOD (Ministry of Defence) records back in the late nineteen-nineties.

He remembered how stunned he had been on hearing the words of his predecessor—*Do not go to great lengths to discover his identity. And if one day you do discover it, be very careful in attempting to assassinate the man, because the storm that failure would bring might not be in anyone's interests.*'

"No. There are always possibilities but I haven't been able to confirm the existence or identity of The Guardian."

"He exists," said Daniel emphatically. "And he has encroached on an important venture of ours. An enterprise that allowed talented minds to be placed in positions that benefit everyone involved. It was a resource destroyed by this man, and I would be interested to know who he is. These 'assets' in Japan will have his guiding hand behind them—which means they form a link to him."

A few moments of silence passed between them before Orlov said, "You're wishing for one of them to be taken alive?"

"The principal objective is obtaining the technology," said one of the masters of the world. "But being able to question anyone who knows of The Guardian would be of great use to us."

Orlov caught the ambiguity of the billionaire's use of the words 'Us' and 'Ours'.

"I will send instructions to our asset."

30

The aquarium provided Ronald Sykes a mesmerising reprieve. Designed by a legendary Japanese aquarist, it created a vision of a miniature mountainous, forest-covered valley not dissimilar to where he was now located.

The Ryukin Goldfish reminded him of humped aquatic peacocks as they danced in a beautiful array of colours.

He had not long finished a phone conversation with the British Embassy lady Miss Ciara Robson, who had interrupted his watching the Bayern Munich v Paris Saint-Germain game, to brief him.

The elation he felt on being told that Ken's family had been rescued was swiftly doused by the news that his son was still in a critical condition.

The guilt weighed on him. Had he shared his knowledge with Ken or put it in a computer file, they might have simply beaten the information out of the engineer.

And Sykes was scared; the Yakuza had not attempted to kidnap him but ordered his death. And if they were to succeed, the scientific principles could take years to be rediscovered.

At the end of the call, she had asked him what had been the background noise that he had muted at the beginning of the call. When he answered, she had said something that stuck in his head.

"Sometimes the defence will converge on a brilliant striker leaving another less gifted player wide open—if only they were passed the ball."

He couldn't stop thinking of this as he watched the rest of the thrilling game. Finally, a while after the game's conclusion he sighed, and rolled over to grab his laptop. As he fired it up, his phone rang.

He answered it with, "Speak of the Devil."

Chisato replied, "What have I done to be called the Devil?"

"It's a figure of speech. It means—"

"I know what it means Ronald," she laughed. "Why were you talking of me?"

"I suppose I should have modified it to 'Think of the Devil'."

"Should I ask how you were thinking of me?"

His smile disappeared in an instant. "Remember how I said that I didn't need to write down or store anything with regards to the project?"

"I remember. You are a genius Ronald."

"That does not mean I didn't"

Alexey Orlov looked out of the chauffeur-driven black Jaguar XJ Sentinel's window.

Now thirty minutes into the forty-minute drive from London's RAF Northolt Jet Centre to Vauxhall Cross, the SVR Chief had asked for a minor diversion to cut through Hyde Park, passing down West Carriage Drive.

He liked the greenery of one of England's most famous parks amongst its densely populated capital. The Princess Diana's Memorial Foundation car park briefly appeared to his left, and Orlov sat back in thought.

He admired the 'old enemy' of Great Britain—a term rarely used by its citizens now, who preferred the United Kingdom; though desires for Scottish and Welsh independence, and a united Ireland, had stressed the idea to breaking point.

His predecessor had once scoffed that, after all their Cold War years of attempting communist subversion to weaken the country, it would be the University professors and students of its own capital that would succeed through the medium of both social and mainstream media.

Orlov was not so sure. Sometimes, the piercing, preaching screams of the loudest minority could solidify the stance of the quieter majority against the message. Subtle subversion was almost always the better course of action.

Despite its relatively small population and land mass, the United Kingdom remained the world's fifth-largest economy. The country also scored high in both income and human development—*Almost forty places in front of my own country.*

As the Jaguar turned left onto South Carriage Drive, he felt a dark bird fluttering in his stomach.

He spoke to the driver in English. "Checked the vehicle for bugs?"

The driver had been one of his predecessor's successes. Rod Smith had lived in England from the age of seven with adoptive parents. His biological father, Ezio Kovalyov, had gotten an English casino manageress pregnant in Copenhagen.

After spending his first seven years in Denmark, his mother returned to London to raise him.

From his pre-teens, the SVR had managed to subvert him to becoming a double agent.

After a stellar international career as a young gymnast, Rod Smith—though known by Orlov as Roderick, the name his father referred to him as—applied for a lowly position within the Government Communications Headquarters, commonly known as GCHQ. This organisation helped process signals intelligence for the UK's military and security services.

Kovalyov's name had been left off the birth certificate, which is why alarm bells had not been rung that the son of an SVR station asset had chosen this career path.

One of the more impressive legends was how Roderick had managed to integrate himself within the Solntsevskaya Bratva's—the true Russian mafia—most feared and influential European brigade. On the day its leader, Ravil Yelchin, had collapsed on a British golf course, Roderick had been assigned to be a member of his security detail.

Though Roderick had not been told, Ravil had assigned another member of his Bratva to act as a wandering bodyguard, and who had been sat overlooking the course. Once the ambulance arrived, it was that member who had insisted on accompanying the Russian mafia boss to the hospital—and it had been that Mafioso who had been murdered by the paramedic-feigning kidnappers.

"It's clean," replied Roderick in the voice of an educated Londoner.

"Give me an update on Opekun."

He thought he saw the driver's shoulder stiffen or maybe he imagined it. Be that as it may, this was the first time he had let Roderick know that his predecessor had passed on the knowledge that Opekun was not just a myth.

Though Orlov knew the answers to most of the questions he was about to ask, it did not hurt to test an agent's knowledge—or indeed his loyalty.

"A few years ago he was brought in from the cold and given the official title of Security Services liaison officer."

"And no one has questioned his background?"

"Whoever has doctored his file has done a masterful job. And the SIS Chief has substantiated it more than once. From what I can gather, he is exceedingly good in this role—at both managing the politics of it, and finding solutions to the various groups' challenges."

"If he is in such demand, then how is he running his dissident group?"

"How do you know he is?" asked Roderick, before adding, "Apologies, sir, I did not mean to ask how, just if you are sure whether he is or not?"

"No apologies necessary. We have a sensitive operation in Japan that has been receiving…interference. I believe this man is responsible."

Roderick answered, "If his group still exists, I believe he is either a very busy man, or he has delegated some of his responsibilities."

"We will have to discover that. No sense in cutting off the head of one snake only to find out there is another."

The sleeper agent did not speak for a moment before saying, "Sir, may I speak freely?"

"Yes."

"Your predecessor expressly forbade any attempt on Opekun's life. This was before he became official, and as such would have avoided heavy scrutiny. At first, I believed Opekun might have been a mole himself, or perhaps he was bribing your predecessor. But the former chief had always run aggressive counter operations, and Opekun's own operations went against Russia's interests, so I ruled out him being a double agent. I thought whatever reason why he had chosen not to assassinate Opekun would have been passed to you."

Orlov considered this point. One of the espionage game rules etched into stone was to keep everything on a need-to-know basis. However, Roderick's star was on the rise within the British security services. So far, the value of the intelligence he provided could only be matched by a handful of assets working within the US and China. And Orlov, despite the continued weakening of the United Kingdom's geo-political powers, reckoned on its resurgence in the coming decades; that meant Roderick would be well-positioned to become the most important human asset the SVR had cultivated—not everything passed through the digital sphere, and when men were given appreciation and respect, they wanted more of it—a positive reinforcement cycle he could use to his advantage.

"It comes from higher above me, Roderick."

"*Blednaya mol* wants him gone?" asked Roderick using one of Vladimir Putin's old KGB names of 'Pale Moth'.

"No," answered Orlov. "In this world, there is no single master. One man's thirst for power is eventually checked by other men's thirst for power—the game remains the same but the players change, either after a short time, or over a long time, but some have held influence in the world for decades."

"I understand, sir," said Roderick. "What would you like me to do?"

"We must take extreme care, Roderick. These people do not know that I—*we* know of Opekun's identity. We need a full and detailed dossier of Opekun to hand over."

"Why a dossier, sir? Don't we have assets ourselves to carry out Opekun's…removal?"

"I would not action this unless I had my best. And my best is currently away on a mission of extreme importance," answered Orlov, before murmuring, "Not that he is 'mine' anymore."

Gorokhov began breathing from his diaphragm to control his adrenaline release.

He had chosen to drive the black Toyota Corolla alone. The additional time it would take to stop the vehicle and get out, in exchange for being confident of another driver stopping it in the optimal position, was time worth sacrificing.

As the ambush point drew nearer, the darkening blue sky began to fade into the green of the forest.

A convoy of four vehicles comprised Ronald Sykes and his protection teams.

The former SVR agent had planted both parabolic and tracking devices to the vehicles two days ago. From these he discovered the Okada engineers were installing the new technology at the Sapporo Kokusai Ski Resort.

Also, today Sykes had arrived to check and sign off on the integrity of the installations. Communications with Kenjiro Uda had gone dark with the rescue of his family.

Thankfully, his services were no longer needed.

Tracking the convoy on a forest road down towards Sapporo Lake, the strike point he had chosen was now fast approaching.

The lookouts he had posted within the forest would alert the main force.

Gorokhov felt the adrenaline—not for his own well-being but for Sykes. If the British scientist died during the extraction, he will have failed to secure the prosperity of his people and the future of his nation.

And he'll have disappointed the old man.

He had considered arming the ambushing party with Tasers before instantly dismissing the idea.

Shintaro Goto had insisted the group were his very best men, accurate with their weapons and not prone to panic. However, Gorokhov knew none had any formal military training, despite Goto insisting that they regularly frequented firing ranges.

He did not care how many died but he did care about failing.

The voices of the Yakuza men filled the Corolla as the lookouts alerted the main ambush party.

He had drilled and rehearsed the men hard. The remote-controlled snap-net would be triggered, catching the front tyres of the lead vehicle and wrapping around them.

The snap-net could stop a two and a half tonne vehicle moving at speed in less than one hundred metres—and it was at that point in the road where Gorokhov had ordered the pair of empty sedans to be situated.

He heard the excitement as a voice came through the intercom in the American-English of a Hollywood film—"Gotcha! Like a rodeo bull."

Gorokhov pressed on the accelerator and heard the night come alive with sounds of horns and then crashing.

The assassin came upon the bunched, static convoy and threw the Corolla side-on to a halt.

His driver's side faced away from the carnage and he leapt out to the sounds of gunfire.

That none of the vehicles had tinted windows was an amateur mistake.

Gorokhov rapidly whipped the three-point sling of the stolen Howa Type 89 assault rifle over his head and arm. Loaded with a thirty-round magazine of 5.56×45mm calibre bullets, he switched the selector to タ (タンパツ)—*three round burst.*

He depressed the pressel on his radio and spoke in Japanese, "Take cover and cease fire, cease fire, cease fire."

The firing quietened, although Sykes's security team took the opportunity to immediately alight from their vehicles.

Gorokhov side-stepped out of cover and began scything down targets.

Pre-neural link, he would never have defied the 'cover and manoeuvre' adage for fire-fights.

However, with his adrenaline raised to this pitch, an instinctive confidence in his ability to defeat them in the open washed over him.

Death hit three of the enemy Gādian as they faced the treeline. Two more got shot in the face while bringing their weapons to bear on him.

A vague awareness of his current Zen-state imbued him—his body reacted with the barest glimmer of conscious thought.

The remainder of the security team now spun their weapons in his direction.

Diving into a diagonal roll, he disrupted their line of sight using the two rear vehicles.

He popped up to see that he had accurately predicted their anticipation of his appearing behind the right-hand car instead of the left.

Three bursts from the Type 89 dispatched the remainder with three rounds to spare in the magazine.

He scanned the kill zone with his eyes and barrel in perfect unison. Satisfied there were no immediate threats, he reloaded and ghost-walked towards the centre vehicle.

The profile of the British scientist's face appeared so calm that for a split second Gorokhov feared him to be dead.

As per his training, he angled his body and gently opened the door with an extended hand.

Sykes raised his .357 Magnum handgun, ensuring the Japanese-Russian had time to side-step the window-shattering, head-severing slug before pulling the trigger.

Gorokhov snatched the middle-aged Brit's wrist like a striking cobra, twisting it around, forcing him to release the revolver before the Englishman's other hand could reach it.

He unceremoniously tore Sykes from the vehicle and thrust the assault rifle into his stomach.

"Come with me or die right here."

The wide-eyed Sykes looked down and with a tremor in his voice said, "I'll die right here."

Gorokhov had reckoned on a one in five chance this would happen. Still gripping his wrist, he wrenched it, spinning Sykes while simultaneously throwing his Type 89 behind his own back. His right forearm wrapped around Sykes's throat, crushing the arteries and veins in the neck.

Blood strangles, though less painful, rendered victims unconscious quicker than air chokes, and Sykes slumped against him in little over ten seconds.

Spinning him back around, he slung the fourteen-stone man over his shoulder as easily as if he were a child.

He turned to make for the Corolla.

"Where are you going?" exclaimed the voice behind him. "The boss says he is to come with me. You know this already."

Without looking back, Gorokhov shouted, "We haven't time for this. Let's go—"

"Drop him, you dirty half-breed bastard," shouted the voice vehemently.

Gorokhov began to turn as he asked, "Then which vehicle should we put him in?"

Knowing his question would engage the brain of his protagonist, and his turning would shortened the time needed to bring the Howa to bear.

Firing from his hip, the three-round burst caught *Kyodai*—'big brother' similar to a Capo in the Italian Mafia—at the point of the chin.

With a flick of his wrist, his second burst caught both the two *Shatei*—little brothers—stood next to him. He snapped back his left side, the return bullet from the falling third man just missing his left pectoral.

Flicking the selector to auto, he fired several bursts into the Yamaguchi-gumi foot soldiers emerging from the treeline.

He turned and ran for the Corolla. Tearing open the passenger door, he roughly bundled the now conscious but nonplussed Ronald Sykes in.

Firing the rest of the magazine at the dark shadows and muzzle flashes of the forest, he jumped into the driver's seat and sped off.

31

Ciara parked the yellow Honda Insight and got out. The looks she received walking across the forecourt from the Japanese yellow and green-overalled garage workers were much more surreptitious than she would expect from their British counterparts. They sat in a gaggle enjoying a cigarette break, and their backs straightened as she stopped in front of them. The Englishwoman noted the absence of any cigarette butts around the chrome ashtray bin.

She spoke in clear, if a little enunciated, Japanese, "Which of you is Momota-san?"

The garage owner had already been contacted by an embassy staffer. One of the men leapt up and ran inside. After a minute, a compact, middle-aged, bespectacled man appeared.

They bowed with equal depth, and she handed him the keys to the Honda.

"When would you like me to pick it up?" she asked in Japanese.

He replied in stilted English, "Tomorrow…tomorrow, before moon comes."

She smiled and said in English, "Tomorrow afternoon."

"Yes, yes, tomorrow."

After a flurry of pleasantries, she left to meet the embassy driver around the corner.

Alexey Orlov sat across from the towering SIS Chief, Miles Parker, in the private restaurant known colloquially as 'The Vaults'.

Beneath a Royal Garden that was once the site of an old London prison, Putin had once told him about this place, but Orlov knew this to be the first invitation extended to a Russian intelligence chief of any kind.

Stone blocks made up the walls, floor and ceilings. The waiting staff—limited to a waitress and hostess—stood at the bar, out of earshot.

Each man had been allowed only a single member of security, and they stood next to opposing pillars, also out of hearing range.

Their suit jackets lay folded beside them.

"What would you like to drink, Alexey? They have an impressive range of vodka."

Orlov knew this simple request formed the opener for the subtle game the two men would play. A man like Miles Parker would have discovered and memorised his drink of choice to be Massandra wine produced in the world's oldest winery near Yalta.

If Parker wished to be underestimated, then Orlov would indulge him.

"Thank you, Miles. But does this establishment have any Ararat brandy?"

"I reckon they have everything, Alexey," said Parker before summoning the waitress.

She skipped over and confirmed they did have the Ararat brandy, and Orlov hid a rueful smile as Parker ordered a Massandra wine for himself.

Once she had left, Orlov said, "I wonder what the honour is to have been invited here. I would not have thought Russians would have been in regular attendance here?"

"The Cold War was a long time ago, Alexey."

"Indeed, Miles. However, I wonder if your attendance at the recent Bilderberg conference has caused this hospitality."

"You know I can't talk about what may or may not be said at those conferences."

"I thought the 'Chathman House Rule' was that you could talk about what has been discussed, but not who discussed it."

"I choose not to, then," said Parker.

The waitress broke the tension by arriving with their drinks and Orlov beckoned his bodyguard. He saw the counterpart take a step forward, only to be halted by Parker's raised palm.

When his bodyguard reached the table, Alexey said, "Mr Chernit has a refined taste in brandy."

His protection officer took a mouthful, before returning to his post.

The Russian Intelligence principal did not touch his drink for a few minutes.

"I do not know whether to feel complimented or offended that you would think I would poison you, Alexey."

"I have not survived this long by taking risks I do not have to. Especially when out of the bosom of my mother country," said Alexey. "Now, what is it you wanted to discuss?"

Orlov's head whipped around at the choked bark. His heart pounded on seeing his bodyguard clutching his throat and sinking to his knees. His security officer's hand began to pat his jacket, and Orlov registered that the signals between his brain and hand had been scrambled, preventing him from drawing his pistol.

"You fucking snake," Orlov hissed, standing up.

A hand clamped down on his shoulder before he could fully straighten his legs, forcing him back down into his seat like an accordion.

Except the hand did not belong to either Parker or his own security agent.

His heart pounded on seeing that it belonged to Opekun.

"Relax, Mr Orlov, your bodyguard will wake in approximately fifteen minutes with a feeling like a hang over," said Bruce McQuillan. "Don't be undignified and attempt to run."

When the Russian gave the subtlest of nods, Miles Parker rose and said, "I'll allow you two your privacy."

The SVR Chief calmed his breathing. The rest of his security knew the latest time he was due to leave, and would intervene if he didn't appear by that time.

Though he recognised all the years in an administration role had softened him, he also knew no truths could be prised from him within ninety minutes if he did not wish them to be.

"Who are you?" asked Orlov.

McQuillan ignored him. "I would ask where Rod Smith is, but you wouldn't tell me."

"Who?"

"The man who drove you from the airport to Vauxhall Cross."

"How would I know the whereabouts of your staff?"

"We've had suspicions Rod Smith might be a back-channel to the SVR. He went missing after the journey you shared. But that isn't what I wanted to discuss."

"You can't make me discuss anything. You yourself have stated as much...Opekun."

McQuillan smiled. "A man once told me that was my moniker within the Russian intelligence circles."

Orlov gave a mild snort. "Circles? There might be ten men who know of that name. And on a single hand I count the people who know—or think they know—that Opekun is you. I protect you for a reason I have never been told, and do not understand."

The Scotsman looked at him, "One day I might tell you the story, Mr Orlov. Right now, all you have to know is that we could be one another's worst enemies or the best of allies."

"Our two nations often have conflicting objectives."

"Sometimes they do. And sometimes, they only appear like they do. Like our mutual need to claim this renewable technology as our own."

Orlov briefly considered feigning ignorance, but said, "Why only appear?"

"This technology would ensure Russia's economic future if it works—if it remains in your hands and not the people manipulating you into doing their bidding."

Orlov didn't speak for a moment. "Those people's objectives align with my own."

"Do they really?" said McQuillan. "I would more deeply examine their motives."

They stared at one another for a few moments, before Orlov suddenly leant forward and said with urgency, "These people control the world."

"You and I know that no one organisation controls the world, Alexey. Like you say, powerful people compete."

Orlov felt a tinge of shame in the face of the calm reaction to his own fearful revelation. Before he could answer, McQuillan continued, "But there are entities in this world stronger than others. And some of those entities care for nothing but their own power, despite what they tell themselves and others. I believe such a person has engaged with you—and you don't like it. Because you know you will be discarded, and not in a most pleasant of ways."

To hear his own fears clarified by another cracked through the walls of his denial.

"What do you propose?"

"Just tell me his name, and I'll do the rest."

Orlov scoffed. "Even if you succeed, his organisation will come for me."

"His organisation will not know. Besides, you know the rules when it comes to bullies, Alexey Orlov—you do not have to be more powerful than them, you just have to make it not worth their while, so that they go pick on another kid in the schoolyard who won't smack them in the mouth."

"You believe if you kill a few of them, they will simply decide to give up ownership of one of the most profitable technologies?"

"It's a means to an end, and that end is to remain wealthy. The people coercing you will sell this technology to the highest bidder, and that won't be Russia, and you know this, Mr Orlov. But if they are led to believe it is destroyed…that is another story."

The spy chief began slowly, "The agent I have sent left the SVR a few years ago."

"You let him do that?"

"I did not let him. After a few attempts to…persuade him back failed, we came to an agreement where I would offer him work, off our official records."

"Why did he leave in the first place?"

At this Alexey burst into genuine laughter. He quickly calmed himself, looked into McQuillan's enquiring eyes and said, "Because you killed his brother—half-brother—near the Thames. And I built…how do you say?…a stonewall around the death to protect you, because nothing would have stopped Gorokhov killing you if he discovered the truth."

A silence fell on the vaults before Bruce murmured, "Makar Gorokhov was working for you the whole time."

"He worked for my predecessor. I inherited him."

"I see."

"Gorokhov took the assignments in the beginning of our new arrangement, but then began to reject them. I offered more and more money, but I one day give up on him. Let him live his life."

"And so?"

"He comes back one day, apologises and says that he is now recommitted as a servant to Russia. And that he will do anything to make himself a more valuable weapon. This is when I knew that Gorokhov no longer felt loyalty towards the SVR."

"What tipped you off to that?"

"Because I had been asked if I had any agents willing to undergo surgery to enhance their abilities. A brain chip. When the body releases adrenaline the chip enhances the reflexes, mental and physical abilities way beyond even a high performing athlete."

After a few seconds, Opekun asked, "What does he use to replenish himself?"

He is a very clever man, thought Orlov.

"In what sense?"

"I have studied physiology extensively. If his synapses, neurons, and contractile muscle fibres are enhanced beyond the level of a highly performing human, he will suffer severe depletion during the adrenaline come down. Aside from carrying the risk of death from that alone, it wouldn't be something to risk in the field."

"Injectable vials. I do not know what is in them."

"Maybe the surgeon does."

"I will not give you that information."

"Then maybe there is a name you'll give me."

Orlov took a breath akin to a parachutist about to jump behind enemy lines. His guard began to stir.

He whispered, "Daniel Fridman."

Connor Reed felt his nerves sing as he approached the roller-shutter doors of the warehouse.

Carlo walked with him, and on reaching it, Connor tapped the pre-arranged signal.

The door began to rise with a sound like distant thunder.

The suited, young Japanese man ushered them both in.

Once inside, they were led around a corner and into a car mechanic's workshop. Work benches were filled with tools placed in such a way Connor reckoned that, back in the United Kingdom, would have hinted at an obsessive-compulsive disorder. He knew, however, this was typically the Japanese way.

Two cars, a yellow Honda Insight raised on a car lift, and a green Mazda MX-5 beneath, were situated at the back of the workshop, along with a stripped Toyota Avalon chassis resting on jacks.

Yasuhiro Takato stood with three of his men who, Connor noted, made no attempt to intimidate.

After greeting him, Connor said to Takato, "This is a friend of mine. He was instrumental in rescuing the Uda family."

Takato took a moment before giving Carlo a simple bow, which the Italian mirrored.

The outlaw leader said, "The media are not aware Sykes-san has been captured. They think it was a gangland shoot-out between our clan and the Yamaguchi-gumi. But the police know Sykes-san has been captured. They have publicly declared war on all Yakuza clans, including our own."

"Why yours? Surely you're exempt from that given that they signed off on you being their protection detail?"

"The media is mighty. The scene has the bodies of the two dead policemen, and lots of Yakuza. The police cannot tell them that we were part of the security team—instead, they tell them that their two brave officers got caught in intergang crossfire."

"Any ideas where the Yamaguchi-gumi have taken him?"

Takato turned to the man on his left. "This man was present. He tried to flank the man but he had Sykes-san on his shoulder. But he witnessed this man also shooting members of the Yamaguchi-gumi."

"Can he describe him?"

"He says it was at a distance but he seemed part Japanese."

Connor felt a flutter in his stomach and took out his phone. After a few taps, he lifted the screen for the man's perusal. The Yakuza soldier's face lit in recognition before Takato confirmed, "He says that is him. Who is he?"

Connor nodded, "I'll be fully briefed later. For now, I've been sent this picture and told he is—or at least was—an SVR agent. Regarding his skillset, I can tell you is that he is nothing like I've ever seen before."

"Do you have a plan?"

"Our embassy has petitioned the Japanese government to post alerts at the borders. But we think he might keep Ronald Sykes in the country."

"Why?"

"He knows Nippon. Spent time as a teenager here and made frequent trips to visit his mother. She is currently on holiday in the States. You should assign a team to watch the house in the small chance he goes there."

Takato's face lit up. "Where?"

"Before that, you have to be aware that this man is extremely dangerous and any thoughts of vengeance have to be put to one side for the common objective, which is to see Ronald Sykes taken back safely."

"Of course," said Takato. "Kenjiro Uda said that he could implement the technology himself. It would take longer but could be done."

Connor had feared this—the notion of Sykes's expendability. If Connor did not dissuade Takato, then the brief to his men might not emphasize just how important it was to keep Ronald Sykes alive.

"As you're aware, Kenjiro Uda's knowledge is primarily centred on the installation of the systems that Sykes has designed—he doesn't know all the internal mechanisms and science behind it. He can't rapidly troubleshoot. Yes, he or others, if given enough time, might be able to reverse-engineer the various components, but that'll take time. If Okada can afford to do that, then by all means—lets go in, guns blazing, and like Drago says, 'If he dies, he dies'."

"Who is Drago?"

Connor blinked, and said, "A famous Russian boxer from the eighties."

Takato nodded, and said, "What do you think is the best way?"

"We need to locate Ronald Sykes, and when we do, you have to allow my friend here and I the opportunity to

292

extract him cleanly before any assault on the Yamaguchi-gumi holding him. Just the same as with the Uda family."

Takato bowed, "As you wish, Reed-san."

32

Ciara sat at the small black glass table beside the Park Hyatt Tokyo window. It framed the setting sun sandwiched between dark blue clouds and the city.

She would ordinarily take advantage of the view's mind-settling effect, but instead the screen of her laptop fixed her attention.

Ciara divorced herself from the feelings quickening her heartrate as she read the English transcription of the recorded conversation in Japanese.

This was a disaster.

Her phone vibrated—it was Connor making her aware he was on his way up, complete with their 'I am not under duress' code. After three minutes, came the predetermined knock at the door. She opened it as trained— arm extended, other hand bracing, and in a crouch.

Connor walked in, looked at her and said, "What's wrong?"

"You need to take a look at this," she said, shutting the door.

He shook off his Barbour jacket, revealing the bandaging resulting from the rescue of the Uda family.

He sat beside her, facing the laptop screen.

"This is a conversation that Takato had with his second in command six hours ago. Jaime has had it transcribed."

Connor turned to her. "How did you get this?"

"Audio bugs."

"I used my genius-like intellect to deduce that—I meant who gave you the….," he trailed off before saying, "Who did you use to bug him?"

"I didn't bug him. I bugged the yellow Honda Insight before taking it earlier in for repair. This conversation happened in the garage after your meeting with him."

He gave a slow nod, "Good."

She reached and tapped the laptop's touch pad.

The conversation began again and the transcription flashed up.

They sat through the eight minute conversation without speaking.

Ciara turned to him. "I don't understand this. They have Sykes in their possession—he won't take long to break. They could have this technology to themselves, but instead they are offering to share it with Okada in exchange for you?"

"It's nice to be wanted."

"I would imagine the SVR being the exception, Connor."

"Or by Operation Yew Tree."

"Can you think of why?"

"I am not sure. The thought occurred to me that Gorokhov might have wanted to even the score after I thwarted his attempt to get at Akio Shigeta the first time. But I doubt he would have got the position if he put his ego ahead of his mission. Besides, I am the one who got—as our American cousins would say—his ass kicked. He isn't the first Russian who's kicked the fuck out of me, either."

A look of confused thought briefly came over his face, and she asked, "What is it?"

She barely heard his murmur of, "Perhaps they all look the same."

Ciara smiled, "Or perhaps relations do."

He turned to her and stated, "Half-brothers?"

She nodded, "He's former SVR agent, Mikhail Gorokhov. Russian father and a Japanese mother. Another Judo and Sambo stand-out when he was young, he joins the army and then the blue beret Spetsnaz, which means he's—"

"I know. Spetsnaz can be separated between the navy and the marines who wear a black beret, the national guard have maroon and the ground and parachute forces wear blue."

"Exactly," said Ciara, impressed by his knowledge. "Gorokhov was in the airborne. After a brief stint, he is transferred to Directorate "A" of the FSB Special Purpose Center, or Alpha Group for short—a counter-terrorism unit. And after the Belsan disaster, Gorokhov was tasked with hunting down Chechen terrorists. His…performances are recognised as outstanding. There was a five-year period of relative peace, and we've found evidence the hierarchy within the FSB have attributed much of this to his actions."

"I told you he was the Russian Jason Bourne," said Connor. "What happens next?"

"Next he is head-hunted into the SVR for special tasks and becomes their go-to man. This is where it gets interesting. His half-brother, Makar, goes into deep cover to penetrate the Solntsevskaya Bratva. Becomes the most feared Avtoritet within the most successful Bratva in the Russian mafia. Obviously, you already know this—the last part at least."

She watched the stoic mask of his face as he said, "So, Makar was a deep cover agent for SVR all along—before we killed him."

Ciara nodded, "Turns out only the Directors of the SVR knew—Alexey Orlov, and his predecessor who originally tasked him. Not even his half-brother knew."

Connor said, "He might have felt he was working under a cloud of suspicion having a brother who seemingly defected. I take it Orlov had to break and tell him the truth when Makar died."

She shook her head. "He didn't. Gorokhov suspected the state had him murdered, and so he left the service."

"And Orlov lets him?" said Connor with a hint of disbelief.

"No. He sends a couple of his best to 'persuade' Mikhail Gorokhov to return to the fold—they didn't come back."

"I see."

"He travels around before landing in Israel. Meanwhile, he and Orlov come to an understanding that he would be offered jobs for money, and that he could work freelance for others, as long as it wasn't against Russian interests. And he agrees to undergo a procedure which leads to Orlov referring to him as *Uluchshen*."

"What is this word?"

"It means, 'the enhanced'."

She noted the edge of elation in his voice as he said, "I fucking told you it was something. What is it?"

"A brain chip. It enhances his nervous system when his adrenaline is triggered to a certain threshold. Not only does he become stronger and faster than normal, but his reflexes and fine motor skills are also heightened to an extraordinary level, which shows in his gunplay and unarmed combat skills."

"Fuckin' A," murmured Connor, before saying, "So his…powers wear off with the adrenaline come-down and—"

"He doesn't simply go back to 'normal'."

Connor slowly nodded. "Every action has a reaction."

Sykes kept his head down but his spirit strong. He knew escaping from the dripping stone walled basement would be near-impossible due to it being two storeys below ground.

After the superman had taken him, he had been passed on to Yakuza guards.

Though he hadn't been told, when he had been pulled out of the car's boot, Sykes had caught a glimpse of a distant airfield he recognised to be Wakkanai Airport.

He remembered a visit to Japan's northernmost city over a year ago. He had stood with Chisato at The Monument of the Northernmost Point of Japan—a set of circular steps with two giant stone spikes touching at the tips.

Despite the sea wind sweeping into their faces, they saw Sakhalin, the largest island of the Russian Federation.

He missed her terribly, all the while knowing the hope of seeing her again provided the sails of his spirit.

33

As Connor hiked through the timber rich mountainside, he lamented on the sharp contrasts between Japan's congested, sensory-loading streets of Tokyo, Yokohama and Osaka, and the serene quiet of its forests and mountains.

His khaki and black-patched lightweight trousers matched the comfortable Merrel hiking boots quietly crunching the vegetation. He had unzipped his olive green jacket to let some of the heat out.

He remembered the adage in the Corps regarding long hikes being '*Start redders* (warm) *become threaders* (pissed off). *Be bold and start cold*'.

The remote Iya Valley on Shikoku Island had been referred to as Japan's Grand Canyon. Though the west part of the valley had become an increasingly popular tourist attraction, this was the eastern area, known as Higashi-Iya, and was difficult to access.

The turquoise lagoon-like waterway below cut through the valley floor to feed the Iya River. Apart from a small hamlet made up of thatch-roofed houses at the beginning of the hike, Connor had not seen any sign of other humans.

His guide had not spoken much to him since he had met him at a small car park made of smooth stones, five kilometres back.

"How much do you know about this place?"

"I know lot," the guide replied in his stilted English. "I have to live in this place for three years."

"Why has he chosen here?" asked Connor.

"Hard for enemy to come, and we do not know for long time."

Connor deciphered this as, 'It is hard for our enemies to approach without us knowing long in advance.'

"I heard that defeated warriors from the past have sought refuge here."

"Taira clan lose Genpei War. Escape. Hide from Minamoto clan."

The Englishman was aware of the civil war which engulfed Japan in the twelfth century. With a feeling of mischievousness, he said, "Some might say the Gādian are hiding from the rest of the Yakuza, especially from the Yamaguchi-gumi."

The guide gave a sound between a grunt and a scoff. "Small Viet Cong hide from big Yankee America. Small Afghani hide from big Russian bear. They hide. They won."

Connor smiled to himself—*That's me told.*

Sensing the guide would be happier if he stopped talking, Connor did so to take in the unfamiliar ambience around him.

When doing his initial studies of the country, Connor read a text stating that the valley exuded *'a majestic mysticism that imprints on your soul.'*

However, Connor did not have a feeling as dramatic as that, and though he liked the idea of being at peace with nature, after absorbing the tranquillity he soon began to pine to get back to the cities. He realised that might be the benefit of the countryside for him—the restorative effect it had before it booted him back out.

His mind wandering, he felt a pang of guilt regarding the black bear he had killed back in Akiogahara. His heart sped just thinking of the moment the beast had charged. He had been the one encroaching on the animal's territory.

Don't worry about it, he thought, *you won't be going to the same place as David Attenborough when you die, anyway.*

His mind began to swirl with thoughts of Grace and his likely son. Of course, he did not know for certain, which provided him with a small comfort for not immediately reaching out to Grace once he learnt that he probably was the boy's father.

Shortly before he had found out, Connor had tortured a psychopathic Serbian war criminal before handing him over to an Albanian associate, Arben Tinaj, for further retributive justice.

His associate had commented positively on Connor's relative freedom of close ties. He had said,

"…parasites like this don't give a fuck about catching hold of a man's wife, girlfriend and kids, and torturing 'em."

Arben had been wrong in assuming that Connor had no one close to him other than the family he had been born into; there was Rayella, now fifteen-years-old, who was the sister of his deceased best friend and whose family treated him like one of their own.

His reverie broke with their arrival at the vine bridge. Though the valley officially had only three of these vine bridges, where it once had fifteen, Connor surmised this was a fourth put up by the Gādian. Aside from their purpose of transporting both people and goods around the valley, the vine bridges had been originally designed to be cut away easily to deny access to invading samurai, and Connor reckoned that Yasuhiro Takato had a similar idea in mind.

On crossing, Connor's trained eyes picked out a sentry high in the treeline with the barrel of an AK variant.

The trees grew denser, reducing the light as the path cut away from the river and deeper into the forest.

As saplings stroked his cheek, he remembered when on various Royal Marine exercises in the UK, the whispers of 'eyes' being passed down the patrol, as in 'Watch for these branches getting into your eyes'.

He recalled a night patrol in Afghanistan, of a Corporal miming the negotiation of a non-existent wire fence before looking back to laugh at the dumbfounded *sprog* looking for it in vain.

After several minutes, he and his guide came to a huge pile of leaves against the mountainside, the colour of which differed in shade to the surroundings. A collection of sticks leant against the rocks like walking canes.

A rustling in the trees behind him caused Connor to whip around with his hand snatching the grip of his pistol. A red-faced, grey-white furred Japanese snow monkey cocked his head and stared at him.

The Englishman turned back to see the guide holding back a laugh.

When Connor smiled back, the man picked up a stick, and poked it through the leaves—which Connor could now see were fake—and hammered against something solid, in what the Chameleon Project agent recognised to be a code, and one which he memorised.

The leaves parted like angel wings attached to smooth wooden doors. Connor barely had time to work out the design as the guide ushered him through with urgency, before quickly closing them behind.

A small, flickering lamp, approximately twenty metres down the stone corridor provided the only light. Though the natural rock of the caves made up the walls, he surmised the unseen floor to be man-made due to its smoothness.

They reached the end, and Connor frowned on seeing the red-eyed security pod and steel door. They stood for a moment, then the door slid back like elevator doors in a high rise office. Stepping in, surprise hit Connor; he had expected a tunnel system akin to those developed by the Viet Cong.

Instead, the cave opened to an area that could fit two football pitches. Sunlight bathed the farthest half from a vast, natural opening situated above, and glinted off the brook dividing the cave floor.

Various powder-coated, black metal partitions littered the sides, where Connor guessed the Gādian soldiers slept.

A chef manned a fully functioning kitchen in one corner, and various steel doors adorned the walls.

The contrast of cave-dwelling with modern amenities jarred the Englishman.

Yasuhiro Takato approached, wearing a pine-green jacket with matching trousers.

They bowed, and the clan chief said, "Glad you are here, Reed-san."

He then exchanged words with the guide, and both laughed. Connor smiled, knowing the guide had told him of his reaction to the monkey.

"How was your journey, Reed-san?"

"Apart from me almost shooting the monkey?"

"Yes, aside from that."

"As I wandered in, I felt a war within me as both the good and evil Kami fought for possession of my personality. Finally, a serene peace stilled my soul as the good triumphed."

A couple of lines appeared in Takato's forehead. "Did that happen?"

"No."

The renegade smirked. "You do not believe in things that your eyes cannot see?"

Connor shrugged. "I believe in the process of actions and inactions leading to different types of actions and reactions. That we are affected by our actions and inactions and by those of others. I think this process goes beyond our level of understanding—which is when people start making references to spirits."

Takato's eyes stared into his with curiosity and he asked, "So, you have never felt the hand of God intervene on your behalf when you have attempted to do good?"

Connor opened his mouth to answer, but closed it. There had been several occasions when extreme fortune had inserted itself into a situation that might have otherwise meant his death.

When he didn't answer, Takato said, "God, Kami, Allah, Greek Gods, Brahman are the spark that help prepared men cross the void to meet great challenges. Your own preparation helps narrow this space, and so less spark is needed."

Connor nodded. "Yes, 'luck is when preparation meets opportunity'—my cousin sends me motivational memes all the time."

"That is good."

"So, none of your enemies have managed to track you here?"

The Gādian clan founder shook his head. "Our disinformation still has them searching the forests of Oyama and Hachikokuyama Ryokuchi. One day, they will find this place but it will be too late by then. Follow me."

Takato led him down beside the brook before crossing it at a narrow point, and leading him to a red stone archway.

The carved face of a deity appeared above the archway like a clever optical illusion.

Connor gestured to it. "Who is that?"

"Taira no Masakado. A samurai who challenged the imperial government of Nippon over a thousand years ago. He conquered much of the land before he died. Now his ghost must be fed or bad luck comes."

Tiny lamps lit the stone corridor intersected with wooden arches.

Connor asked, "How do these lamps remain on all the time without being wired to a central system? Batteries?"

"Okada magic batteries. Making batteries needs massive energy—they are bad for the environment—contribute to global warming."

The Japanese outlaw stopped at a steel door, pressed his finger down on a mounted scanner and the steel jaw opened.

Takato entered and Connor followed. The door closed and the lights came on.

The Englishman curled his toes hard in the face of Gorokhov and three other men that Connor instantly recognised as Russian.

One looked vaguely familiar.

No one spoke or moved for a moment, and Connor recognised they expected him to.

"I see," said Connor looking at Takato. "This Russian made you an offer you couldn't refuse."

"I could not risk Sykes-san dying in a hostage rescue. You convinced me of his importance."

"I am sure you all will work it out amicably and share equally—a bit like you do the Kuril Islands."

Connor knew it to be churlish to bring up the sovereignty dispute between Japan and Russia, but he wanted to make a point.

"Who has rule over the technology is of tiny importance compared to its existence."

In that one sentence, Connor went from despising Takato to respecting him more than ever. The black operations agent knew the financial windfall the Okada Company stood to receive would make it the largest in terms of gross revenue, and perhaps the most profitable too; by proxy, the Gādian would become the most powerful outlaw syndicate in the world. If they allowed the Yamaguchi-gumi and the other Yakuza clans to exist, it would only be on the proviso of their subservience.

And yet, here he was, willing to sacrifice all that to ensure the technology's survival.

Connor asked, "If that's the case, why not just have helped them escape the country with Sykes."

Gorokhov answered, "Because I refused to give up Mr Ronald Sykes's location until I had you in my possession."

"Being trapped in this room with you and three of your Spetsnaz goons isn't a nice feeling. But knowing you would take this risk just to get me back for making you run away that night gives me a certain satisfaction."

Gorokhov smirked, "I think my hitting you has affected your memory. And it is not me that wants you. You must be a significant man for my boss to request you."

"Vladimir Putin wants to speak with me? Now I know I have arrived."

"Our president does not know of you. The higher power goes, the less you can see who has it."

"I take it that postponing this meeting to return some overdue library books isn't an option?"

"A man always has options," said Gorokhov flatly.

"You know, I haven't been to Russia before. Always been curious as to what it's like. Although my imagination always conjures up images of fucking a Russian bird—girl rather—while she wears one of those furry ushanka-hats complete with the soviet military star in the centre."

Gorokhov smiled with his eyes. "Let's hope your humour stands up in the face of adversity."

That's when Connor understood the Russian knew of at least some of his background.

One of the tenets of the Royal Marines Commando spirit was *Cheerfulness in the face of adversity.*

34

Connor's heart began to beat harder as Gorokhov held up the straight-jacket.

"You're not putting that on me," said Connor almost reflexively. The thought of being so restricted amongst enemies made his stomach lurch.

"We are putting it on you, Mr Reed. You can resist—put up a good fight, but in the end you will be wearing it and in an impaired state to what you are in now. Both a painful and tactically unsound choice."

The Englishman recognised the logic of the former SVR agent's words—*fuck.*

He stripped off his outer layers down to his t-shirt before holding out his arms—the upper left being covered by a black tubular bandage from the triceps down just past the elbow beneath.

"James Bond gets Famke Janssen trying to suffocate him with her thighs when he encounters the Russians, and I get a dirty straight-jacket. The inequality, eh."

Gorokhov looked at him without a flicker of expression and said, "Xenia Onatopp was born in the Georgian Soviet Socialist Republic, not Russia. And in 'Golden Eye' she was part of the crime syndicate Janus, not 'the Russians' as you have said."

Connor raised his eyes in appreciation—*He either has a photographic memory or loves films.*

"How bad is your arm?" asked Gorokhov.

"I would appreciate the straight-jacket being applied as delicately as Russian fingers will allow."

Gorokhov spoke in rapid Russian, and one of his men lifted the straight-jacket.

As surreptitiously as possible, Connor expanded his diaphragm with air, and forced his elbows out against the fabric as it slid over his frame with—to his surprise—a certain degree of care.

He noticed the Russian leader had a strange look on his face but did not say anything.

The sounds of laughter and Japanese permeated through the stone ceiling. Sykes had given up attempting to decipher the muffled words.

He took heart in the fact that not only was he still breathing, they hadn't tortured him. He'd even been allowed to shower, given a clean kimono and been fed basic but good Japanese food.

In truth, Sykes's sense of patriotism had receded the more time he had spent in Japan. He liked certain things about his native Britain; the black humour of its television comedy dramas being one. He could never quite get the American comic buoyancy in some of their shows. He had theorised that with their overtly politically biased news channels pumping out so much melodramatic negativity, the average American could not stomach it in their comedy too.

Aside from the humour, Japan had almost everything that made Britain attractive—politeness, vibrant cities contrasting with peaceful countryside, a rich history and some extraordinary architecture.

Sykes had been happy when Okada and the British consortium had reached their historic agreement to share the renewables project. That a third entity now sought to steal it when they were so close, had filled him with a rage, feeding his stubbornness.

However, he knew he was no 'tough guy', and might not hold out for long under any kind of torture. In truth, the most important thing to him now would be that the technology thrived, and if that had to be under someone else's banner, then so be it.

One truth he could never utter was Chisato's knowledge of technological aspects—he'd rather just give them what they wanted.

He tilted his head up at the sudden quietening of the music and talking.

The lock clunked before the door opened. Instead of the Yakuza, three men dressed in military garb with faces of pale stone stared back at him.

The one in the centre barked in Russian-accented English, "Stand up. Come with us."

As Connor began his attempts to create space within the jacket, he lamented how this had been the second time he had been blindfolded, put in a vehicle and taken to an unknown destination within the space of six months.

However, whereas on the previous occasion he had been merely unsure of the intentions of the man he had been taken to see, this time he would be in for a rough time, followed by his death.

Following an extremely awkward and uncomfortable hike back through the Iya Valley, he had taken advantage of the opportunity to sleep after once again being blindfolded and this time placed in the boot of a dark blue Nissan Altima.

Now fully awake, he thought about how many times he had faced death in the last few years. And why he kept on doing so.

He knew if he asked Bruce for release from working for the Chameleon Project, the Scotsman would do so with no hard feelings other than the disappointment of losing a good agent.

If he survived this.

He thought about Grace and her son—very likely his son. If the baby was his, would Grace accept him into their lives, given what she knew about him? Maybe she would. What would he do for a living?

Thinking of the options made the ice-winged butterflies glide around his stomach.

The obvious choice would be to immerse himself in the family business. However, to do so would be to defeat the purpose of avoiding danger. And he'd have no means of paying off the karmic debt of distributing drugs.

What then? Private security? Be boring as fuck and just for money.

Connor realised daydreams like this were just that—dreams. If he didn't want to truly leave, despite being a straight-jacketed hostage of a SVR super-assassin, then he never would.

The car seemed to be slowing down and he made a conscious effort to box-breath through his nose.

The vehicle came to a halt. The sound of the boot lifting accompanied the cool air enveloping him.

Seized by his arms and legs, they lifted him out and placed him on his feet.

He recognised Gorokhov's voice bark a command in Russian, and then felt the retightening of the back and crotch straps—*bastard.*

The light attacked his eyes on removal of the blindfold.

After a few seconds, they adjusted and his legs went hollow on absorbing the scene. The red-faced HA-420 HondaJet stood on the runway like a sprinter in the blocks, and Connor knew it had the range to comfortably reach the southern tip of Russia's eastern seaboard.

Despite his time in the boot, he still had confidence in his sense of north and of the amount of time travelled, and deduced the location to be on the Japanese west coast not far from Tottori.

To his nearby left, lay two metal steeple-roofed buildings. Neatly cut grass circled the entire airfield.

The Russians formed a loose semi-circle around him. A chip of ice appeared in Connor's brain as he tried to recall where he might know the familiar face of the soldier. Apart from his hair being longer, he matched the others in both physique and bearing.

He turned to Gorokhov. "Not sure why the blindfold was left on for journey inside the car but taken off now. Not that I am complaining."

"I thought it would be nice for you to see a scenic view from the air"

The statement—delivered without any intimidation or ego—was as chilling to Connor as any threat made against him. The former SVR agent had not needed to add *'one last time'* for the Englishman to catch the inference.

"Thank you."

"Before we take off, please follow me."

Gorokhov led the way into the left-hand building. Connor noticed that although his men hovered around him, they were never in one another's line of fire.

They entered. A control unit made up of various screens, keyboards and dials skirted the front edge to his right.

Steel countertops ran down the edges on either side, with a collection of lockers, a calendar, and hung up jumpsuits to the rear.

Gorokhov gestured to a round tuffet-like chair. Connor obliged him.

With the straps loosening, he felt a bitter breeze wash over him. The room felt colder as the jacket came off.

As Gorokhov asked, "Do you want to take off your bandage yourself?" Connor's stomach lurched.

Recognising the jig was up, he complied. Though the thumb of raised flesh might have seemed more prominent to him than it really was, the SVR agent said, "We must cut it out."

"I think I'd do a better job of it."

"Giving you a knife would not be professional," said the Japanese-Russian, revealing a short Tanto blade from a scabbard in his waistband.

Connor knew that, although his fear would not be discernible to a civilian—it would be obvious to Gorokhov.

He attempted to relax in the knowledge his choice was limited to suicide and mission failure, or sitting still and giving himself up to Gorokhov's intentions.

He chose the latter. As the assassin grasped his left wrist, one of the soldiers pressed the barrel of a gun into the base of his skull.

With the gentleness and precision of a surgeon, Gorokhov removed the microchip stapled underneath his skin.

The former SVR agent stepped away and barked in Russian. Connor was able to translate the order as "Start the Jet".

Gorokhov examined the device between his finger and thumb.

"Must be very sophisticated to have the capacity to track you despite being this small. There will be people eager for this to be reverse-engineered," said Gorokhov, the words hurting Connor more than the knife had. "But no one will be coming for you now, Mr Reed."

As the straight-jacket struggled back over his arms and torso, it took all of his strength of mind not to allow the panic to consume him.

35

The HondaJet did not fly north-west over the Sea of Japan, but instead contoured the Japanese west coast.

As it came in to land, Connor estimated the flight to have taken around three hours, and roughly knowing its cruising speed to be over 400 knots (over 460 miles per hour), he guessed they had set down on the northern tip of Japan.

He looked out the left window opposite the side where he sat, and could make out two islands and realised they could be Rebun and Rishirfuji.

We are landing at Wakkanai, he thought.

This heartened him, as when on approach, he had expected the jet to fly straight for one of the Russian-controlled islands.

The landing felt like a hundred-year-old wooden rollercoaster, and Connor could see the disrepair of the short landing strip.

Back in the jacket, and manhandled off the plane, he surveyed his surroundings.

A small isolated multi-storey building lay in front of him. The lower levels were made up almost entirely of glass, with the upper floors comprising white-painted brickwork.

Though he could not translate the signage, he knew the black cross within a downward facing pointer denoted a hospital.

It dawned on him—a psychiatric hospital.

Why did a funny farm once need a jet runway?

Instantly, he realised this to be the Hasegawa psychiatric hospital named after Taro Hasegawa, a deceased electronics tycoon. Hasegawa had paid for a complete renovation of the hospital back in the eighties when his son had been committed there. The runway had been needed so that Taro could more rapidly visit from Tokyo. Connor had also read rumours that the hospital helped hide the

Wakkanai Underground—a disused nuclear energy facility once run off the books for the Yakuza.

Connor nodded in his admiration for the plan—*this is why they got changed.*

With his lack of Japanese, even if the hospital staff were not aware of his 'hostage' status, he would not be able to convince them otherwise.

"Let's go, Mr Reed," said Gorokhov.

Connor could see faces of mild inquisitiveness and dull boredom in the people staring through the glass.

The group led him around the side where the trees brushed closer to the building.

They stopped at oak panels leading beneath the building.

Gorokhov stamped on them three times, and they opened like the yawning of dragon's jaws.

Instead of hospital staff, Connor instantly recognised the dark-suit, slick-haired man who had opened it to be Yakuza.

The discussion in Japanese between the man and Gorokhov seemed heated, until the assassin growled something, and the Yakuza's posture and eyes became submissive, before stepping aside.

The white paint on the walls had peeled, illuminated at intervals by naked white light bulbs.

They stopped at a room he recognised to be a make-shift recreation room. Though Connor could not see the television, on hearing the distinctive voice of the ring announcer, Lenne Hardt, he knew the men within were watching a Pride Fighting Championship match.

However, the sound cut off and the men stood in silence like meerkats.

A few more exchanges in Japanese before Connor felt a shove, pressing him onwards.

The corridor split left and right, and the hand guided him to the right, and then almost immediately to a door on the left.

314

The Yakuza man opened it to reveal a room with a steel box cage.

Connor turned to Gorokhov, "A straight jacket and a cage. A little OTT don't you think?"

"OTT?"

"Over the top."

"You are a dangerous man, Mr Reed. I cannot show myself to take chances."

The wording seemed strange to Connor—'*I cannot show myself…*'

"I take it I'll have to shit in this jacket if I can't hold it any longer?"

"Of course not," said Gorokhov. "I am not an animal. Do you need to go…for a shit?"

"Please," he answered. "Have you got a cereal box or something else I could read?"

Gorokhov ignored him, and called out to his guards. Connor knew if he went into the cage, his chances of escape would be almost nil.

Three of the men formed a triangle around him, and walked him further down the corridor.

The man with the familiar face stared straight ahead as Connor attempted to picture where he knew him from.

They rounded the corner, entering the room where the sight of the traditional Asian squat toilet—though largely replaced in Japan by the 'western' toilet—made him briefly squeeze his eyes closed.

What sounded like a debate—in Russian—began behind him.

When it stopped, he felt the straps of his straight jacket begin to loosen.

Yep, no one fancied wiping my arse then, thought Connor.

Two of the men, including the familiar one, stepped back around the corner, with the remaining guard levelling a pistol at him.

Connor suppressed a smile that his captors had to watch him shit.

315

Afterwards, as he began to wash his hands, a scene from the past sprang to mind. Over two years ago, just before he had lined the cross-hairs of a modified sniper rifle onto the throat of a Ravil Yelchin—the now deceased leader of the London brigade of the Russian Bratva, Connor observed the crime lord's bodyguard stepping back.

The same man stood outside now.

Warm liquid sprayed over Connor's face. The guard holding the pistol collapsed to reveal the familiar-faced man—with a face even more blood splattered than his.

He spoke a London-accented English, urgently whispering, "We don't have much time. Pick up his gun."

The man slipped around the corner to reappear dragging a dead body by the wrists.

"Can I ask who you are?"

"I am a friend of Bruce McQuillan."

Gorokhov felt uneasy leaving Connor Reed. He controlled his disquiet with logic—*He is in a straight-jacket, in a cage guarded by Spetnaz and Yakuza.*

He did not know why Daniel Fridman had insisted on taking Reed into their custody; Gorokhov would have preferred him dead.

With Ronald Sykes being the priority, the assassin began the hike through the forest to the other side of the complex.

Fridman's solicitors would arrive and oversee the legalities of signing the documents to secure the rights of the technology.

Once that had been completed, he hoped he would have some respite before being given a new mission.

He remembered waking one morning in a rented apartment in Tel Aviv, unsure of how he got there but feeling desperately bereft of purpose. It had been that day he had met Daniel Fridman.

The mysterious geo-political billionaire offered him missions on his own terms that would be issued to him under the guise of the SVR.

Much later, when a procedure to make him as "...*sharp as a Nihonto blade...*" had been offered, he surprised himself in accepting instantly.

His thick black hair hid the scar where the chip had been implanted. In truth, he had doubted the benefit. Until the day he found himself in a firefight with an element of the PLA's (Chinese People's Liberation Army) Special Forces guarding one of its facilities specialising in AI.

It had been exhilarating, as it seemed the connections between his mind and body were shortened to the point of automation. The action did not slow down exactly, only that his body found it easier to keep up.

Not that he hadn't been a superb soldier, fighter and agent beforehand. For many years he had been the SVR's go-to man when it came to highly sensitive operations. He had even been opportunistically used—despite never receiving formal training—as a 'Raven' on occasion, the male equivalent of the more prevalent 'Swallow'—an agent who seduces an enemy asset to glean information.

However, being forty years old with over two decades of a hard career settled in his bones, it gnawed at him that the Englishman might have gotten the better of him that night had he not been enhanced.

Gorokhov hiked harder to shed the thought. He had memorised specific trees and the distance and direction to the next tree on the route.

After fifteen minutes through the dense forest on the mountain slope, he came to the clearing.

He lifted his wrist to his mouth to speak Russian into the communications strap.

"Kay One approaching."

This alerted the guards at the high gate and the sniper pair just over two hundred metres within the forest to his right.

317

When the affirmation of his presence sounded in his ear, he made his way out.

The Spetsnaz soldier—though not denoted by any insignia—opened the gate.

It gladdened Gorokhov that only Russian Special Forces protected this part of the massive complex, as much as it vexed him to leave Connor Reed minded by the Yakuza-controlled section.

Still, he had left a trusted complement of three, and with Reed straight-jacketed and in a cage, he decided not to dwell on it.

Connor felt a sense of control return as the man handed him one of the dead men's MP-443 Grach pistols.

He had only fired the 9×19mm semi-automatic once on a range, and remembered that it was the only dual-feed pistol he had ever fired.

Connor checked the eighteen round magazine and said, "Take it I'm following you?"

"Correct, the more distance from here until they discover these bodies, the better."

"What's your name? Unless you want me to refer to you as mate."

"Rod. Let's go."

Connor shadowed his rescuer as he turned left, away from the gathering of Yakuza down the opposite end.

The man led Connor through a maze of corridors, until they reached the bottom of a ladder leading up to a cargo hatchway similar to those he had seen *on ship* while in the marines.

"The last time I saw you was over three years ago— on a golf course where I was picking up Ravil Yelchin in an ambulance. You loaded him on, but didn't get in."

Rod turned slowly but made no attempt to level his weapon at Connor.

"Jaime told me not to."

The reply stunned Connor for a moment—*he's a Chameleon Project agent too.*

Connor nodded, "What's the plan?"

The man turned and spoke to him clearly but urgently. "Ronald Sykes is being held on the other side of the complex. A meeting will commence in Tokyo where the rights to the Okada technology will be shared with a third party—except, Ronald Sykes will be taken to Russia afterwards. We can't let that happen."

"Then let's get him out of there."

"We will try, but a Spetnaz security team guards him."

Connor gave him a brief frown. "I guess we should just fuck off home then."

"I didn't say that. I am just making you aware."

"I am aware. We are on a suicide mission. But there're some things worse than dying."

"Bruce said you'd say something like that."

"I suppose it's too much to hope the half-Japanese-half-Russian *Universal Soldier* has been called away?"

"Yes it is too much to hope," said Rod as he squirrelled up the ladder and began to turn the wheel. "But he has his own Kryptonite. I will explain."

Japanese shouts boomed down the corridor, setting off a flare inside his stomach and extinguishing his intrigue at Rod's words.

36

Ronald Sykes sat on the floor of his cell, the repurposed, disused nuclear reactor control room.

They had unceremoniously taken him from his previous cell and force-marched him through a forest with a blend of threats, rifle prods, drags and pushes for well over twenty minutes until they got him here.

Sykes had been aware of the story behind this nuclear power plant. After the Fukushima Nuclear Accident, an emergency review had been made of other Nuclear Power Plants. This one—known colloquially as the Wakkanai Underground—had been found vastly wanting, and was immediately shut down.

Sykes had treated the rumours of the Yamaguchi-gumi clan buying the plant at a dirt-cheap price, as just that—rumours.

However, on noticing the mix of Yakuza guards and Russian soldiers milling around the place, and rooms filled with brown paper-wrapped packages the size of bricks, he realised the truth of the stories.

His head rested on a traditional Japanese pillow with two books—English translated copies of *The Tale of Genji by Murasaki Shikibu* and *A Book of Five Rings by Musashi* lay by his side.

Earlier, he thought he'd heard a plane landing and braced with anticipation. However, nothing changed and a few passages of the latter had helped him not fall into the pool he had been desperate to wallow in. Every time he found himself sliding in, he'd swim back and pull himself out.

Chisato remained safe, and as of yet, nothing had really happened to him. His captors had treated him with only a rough indifference.

All he had tried to do for the last decade had been to work towards helping the planet sustain itself. And now they were on the brink, he found himself a pawn in a deadly game.

If he had disseminated the information more in the beginning, then he would not have made himself such a prized target for every power-hungry person and organisation on earth. He had not realised just how far they would go—but now he did, and despite his predicament he was glad of the decision he had made.

You didn't come this far just to come this far Ron.

Sykes did not kid himself that implementing his technology would eradicate fossil fuel usage. Still, he knew it would slow it down to the point where others in the world would have time to apply their own technological breakthroughs.

He would like to witness it if he could. Like to be a part of it. But his goal was to keep the secret that the information no longer lay solely in his head.

The door opened to reveal the hāfu leader. Sykes creakily stood, and the man said in English, "It should not be long now."

"Until my release?"

"Yes."

"Forgive me, but I do not believe you. It doesn't make—"

"You will be transported to Moscow to work with us there. You and Fukuhara-san will live like royalty—we Russians have not forgotten such things."

Sykes's stomach lurched on hearing the man use his girlfriend's name.

"If you think my loneliness will overcome the concern for Chisato's safety, you are very much mistaken. Unless you're going to attempt to kidnap her again."

"I see that the British propaganda has planted itself in your mind. In Moscow, you and Fukuhara-san will be afforded the great respect you deserve—unlike in your home country."

"May I ask your name?" asked Sykes.

The man seemed to hesitate for the briefest of moments, before answering, "Mikhail Gorokhov."

"Suppose you were just the man for this job—half Russian, half Japanese, both your countries will now prosper. Well…at least on the surface that is how it will appear."

Sykes caught a ghost of a frown come and go before the man said, "Appear? They will benefit."

"The Russian in you should know that although this technology will benefit everyone—literally—there will only be a select few who profit. And that won't be you or I. If you questioned the motives for whoever sent you, you would know that, if you don't already."

"I do my duty for my country."

"I notice you said 'country' and not 'people'."

"And you think Great Britain is different?" said Gorokhov with a faded sneer.

"My goal is for the implementation of this technology while we still have time. Frankly, I do not care who has the rights to it, as long as it exists. Nor do I care who has credit. All you have done is delay the project, wasting precious time—for what? To carry out orders in the name of either a national or someone else's self-interest?"

He caught the Russian's strange expression. The abrupt opening of the door revealed a soldier who spoke in urgent Russian.

Gorokhov said, "Thank you for the discussion," and left.

Connor could hear Rod's heavy breathing when he had finished talking as they cut through the forest. The Yorkshireman found the pace only mildly challenging and judged Rod's physique belied only an average cardiovascular system.

After fifteen minutes Rod slowed before indicating they stop.

Once they had taken a knee, Connor asked, "Why have we come this far into the wood?"

"There is a sniper pair not far from here. I only know approximately where they are."

"So, you're saying that you and I, wearing clothes that in this environment make us stand out like a prick at a eunuch's convention, are about to hunt a camouflaged Spetnaz sniper pair who are now probably aware that I have escaped with your help?"

Rod took a moment to answer before saying, "Yes."

"Okay. Just so I know," sighed Connor. "Take it you still remember the principle of 'cover and move'?"

"Yes."

That his new battle partner did not seem to take offence at what was meant to be a light jibe, disturbed him.

All you can do, is what you can do, thought Connor before saying, "I'll take point."

Gorokhov alerted his men to the Englishman's escape, before taking a moment to consider his orders. His two options were to post a portion of his men around the perimeter of the forest and use the remainder to perform a sweep. Daniel Fridman had been adamant the apprehension of Connor Reed was just as important as Ronald Sykes's.

Any man in Reed's position would take the opportunity to escape. Still, Gorokhov's instincts gnawed at him that despite the odds, this animal would attempt to take back custody of Sykes.

If that proved to be true, the best option would be to bolster the complex's defence.

No, even if he comes here, there are only two of them armed with pistols, he thought.

He began issuing clear and concise instructions, before realising a part of him was glad a final confrontation with the Englishman might be had.

His secure tactical phone began to vibrate against his hip in a pattern that denoted Daniel Fridman on the other end of the line.

Connor could not map in his head the route to afford him the best cover, as he did not know the position of the sniper pair.

Rod informed him the pair were providing overwatch. They crept to a point just back from the edge. Being sniper-trained himself, Connor began to scan the far edge of the treeline in relation to the complex's main gate to ascertain where he would have set up.

In a battlefield setting, a good Spetsnaz sniper might forego the position affording him the best vantage point of the area, as potential counter snipers could predict it. However, Connor surmised in this situation they wouldn't have expected counter snipers, or, given the expected time-frame, have built a real hide, either.

Connor closed Rod in on him with a hand signal, before saying, "See the small nook, three fingers right from the edge of the wood?"

"Three fingers right?" asked Rod.

The former Royal Marine hid his concern at the question and said, "Extend your arm while holding up three fingers compressed together. Put the left edge of 'em in line with the edge of the wood—the nook should be on the right hand edge of your fingers. Seen or not seen?"

Rod did so and said, "Okay, I see it."

Connor held back reprimanding his new battle partner for not saying 'Seen'.

"We'll hike around hard before dropping in on them."

Rod pointed to the entrance and said, "We don't have much time."

Connor followed his finger to see soldiers pouring out of the buildings behind the wire fence-line.

He took a deep breath and said, "Let's skip the cover and manoeuvre. Our only hope now is to reach those sniper rifles."

An idea from the back of his brain punched itself to the front.

"Wait a minute," Connor said. "I have an idea."

37

The older man stole a glance at Evengy to see him frown at the static sounding from the headset.

Igor returned his focus to the open area in front of him, over the Dragunov sniper scope and asked, "Anything?"

"It's garbled again. I thought the Japanese were the best at electronics."

"It's the power lines feeding the place—the electrical interference."

"We'll be returning to Russia with brain tumours."

"You'd need a brain for that," said the older Igor, and Evengy smiled.

Usually, the more experienced man acted as the spotter. In addition to estimating the distance to the target, wind strength and direction, his duties also included watching the fall of the shot and making corrections in light of any misses. But in this instance, the pair decided to swap in hour intervals.

Spetsnaz sniper teams were traditionally made up of three men. The third was a flanker, responsible for the team's security and usually placed at the rear.

However, with this not being a war setting, they had given Aslan a VSS Vintorez silenced sniper rifle—the rifle most of the younger generation of Spetsnaz liked—to provide overwatch from the tower roof.

Igor swore under his breath, seeing yet another scope-reflected sun glint from Aslan's position. The third in as many hours.

The thought had passed through the veteran's mind more than once that the new Russian *Ratnik* combat system was so advanced it might have bred a tinge of reliance in the younger generation. For this operation, they hadn't been permitted to wear it or any insignia identifying them as official Russian soldiers.

Also, the briefing given to the team before leaving for Japan had dripped of nonchalance— *'Go over there, intimidate these Japanese soft Kung Fu gangsters so that they don't think of reneging on our deal, and then bring both the British scientist and agent back.'*

Despite his caution, Igor felt that, though up to now professional, the squad were missing the danger-sharpened edge of their other covert missions.

"There must be something happening," murmured Igor, observing the boys forming up behind the gates.

"I thought the package wasn't going to be moved for another two hours?"

"Looks like the plan might have changed," Igor shrugged, before thinking for a moment. "Go back to the place where you last carried out a communications check. There is little point us sitting here without knowing what is occurring."

"It was a hundred metres back," said Evengy, with a hint of concern.

"Then you'd better get moving. Keep your wits," said the veteran, before hissing, "Quietly!"

Evengy sloped off, and Igor kept his eyes peeled. A furrow of confusion and concern rested on his forehead, watching both his countrymen and the Japanese gangsters pour out of the compound to form a line abreast.

If he had to guess, he'd have thought Gorokhov had augmented the Spetsnaz soldiers with Yakuza to perform a sweep of the forest. If this was true, then that meant that an enemy, or at least a potential enemy, was out there—and he had just sent Evengy off on his own.

There was nothing he could do now but wait for his return.

His keen eyes picked out a rustling in the treeline thirty metres to the north-west. Slowly, he changed the angle of the Dragunov towards it.

Like a ghost from the darkness, the blood-splattered face of the new guy—Roderick—appeared in a daze. His hands, completely relaxed by the sides, were empty. He wandered aimlessly into the open ground.

Igor could see the Spetsnaz soldiers, some four-hundred metres away four-finger-pointing to their fellow soldier.

The veteran soldier barked, "Halt."

The words seemed to barely penetrate the stupor that had seized his countryman.

Igor caught a noise from behind—the last sound he ever heard.

Connor dropped the blood-stained rock and snatched the Draganov from Igor's lifeless fingers, rolling the corpse away to his left and stealing its position behind the tree.

As he lay behind it, he yelled to Rod, "Back into the woods and converge on my position."

Their distraction had worked too well—he had told Rod not to come out of the treeline; not only had it drawn the attention of the sniper he had just killed but also the men immediately outside the compound.

And probably the sniper whose scope he had earlier observed reflecting on top of the tower.

The top of Rod's head skimmed off like a bloodied Frisbee and Connor's rescuer collapsed.

Evengy hurried back to Igor's position to tell him the news—the 'dangerous' prisoner had escaped, either with the help of the new guy, Roderick, or by taking him as a prisoner.

He cut through the trees, only to be momentarily frozen by the sight of another person lying in Igor's place with his mentor acting as a spotter.

Creeping closer and observing Igor's slumped and misshapen head, it dawned on him that his friend was dead and the man beside him had killed him.

Evengy raised his AK47 and took aim—*No, capture him. Gorokhov wanted him secure for a reason.*

The Spetsnaz soldier began to stalk forward.

38

Sykes's heartrate and breathing remained unsettled from the moment his meeting with Mikhail Gorokhov had been interrupted.

The Russian commands and Japanese shouting, both near and far, filtered through the heavy doors.

Were they under attack? Or were they preparing to move him?

The door opened to reveal Gorokhov with an expression of reluctance and determination alternating on his face like a kaleidoscope.

His right hand gripped a pistol.

Connor, ascertaining the tower sniper to be the most dangerous man on the battlefield, focused his scoped view onto the top of the tower. He lined the intersection of the crosshairs on the targets' head, expelled his breath and smoothly squeezed the trigger.

The head exploded like a grenade inside a watermelon.

The former Royal Marine sniper switched his attention to the targets below, as the Russian soldiers moved aggressively towards his position.

His two options were to either begin shooting now, out in the open—inviting the return fire of multiple weapon systems—or bolt back deeper into the wood and change his position.

Fuck it—he thought—*you're behind a tree, and have the high ground.*

The moment he killed one, a wrathful avalanche of gunfire returned.

Connor picked off two more but the accuracy of the enemy fire coerced him in to moving. He forced himself into a crouch before turning to run back.

The dead body, not more than five metres away, startled him. He quickly realised the man must have been creeping up on him, only to be inadvertently killed by the rounds of his own men.

The Englishman grabbed the AK and ran into the forest. He understood there were guards on the outer edge. He had to move quickly and take the risk that the outer cordon was not closing in.

He sprinted hard back along their initial route in—
Better not be any more fucking bears.

Now out of the firing zone, he wanted to position himself behind the sweeping force.

With his actions now reactive, and without a definitive plan, he bit down his panic. He could not simply run across the open ground to a compound guarded by a locked gate and two armed guards.

The Japanese voices alerted him to the presence of the Yakuza contingent. His eyes snapped back and forth, looking for a way out.

With a weapon system too unwieldy to bring to bear on multiple targets at close range, he recognised the tightening of the snare around him.

He briefly considered shooting as many as he could before going down in a blaze of glory.

However, they were just criminals looking after their interests like criminals do—if he shot them, knowing he could not achieve the objective, would he be simply committing murder?

His indecision clawed at him—surrender and accept whatever circumstances might play out, including his instant death, or start shooting?

He caught glimpses of them through the trees and felt the butt of the sniper rifle slip from his shoulder.

Explosions reverberated underneath his feet to the sound of Japanese screams, followed by small arms fire, and then quiet.

"Connor, it is me. Behind you."

He recognised the Italian's voice immediately.

He turned to see the 'Ndrangheta assassin in dark military-style garb galloping down the hill like a child running to a funfair. He carried two Howa Type 20 assault rifles, one in his shoulder and one in his left hand.

That fucking bloke is mental.

The Englishman refrained from asking any questions not immediate to their survival.

"I can't see a way into the compound," said Connor.

"Aha," beamed Carlo Andaloro, reaching back to tap his backpack. "I have something that will open sesame."

"Okay," said Connor. "Help me strap this Dragunov to my back."

"You want to take it? It slows us down?"

"Range will be the only advantage we have now," said Connor, and then after doing his obligatory checks of the Howa, "Let's get going."

As the former Legionnaire and Royal Marine Commando set off in a perfect demonstration of cover and manoeuvre, Connor briefly thought of how unfazed he had become to the sight of freshly murdered bodies—and how much of his soul he might have lost.

When the sounds of quietly spoken Japanese commands filtered through the forest, the pair slowed and took positions behind broad tree trunks.

Not knowing the exact distance of the Spetsnaz sweeping party to their rear sent a swirl of cold anxiety around him. He gripped the emotion by concentrating on the immediate threat.

He knew Carlo's professionalism well enough now to know he would not fire until the last possible moment to draw as many of them into the killing zone.

Slowly, one walked into his field of fire, followed by another. For a moment, Connor wondered if they were pretending not to see him, such was their apparent lack of tactical awareness.

Finally, when five had stepped into his field of fire, one locked eyes on him only to die in the next instant.

The forest came alive with the snaps and wisps of small arms fire, and the cries of shot Yakuza soldiers.

When the firing had ceased, Connor shouted, "Carlo, what's your status?"

"Four magazines. Okay."

Connor had taught the former Legionnaire a way of reporting ammunition and well-being status, except that back in his soldiering days, 'Four magazines' would have been how many he needed, whereas now Carlo was telling him how many he had.

"Prepare to move," bellowed Connor, now that the firefight had removed the need for quiet. "Move."

Carlo moved first with Connor covering. When his counterpart took up a firing position, the Englishman sprinted in a zig-zag.

A sledgehammer blow smashed the sniper rifle into his latissimus dorsi muscle, flinging him forward. He couldn't draw the breath to summon an alert to Carlo.

Though pain pounded his shoulder, he found himself able to work his right hand enough to take the strap of the sniper rifle from around his head. He ignored the pain in the upper-right-hand part of his back to roll over to face the direction of the bullet.

Before he could bring the Howa to bear, a Spetsnaz boot stamped on his hand, and thumped the muzzle of his rifle into Connor's sternum.

The soldier bawled in Russian, no doubt alerting his comrades of his capture, before his lower face vacuumed inwards, spewing out blood, teeth and bone fragments.

Within seconds of the body falling, Carlo skidded beside Connor.

"Upper back on my right side," gasped the Chameleon Project agent.

333

The 'Ndrangheta man roughly quarter-turned him, and said, "No holes in the clothing. Sniper rifle took the impact. God smiles on you. Let's move."

As Connor shunted to stand, he caught sight of movement and fired a couple of bursts along with Carlo.

They fired and moved backwards, using the *'leap-frogging'* method instead of *'pepper-potting'* to cover as much ground as possible.

As the weight of return fire tore up the forest around them, an internal dialogue leapt uninvited into Connor's mind

We're fucked, we're fucked, we're—shut the fuck up, you're still breathing.

One of Carlo's grenades dashed itself amidst the Spetsnaz dragons, temporarily halting their advance.

After three minutes of hard running, the fence-line of the compound appeared on their right side.

Connor slowed and whispered, "Where's the open sesame?"

Carlo dumped his assault rucksack and pulled out what looked like four wrapped cocaine bricks attached to wires with a toggle drawing them in.

The Italian rapidly pressed them onto opposite points on the fence, before his thumb pushed what Connor thought to be a detonator, causing the Brit to flinch.

Carlo smirked at Connor's reaction, as the block and the metal they were attached to began to dissolve in a hissing burning.

As the opening appeared under the burn, Carlo rooted inside his bag and pulled out two headsets.

"Ciara said to wear these and let 'The Wizard' guide you."

They both donned them, switching on via a smooth button integrated into one of the earpieces.

The computerized voice came alive in his left ear. Connor and the voice went through a code sequence to establish it was indeed Jaime, the Chameleon Project's tech guru.

Then the voice said, "I can guide you through the complex. The headset has inbuilt GPS and the architectural plans I have are relatively new, but I do not know the positioning of any other humans in the building."

That Jaime delivered his last sentence almost apologetically briefly made Connor wonder if that was possible.

"Roger. Where do we enter?"

Jaime guided them around a metallic housing for a giant fan to a trap door.

Connor opened it with Carlo covering. With no gunfire or noise forthcoming, the Brit said, "I'll go point."

He quietly took his footing on one of the ladder rungs. Without the light emanating from the opening, he was unsure how dark it would be when the hatch closed. However, knowing the Russian Special Forces patrol tracking them must be close by, he said, "Close it behind you."

The gaps beneath the twin steel doors to their right and left provided enough ambient light to make out shapes.

He covered as Carlo descended, who, when landed, whispered, "Déjà vu, no?"

Connor smiled—they had been thrust into a similar situation on their first meeting. It was also the time he had come closest to death. The faint shrapnel scars acted as reminders.

They stacked on the door, before Connor rolled on it and entered.

The voice sounded in his ear. "Straight down the corridor. Fifteen metres to your left is a door with the code 27022009. It opens out into a multi-floor complex. My best guess is that Sykes might be held in one of the rooms in the north-west quadrant."

Connor looked at Carlo, who nodded his acknowledgement of what Jaime had said.

The Englishman tapped in the code and opened it slowly with the Howa up on aim.

Connor's nerves sang on entry. He had expected to see signs of life, instead of this eerie quiet. He compartmentalized the pain in the back of his shoulder as much as he could.

The area opened out into an expanse. Connor estimated it to encompass over one hundred square metres of cylinders, turbines, safety railings, gridiron flooring and fuel rods—perhaps defunct but maybe not—going several levels deep, and joined by corner stairs.

The centre opened out to the size of a standard living room to accommodate a tower, exiting through a similarly-sized opening in the roof.

The Chameleon Project agent could already ascertain the great danger. In such a massive space, with so many blind spots and obstacles, it would take twenty men to clear the first floor alone.

He briefly looked up to see various ledges where a solo enemy could be in wait.

Connor indicated to Carlo that they would skirt around the perimeter to cut down on the target they offered.

They moved with the Yorkshireman facing forward and the Calabrian side-stepping in time with him.

The pair flinched at the tannoy-amplified voice.

"Weapons around a nuclear reactor. Very unwise."

As Connor began to compute the words, metallic clanks sounded all around. Hearing bursting hisses, the billows of smoke came as no surprise.

Just a moment before the smoke grew to its vision-obscuring, choking maximum, Connor whispered, "Move three paces to the left."

Between their second and third pace came a flash of movement, with sounds of impact and expelled breath.

Connor spun to see Carlo in a semi-crouch, awkwardly holding his Howa.

"What happened?"

"It…he, tried to take my weapon. My trigger finger is broken. I can switch."

The Englishman, watching Carlo switch the assault rifle into his opposite shoulder—which had its ejection port on the right side, so awkward to shoot for left-handed firers—realised they were trapped down here with Gorokhov.

Stop it. The cunt is trapped down here with us.

Connor felt an uncertainty—why hadn't he shot them both?

The voice out of the smoke confirmed his thoughts, "There are too many dangerous fission materials down here for a gunfight. I am prepared to fight like a man if you two men are. If I wanted to shoot you, I would have. What is your answer?"

Connor snatched a look at Carlo, whose confused face then broke into a smile.

Connor shook his head and whispered, "This cunt is like M. Bison. It's not a—"

"Who is M. Bison?"

"Never mind. There're levels to unarmed combat and this fucker belongs in the UFC."

"But there are two of us."

Connor nodded before calling out, "We accept."

His blood frosted as the smoke cleared to reveal Gorokhov, ripped torso bared, wearing khaki trousers and boots.

It took all of Connor's sense of honour to overcome his thirst to win and shoot Gorokhov.

Instead, the pair stripped themselves of their weaponry.

So the fate of the world's sustainability comes down to this? A fistfight, thought Connor as the teeth of his nerves sunk in.

He murmured to Carlo, "Let's keep on opposite sides of him."

Connor had no real idea of the Italian's unarmed fighting prowess.

337

Gorokhov's face showed no tension as he slid his foot back into a fighting stance on Connor's approach.

The Brit's chin neared his collar bone and his hands rose. Carlo moved behind the Japanese-Russian, who showed no hint of concern.

Connor initiated the fight, but mid-feint Gorokhov attacked simultaneously with a kick to his torso and a punch to the face.

Unable to pull back in time, he slipped the punch, but the kick shunted him back a few steps.

Then, with the dexterity of a high-level Taekwondo practitioner but the force of Muay Thai specialist, Gorokhov hit Carlo's head-guarding arms with a left kick.

He switched with rapier speed to a calf kick with his right foot, toppling the Italian.

Connor dived at the Russian's legs, executing a double leg takedown, only to find his throat compressed by an arm-in guillotine. He gripped the wrist with both hands to perform a 'turn-out' but Gorokhov's unnatural strength felt vice-like.

Just as the oxygen debt began to elevate him into a floating dimension, Gorokhov threw him into one of the steel cylinders.

Connor ignored his screaming shoulder, to force himself up in time to witness Carlo retreating under a flurry of strikes. An upward elbow to the point of the jaw and a foot sweep felled his battle partner.

The Brit ran at his opponent to draw the lead. He pulled back at the last moment, avoiding the punches.

He stepped back in to spark off a crunching exchange of blows.

A reverse elbow caught Connor in the temple, rendering defences groggy to the following hip throw smashing him into the ground.

The weight on top of him painfully doubled as Carlo jumped on their antagonist's back, punching a striated forearm around the Japanese-Russian's steel-cabled neck.

Gorokhov easily stood up, deflecting Connor's attempted up-kick aimed at his groin with his knee. Then, gripping the former Legionnaire's hand off the top of his head, Gorokhov crushed the fingers. Next, he pulled his arm down and used his Terminator-like strength to torque out of Carlo's rear-naked chokehold.

He snatched the 'Ndrangheta assassin by the throat, lifting him off his toes Vader-style with a single choking hand.

Connor took the force of his thrown *Oppo* in his grasping arms and chest, only to be punched in the eye with terrific velocity, swelling it immediately.

Tucking his chin and hunching his shoulders against an anticipated barrage, a boot to the chest threw Connor onto his back.

He craned his neck to see Carlo's left punch caught by the wrist, before the former SVR assassin snapped the arm by the elbow with a hammer fist.

Gorokhov blocked Carlo's right-hook with an oak-like karate-style block before whipping an overwrap on the arm and cranking it.

The Yorkshireman dashed forward, leaping into the air to drop-kick the pair to the floor, splashing surprise across their faces.

Gorokhov, with his wrapping arm pinned beneath Carlo, could not scramble to his feet before Connor. The Chameleon Project agent threw his legs around the former SVR agent's in an *Ashi Garami* entanglement.

He wrenched on an inside heel hook.

Gorokhov failed to suppress a growl of pain and fury. The Sambo master pointed his toes, twisted his knee back in, and Connor felt the heel rag free from his adrenaline-frayed arms.

Despite any damage he might have caused to Gorokhov's knee, his adversary still jumped to his feet quicker. He struck Connor's jaw with speed the former amateur boxer had rarely before encountered, sagging him back to the floor.

Carlo threw himself at their enemy's ankles, only to have Gorokhov keep his balance with a hand clamping down on his neck and kicking his leg free. When the former Legionnaire tried again, his throat became snatched up in a guillotine choke.

The former Royal Marine struggled to his feet as Carlo's body became limp. Gorokhov dropped Carlo like a sack of cement as Connor approach once again.

The Chameleon Project agent noticed a hint of weariness in the Japanese-Russian's expression.

39

Gorokhov began to feel his system deplete. He could have finished the pair early, but allowed the enjoyment of his dominance to overcome him. Why Daniel wanted Connor Reed alive, only he knew, but this other man—Italian if he had to guess—was not afforded the same reprieve.

However, just as his victim's life began to ebb under his choking forearm, Reed stood and came towards him like a zombie forcing him to drop the man.

The former SVR assassin again felt a tinge of inadequacy knowing he might have lost to the man if not for his enhancement. And had the Brit not been harried through the forest by the Spetsnaz teams?

The inside of his knee throbbed, warning him of the future acute pain and possible surgery. Despite this and the fatigue seeping into his bones, Gorokhov knew the Englishman would be worse, despite his expressionless face.

"Why are you fighting the inevitable?" asked Gorokhov.

The sneering reply of, "Shut the fuck up and fight," singed his sense of honour—*I shouldn't have had to ask him that.*

He parried the jab to his stomach that came after the feint to his head. But the following right hand caught him with a glancing blow on his cheek.

With his knee inhibiting his movement, he grabbed the upper arms and reaped out his opponent's leg with an inside trip.

As they fought on the floor, Gorokhov felt an unfamiliar bile of fear bolt into the back of his throat. His reserves were diminishing, and he needed to finish the Englishman quickly.

With Reed's legs clamped around his waist, he postured and delivered a blitzkrieg of pile-driving blows into the fading Brit's ribs and face. The legs loosened and Gorokhov broke away.

Not trusting his energy reserves, and seeing Connor Reed in no state to attack him, he delayed his plan to secure his prey. Instead, he limped his way to the satchel containing his nourishment vials.

He hated his reliance on them—to the point he felt low-level anxiety if they were not in sight, which had been frequent in the last two days, as they had been under the care of his team.

The assassin pulled the satchel wedged between pipes out and slid the needle onto the vial. In the low light of the room and with his tiredness becoming more acute, the liquid looked a little different but sparkled with its revitalising promise.

He found a vein and plunged the needle in. His heartrate increased a few beats from the anticipation.

Icy branches of pain and shock spread across his chest, robbing him of his breath. Finally, he took the pressure off his knee to slowly sink to the floor.

He focused on his breathing to ignore his vulnerability in this state. He failed as the two pairs of feet appeared.

His ears still worked fine.

"What has happened to him?" rasped the Italian.

The Englishman replied, "The man who freed me—Rod or Roderick to our Russian friends—was a deep cover agent for my boss working against the SVR. We discovered this *Shredder* needed these vials to replenish himself for prolonged bouts of extreme exertion, and so Rod refilled the vials with cola. I do not think it is friendly to your blood. I mean I am sure there're more than a few smackheads who've shook it off, but maybe not after a fight like that. If too much got injected the carbonic gas expansion would finish him off with a heart attack. "

"Your idea?"

"No, my boss. She's proving good at what she does."

Carlo smiled, "I like Pepsi—more zip."

Gorokhov lifted his head with a great effort and rasped, "You will not escape. Spetsnaz surround you."

The Italian gave a low chuckle and said, "They are taking their time, are they not?"

Connor Reed said, "You know something I don't?"

The Italian said, "They were going to transport signor Sykes by helicopter over to the Kuril Islands for Russia. But it could not come in until the area was secure. I guess Russian helicopters in Japan would be a little embarrassment for Russia."

"So, it's waiting for the area to be secure?"

The Italian shook his head. "I think Japanese Special Forces have arrived. I was sent only to delay the helicopter until they arrived."

Gorokhov's heart sank in time with Connor Reed's knees, who squatted to make eye contact.

"You don't even know why you're upset, do you, Gorokhov?"

His breath had marginally improved, and he said, "Because I failed."

"Failed at what?"

"My mission."

"And what was so important about this mission?"

Gorokhov's brain scrambled for an answer he couldn't find.

The Englishman continued, "Apparently you were content in retirement. Can you pinpoint what made you decide to come back?"

He couldn't answer that either.

"Where is Ronald Sykes? We'll find him but it'll save us fucking around."

"Please…allow me to take my own life."

"As much as I admire that 'Go hard or go home' attitude, I think my boss is too interested in your boss to allow that to happen."

"I would not talk."

"Bet you never thought you would inject cola into your veins, but it happened, didn't it," said the Englishman.

Gokorov shot defiance through his eyes, and Connor said, "One of the perks of this profession for me was getting to torture evil men. My boss, or bosses, turn a blind eye to it I reckon. Very few things make me happier in life. I know, no man is purely good, and no man is all bad—the word on the street is that Hitler turned vegetarian 'cos of animal welfare. Still, some men are beyond redemption."

He gripped Gorokhov's hair, forcing the maintenance of eye contact, and continued, "But you're a strange case—I've been to the island where you were brainwashed, I know how they did what they did to you. I don't think my heart would be quite in it to punish you gratuitously. Plus I haven't the time. So I am asking you please, with sugar on top, where is Sykes?"

A glimmer of triumph flickered in Gorokhov. "Ronald Sykes is dead. I was ordered to kill him if there was any danger of rescue before transporting him to Russia. You should have escaped instead of coming here."

Despite Reed's relative lack of expression, Gorokhov, even in his current state, due to years of training and experience, could tell the news hit the Englishman hard.

The Brit finally said, "You have been looking to meet my boss for years."

"I...do not...understand."

"You've been looking for the man who killed your brother. I have to say you Gorokhov brothers are the best fighters I've ever fought on the street—your older brother would have killed me if my boss had not shot him."

The surge of hatred and rage dragged the last energy reserves from him. Connor Reed stood, and a vision of him screwing a needle into a fresh vial began to blur.

However, the Englishman's voice rang glass-like in his ears.

"This will give a new meaning to the phrase 'Died of a coke overdose'. Pin him down *Amico*."

Gorokhov did not have the strength to resist, flopping over like a rag doll as the shaven-headed Italian sat on his chest with knees pinning his arms.

He barely felt the needle plunge into a vein in his right forearm.

However, he did feel a black hand snatch a grip of his heart and lungs, squeezing him into an agonizing darkness of death.

40

Three Days Later

Daniel Fridman acknowledged that although his mind could be as sharp as ever, he tired much quicker than he did even ten years ago.

He had just given his speech at the Courageous Rats Foundation annual convention. These specially trained rodents had the dual role of detecting landmines in post-conflict areas and also aiding research into tuberculosis. The estimated number of lives these rats had saved ran into the tens of thousands; a point he emphasised in his speech, eliciting a standing round of applause from the glittering women and pristinely dressed men.

Though totally unnecessary, these events were almost always outlandishly lavish, befitting their wealthy attendees, all looking for a tax loophole dressed as a good deed.

And that was how it should be, he thought.

The value of these functions was they allowed him to identify and gauge the movers and shakers of this world. The benefit of any speech he gave was the guests witnessing his command of the room, incentivising them to court him afterwards.

As he had always done, Daniel put on the pretence of being impressed and grateful for the attention he received from these individuals. Down the line, this first impression lent itself into his greatest strengths—to make the powerful do his bidding and be convinced it was their idea all along.

After several rounds of schmoozing, the eighty-nine-year-old beckoned to the head of the security team.

"Any news from the far east?"

"Not yet, sir. Do you want me to check in?"

Daniel smiled and said, "No news is good news in that regard. At least until the morning."

He gestured he was to indulge himself in his customary cigar, and that no one was permitted to disturb him.

The octogenarian shuffled his way to the back of the enormous mansion, to his room and out onto the balcony.

The echo of the crowd's hum died in his ears, and he lit his cigar. He looked out onto the silhouettes of the Belgian countryside, and enjoyed the stillness of the night. It mirrored the tranquillity of his heart, knowing that as he approached the end of his life, he had secured the legacy and prosperity of his family. His sons, grandsons and granddaughters, held positions of influence in the halls of investment banking, corporate America and Europe, and politics.

He jumped at the voice.

"Gorokhov won't be reporting in."

Daniel forced himself to relax. He turned slowly.

It was not just the calmness in the grey eyes that ran his blood cold—it was the waiter's uniform the British Security services liaison officer wore.

"Ahhh. Not the circumstances I thought we would ever meet," Daniel said as calmly as he could.

"You envisioned our meeting?" asked the tall, lean man in a west Scotland brogue.

"I thought it might be a possibility," said Daniel. "Are you here to kill me?"

"What makes you say that? I am merely a civil servant."

Daniel smiled, despite himself. "Mr McQuillan. You ascended to that position seemingly from nowhere. I had my suspicions, but it is only now I realise you are the one whom the Russians called Opekun—'The Guardian'. My wonder now is why they protect you? Maybe you will indulge an old man?"

"That's a long tale involving a stolen nuclear weapon back in the nineties. I doubt we have time for it, especially as there are questions I wanted to ask, like why you had the man who held the key to the planet's sustainability killed?"

The urge to lie evaporated as quickly as it came.

"The original strategy was to have Mr Sykes brought to the EU and convinced to divulge his findings here, or at least have him hand over files. But Mr Kenjiro's claims that Mr Ronald Sykes kept most of the principal information in his head were substantiated."

"And with the time allowed, you ordered Mikhail Gorokhov to assassinate Sykes."

Fridman took a puff of his cigar. "He is a faithful agent."

"Faithful agent?" said the Scotsman, "That's one way of saying 'brainwashed puppet'. Though Tareq Nabil, the foremost advisor for the Chief of Saudi intelligence, knows all too well why he is doing what he is doing. Your fifteen-year-plus cultivation of a man influencing other men without them seeing your hidden hand is truly impressive. Having him advise Prince Nawwaf bin Salam to assassinate journalists and ascend power, and also fund Mikhail Gorokhov's campaign so that any trail leads back to Saudi Arabia but not you, has a touch of the evil genius about it. Though you've had that MO since at least the seventies."

"Whether an act is good or bad is dependent on the result," said Fridman. "So, why do you think I planned this?"

The Scotsman answered, "Well, being the most influential geopolitical advisor in Europe, my guess is you didn't want the applecart of world power tipping further away from the EU."

Fridman brushed a speck of ash off his suit and said, "Japan and Russia signed a secret agreement two years ago. Russia would return the Kurils and heavily discount natural gas prices to Japan in exchange for implementing the new technology, to be distributed all over Russia first. You should be aggrieved. They were going to cut the United Kingdom out."

The grey eyes peered into his, and McQuillan said, "So, your…faithful agent was never going to complete Sykes's extraction back to Russia?"

"Correct. Measures were put in place," said Fridman, taking a draw and billowing out the smoke. "With the Russian economy no longer reliant on their natural gas reserves, they would form a stronger coalition with China. Thus weakening our position. An intelligent man like yourself might understand the need for a strong Europe in theory, but you never experienced being forced to flee from your family home to a foreign land while your father is left behind to fight an unwinnable conflict."

Fridman thought he could see the shadow of a wry smile briefly appear.

"So, you would rather the planet rot in unison than for other countries outside of Europe to profit from its safety. The ultimate in cutting your nose off to spite your face."

"Reports of the world's demise have been around since Noah built the ark. You should know better than most that to react to every doomsday prediction would plunge one into a pool of anxiety."

"True," replied the Scotsman. "But when ninety-seven percent of the world's scientists are in agreement of the dangers of global warming—albeit some disagree on timelines and severity—I am inclined to believe a technology which would have allowed for the complete electrification of the world's air travel, with a fraction of the damaging waste, would be a good thing."

Fridman's heart stilled and he said, "Beneath the former Special Forces soldier aura, I can see that an idealist heart beats within your chest."

McQuillan slowly raised his chin a few degrees. "I might have inherited that from my father—Arthur McQuillan. Though that wasn't the name he went by—his

349

da', my granda' was also called Arthur and my da' did'nae want to be known as a junior."

His next words sent an ice-snake slithering over Fridman's diaphragm. "Everyone knew him as Don McQuillan."

Fridman's mouth slid open before murmuring in his now dream-like state. "His accent was quite a bit stronger than your own."

"Aye. He travelled a lot but he wouldn't have dreamt of leaving Glasgow. So I've been told of course—I was only six when he 'passed away'. My sister claims to have memories, but I reckon they are mostly imagined, as she was four."

After attempting to grip his current situation, Fridman asked, "How did you know I met him."

The smile did not reach the younger man's eyes.

"Not knowing your name, he described you as 'David Bowie'—took me a while to realise it was because you both share heterochromatic eyes. I couldn't work out his description of you being part of the 'TOR mafia' at first. Then it clicked that he was referring to 'The Treaty of Rome'. A few other bits came together to confirm."

The vulnerability he now felt transported Fridman back to his childhood. A state he had fought long and hard never to feel again. An anger rose inside him as he spat, "Your father could never understand that instead of harassing the political figures, he could have become one himself and affected change. That's what killed him in the end—'you get more flies with honey than with vinegar' is an expression you will be familiar with."

The atmosphere seemed to cool.

McQuillan said, "Honey? You following a narrative instead of searching for the truth?"

After a lifetime of strategy-influenced speeches, Fridman's fear-mixed ire acted as a truth serum.

"Your father was killed because he had procured interviews with media groups, based on conjecture and rumour. Too much British and liberal arrogance, and too little foresight. Activism is one thing, espousing half-cooked theories is another."

"Like a western-sponsored sniper killing a popular Lebanese mayor and thus sparking a civil war?"

"Yes."

"Half-cooked does not mean untrue."

"No, it doesn't. But there are truths that destroy and lies that protect. Morality is rarely black and white."

"And what were the morals behind kidnapping innocent people, taking them to an island and brainwashing them to do your bidding?"

"Those people were more of an asset to humanity than they ever would have been otherwise."

A ghost of a sneer appeared and died in an instant on McQuillan's face. "Was Mikhail Gorokhov an asset for humanity? A man who you contracted to kill Ronald Sykes?"

"Yes."

The former SAS soldier did not speak for a few moments before saying, "Why would you tell me that you were responsible for my father's murder?"

"Because…what does it matter? You don't have the time to torture me. I am an old man with cancer," said Fridman, looking at the moon's glare over the rooftops. "If I die in my room, there will be an investigation, which is not something a man like you would risk, given your responsibilities. I have helped stabilise Europe and brought peace to the world by being able to see into the future."

"And that you're buying time for security to check on your welfare—since your cigar sessions typically last for fifteen to twenty minutes but no longer," smiled the Scotsman. "You're right, I don't have the time to interrogate you, but what I can do is destroy your reputation. You see, the photograph you signed earlier was actually a hidden letter now resting beneath your pillow."

Despite himself, Daniel Fridman's eyes flicked towards his bed. Indeed a corner of an envelope mocked him from the pillow.

McQuillan continued, "Your preference for beautiful handwritten letters has—reluctantly I imagine—given way to typing with the decline of your hands' dexterity. The letter lists your crimes and accomplices. Only a fraction, as rooting out all your misdeeds along with every man and woman who has aided you might take years—but I know enough. It is one of the better suicide letters I have had concocted."

"That letter will never see the light of day. You know that, Mr McQuillan."

"Perhaps you are right—too many powerful people stand to lose too much," said the Scotsman. "But it will perform the dual purpose of cutting short any investigation and for certain powerful people to be less inclined to assist the Fridman dynasty. And after copies of the letter are leaked, some may even seek to knock your kin off their lofty perches. You know how it is Daniel, the generations that come after are always a little softer than the one which forged against resistance."

Anxiety billowed in his diaphragm as Fridman thought of the lifetime of toil, sacrifice, and political manoeuvring. He'd put his ego to one side to placate men he neither liked nor respected. The dread of the end goal being snatched from him at the literal and metaphoric death, tightened its black soot-covered fingers around his throat.

He remembered the vow he made to himself in the scramble to get out of Poland. A promise that he would never leave his family without the shelter of power like his father did to them.

"There must be something you want?"

He felt a small relief when McQuillan nodded. "Two things. One is for you to know that before his death, Ronald Sykes wrote a full-bore explanation of all the principles relating to the amplification and storage of clean, renewable energy. He sent them to Chisato Fukuhara and Kenjiro Uda.

They have both been granted asylum in the United Kingdom. They are grieving, but determined to stop at nothing to see this technology realised. You have delayed it, but let's hope not significantly."

This news would have hit him in the stomach a minute ago, but his next question floated on hope. "And the second?"

"To deny you the time to think of a solution."

The former Special Forces soldier leapt forward like a grey wolf and seized him.

Launched like rag doll over the balcony railing without even touching it, Daniel Fridman's cry for help hurtled down with his fall.

The huge, wet, metallic-sounding impact did not immediately switch off his brain despite the death of his body. His eyes took in the sight of McQuillan scaling around the tower's side before nothingness settled on his senses.

41

Grace offered Mark her cheek as he said his goodbyes for work. Feeling his wet, rotating lips on it she lamented on how the practicalities of life stamped out girlish notions such as 'soulmates'.

She admonished herself for thinking like this as she watched the kind-eyed man crane over Jackson's crib. Then, he began saying goodbye in a 'baby language' that made her cringe. In addition to being tall, dark and handsome, Mark held a well-paid position within a nationwide gas company and doted on her and her son.

You should be counting your lucky stars, she thought, smoothing her green, fleece-lined dressing gown.

But she wasn't.

Though he had not officially moved in, he had been stopping the night more and more. She knew this was Mark's way of asking without asking, which vexed her but he was so good with Jackson that she had let it slide until now.

I'll tell him at the weekend that it's not working out, she thought, replying to his enthusiastic "Byyyeeee" with a tight smile. *Actually, I'll tell him tonight.*

Though she hated how some women shunned perfectly good men in exchange for 'bad' ones due to a 'lack of chemistry', she also knew that a lack of respect for one's partner could quickly disintegrate into contempt.

Grace finished the peanut butter on toast, drained off the rest of the coffee, and wiped her mouth. She had booked one of the nurses in for a tattoo in a quarter of an hour.

Approaching the crib, she felt her heart melt on looking at her son's peacefully sleeping face. Restraining herself from waking him up, she thought about how much he looked like his dad, despite only being a few months old.

It had been Jackson's father who once told her that babies—even girls—looked like their father so that '...*Fred Flintstone could tell that Pebbles was his, and Wilma remained safe from a clubbing.*'

She smiled—he always had a way with words. She hated that after he risked his life saving hers and a slew of children from a psychopathic, child-murdering warlord, she had given him an ultimatum.

However, though the trauma she had been through proved horrendous, watching him tie the twisted madman to the axle of a vehicle and dragging him to his flesh-stripping death had been repulsive to her. Despite what the beast had done.

Now, with both time and distance, she did not feel as strongly, but still recognised that she and Jackson might be best off without him—as much as she wished that was not true.

The knock at the back door made her jump before glancing at the Albani wall clock and scowling—her appointment must be early.

She composed herself and went to the door. Opening it, her insides iced her mouth open.

Connor stood with his palm raised, "I just wanted three minutes, then I'll be out of your hair, scout's honour."

The yellow-edged, purple bruising indicated the impact to his eye was now several days ago.

She floated backwards without saying anything, and he came in.

Finally, she asked, "Why did you go to the back door?"

She felt vaguely self-conscious of her hair and make-up not being done.

"I didn't want anyone seeing me come. And I had to wait until your boyfriend left."

"He's not my...thank you, very considerate of you," she said, attempting sarcasm but achieving sincerity. "What happened to your eye?"

He shrugged, "Some women don't understand that 'No' means 'No'."

She frowned and asked, "Why have you come?"

Her heart fluttered in anticipation of his renouncement of his sadistic edge and his insistence they should be together. Then she would tell him the news.

"A year or two ago, my gran made friends with a lovely lady named Rene. I visited her house after we helped renovate her kitchen. Almost spilled my coffee on entering her living room."

It took a few moments to answer, but all she could summon was, "And?"

She caught his ghost of a smirk before he asked, "Is he mine?"

She blinked in rapid succession. "Yes."

"Am I that much of a bastard that you thought it best not to tell me I had a son?" he said, before waving his palm in front of his face. "Unless he's like…like…I know I sound like Forest Gump when he found out he had a kid…unless he's, you know?"

"Know what? Are you asking me if he's disabled?!"

"No! I could handle that. I was worried he might have inherited your ginger hair."

She failed to keep the smirk from breaking out on her face.

"Unless it changes with age, he has inherited your hair. And eyes. And everything."

Connor murmured, "Lucky bastard."

"Let's hope he inherits your supreme, if slightly misguided, confidence."

He looked at her with a smile, "It's good to see you again."

"You too," she said, meaning it. Then held her nerve to say, "I never actually thanked you for saving my life—our lives. I was…such a bitch…It's hard for me to say, but I am sorry, it was just that—"

"Stop being silly, Grace. I should imagine that being kidnapped by a child-murdering psychopath would stress most people out. I am more annoyed that you haven't offered me a cuppa. And there're words much harder to say than 'sorry'."

"Like what?"

"Like Wor-ces-tershire Sauce...yeh, worcessst...fucksake, Worcestershire Sauce, there, did it."

She smiled, "Tea or coffee?"

"No, I can't stop long."

Bastard, she thought.

"Do you want to see him?"

That he didn't immediately answer in the affirmative surprised her. After a few moments he said, "Yeh, sure."

"Calm your enthusiasm, Connor."

He replied with a tight smile.

She led him to the crib, and looked at him looking at his son properly for the first time. His face became a painting, expressing happiness and sadness at the same time. He stroked Jackson's cheek with the back of his fingers before retracting them as the baby stirred.

Finally, he said quietly, "The more I am around you and Jackson, the more I am putting you in danger."

"What is it that you do?"

"I...I am trying not to sound corny...I suppose I help provide a check against evil. I like to think so anyway."

"You work for the government?"

He shook his head. "I work for a man who works for the government. But sometimes his agenda conflicts with theirs."

"Very cryptic."

"Yeh, I know."

"Can't you quit and let someone else be a 'check against evil'?"

His eyes held hers. "You know who my family are and what they do. This gives me the freedom to go to certain areas and mix with certain people without

357

suspicion—there are other agents—perhaps even more capable than me, but they don't have the background I do. There is nothing else I can do in life that would affect change for the better than what I am doing now."

"And that you love doing it," she stated.

"Yeh," he said. "But I would have given it up for you and Jackson if I didn't think what I was doing was important. Or that I could produce a similar effect doing something else."

She fought to keep a neutral expression despite the tears swirling beneath her eyes.

"Does anyone else know about Jackson?"

Connor sighed. "My gran knew as soon as she picked him up. And she's not going to let this go. I've told her the situation—made her understand, but Jackson is her great-grandson and she'll treat him accordingly. So, you accept any 'gift' she gives you, because it'll be coming from me."

"Connor, I don't need money, I work two—"

"It's money to help secure his future. Mixed Martial Arts classes can cost quite a bit."

"You mean university or college can cost quite a bit?"

"Of course, that is what I meant."

"Quite the coincidence that your gran and mine should meet."

"Yes…very *Adjustment Bureau*."

"An underrated film," she said.

"Yeh, I liked it. That had a happy ending."

She felt a lurch in her stomach at his last statement. Grace took a while asking the next question because she didn't want him to leave.

"So…this is it? I'm not—we aren't ever going to see you again?"

"Grace…some of these people I deal with wouldn't think twice about hurting the people I love. Now my family are my family—they are known to whoever cares to find out, but you and Jackson don't have to be put at risk. I won't put my desire to be involved ahead of your safety."

She did not trust herself to speak. Before her silence became awkward, she slid her arms around him and kissed him deeply.

He responded and hugged her so tight it hurt. His fingers slid into her hair.

Finally, the kiss broke, and she choked, "Just leave now before it becomes harder."

He stepped back, ashen, turned and walked out the door.

AUTHOR'S REQUEST

Please leave a review of The Puppet Master

As a self-published author, Amazon reviews are vital for me getting my work out as many readers as possible.

By reviewing it means I can continue to write these books for you.

Thank you so much

Quentin Black

The Puppet Master Review

GLOSSARY

Ashi Garami— A leg entanglement designed to lock the opponent in place for grappling-based leg attacks.

Avtoritet— A Brigadier within the Russian Bratva. Similar to a 'Capo' in the Italian-based mafias.

Bobby Dazzler— A person or thing that is outstanding or excellent. Or a boy or youth that is smartly dressed.

CQB— Close-quarters battle. Fire-fights conducted at close range, usually in and around buildings.

Div— British slang for a stupid person. Origins disputed but one theory is that the simplest jobs in prison was the insertion of dividers (divs) into cardboard boxes.

Éminence grise— The decision-maker operating in the shadows, usually behind a 'puppet'.

Keffiyeh— A type of headdress worn in the middle-east or by persons with ancestral roots there.

Gaijin— A foreigner in Japan.

Ghillie suit— An all-in-one camouflaged outfit typically used by hunters or snipers.

Gipping— To gip is to retch. So, something that is 'gipping' is something that induces retching i.e 'He has a gipping body'.

Greet— Scottish slang for 'Cry'.

Irezumi— A form of Japanese tattooing using wooden handles and metal needles attached by silk thread.

Hiding— British slang for a beating.

Katagi no shu— Citizens under the Sun

Interi Yakuza— Intellectual Yakuza

Keizai Yakuza— Economic Yakuza

Kami— Sacred spirits of the Shinto religion which take the form of concepts such wind, rain, mountains, trees, rivers and fertility.

Leap-frogging— A method used by infantrymen moving over ground during 'fire and manoeuvre' or 'cover and manoeuvre' scenarios. Leap-frogging refers to the practice of the moving soldier running past the covering soldier before switching roles until the ground is covered. **Pepper-potting** refers to the practice of the moving soldier stopping in-line with the covering soldier before the roles are switched. (Yes, I would just Google it too).

LOD— Line of Departure, starting position of attack on enemy positions.

Maw— West of Scotland slang for Mother.

Oppo— An affectionate term for a friend within the Royal Marine Corps—an opposite number.

Pish— Slang word used in Glasgow and other parts of Scotland meaning 'nonsense' or 'without competence' i.e 'He's talking pish' or 'They are playing pish today'.

Rash guards— A top made out of elastic fibres to protect the wearer from abrasions.

Shinnies— Shinpads.

Shredder— the Japanese supervillain from the Teenage Mutant Ninja Turtles franchise.

Sosai— Roughly translates to 'president' or 'director-general'.

Spats— Akin to leggings worn to prevent rashes while grappling.

Sprog— An inexperienced Royal Marine. Also British slang for a child.

Tengu— In Japanese folklore they are ghosts of angry, vain, or heretical priests who had fallen on the "tengu-realm".

Universal Soldier— The Universal Soldier film franchise revolves around a programme that reanimates dead soldiers into superhuman agents and unquestioning killing machines.

Wasp— A description of a fired round passing close due to its sound.

Wean— West Scotland term for child, pronounced 'Wayne'.

THE NEXT BOOK

Available on Amazon

The following is the first chapter of Quentin Black's follow up novel—*A King's Gambit*

1

Standing on the dais, David Franklin felt the warmth of pride as well as the Costa Del Sol sunshine. The ocean breeze blended with the sharp scent of freshly cut grass and combed through his strawberry-blond hair.

Behind him lay the enormous, majestic golf course, its fairways tapering towards a series of lakes and, finally, the simmering Mediterranean Sea. Before him stood a bevy of regional and Irish journalists, a multitude of tourists and local golf enthusiasts, as well as several lieutenants and underlings of what the media were dubbing the Franklin Organised Crime Group.

His identical twin, Dion, had gotten a kick out of referring to the organisation as the FOC, a moniker which had spread.

That morning, a cocaine hangover had cemented his brother and his hired lover to his massive black velvet bed.

With the golf course being just one of a slew of grand openings of casinos, apartment complexes, strip clubs and shopping centres in the coming months, David had reluctantly agreed to stand in for him.

"Yer a lazy bastard, so you are," he had told Dion.

"Yer need to learn how to blather in front of a crowd," came the reply from beneath the pillow, and that was that.

To protect himself from his nerves, David had decided to impersonate his brash brother and not tell anyone—though some of the FOC boys probably guessed. Dion had a huskier build, and though both brothers stood an inch or two under average height, David took to wearing internal heels to elevate himself. His skin also lacked the pockmarks smattering his brother's face, though he guessed the gathering to be far enough back not to notice.

Clutching a giant pair of gold-plated scissors, he filled his lungs. Accentuating his now watered-down Dublin accent to match Dion's, he announced, "Welcome to the opening of Moonray Golf—the first golf resort where a person can play day and night beneath the stadium lights. Complete with fully interactive virtual reality indoor systems for those who believe fresh air is overrated."

The crowd rewarded him with a chuckle. He turned theatrically and ceremoniously cut the white satin ribbon strung between two shiny poles. A collective cheer rose from the crowd.

"Now," David continued, snapping his fingers at the head waiter. The waiter was poised in the complex's doorway beneath its slanted terracotta roof. It struck David as odd that the head waiter seemed incapable of balancing his silver salver as elegantly or deftly as other waiters he had seen in the resort or anywhere else.

He frowned as the waiter headed a procession of equally inept waiters—none looked like Spaniards or even particularly tanned.

Closer still, and not only did he look too old to be a waiter—he seemed vaguely familiar. And he was staring directly at David with such defiance it made the Dubliner's stomach lurch.

David recoiled on seeing the silver salvers' domed lids lifted en masse. Time slowed as the shock sank in; beneath the lids lay guns, not the anticipated hors d'oeuvre.

He turned to run but barely got into his stride before the air split with the fury of several Ingram Mac 10 submachine guns.

Four invisible hammers punched into his back to a crescendo of background screams.

The thudding pain began to scorch into something more acute. He slumped to his knees. He sensed someone running towards him. Craning his neck, he gazed into the barrel of an SMG.

The owner's Northern Irish-edged voice said, "What is a man without honour, Dion?"

Those were the last words David heard.

ABOUT THE AUTHOR

+ Follow

Follow me on Amazon to be informed of new releases and my latest updates.

Quentin Black is a former Royal Marine corporal with a decade of service in the Corps. This includes an operational tour of Afghanistan and an advisory mission in Iraq.

AUTHOR'S NOTE

Join my exclusive readers clubs for information on new books, deals, and free content in addition my sporadic reviews on certain books, films and TV series I might have enjoyed.

Plus, you'll be immediately sent a **FREE** copy of the novella *An Outlaw's Reprieve.*

Remember, before you groan 'Why do I always have to give my e-mail with these things?!', you can always unsubscribe, and you'll still have a free book. So, just click below on the following link.

Free Book

Any written reviews would be greatly appreciated. If you have spotted a mistake, I would like you to let me know so I can improve reader experience. Either way, contact me on my e-mail below.

Email me

Or you can follow me on social media here:

IN THE CONNOR REED SERIES

The Bootneck

How far would you go for a man who gave you a second chance in life?

Bruce McQuillan leads a black operations unit only nown to a handful of men.

A sinister plot involving the Russian Bratva and one f the most powerful men within the British security ervices threatens to engulf the Isles.

Could a criminal with an impulse for sadism be the nly man McQuillan can trust?

When the ruling class commoditise the organs of the desperate, who will stop them?

When Darren O'Reilly's daughter is found murdered with her kidney extracted, he refuses to believe the police's explanation. His quest for the truth reaches the ears of Bruce McQuillan, the leader of the shadowy Chameleon Project.

As a conspiracy of seismic proportions begins to reveal itself, Bruce realizes he needs a man of exceptional skill and ruthlessness.

He needs Connor Reed.

Ares' Thirst

Can one man stop World War Three?

When a British aid worker disappears in the Crimea, he UK Government wants her back—quickly and quietly.

And Machiavellian figures are fuelling the flames of slamic hatred towards Russia. With 'the dark edge of the vorld' controlled by some of the most cunning, ruthless ind powerful criminals on earth, McQuillan knows he leeds to send a wolf amongst the wolves before the natch of global war is struck across the rough land of Jkraine.

The Ryder crime family are now at war...on three fronts.

After ruthlessly dethroning his Uncle, Connor Reed must now defend the family against the circling sharks of rival criminal enterprises.

Meanwhile, Bruce McQuillan, leader of a black operations unit named The Chameleon Project, has learnt that one of the world's most brutal and influential Mafias are targeting the UK pre-BREXIT.

Counterpart

Can Connor Reed survive his deadliest mission yet?

Bruce McQuillan's plan to light the torch of war between two of the world's most powerful and ruthless Mafias has been ignited.

Can his favoured agent, Connor Reed, fan the flames without being engulfed by them?

Especially as a man every bit his equal stands on the other side.

"When there is no enemy within, the enemies outside cannot hurt you."

Reed, a leader within his own outlaw family, delights in an opportunity to punish a thug preying on the vulnerable.

However, with his target high within a rival criminal organisation, can Reed exact retribution without dragging his relatives into a bloody war.

The Puppet Master

For the first time in history, humanity has the capacity to destroy the world.

When a British scientist leads a highly proficient Japanese engineering team in unlocking the secrets to the biosphere's survival, some will stop at nothing to see the fledging technology disappear.

In the Land of the Rising Sun, can Bruce McQuillan protect the new scientific applications from the most powerful entities on earth?

And can his favoured agent Connor Reed defeat the deadliest adversary he has ever faced?

Can the Ryder clan defeat a more ruthless organization that dwarfs them in size and finance?

When the **dark hands of a blood feud** between Irish criminal organizations begin to choke civilians, and strategies to halt the evil fail, fear grips law enforcement in the United Kingdom, the Republic of Ireland and continental Europe.

When this war ensnares the Ryder clan, Connor finds with the choice between trusting the skill and mental fortitude of untested family members, along with the motives of his enemy's enemy.

Or the complete **annihilation of his family.**

Printed in Great Britain
by Amazon

38223972R00219